An Angel On Her Shoulder

Dan Alatorre

Cover by DAVID DUANES DESIGN

Edited by Allison Maruska allisonmaruska.com

If you enjoy this book, please stop by and say a few kind words at Amazon! 5 stars is always appreciated, too!.

Praise for *An Angel On Her Shoulder*

Alatorre's best yet!

I wanted to keep reading. Good job.

- Molli Nickell, The Publishing Wizard and former Time-Life acquisitions editor

Alatorre weaves a tale of mystery and suspense tied together by the heart of a loving father.
Doug is an average family man who experiences strange disasters, all surrounding his daughter and all occurring around the same time of year. Finding no answers in the physical world, he faces his own disbelief and seeks them from the supernatural one, taking him down a path darker than he ever expected.

With echoes of King's *The Shining, An Angel On Her Shoulder* will keep readers guessing and challenge what they believe is real. This exciting story is one readers won't soon forget.
- Allison Maruska, bestselling author of *The Fourth Descendant*

A brilliant work. Haunting, fast paced, multi-layered.

Alatorre has outdone himself with this chilling tale of paranormal suspense. If you loved *The Shining* or *A Change Of Seasons'* The Body (also known as the movie Stand By Me), you'll love this book.

- Lucy Brazier, author of the *PorterGirl: The Vanishing Lord* and *PorterGirl: First Lady of the Keys*

Chapter 1

"Call 911! *CALL 911!*"

The man's shouts ripped through the tasting room of scenic Hillside Winery. At the counter, Mallory lowered her brochures for 2017 vintages and glanced over her shoulder, unable to see who had called out. The other customers, two dozen or so elderly tourists and a smaller group that called the server by name, were looking around, too.

With confusion working its way into their expressions, nobody moved or called 911.

The man's voice rose, straining with fear and urgency as his words boomed down the hallway and spilled over them. "Somebody call 911! There's been an accident in the parking lot!"

A robust fellow, gray at the temples but broad in the shoulders and belly, pushed away from the tasting counter and headed toward the shouts.

"Martin." The woman next to him reached out for his arm. "Don't. You're not on duty."

He didn't break stride. "A cop is never off duty."

Rejoining the others at the granite countertop, his wife muttered to herself but for the benefit of anyone within earshot. "Retired ones are."

Mallory set down her Virginia Wine Country pamphlets and smiled at the woman.

The officer's wife sighed, having found a willing audience. "He just can't relax. He'll—"

"Jenny!" From the window, Martin wheeled around, his eyes wide.

"Tell the bartender to call an ambulance. Now!" He lumbered toward the front doors at a pace slowed only by his age and size. "Tell them there's an accident with severe injuries and we may need a medevac unit."

In a wave, curious winery patrons moved from the counter to the windows, gathering close to view the parking lot as Martin rushed outside.

Mallory moved with the mob, checking around the tasting room as she did. No sign of her husband and daughter. She clutched the brochures to her chest, a tiny knot of fear gripping her belly.

Behind the bar, the server picked up a telephone. "Where's Mr. Hill?" His finger hovered over the buttons as he directed his gaze at the closest employee, speaking with hushed urgency. "Avery—anybody know where Mr. Hill is?"

Carrying an unopened case of wine, Avery did his best to shrug.

"Okay . . . grab any other volunteer firefighters from the warehouse crew and get out to the front parking lot. See what's going on."

"All right, Mike." Setting down the white Hillside box, Avery scurried into the back room. "José! Ron!"

An uneasy feeling gripped Mallory. Her eyes darted around the room as she held her breath and searched for her family. She'd said goodbye to her husband and three-year-old daughter a moment ago, but how long had it really been? A few minutes? More?

Her stomach tightened as the wave of uneasiness swept through her. She recounted her conversation with Doug. He had gone to get their little girl something to eat from the car—their rental van—for lunch. *"We'll have a little birthday picnic in the parking lot. Does that sound fun?" He flashed his amazing smile at their daughter. "It's nice out. Maybe we'll open the van doors, sit outside on the cooler, and watch a DVD."*

Mallory grinned as her daughter's blonde ponytail brushed the collar of a new yellow dress. Hand in hand, her man and her baby strolled past the racks of t-shirts and souvenirs, then Mallory returned her attention to the tasting list.

A few moments later, a loud crash. The vibrations came right through the floor, but she and the other customers ignored it. In a bustling winery warehouse filled with forklifts and trucks and massive juice pumps, loud noises weren't unusual.

But panicked shouting was.

Her heart in her throat, Mallory tried to press through the curious onlookers gathering at the windows. A quiet morning at a picturesque Virginia winery was turning into chaos. Straining on her tiptoes to see past the others, she caught a glimpse of the scene.

Enough to make the hairs on the back of her neck stand on end.

A pickup truck with the Hillcrest logo on the door had somehow wrecked into several cars in the lot. *Her car*. The van she and Doug had rented for their vacation. The entire side was demolished, the windows shattered. Broken glass covered the pavement all around the vehicle.

Pulse racing, she grabbed the shoulder of the man in front of her, craning her neck to get a better glimpse. She couldn't see her husband or daughter anywhere, but too many gawkers blocked her view through the small window. Outside, volunteers and arriving customers gathered in the lot, further obscuring her line of sight.

An audible groan escaped as she clutched her aching gut. Where were Doug and Sophie?

Outside, Avery reached the gathered onlookers and immediately turned white. He stepped back, almost losing his balance for a moment, then shouted at the windows. "Tell Mike we need an ambulance! Tell them to hurry!"

Inside, each customer moved forward to look past the others, jamming the space in front of the windows and blocking the hallway that lead to the front door. People trying to get outside to help ran into people straining to see. Everyone rushed to get through the door at the same time, so no one did.

Mallory was pinned to the wall. The fear inside her was mounting to an uncontrollable level.

"How many people were hit?" Somebody asked.

"I can't tell. A few," another voice replied.

A man near Mallory put his hand to his mouth, gasping. "My God, there's a girl pinned under the van!"

His words ignited the surging panic inside Mallory. She heaved against the rotund man next to her. "Let me out!"

Wedging her arms and lowering her head, she forced her way out of the crushing mob and into the tasting room. Not stopping to catch her breath, she ran at the packed entryway, clawing her way through the crowd of curious onlookers.

An elderly woman came in the front door, wringing her hands, her mouth agape. "Oh, my God, I've never seen such a thing." She shook her head. "That car hit her and she flew right up in the air!"

"That girl is going to die." The man behind her muttered.

Surely, they can't be talking about my daughter.

"It plowed right into them! It didn't even slow down!"

The exit hallway was completely blocked. Mallory's heart pounded. She looked around, frantic.

"I don't know how anyone could survive that."

Mallory tried to see out the hallway window. She strained, on tiptoe, looking over shoulders and between bobbing heads. She swallowed hard, pushing down the panic welling inside her.

"Okay, I'll go feed Sophie her lunch. You come out when you're finished." He turned to their daughter. "We'll have a little birthday picnic in the parking lot. Does that sound fun?"

Mallory craned her neck to catch a glimpse of anything. Inside, too many people blocked her view. Outside, too many helpers crowded around the victims. There were tire marks showing the path the truck took, straight into her rental van and the car next to it.

Fear rose up in her throat. She fought her way through the crowd to the door.

Where is my baby? Where's Doug?

She clawed her way to the next window. It gave fewer answers. The volunteers had rolled someone over, but there were too many people in the way to see who it was. The others worked to get the girl out from under the van.

Her van.

Putting a hand on the wall to keep from falling, the elderly woman shook her head. "My God, the blood . . ."

A volunteer by the vehicle moved. Mallory caught a glimpse of the blood splattered clothing—a bright yellow dress—and a stream of blood running from it to the parking lot gutter.

She gasped in horror.

Panic and adrenaline took over. Mallory had to get down the hallway. She had to get outside. She shoved and punched at the onlookers, but everyone else seemed to be moving in slow motion. "Let me out! You've got to let me out!"

Shouts from the crowd obscured her cries.

"We need some towels for them! Get some towels!"

"Where's that ambulance!?"

Tears streaming down her face, Mallory squeezed between the wall and the last customer in the hallway as she grasped for the door. "Please! I've got to get outside!"

She fell forward, latching onto the large iron door handle. She squeezed her eyes shut and took a deep breath, desperately whispering a prayer. "Please, God. Don't let this be happening to my family."

Please.

Chapter 2

We would never have called it bullying.

Not back then, when Nixon stepped down as our president and plaid pants dominated the business fashion world. In Millersburg, Indiana, whining about being bullied would get the crap kicked out of you.

Some kids were towel snappers in the high school locker room, but they were usually fifteen or sixteen years old. Jimmy was already there when we were ten. He was my best friend, and even though he was a little small for his age, he made up for a lot of that in effort. He had to. It would be a long time before we were as big as our older brothers, if we ever got that big. And like a lot of older brothers, Jimmy's was pretty ruthless on him in public. It was one of those, "I can pick on my little brother but you can't" things. Only, Jimmy's older brother didn't care who else picked on him.

It wasn't bullying. We called it "teasing" or "tormenting." That was some sort of parental code for getting close to the line but not quite crossing it. If you got punched, it was in the arm, as part of a "game." Your grade school friends might give your triceps a good shot playing slug bug while riding bikes, but if you hit a kid hard enough to make him cry or wreck his ten speed, you probably paid for it when you got home. Nobody got punched in the face or drew blood—not on purpose, anyway. Accidents happened all the time, but a cut caused by a go-cart with no brakes that crashed at the bottom of a hill, that bleeds differently than a cut caused by a tough kid at the park with a pocket knife or a broken bottle.

Jimmy might get his butt kicked, but he would get right in there if a confrontation occurred. That impressed me about him. I could never do that. If I rode my bike to the park and there were some rough-looking older kids there, I would go home and come back later, or maybe wait for another day. Jimmy would stay there and ignore them, deciding that we'd come to test our bikes on a makeshift bike ramp or to hike the trails through the woods, and we were gonna do just that. It never bothered him that the rougher kids were around. If it did bother him, he never let on.

He never had to. I would always mention it.

"Aw, come on, Dougie, ignore them." Jimmy would say. "Let's splash some rocks in the deep part of the creek."

They were only a few years older than us. Punks, as my brother would later call them when he grew up and joined the Millersburg police force. But at that age, when we were barely ten years old, a few years makes a big difference. An extra thirty pounds and eight or ten inches of height can make for a pretty unfair fight. The tough kids were bigger and stronger than us, and they had been around. They probably actually knew what to do in a fight.

I never saw Jimmy's attitude toward them as being brave. It was, but it was also a kind of nonchalant. He was indifferent, somehow not seeing them as a potential threat. He'd heard the same stories I'd heard, about kids getting beat up and having their bike stolen or something. Jimmy was patient, taking in the situation like all good hunters learn to. If those kids wanted to smoke cigarettes or read a stolen *Hustler* magazine, they didn't want a bunch of us younger kids around watching. They would leave. And Jimmy always seemed to know that.

One time, my family went to a fundraiser for our church. We were always selling raffle tickets or chocolate bars or some damn thing for St. Matthew's. Going door to door asking strangers if they wanted to buy an overpriced candy bar so we could get new basketballs. It never ended. I was the worst at it, too. I ate as many candy bars as I sold; probably more. I'd come home with ten dollars in cash and twenty dollars in missing chocolate, and Mom would know that she was going to have to write another check. Jimmy moved his allotment of candy, but his mom helped. She worked in a big office, so she pushed it to the other employees. Jimmy almost never had to go door to door.

My mom helped me by driving me to neighborhoods I hadn't door-knocked yet.

Hawking chocolate bars for the church was lousy, but the church festivals were great. Candy selling was a lonely business, done by yourself or with a friend across the street, but the festivals were packed with people. There was music, bright lights, and games of chance. They had a big spinning wheel lined with poker cards. There was a ring toss, where you could win a huge glass bottle of Pepsi if you could get the little wooden ring to land on its neck. I don't think they make them anymore, those big glass bottles. They must have been almost as big as the plastic two-liter ones they sell now. A kid who could get the little ring to stay on the neck of the bottle got to walk away with an enormous warm soda to share with their friends. Winning a big Pepsi was a really huge deal—those little rings never stayed on when you threw them. They always bounced crazy and landed on the floor of the booth, so players would end up paying two or three bucks for a one-dollar bottle of soda. Kids didn't care, though. We never got soda at home unless our parents hosted a big party with all our friends and relatives, like New Year's eve or something. Winning the massive Pepsi was a treasure for a ten-year-old kid.

Like a lot of small cities in southeast Indiana, we had a large German population—and our church festivals showed it. There was always a long line at the beer booth, and they sold nasty smelling stuff in the cafeteria: sauerkraut, turtle soup, red cabbage—stuff like that.

Jimmy looked at the sign as he sipped warm Pepsi from the enormous glass bottle. "'Rathskeller?'"

"That means rat cellar." My knowledge of German was embarrassingly weak, but overhearing Mom and Grandma when they played canasta at holiday get-togethers, I'd picked up a few words.

"Rat cellar?" Jimmy snorted. "It doesn't mean that."

"It does." I eyed the sign and reached for Jimmy's big glass Pepsi.

He shook his head. "Why would you call the cafeteria the 'rat cellar'? That sure doesn't make me want to eat there." He glanced at the windows of the darkened upstairs. A thick metal wire mesh protected them against errant baseballs from the asphalt playground that doubled as the parking lot. "Do they cook rats in there?"

"Worse." I gulped the warm Pepsi. "Turtle soup. And sauerkraut."

"*Turtles*? Yuck!"

"Yeah." I held the thick glass bottle in both hands, waiting for the fizz to stop hurting my throat from taking too big a swallow. Jimmy could hold it with one hand sometimes, and even drink from it that way.

It was too heavy and awkward for me to do that. "I tried turtle soup once. It's pretty awful. And the sauerkraut is just as bad."

"I like sauerkraut." Jimmy took the Pepsi from me and sipped it without wiping it on his shirt first.

"Man, I hate sauerkraut. That *smell*." One of the true blessings in our house was Mom didn't cook traditional German food very often. Grandma did, though, and her house always smelled . . . stern. The pungent nasal assault of her homemade pickles and sauerbraten reminded her many grandchildren that rules were strictly followed in that house.

Jimmy and I walked between the rows of boardwalk style festival games, trying to out-burp each other. Our whole church parking lot had been transformed for the weekend, giving it a surreal, fun feeling it didn't have most of the rest of the year. Happy, as opposed to respectful and somber. Even the girls from our class seemed different. At the festival, they would be in shorts or jeans, not the school uniform—a dull, blue-gray plaid skirt and plain, white collared shirt. It would be another year or so before those boring skirts would be the highlight of my school day.

Popping six balloons with six darts would earn a festival goer a giant teddy bear. The overstuffed monstrosity was huge, like three feet tall. I practiced on the dart board Dad hung in our basement. It had real darts, too; not those toy darts with the suction cup tips. I worked on my dart throwing skills as I stood between my old toy box and our upright piano, waiting for my chance to impress some lucky girl one day.

"Wanna try it, Dougie?" The booth attendant grinned at me. Small town. I didn't recognize him, but he probably knew my dad, which meant he knew our family. Everybody kind of knew you in a small town, but if you were a doctor's kid, they all knew you *for sure*. Dad had so many patients that knew him and loved him, I couldn't ever misbehave. When everybody knows you, you can't get away with anything. It felt like my parents had eyes all over town, and at that age, I believed that they did.

When we got older, we'd figure things out differently.

But the dart game cost too much and my allowance was too small, and I said so. Besides, I didn't have any girls to impress just yet. I thanked the booth attendant, though.

Manners. Maybe he'd let mom and dad know I was polite. *"That boy of yours sure is polite, doctor!"*

Jimmy and I moved on.

"Hey," he said, stopping and turning to me. "Did you really eat a turtle?"

I nodded.

"Damn." He kicked at a stone, watching it roll away under the bushes. He used to have little green turtles in a small aquarium, and sometimes we'd catch box turtles in the creek that ran behind our houses. It was an odd thing for us kids to think that some people ate them, but turtle soup was a kind of delicacy among the German people. It was part of the ambiance of the festival, and my mom got some once and let me try it. I don't know if I liked it or not; I couldn't get past the thought of eating little green reptiles. But somehow, trying the soup was like being brave. So I did it. I didn't know "mock" turtle soup meant "pretend."

The festival games stretched beyond the cafeteria to a grassy area where they had a "smash car"—an old car for you to hit with a sledge hammer. The windows had been taken out, so you wouldn't get cut by breaking glass, but for twenty-five cents you could whack the car three times. There was even a "barker," a man with a microphone who explained the game over the loudspeakers. I guess it was a show of strength to see which man could put the largest dent in the car. To a kid, the idea of smashing anything was pretty appealing—and the thought of putting a memorable dent in a car on purpose was, too. Stray baseballs and other sports activities on Reigert Drive had put a few dents in a neighbor's car from time to time. This was all sanctioned. Pre-approved destruction. What could be better? The smash car was fun for boys of all ages.

The barker's job was to draw a crowd. He would goad men into playing, then cheer or mock them over the loud speakers when they did. The crowd loved it. He'd call a really big guy "tiny" and really little guys "King Kong." He announced the play by play as men tried to outdo each other damaging the smash car, but mostly he tried to get the crowd to laugh by making fun of the players. It was great entertainment.

The sledge hammer was really heavy. At that age, I didn't know they made them in different sizes and weights. The one at our house was heavy enough, but this was even heavier—and the players were surprised by it when they went to pick it up. That was the first trick up the barker's sleeve. Men would attempt to wield it without showing that they were straining, but smart observers would see that even big men had trouble guiding the heavy sledge to its target. To us kids it weighed a ton, so we got to swing it one time for a nickel. Most kids my age couldn't even do that.

"Whoa, big fella!" the barker would say to a kid. "You're supposed to swing the hammer, not let the hammer swing you!"

I had never picked up a sledge hammer except to carry it from the garage to the back yard for some Saturday afternoon project my dad was working on. Even then, it seemed like too much weight for a kid. This one was extra heavy, so the adult men couldn't swing it too hard or too many times.

"Can we get this guy some help?" the barker would ask the crowd. "I'm not sure he can pick up a mallet this heavy."

Then he would find a pretty girl in the audience. "Maybe you can help him, dear. With a dress like that, you could pick up anything!"

The crowd would roar.

If he embarrassed her enough, she would walk off and he would stop the game. "Just a minute, folks, just a minute." He'd take off his hat and hold it over his heart, shaking his head and leaning over dramatically to stare at her behind as she sauntered off. Then he'd hold up his microphone and say, "Bless you, dear."

Laughter erupted from the crowd again.

The barker knew his stuff, and the audience enjoyed it, even if he had been using the same lines for twenty years. By the time I was a senior in high school, I could recite the lines along with him. Still, if guys made enough visits to the beer booth, the barker was always able to draw a crowd and get them to beat on the smash car.

He made guys feel like they were in a competition with each other, and with the big sledge hammer, there was a thrill factor for the audience.

Men would hoist it waist high, get a feel for its weight, and then walk around the car looking for the best spot to inflict damage. Then they would raise the giant hammer over their heads.

There was always a slight pause at the apex, the point between the giant hammer going up and it coming down, as the player attempted a last bit of aim. The crowd would draw quiet then. But it was only for a moment, and then the man would bring down the mallet with great force and a grunt, crashing it onto the car.

A sizeable dent would be met like impressive fireworks. The crowd would all say "Ooh," in unison. A lame dent, or—God forbid—a miss, would be met with chuckles.

And some teasing by the barker. "Maybe you should have your mother help you next time, pal."

It was a balancing act for the barker, keeping people entertained while continuing to draw in more, so he never let things go too far. One of the smaller—and drunker—contestants bounced the sledge off the car and into the dirt, taking the man with it. Not only did he not leave a dent in the car, he put a hole in his pants leg and skinned his knee.

The barker jumped in. “Hey, let’s have a round of applause for our friend here!” Leaning down, he put a hand under the small man’s armpit, helping him to his feet and raising one of his hands into the air. “It’s harder than it looks folks! Harder than it looks!” While getting the crowd to applaud, the barker slipped the sledge hammer out of the man’s grasp, avoiding a scene. “Good try, sir!” The barker put the microphone up to the man’s mouth. “It’s a lot harder than it looks isn’t it, fella?”

Taking the hint, the little man wiped his brow. “It sure is.” He even managed to muster a smile.

“What a good sport!” The barker waved to the crowd. “How about another round of applause!” The circle of festival patrons complied.

Changing gears, the barker went back to work. “Who thinks they can do better? You, sir, how about it? Impress the little lady!”

Step right up!

What a great time the festivals were. I could practically still hear the barker’s jokes echoing in my ears as Jimmy and I breezed into the park on our bikes a few days later. A sunny, warm morning, I was certain I’d find some rare dinosaur teeth or other treasure in the creek there.

A few tough kids were milling around up on the park’s far hill. They were probably waiting for their friends, but they kept staring at Jimmy and me as we walked our bikes over the rocky creek bed. I lowered my head and acted like I didn’t notice them, trying to glance in their direction without making it obvious. I pretended to scour the water for fossils and ignore the knot growing in my gut. Jimmy just shrugged and said the punks wouldn’t be a problem until a few more of their friends came.

Taking a long look at my green Schwinn, I eased it against a thin maple tree.

I winced and rubbed my stomach, unable to shake the growing feeling that something wasn't right. To me, if anybody else showed up, we should have already been long gone.

Chapter 3

There had been a recent rain, so Jimmy said we might find some good stuff—fossils or whatever—among the rocks in the creek bed. The three-inch-long, cone-shaped pieces we collected each summer *forever* were really only worthless horned coral or petrified squids, but we didn't know that then. We were certain each one was a tooth from a massive Tyrannosaurus Rex and we tried to fill a shoe box with them.

Two other small creeks joined ours near the park by our house, so it wasn't unusual for things to just kind of appear there. Tributaries in southeast Indiana were prone to flash floods, and anything we left in our creek would be gone the next day if it rained overnight, swept straight into the Whitewater River. That was a harsh lesson to learn with a new G. I. Joe Jeep or the scale model aircraft carrier we spent weeks building and painting. Even the smallest rain at our house might have been a big storm upstream, causing our little puddle of a creek to become a raging monster, gushing south to the Whitewater and then into the Ohio River, right down the Mississippi and ending in the Gulf of Mexico. And we just knew some kids with a net in New Orleans were snagging all our best toys as they floated by on the way to Cuba.

Sometimes a summer rain would wash a tree off the hillside. Other times, all sorts of strange rocks and fossil treasures might appear. Beds of blue clay on the creek bottom would be exposed by one spring shower, then buried forever by the next.

It was a minor adventure every day, going to our creek, and we played in it as often as we could—nearly every day in summer. We never knew what it would show us. At the north end was a deep green pool where a stone bridge used to be. At the south end, our neighborhood park. On lazy fall days, we'd meander among with the puddles of tadpoles and minnows to the grassy triangle where the three creeks converged.

It wasn't a standard park by any measure. It was a long, odd shaped triangle, with some rusty old swings up the hill at the street entrance, and a large flat area behind them that ended where the three creeks came together. The tip of the triangle disappeared into a wooded hill we would sled on in winter, and across the creek in the other direction were the railroad tracks.

There were nicer parks nearby, so parents never took their kids to this one. That made it ideal for juvenile delinquents and teenagers looking for a place to smoke or drink. There were "Indian caves" in the side of the steep hill past the first ridge, but when we went to investigate them, they seemed to be big holes that somebody had dug into the soft dirt. On a dare, I crawled in one about five feet. The back wall lay another five feet or so beyond me, but the cave was cramped and smelled musty, like if you took a deep breath you'd get mold spores growing in your lungs and die—so I got out. Beer cans and nudie magazines littered the two or three holes that dotted the side of the big dirt slope. Supposedly, a dead body had been found in one once, but that was probably a story the older kids told us to keep us away from their party spot.

It wasn't a big surprise when we rode our bikes down to the park and found an old abandoned car there. We figured somebody got tired of having a junker like that around, and dropped it off at the park like the old washing machine we found once.

The very sight of it made me forget all about the tough kids watching us from the hill. I don't know how long it had been there; we hadn't gone down to the park in a while. The old car was right there in plain sight, way in the back of the park, where the creeks came through. The antennae was gone and the windows all smashed out. We propped our bikes against the maple tree and had a look inside. Bits of green windshield covered the seats. Outside, the finish was splattered with dirt from where somebody had been using it for mud ball practice. It had dents everywhere, probably from rocks, and the parts that weren't covered in mud were spray painted with graffiti—dirty words, and stick figures with boobs—probably by the punks watching from the hilltop.

There were no headlights or tail lights anymore. The driver's side door was stuck open like it had been bent too far, and the trunk lid was missing. It was a rundown, rusty old piece of crap that somebody had dumped in the back of our park.

And it was perfect.

We didn't have a barker, but now we had our very own smash car.

I glanced around for anything that could be used like a sledgehammer on it, to bash it like the one at the church festival. There'd be fallen branches under the trees, and large rocks would be down by the creek. I started searching.

Jimmy said he wanted to check the car over to see if there were any interesting parts left to take home. The passenger side mirror was still intact. The ball hinge holding the mirror to the door just needed some leverage to pop it off. With both hands on the mirror and a foot against the side panel, Jimmy dropped all his weight downward and grunted. After a few attempts, the mirror broke free—and dropped Jimmy on his butt with a thud.

He stood up, dusting off the back of his pants and acting like it didn't hurt, but it had to. The ground was pretty rocky. After a minute, he looked inside. The dashboard would have interesting items to pry off.

After a few knobs and a pen had been procured, Jimmy exited the vehicle and turned his attention to the car's hood. It was stuck shut. Meanwhile, I had found a decent sized limb to put some dents in the roof. I climbed up the back of the car and stood, raising the limb over my head. I brought it down with all my might, the way I'd seen the men do with the smash car.

The tree limb bounced off the roof and almost took me with it.

Jimmy laughed as I rubbed bits of bark out of the palms of my stinging hands. We needed something heavier.

There were bigger limbs under the trees, but Jimmy went for a rock. Kicking over a few baseball sized stones, he searched until he spied a large, flat mini-boulder the size of a dinner plate. It was about three inches thick, so it was ideal—any smaller and it wouldn't do much damage, but any larger and he probably couldn't pick it up. I scavenged under the trees to find a thicker limb, anxious to get my shots in.

We were having a blast, beating the crap out of our own private smash car, just like at the festival. We wore ourselves out on that thing.

Over my shoulder came a car noise, so I turned to see what it was. We had seen a city maintenance worker on a converted golf cart vehicle once, but this was louder and faster. In the distance, a dark sedan sped down the dirt path, bouncing along as it went and kicking up a trail of dust. That was unusual. People never drove back here. On occasion, a cop might roll through the upper area by the swings, but that was only about once a summer. And cops don't drive fast in a park.

As the sedan got close, the punks on the hill disappeared. Then I looked back at the car. It was speeding up the dirt bike path and came to a sudden, noisy stop. A heavy, middle aged man scrambled out, eyeing the abandoned car.

"God *damn* it." His face was bright red. That got my attention.

I'd been under a tree trying to find a bigger stick, but Jimmy was banging on the car's fender with his massive rock.

The man glared at Jimmy. "Hey!"

We both froze.

The stranger ran towards Jimmy, but it was loose, rocky ground. He slipped on the shifting rocks and nearly fell. As his eyes took in the dents and graffiti all over the abandoned car, his jaw dropped. "God *damn* it!" Stopping for a moment, he grew redder.

I had an uneasy feeling rising up in my stomach. Something seemed wrong with this man.

"Son of a bitch," he groaned, walking around the car. *"Son of a bitch!"*

I didn't know why he was so upset, but it made the hairs on the back of my neck stand on end.

Jimmy set down the rock and backed away. The man was red-faced and sweating. He leaned on the car door and peered inside at the broken glass. Then he reached in and pulled out a floor mat. It was like he was in a momentary daze.

Raising the mat over his head, he flung it to the ground. "God damn it!"

He turned his gaze to me. I was standing there with a tree limb in my hand. The stranger's bloodshot eyes narrowed. My stomach tightened.

"I know you." He growled, pointing at me. "You're the doctor's boy."

My heart jumped in my chest.

I nodded, my breath coming in short, shallow gasps. I had no idea what to do. Lots of people around town knew me through my dad, but this . . . this was different. A twinge of fear went down my spine.

The stranger eyed Jimmy. "You God damned—" He took a few steps in Jimmy's direction, then stopped again and looked at the fender Jimmy had been pounding on. It was pretty dented up and a lot of paint had been knocked off.

The man shouted again, a loud, guttural groan. Another shiver went through my gut.

"You!" He yelled at Jimmy. "Come here!"

I swallowed hard. *Don't move, Jim.*

Jimmy didn't budge. I found myself walking out of the woods toward the scene. The man spun towards me.

"I know you're the doctor's boy." He wiped the sweat from his brow with his thick forearm, wagging a stubby finger at me. "I *know* it." Then he turned back to Jimmy. "Who are you?"

My heart was slamming around so hard I could feel it in my throat. I held my breath. None of this made any sense.

We didn't speak. I was too terrified. There didn't seem to be any answer that was going to calm him down, and he looked ready to explode. Anything we said or did might set him off.

My mind raced, wondering what he would do to us. We were completely outmatched.

"Doctor's kid." His red eyes narrowed again, making the terrible feeling in my stomach surge. "*Rich* kid!" He spat, pointing at the car. "I don't have money like your daddy! This is all I've got!"

He slurred his words a little. That scared me more. I knew people had less control when they were drinking. I needed a plan, but I couldn't think. Every time I thought about running, the man glared at me like he knew what I was thinking. So I stood there, paralyzed.

And he stood there, forehead covered in sweat, staring at me. Rage seemed to be boiling up inside him.

I had no idea what to do. I stood there with my mouth open, my mind a complete blank. Jimmy inched his way back from the car, never taking his eyes off the stranger.

"You son of a bitches, don't you move." The man's face turned to a frown as he stared at the smashed vehicle.

Then it dawned on me. This was *his* car. Somebody had stolen it and dumped it here in the park.

Lightning shot through my stomach and down to my toes, making me want to vomit. He thought we stole his car.

Jimmy must have already figured that out.

Somebody had stolen this man's car, and now he thought he had found it—and the kids who had stolen it. And he meant to get some justice. Far from the road, in the back of the park, nobody would see.

Sweat dripped from his chin. "God damn it!" He kicked the car. His car. It was an act of anger and futility.

I didn't even breathe. I couldn't. The only thing louder than the raging lunatic in front of me was my pulse throbbing in my ears. I absently wiped my sweating palms on my shorts.

Jimmy never said a word. He silently made his way to me. Together we waited to see if we could—or should—make a run for it. Kids didn't disobey adults. We couldn't leave our bikes anyway, and trying to run over and grab them would give the man enough time to catch us. The fact that he hadn't laid a hand on us yet was good; maybe he wouldn't. But I didn't believe that, and the expression on Jimmy's face said he didn't, either. We would stand there like the man said to, like the good boys we were.

For now, the man kept us in Hell, yelling at the car and then at us, while he seemed to be working out what punishment to administer.

Then his eyes got big—too big. The whites showed and a sickening smile tugged at the corners of his mouth, sending a shot of fear straight through me. My ears were ringing and the nausea building in my stomach swelled. A hazy red dot formed in the corner of my eye.

I tried to ignore it, but I couldn't. I squeezed my eyes shut, putting my hands on my stomach and hoping the strange feeling consuming me would go away. The man's tirade roared through my head as a red cloud crept across my vision. I forced myself to take a deep breath to make it go away, but it wouldn't go. It controlled my eyes from inside. I wanted to shake my head back and forth but I was so dizzy and sick I knew I'd lose my balance and fall down.

The ringing grew louder, the red patch overtaking my eyesight and squeezing the breath out of me.

I had to look at it, look *through* it, to what it wanted me to see. I was afraid, but it wouldn't let go.

In the red haze, the color of the lunatic's bulging face changed. An eerie blue glow flashed across it, fast as lightning. As soon as I realized I was seeing it, it was already gone.

Then I was seeing his sedan. The inside. Under the driver's seat.

A long, thin wooden bat, like the kind police carried in old movies, lay tucked up under the cushion. It was shiny and black, with a thick leather string running through the handle.

Then the redness was gone and I could see the park again.

Covered in sweat, I stood there shaking.

The stranger nodded, a string of drool hanging from his mouth. “I’ll show you little bastards!” He stormed off toward the sedan.

I swallowed hard, frozen in place, barely able to breathe. With all my might, I managed to squeeze a few words out of my mouth. “He’s got a night stick.”

Jimmy’s jaw dropped. His eyes went to the raging lunatic.

In my mind, that bulging face glowed as he raised his big arm, bringing the club down on us again and again as we lay cowering on the dry creek bed, bones breaking and blood spewing in the assault.

He never got the chance. The tough kids had appeared on the ridge for their afternoon beer party. They were here to meet their pals, but they had stumbled onto quite a scene.

Their presence seemed to jolt the stranger back into reality. It didn’t occur to me, but it must have occurred to him that now *he* was outnumbered. He might have thought the tough kids were with us, or he might have realized there would now be witnesses to tell the police what he did to the two ten-year-old boys.

Stopping on the rocky ground, he stared up the hill at them. “Hey.” His voice now seemed weak. He said it again, louder, with the menacing growl. “Hey!”

That was all they needed. The punks on the hill didn’t want adult eyes of any sort observing their activities. They turned around to leave.

“Hey,” the stranger shouted again. “Get back here!” He started after them. The stranger’s big belly bounced, slowing him more than enough for the other kids get some distance. He stumbled on the large rocks of the dry creek bed, grabbing at his car to avoid falling.

That was our chance.

"Dougie! *Now!*" Jimmy dashed toward his bike. I was right on his heels. With my heart pounding, I grabbed the Schwinn and stormed up the sled riding hill. We pushed our bikes in front of us as hard as we could, not wanting to slow down for even the few seconds it would take to get on. The stranger couldn't easily chase us up the hill on foot, and it was too steep for his car. We could escape back to our houses through the woods.

As the leaves crackled under our racing feet, we heard the man rage at being outfoxed. "Get back here, God damn it!" His tortured voice bounced through the woods. "Get back here!"

No chance. Once we were up the hill, we jumped on our bikes and pedaled as fast as we could.

The stranger's howls echoed through the trees behind us as we sped away.

Chapter 4

We stopped to hear if the man from the park was coming after us. Staring at each other, we held our breath and focused on what terrifying noises might come to us through the trees.

Nothing.

Jimmy took a deep breath and pulled his t-shirt up to wipe the sweat off his brow. "We got away."

I don't know how he managed to get anything other than a grimace onto his face. My stomach still hurt, my chest was thumping, and my t-shirt was soaking wet. I couldn't stop sweating.

Jimmy hopped up on his pedals and rode away, taking the hiking trail towards home.

Once we were sure we had ridden far enough from the stranger, we worked our way down the hill and across to our side of the creek, the side with mowed lawns and paved streets.

And our houses, right next door to each other, just a mile or so away.

When we finally got onto Reigert Drive, Jimmy rode his bike home like nothing had happened. He leaned back and lifted his palms off his handle bars, riding hands-free. He was better at it than I was, of course.

He took a quick glance at me. "How'd you know?"

Easing my hands away from the handlebar grips, I sat upright but still let my fingertips touch the cross bar. I pretended I didn't know what he was talking about. "How'd I know what?

Jimmy dropped his hands to his sides, riding effortlessly. "About that guy having a night stick."

"I don't know." I slid my hands back to the rubber grips, squeezing them. "I just did."

It was a lie. I didn't want to explain how I knew about the night stick. I didn't want my best friend to think I was a freak.

Some secrets don't get shared.

It wasn't a complete lie, though. I didn't *really* know how I saw the night stick, or what the red haze was. I overheard Mom on the phone with aunt Amy, whispering about panic attacks. Maybe it was one of those.

It happened to me at St. Matthew's once, too, in the middle of mass. An old guy in a baggy, dark suit sat down a few rows behind us, and a strange feeling crept right onto me the way heat does when the oven door opens. I tried to ignore the sensation, but the little blotch appeared in the corner of my eye and seemed to force my attention to it then, too. I *had* to look because not looking was like trying to hold your breath after running wind sprints in gym class.

I tried not to see it. I squinted, focusing on the priest as he rambled through his sermon. I forced myself to take deep breaths, swallowing hard and hoping to push the crimson fog out of my eyes. A ringing grew in my ears and my stomach felt queasy. The whole church rocked like a boat and became hot and stuffy.

The priest blathered on, calmly gesturing in his flowing robes, but his words were crowded out by the insane ringing that pounded through my head. As the redness swept over my vision, I gripped the back of the pew in front of us, convinced I was going to throw up or pass out. With my eyes squeezed shut as tight as they would go, the pressure lifted. I could see the wrinkled old man in the baggy suit. I was now next to him, but we were in his house, next to his bed. He held up a pillow and lowered it over his sleeping wife's face.

Sweat covered my brow. I shook my head back and forth as hard as I could, nearly falling onto the old red carpet at St. Matthew's as I tried not to see the kicking elderly woman clawing at the pillow.

When I opened my eyes, the wrinkled old man was gone and the ringing was, too. The priest was still in the middle of his sermon. I sat there, drenched in sweat and staring at nothing, gasping for breath as my mother's voice urged me to calm down.

You're okay, Dougie. Take a deep breath. You're okay.

It was the strained tone adults used when everything's *not* okay.

Jimmy didn't need to know about that episode, either.

It was still pretty early when we got home from the park, so we dropped off our bikes and headed down to our creek. A day or so before, we had strategically stashed a plastic model aircraft carrier we had built and a few G. I. Joes. That is to say, we had left them near the creek when our moms called us for dinner, and we forgot to bring them up to the house later. We had to make sure that kid in New Orleans didn't have them now.

Living next door met the requirement for Jimmy and I to be friends. To be *best* friends, secrets had to be shared and trusts had to be constructed, done through years of playing together. The confrontation in the park had been one of many things that had cemented into a solid friendship.

But like most things with ten-year-olds, all that would soon change. After Jimmy moved away, it would be a long time before I made another friend that close—if I ever did.

The kid I knew was always outside learning about nature while I was always inside teaching myself how to draw. While he practiced bow hunting with razor tipped arrows, I went to swim meets and read books between my events. He learned how to use his dad's sharpening wheel to hone the blade of a pocket knife (allegedly he could shave with it—if we needed to shave) and could skin a rabbit and store the meat. His older brother showed us how to do it once. It was fast and almost bloodless, not at all what I expected. Once started, the skin seemed to slide off the rabbit like you'd pull off a t-shirt over your head.

I never had a pocket knife. Eventually, my dad bought me an Xacto knife at Pfirman's Hobby Shop that I was allowed to use when I built model cars.

Our hikes were a different story. We were almost always a kindred spirit in the woods, walking and talking about the important things that ten-year-olds talk about: comic books, movies, and sometimes girls. We also had a question and answer game that we invented, and we played the game while we hiked the narrow trails through the woods.

Jimmy poked at the capsized aircraft carrier with a stick. "Hey," he said without looking up. "Would you kill Hitler?"

It was the way we always began our question and answer game. I was tired and didn't want to play. A massive amount of mud had somehow gathered under my fingernails and needed attention.

"C'mon." He turned around to face me. "Let's play."

He stepped onto a rock in the middle of the creek, attempting to find enough to cross without having to walk down to the shallow part. "Would you kill Hitler?"

I leaned forward, accepting the challenge. "Of course. No hesitation."

Arms held out to balance himself, he glanced up and smiled. The game was on.

He hopped back to the other side of the water. Somewhere in the next ten minutes or so, he would try to have me saying that I would do something crazy. That was the game.

We didn't know who Hitler was at that age. Not really. It was a bad name for our game, but that's what we called it. It was our way of being a little bad, I guess, naming a dumb game after someone like that.

The hill by the creek was grassy and soft. Sunlight filtered through the maple trees to illuminate varying patches of the green turf. Small clusters of orange and red leaves glided to earth with each gentle breeze. Jimmy was thinking up the next question—if he hadn't prepared one already. Usually, he was working toward a point.

The game was as simple as Tic Tac Toe. Jimmy was good at it, but I was better, like a good offense against a good defense. That made it all the more important for him to beat me. Him beating me at Killing Hitler would be like me being a better shot than him with our brothers' BB guns. Ten-year-olds have to try to stake out their own "bests," especially if they have older brothers.

Jimmy strolled along the creek bank like a lawyer preparing a cross-examination, wagging his finger in the air. "Would you . . . kill Hitler if you knew they would catch you?"

"Oh, sure." I picked up a stick and pushed it through a yellow leaf, spinning it like a pinwheel. "Hell, I'd *expect* to get caught." It was easy to be brave in theory, when life and love were hypothetical. Or to use cusswords like "hell" when you knew no parents could hear you.

Nodding, Jimmy turned and paced back the other way. "What if the Germans had spies that took your mom and dad hostage?"

"I'd still do it." I shrugged. "Besides, if I could sneak in close enough to kill Hitler, I could probably sneak out and nobody would know."

"Oh, they'd know all right." Jimmy chuckled. "He's in charge of the whole country. They'd know."

I thought my answer was pretty solid. "I'd have to do it. He was a bad guy. He killed a lot of people. I would be a hero for killing him."

"Oh, a *hee-ro*!" Jimmy laughed. "You're a tough guy, huh?"

"No..." I tossed my stick in the water and watched it drift towards New Orleans. "Not tough. Smart."

"Right. Smart." He sauntered over the rocks for a moment before perching himself on a small boulder jutting out of the hill. "You might be smart but you aren't sneaky."

I didn't know where he was going with that, but we were off track. "C'mon, you aren't playing the game."

"Okay, okay." He had probably already thought of his good question, and now he needed time to remember it. His attention appeared consumed by a few passing minnows as they darted around in the stream, then his eyes narrowed. "Okay, so if you were sure to get caught, you'd still kill Hitler, right?"

"Right. No question."

"What if the Germans were going to murder your parents if you killed Hitler?"

I was ready for that. "I'd still have to do it. Two people for the price of a million people is a good trade."

"So you'd sacrifice your mom and dad, just like that?"

"Well . . . I think you'd have to. Heck, for a million lives? You *do* have to."

His head bobbed, seeming to agree with that math.

"Besides." I grinned. "Then I could run the damned air conditioning in my room."

We laughed. His bedroom was as hot and stuffy as mine. For some reason, our parents wouldn't run the air conditioning in summertime until after dinner, not even the window units upstairs where the kids' bedrooms were—the hottest part of the house. They said electricity was expensive, but maybe it was a ruse to keep us playing outside.

"Hey, no." Jimmy waved his hand. "You wouldn't get any air conditioning. You'd be dead already, remember?"

"No, I think I could still sneak out if I was able to sneak in."

"Uh-uh." He shook his head. "You can't sneak out. They have too many guards. You definitely get killed."

I nodded. "Okay..."

"Okay. So . . ." He squatted, resting his arms on his knees. "What if they . . . if they also kidnapped your aunts and uncles, and all your cousins, and they were all gonna get killed, too?"

"Hah. Take 'em."

"Boy, it's a good thing you don't have a dog." He stood and threw a rock into the creek. A tall column of water splashed up with a *bloop*. The water was deep where the stone hit. A smile crept across his face. "Suppose they also grabbed Sheila McCormack." He glanced my way. "And they were going to kill her, too."

I opened my mouth but didn't speak. I didn't know he knew about Sheila.

Jimmy hopped back onto the rock in the middle of the creek and made kissing noises. "Ooh, Shee-lah. Oooh!"

Leaning back on one shoulder, I tried to play it cool. "Whatever. Take her."

He raised his eyebrows. "Really? You'd let them kill Sheila McCormack!?"

"Well." I inspected the mud under my fingernails. "Do I get to kiss her first?"

"You sure do." He was wearing a huge grin now. "Maybe more than that."

"Okay, then. Hitler lives."

"Bwah!" Jimmy laughed, nearly falling off the rock. "I knew it!"

That was his goal, to find out if I liked Shelia McCormack. That wasn't usually how we played the game. Typically, we'd start out by asking if you would, say, rob a bank. You'd say no. Then we'd say, what if bank robbers had kidnapped your parents and they would kill them if you didn't rob the bank. Maybe you'd consider it then. The goal was to get you to admit that you'd do something that you originally said you wouldn't. Something you'd never think of doing in a million years, and suddenly in a few questions, there you were, admitting that you'd definitely do it.

But it was a game, a joke. I always knew we had no chance to do something heroic like killing Hitler, the way I knew I probably had no chance of kissing Sheila McCormack. But it was a fun way to trick your pal if he played along. And sometimes it was just funny.

"Would you ever peek up an old lady's dress?"

"I *have* peeked up your mom's dress. Yuck."

"HEY!"

Sometimes it went off the rails right from the start.

"Would you ever kill a person for a dumb reason?"

"I'd kill you for telling me it was too hot to wear pants today. I tore the hell out of my legs shinnying up that tree."

Sometimes it tested our limits.

"Would you kill the President for a million dollars?"

Digging clay and sand out from under one fingernail by using another fingernail took it from one and wedged it under the other. "Kill President Ford, huh?" I peered up at the sugar maples, their leaves turning orange and yellow and red with the onset of fall. "He just took over. Would I get caught?"

"Nope. But you'd spend the rest of your life on the run."

"I don't know. A million dollars is a lot of money. If I could get a million dollars and get away with it . . . I don't know."

Usually it was like Tic Tac Toe—it didn't get far, and it didn't get complicated. But sometimes, it opened doors that were better left shut.

"You couldn't do it." Jimmy scanned the bank for another baseball-sized rock. Finding one, he heaved it into the deep part of the water. *Bloop.* "No way."

I watched the ripples from the splash fade and the water become a clear, blue-green tint again. "I bet I could for a million dollars."

"No, you couldn't. Not you."

"Why not me?" I placed my hands in the grass and righted myself. "A million dollars is a lot of money. My brother said that if you had a million dollars and you put it in the bank, you could spend a thousand dollars a week for the rest of your life and never touch the original million."

"Yeah?" Jimmy narrowed his eyes. "How do you figure that?"

"Interest. The amount of interest the bank pays you is so much that you could take a thousand dollars a week out and never go broke."

He stared at the water. "Man, a thousand dollars a week." That was a lot of money to kids who were lucky if they earned five bucks for mowing the lawn on Saturday—and that took most of the day.

"Yeah, you could have a Corvette and a gullwing Mercedes." Those were our favorite model car kits to build, so of course we'd buy them for real if we could. Things like food would still be provided by mom and dad, of course.

He nodded. "I'd definitely get a Corvette. Maybe a convertible one."

"That won't work." I smirked. "You can't fit a gun rack on the back window of a convertible." He didn't like redneck references. They hit too close to home.

"The heck with that." Jimmy hopped onto the midstream rock, throwing his arms out again to balance himself as he eyed the next stony foothold. "Besides, if I had a million dollars, I could get somebody to make me a custom rack for my convertible corvette, that's for sure."

"And a CB radio?" Holding a fist to my mouth, I pretended to hold a receiver. "Ten-four, good buddy!"

Finding enough dry rocks so he wouldn't slip, he bounded over the water and landed near me. "So? What would you put in yours?"

"If I had a Corvette?" I thought for a moment. "I don't know. They're pretty cool the way they come."

"You wouldn't customize it?"

"I don't know . . ."

"You wouldn't." It was a statement, not a question. Jimmy stretched out on his back, put his hands under his head, and stared up at the tree tops.

I never did that. Bugs might get in my hair.

"Why not?"

"Because you wouldn't get a Mercedes or a Corvette."

I put a hand in the grass and turned to him. "Why *not*?"

"Because you couldn't kill anybody."

"For a million dollars I bet I could!"

"No, you couldn't." His tone had changed. Now he was almost sneering. Maybe the redneck stuff had been over the top after all. He sat up and eyed me. "You couldn't do it. You could never do something like that."

"Why not?"

"You know why." He spat, not at me, but to emphasize his point. His sneering pissed me off.

"Why not?" My cheeks felt hot with embarrassment.

Just then, the voice of Jimmy's mom pierced the woods. Supper time.

Hearing it, he took off like a shot. I'd get called soon, too, but if Mrs. Marondeck thought Jimmy was up in the woods somewhere, she would let him stay out for a while. So he scampered off, across the creek and up the hill, disappearing into the woods and the farmer's fields beyond, allowing me to lie to his mother without *really* lying. If she saw me coming up from the creek to my house, I could tell her that Jimmy was up in the woods. The kitchen windows of these houses were strategically placed so moms could see the kids in the yard. By the time Mrs. Marondeck saw me, what I'd tell her about her son would be true.

I had to eat fast or I'd be late for swim practice. A whole hour of my head immersed in water, with very little talking. It was a lot of time to think. Too much, really. At least my fingernails would be clean when I got back home.

As I swam, I thought about the game.

Stupid as it was, Jimmy and I liked playing the question and answer game mostly because we had invented it. But there was never a real point in the line of questions, because if you think about it realistically—like considering if you really went back in time to kill Hitler—the game took on a whole other dimension.

You'd have to do it before he came to power, before the damage started. You'd have to do it before Hitler was Hitler. That means doing what most people would consider an insane act, killing a harmless politician. You would become an enemy of the people for killing a person like that. No one else would know what he becomes.

It was a long practice. Mr. Holtzman has us doing sets of 200 yards and distance swims. He must have had a bad day at work. Churning my arms through the chlorinated water at Highcrest Swim and Tennis Club, the questions bounced in my head.

If somebody showed up on your front door on a Saturday afternoon and said, "You have to kill this stranger to save millions of lives . . ." Hell, you'd laugh. You'd freaking call the police on them. Nobody would ever really do such a thing, and the few who did—aren't they the ones we read about? Charles Manson, Jim Jones, David Koresh . . .

When swim practice finished, I was tired mentally and physically. We drove home in near silence, listening to Easy 105 FM on the radio. An old *Carpenters'* tune, done as an instrumental, filled our station wagon. Our little town only got rock n roll on one AM channel, and my parents never played that. I stared out the window and watched the houses roll by in the dark, my cold, damp hair clinging to my head.

After watching some TV, I went to bed and stared at the ceiling of my room. Model airplanes pinned with strings created a frozen dogfight overhead, but the questions wouldn't let go.

If the bad acts aren't random, if they're not crazy people going crazy, *if that's not what they are,* then—what are they?

I rolled over and adjusted my pillow, shoving an arm under it. The headlights of an approaching vehicle shined around one edge of my window shade, casting long white rectangles onto the far wall of my room. As the car rounded the curve on Reigert Drive, *Benny And The Jets* became audible, fading as the traveler continued up the hill.

In Millersburg, kids had to wait until they were practically sixteen and had a car before they could listen to any good music—unless they stole an older brother's portable radio for the afternoon. Mostly, we were limited, and we accepted it. We never tried anything. We never stole a car or skipped school or smoked. We rode bikes and played in the woods and climbed trees. We were supposed to be good kids who grew up to be good adults.

We played our little question and answer game to amuse ourselves. We never played it with other kids. We chose to just play it between us.

Until we got too big for it. Then we chose to do other things.

One of us chose college in Florida, graduate school, and marriage. The other chose very differently.

Chapter 5

It looked a like a castle.

At almost four years old, anything princess-oriented was a big hit with our daughter. While Mallory stood at the massive front gate to Hillside Winery and snapped a picture, Sophie bounced up and down in her car seat. The castle was real, and she was finally here.

The morning sunlight sharply illuminated the rows and rows of majestic grape vines leading up to the regal building. Its tall roof and circular front spires were something right out of a story book—which was all Sophie needed.

Her tiny mouth hung open as she gazed at the ornate building. “Does the princess sleep in that tower, Daddy?”

“Hold my hand, sweetie.” I wiggled my fingers at Sophie as I stood in the parking lot, waiting for her small hand to take mine. Mallory shut the van door and gazed at the big building through sunglasses, admiring the winery-castle and no doubt contemplating the many fermented treasures waiting for her inside.

“Let’s look both ways here.” The instruction was for our daughter but a reminder to my wife as well. Either could wander into a busy parking lot while distracted by what lay on the other side. Bold knights in shining armor for one, bold merlots in shining glass for the other.

Holding hands and swinging arms with Sophie, I led the way as we crossed the lot toward the massive wooden front doors. “Cars are looking for parking spots. They aren’t watching out for little girls in pretty yellow dresses.”

With her own face buried in the brochure, Mallory strolled across asphalt, more or less in the general direction of the winery entrance.

"Hey." I chuckled. "They aren't watching for pretty ladies in blue jeans, either."

"What?" Mallory let the brochure flop downward and raised her eyebrows. Her mind was elsewhere. On a vacation, that was a good thing.

I may have suggested to our daughter, through a series of carefully directed questions during our long drive from Tampa, that Hillside wasn't a winery at all. Instead, it might contain all sorts of magic, good and bad, inside its tower walls.

It looked like a castle on the internet, after all. As my Sophie sat on my lap in her princess pajamas, we scrolled through the pictures on the Hillside website. I didn't have to do much convincing.

"Is that a Rapunzel tower, Daddy?"

"Hmm. Could be."

"Oh, and is that there where the princess carriage goes?"

"Wow, I bet it does."

For my niece's wedding in Millersburg, we plotted out a meandering, scenic journey from Tampa to Indiana and back, stopping in on Virginia's wine country "on the way."

We saw a bear cross the road in front of us outside of Nashville, but Sophie had been more impressed by the *real cows* grazing near the dairy cheese shop near Macon. She also enjoyed spearing assorted cheese samples with toothpicks and offering them to anyone and everyone in the store.

Winery trips and the accompanying excursions were a welcome pressure release from the stresses of Mallory's job. We even rented a minivan for the occasion—something I originally balked at.

"Why do we need a *minivan*?" The word invoked an utter lack of coolness that I was not quite ready to embrace.

Mallory raised her eyes from her wine brochures long enough to give me the *wife* look. "To have some space." She continued sorting the colorful collection of glossy pamphlets in front of her—an odd paper-bound method for a tech person. "You'll be driving, but Sophie and I will be cramped into a small back seat if we rent a sedan. After we load in enough suitcases for a two-week trip and start packing in cases of wine, we'll be sardines."

Shipping multiple cases of wine gets expensive fast, so on last year's vacation trip to California, she had to be selective about our purchases.

Our annual vacation had evolved, like a lot of other things, to encompass our young daughter. Kids at that age can only do so much before needing a long nap or food; that left a lot of vacation choices off the table. As Sophie's endurance expanded, so did our vacations, but there was nothing wrong with folding her interests into ours, or Disney World and Sea World would be the only places we'd ever go.

That compromise eventually led us to Virginia wine country, to round out a trip in our rented minivan to attend my niece's wedding and to see my family—especially my dad. Sophie's grandpa had the ability to make *each* grandchild feel as though they were his favorite.

Sophie generally did fine in cars, so the trek to Indiana went well, but nobody can take a thirteen-hour road trip without stretching their legs. To accommodate that, Mallory arranged for a roomy vehicle and some stops—wineries, usually—along with a few touristy destinations for our daughter. Plus a cooler full of kid snacks. With the van's DVD player, our daughter was pretty well set.

The routine at a winery varied depending on Sophie's mood. Sometimes she would fall asleep in the stroller, so I'd park under a tree and read a book. Other times she played quietly in the tasting room while Mallory and I both did a tasting.

The return trip to Florida was well mapped out, designed to sample numerous award-winning wines from Virginia's wine country.

One winery was like a castle. That alone might be enough to keep Sophie interested for an hour, but mentioning that we'd go there on her birthday made it an over the top exciting event. *Was it really an old castle that they made into a winery? Do you think it has a king? Is there a princess in a tower?* Only a visit would say for sure.

Each day, as we made our way to other wineries, Mallory primed Sophie. "Pretty soon we're going to the castle for your birthday!"

Sophie couldn't wait. Each morning she would wake up and ask, "Are we going to the castle today?"

The newspapers I'd read online said that Hillside Winery had existed for many decades in the wide open spaces of Virginia's wine country. Beautiful in every picture taken over the years, Hillside was proof its owners, Mr. and Mrs. Hill, had created a winery appealing to the eye as its esteemed wines were to the palate. From the huge iron gates of the entry, to the stone walls surrounding the campus, to the wooden floors of the tasting room, everything was done well.

It certainly appeared to be the result of an owner who loved his winery.

The articles indicated Mr. Hill's business had prospered along with the growing town over a half century, making him a pillar of the community. He studied what the successful wineries in California were doing, and he did what they did. Tourists wanted a winery to visit, but they needed a restaurant to eat in and a hotel to sleep in, too. A hard worker and a quick learner, Mr. Hill saw to it that partnerships were formed, hotels were built, and the area thrived.

The last article I read was about a traffic accident a year ago—and the lawsuit that followed. It wasn't flattering to Mr. Hill.

The police reports blamed a light Virginia rain, or maybe the fog that had burned off hours before, for making the roads slick. A car came through a traffic light and Mr. Hill's pickup collided with it, smashing the truck and him with it. Doctors feared he would never walk again.

When we finally toured the winery in person that sunny fall morning, I noticed a hallway lined with pictures of his recovery, from hospital bed to standing with the use of two canes. A framed local newspaper clipping noted that getting up and down from chairs was now difficult for the old man, and his new pickup truck had to be fitted with hand controls for the brakes and the accelerator.

I strolled around the winery that morning, holding my daughter's hand and wondering if he still worked there.

That's why he walked across the tasting room with the dolly. Loaded with four cases of wine, no other employee would be allowed to do such a thing with paying customers present. Cases for delivery were to go out the back, but Mr. Hill's car was parked by the front door—in the handicapped spot—closer to his office and closer to the walk up ramp.

"Going over to Bertram's for their delivery," Mr. Hill grumbled to his wife, letting Avery stack the last case of wine onto the dolly.

Mrs. Hill looked up from her desk full of papers and peered at him over her glasses. "Bertam's? That was supposed to be delivered yesterday."

"Yes, Bertam's!" He grabbed his keys off his desk. "That moron José missed the delivery. *Again*!"

Avery patted the stack of wine cases. "I can load these for you whenever you want, sir."

"I can do it!" Hill narrowed his eyes. "My knees and back might be on fire with pain, but I can still outwork you any day." He yanked open a desk drawer and pulled out a brown pill bottle, stuffing it in his pocket.

Avery recoiled. "Yes, sir. I didn't mean—"

The old man yanked the dolly out of his employee's hands and stormed out of the office.

"I'm sorry, ma'am. I didn't mean to insult him."

"Go on, Avery. He's just in one of his moods." Picking up the time sheets, Mrs. Hill flipped through them. José was scheduled off yesterday.

I had to pull my daughter away at the last second to prevent her from running into the dolly as it sped across the room.

Lifting her to my arms, I swept a strand of blonde hair from her eyes. "You know how we look both ways before crossing a street or parking lot? We have to look both ways before crossing a winery lobby, too!"

She wasn't amused. I figured she was starting to get fussy for lunch.

As I lowered Sophie to the ground and took her hand, the hairs stood up on the back of my neck. I shuddered, glancing around the ceiling of an air conditioner vent that must have kicked on.

Sophie tugged my hand, visibly upset.

"Okay, okay. Let me tell Mommy we're going outside and then we can get something to eat."

The scowl on the face of the old man with the dolly was a real surprise. I didn't know who he was, but he seemed to be a very unhappy employee. Unusual, for a customer service area. I don't remember seeing any unhappy employees at the Napa wineries.

At the counter, Mallory was about to start sampling the wines. I informed her of the pint sized mutiny happening, and she agreed to stay behind and make sure the 2017 wines weren't adversely affected by the weather or something.

"Okay, I'll go feed Sophie her lunch. You come out when you're finished." I turned to our unhappy princess. "We'll have a little birthday picnic in the parking lot. Does that sound fun?" I smiled in an attempt to brighten her mood. "It's nice out. Maybe we'll open the van doors, sit outside on the cooler, and watch a DVD."

It didn't work. Sophie had grown restless, launching into a near tantrum.

I'd better hurry with that picnic.

Mr. Hill wheeled the heavy dolly down the ramp, and stood it next to his grey truck. He placed a hand on it to steady himself while he dug for his keys in his jacket pocket. Pulling them out, he dropped them.

"Damn it!"

A group of young customers, two couples, had just finished their tasting. Early birds, one couple wanted to get to as many wineries—and as many tastings—as they could in a day. The other couple was considering whether to break for lunch. The men smartly decided to let their ladies decide, as they loaded their purchases into the trunk of their sedan.

"Come on, Sherry." Abigail giggled, tugging on the sleeve of her red-haired friend as they stood by the driver's side door. "We can eat any time. I wanna get loaded!"

The men laughed. They agreed with Abigail, who had already consumed enough alcohol to no longer whisper quietly. As the men made room among their cramped suitcases for their wines, the ladies continued.

"Aren't you guys hungry at all?" Sherry asked.

"Sherry-berry." Abigail wobbled as she spoke. "There's gotta be a fast food place on the way to the next winery."

Across the lot, Mr. Hill painfully stacked the delivery cases into his truck. Each one was an aching challenge. His knees burned from squatting to get the dropped keys, but that was the best he could manage using the canes. His back would soon hate him for lifting the cases instead of having a helper do it, but he was too proud and angry to admit to needing help.

The sedan trunk slammed shut. "What did you guys decide?" Steve put his arm around Sherry. Tyler leaned against the trunk as they waited for an answer.

Abigail stuck out her lower lip and pouted. "She's being no fun."

"I think we should eat pretty soon." Sherry sighed. "Or we'll all be three sheets to the wind like somebody I know."

Steve nodded, digging his phone out of his pocket. "She's got a point. Why don't we check at the map and see what's around here?"

Across the parking lot, Mr. Hill started the pickup. He glared at the hated hand controls of his truck, grasping them in anger.

"I think there's a historic church nearby," Sherry said. "And an old antebellum house . . ."

The others groaned.

Mr. Hill swung an arm over the passenger seat. As he looked backward, the truck engine roared. The wheels screeched and the truck lurched backwards, speeding across the parking lot in reverse. The old man's knuckles turned white as he clung desperately to the hand controls.

At the squeal of the tires, Sherry glanced at the gray truck that sped towards them. Its tail lights never lit up to indicate that it was slowing down. Instead it came faster. Her eyes widened as she opened her mouth to scream.

Panicking, Mr. Hill gripped the controls even tighter. The truck accelerated faster.

The look on Sherry's face made Tyler turn around. The tailgate of the truck was coming right at him. He flinched and turned away. Tires still screeching, the truck smashed full speed into the sedan. Glass exploded everywhere. The impact slammed Steve into the van in the next parking space and heaved Sherry into the air. She was like a matador being thrown by a raging bull in one of those "Animals Gone Crazy" videos.

Eyes bulging, Hill still gripped the accelerator, shouting as he bounced around the cab of his pickup. The engine raced as the truck forced its way past its victims and into the small grassy patch in front of the vineyard. The truck had barely slowed down on impact. It plowed backwards, churning dirt into the air, as it sped toward the vineyard. Engine whining, it smashed through vines and fences and irrigation posts, revving higher as it went, until it finally got tangled up in enough debris to stall out.

It was as though its driver had maniacally intended to kill everyone present.

Chapter 6

"Hey."

One simple word could not have meant more to any other person in their entire lives.

Mallory turned to the voice and saw me, her smiling husband, holding our daughter in my arms. She ran over and grabbed us both, hugging the two of us tighter than she ever had before. "Oh, thank God!"

I'd been smiling upon seeing my wife. I was now concerned. "What's the matter?"

"I didn't know it wasn't you." Mallory glanced at me and then out to the parking lot. "I mean, I thought it *was* you, the two of you, out there." Tears welled in her eyes. She buried her face in my chest. "I didn't know you two were okay."

I put my arms around my wife as she continued to squeeze me and our daughter. In the winery doorway, the three of us embraced, a family reunited after only minutes, but to Mallory it must have seemed like hours. I'd never seen her like this.

"I heard somebody yell for an ambulance and when I got to the window I saw somebody laying on the ground and . . ." The words caught in her throat. "Her dress was the same color as Sophie's."

"It's okay." I rubbed her back, feeling the tension draining out of it. "We're okay."

She kept hugging us. "I've never been so scared!"

I gazed out the doorway at the carnage. The crowd around the victims obscured almost everything except the blood. Small pools of it streamed across the lot to the storm drain. It was different from the blood they show in movies.

That, and the damage to the cars in the parking lot, did a lot to fuel my wife's impression that she'd just lost her family.

What a scene. The entire sedan was smashed like a soda can. The trunk was crumpled but the car had been forced around backwards so now the hood faced the winery and the trunk faced the vineyards. Our rental van was demolished. The side nearest the sedan was almost completely torn away.

Knowing that and feeling it are two different things. I was so concerned about keeping Sophie from seeing it, I didn't react at all to what I'd see—and what had almost happened to us. Had we been sitting there for our picnic, we would have been killed.

Heaving against my chest and covering our daughter in kisses, Mallory thought we had been. But it didn't register with me. Not yet.

I suppose I never felt we had been in any danger. Sophie and I never made it to the van. A distraction—a little temper tantrum—had slowed us long enough to avoid being victims of the wreck, but I had witnessed all the shocking carnage. I pulled open the winery door and the gray pickup truck squealed its wheels. It launched across the parking lot like a rocket, smashing right into the sedan—and the people. I saw it all and was able to turn Sophie away so she didn't see any of it.

"I heard somebody yell for an ambulance." Mallory shuddered. Holding our daughter, she paced back and forth in the entryway as people rushed in and out to help attend to victims—or to get a better view of the macabre scene still unfolding outside. "That was me," I said, trying to comfort her. "I was the guy you heard shouting."

Mallory gazed up at me, her mouth open. She wiped her eyes, smearing mascara onto her cheeks.

"I saw the whole thing from right here. I didn't want to go out and help because I didn't want . . ." I paused and nodded at our daughter, lowering my voice. "I didn't want this one to see that lady and all the, you know. B-L-O-O-D."

Certain the young woman had been killed, I didn't want our child to witness that first hand—or hear the screams from her friend, the shouts from the volunteers . . .

"I'm so glad you're both safe." Mallory hugged and kissed us both. She held back her emotions as best as she could. To go from terror to joy was a sudden turn, and no one could blame her for crying a little in the process.

Volunteers rushed in and out, getting towels and water for the victims' wounds. We needed to move.

I scanned the winery. "Why don't we . . . why don't *you* take Sophie back into the lobby. I'll go see if I can help outside."

Mallory took a deep breath and nodded, appearing happy to get away from what she could see in the parking lot.

The police would probably want a statement from an eye witness when they arrived. I stepped out the door and made a slow circle around the crowd, thinking about ways I could help but not really wanting to see the dead woman or her friends' injuries. With my hands in my pockets, I crept toward the wreckage that had been a peaceful parking lot moments before.

The young lady was on her back, surrounded by her friends and the volunteers, her yellow dress stained with blood. Several of the winery's employees were administering makeshift bandages to the victims, using towels and cleaning cloths. The way the employees spoke to the victims was the way we'd been trained to when I was a life guard in high school. Keep them talking, keep telling them they're okay, and do it in reassuring tones.

A man wearing a volunteer firefighter t-shirt kneeled closest to her. A barrel-chested man and a few other customers had jumped right into action when they heard me call for help. They seemed to know what they were doing, too. Calm voices. Several asked each other for a towel or water, addressing each other by name.

I hoped the girl had survived. It was incredible, to see her tossed into the air like a doll, then come crashing down between the two cars as they smashed together. I was sure there was no way she could have survived, and the streams of blood indicated I was right. With all the damage to the vehicles, and the way the truck plowed right into the people, it was difficult to think any of them had survived.

But they had.

Her friends had all miraculously escaped much harm. Bruises and a black eye for the one; a few scratches for the others. They stood vigil over their injured friend in the yellow dress as the volunteer firemen steered her away from going into shock and tried to keep her conscious.

She should be dead. Ironic, but she has no idea how lucky she is today. She won't think that, but it's true.

There was no way anybody should have survived it.

That's when the realization struck me. It came with such blinding force that I blinked, unable to breathe.

This is how close you just came to getting killed, yourself. To having your insides splattered all over the side of the van.

I would have been sitting right between the cars, on the cooler, like we had planned . . .

Sophie probably would have been on my lap.

That made the air rush out of me. I put my hand out, knocking into some people, staggering to find a solid place to hold myself up. I leaned against one of the other cars in the lot, trying not to think about the possibilities, but they came rushing into my head anyway.

I turned away, but the image was already imprinted on my memory. Sophie would have been killed. My sweet little girl, dead.

Even if an adult could survive, could a child? Being smashed by a truck at full speed? They worry about kids becoming fatalities in twenty mile per hour crashes! There was no way she would have made it.

I thought about our daughter being thrown into the air the way the young woman had been. The image caused an awful blackness to swell inside me. I wiped my eyes and forced myself to refocus. There might be help I could offer. Inbound cars full of customers, not aware of the accident that had just occurred, were trying to pull into the parking lot.

Where was the ambulance?

Employees directed traffic. Chairs were brought out to block the wreck area. I walked to the parking lot entrance to direct any new arrivals to the rear lot.

But I couldn't help surveying the damage again.

The gray truck was buried a hundred yards into the vineyard. The sedan was crushed and turned around. Our rental van was demolished on one side. Glass was everywhere. Huge black tire marks showed the path the truck had taken, directly from its handicap spot to the sedan, then it had plowed up huge chunks of grass and dirt all the way to its resting place deep among the vines. A winery worker had gone over to help the driver.

Good idea. That old guy was probably having a heart attack when he did all this, and if he didn't have one then, he might have one now.

The worker opened the truck door and reached inside. The driver, clad in drab clothes, came out of the vehicle. He fumbled a bit as he exited the pickup. Probably a concussion.

Steadying the old man, the employee produced two canes from the truck bed. The driver began to walk with them, hobbling toward the parking lot. He shrugged off the worker, batting at him with one of the canes.

That was odd. The guy was only trying to help.

It was a curious moment, but I didn't give it a second thought. Sirens in the distance indicated help was finally on the way.

I returned to the tasting room to give Mallory an update. She had commandeered a t-shirt display table as her command post and was already working on getting a replacement rental van. Whether she was working hard at distracting herself or already over the excitement, she looked busy.

"Sophie's getting fussy." Using the tasting room's fireplace hearth for a seat, Mallory held her cell phone to her ear and bounced our daughter on her knee. "Why don't you see if any of the stuff in the car is okay? The cooler and the snacks. Maybe we can get her something to eat."

The winery only sold exotic cheeses and bottled water, and maybe some wine crackers. Our picky girl wouldn't eat any of that.

"Okay." I walked back out to the van.

I stepped around the glass and the blood soaked paper towels that had been discarded by paramedics. Somehow, getting into the van at this moment, with the young lady lying right there on the other side, it seemed . . . rude. While paramedics tended to her wounds, I was trying to get a snack.

I tried to make it less uncomfortable on myself by going to the driver's side. As if I could have gotten into the passenger side anyway.

Opening the door shocked me.

The van's interior was pristine. The wreckage to the outside was completely masked on the inside. There were broken windows but no bits of glass on the seats. No smashed bottles of wine leaking from the many cases stacked by the suitcases. Nothing really out of place.

Outside, chaos, demolished metal and debris. Bloody victims groaning as emergency workers tended to them.

Inside, quiet and calm. The car was peaceful and . . . a little stuffy.

I reached in and grabbed the cooler. As a passing thought, I popped open the glove compartment and pulled out the rental contract paperwork. We'd be needing it.

As I stepped back and went to shut the door, it pushed back. It wouldn't close. I stared at it for a moment. The impact of the crash must have twisted the support frame. I shook my head. How amazing that the wreck could bend the sturdy steel frame and not break a single glass wine bot—

A wave of nausea hit me. My head became uncomfortably warm, almost dizzy, and a queasy feeling swept through my gut. I put my hand on the side of the vehicle to steady myself, drawing deep breaths. The air outside was cool but in my nose and throat it felt stuffy, like the inside of the van a moment ago. I swallowed hard. All the excitement must have finally been getting to me. A delayed reaction.

"Excuse me." A tall young man in a dark blue police uniform approached me.

I righted myself, taking another deep breath. "Yes, officer?"

He glanced at the van. "Is this your vehicle?"

"Yeah." I looked it over. "What's left of it."

The queasiness wouldn't leave. For a second, I thought I might throw up right in front of the officer. I swallowed again, trying to force back the uneasy feeling.

"Are you okay, sir?"

I nodded. "I am. A little motion sickness. It'll pass." His name badge read SGT. TAGGART.

He watched me for a moment, then took out a notepad. "Did you see what happened?"

"Actually, I did." Putting a fist to my lips like I was going to cough, I tried to assess whether the sick feeling was growing or passing. It did neither. Maybe talking would help. I pointed to the winery building. "I was in the doorway, coming out into the parking lot. I saw the whole thing."

Sergeant Taggart peered over my shoulder. Behind him, the drab old man used his two canes to slowly work his way back toward main building. The winery worker trailed a few steps behind him.

"We're going to need you to make a statement. Would you mind?"

"No problem."

"It's going to be a few minutes since we have the situation with the other people . . ."

"Oh, I completely understand." I said. "You go ahead and take care of that. I'll be around when you're ready." I hooked a thumb at the van. "We aren't going anywhere for a while."

The old man and his canes hobbled through the grass and disappeared behind the building. Aside from the winery employee following him, nobody seemed to notice. Everyone's focus seemed to be on the victims, and rightly so, but . . . With a quick change of clothes, he could practically disappear. The driver of the pickup truck that caused all the carnage could walk right through the parking lot and nobody would be the wiser.

The nausea swelled inside me and my ears began to ring.

"Well," Taggart said. "Maybe we can call a wrecker for you and have one of our officers drive you to the rental car office in town."

And get your snooping eyes out of here.

I didn't hear the words as much as I . . . felt them. The officer was no longer talking. My stomach churned harder and the ringing in my ears became a nonstop cymbal crash.

"A rental car? That would be great!" He had to notice me sweating and my panting breath. "But, do whatever you need to first, with the other folks. I have to call our insurance and see how they want us to handle things."

"Sure," he said. "But briefly—what did you see?" *So I know which witness reports to file and which to misplace.*

It was an overactive imagination run amok. Shock from the sight of the blood. Post-traumatic stress, maybe. I was losing it. The emotional reactions I didn't have at during the carnage—like Mallory had felt seeing the wreckage—were they going overboard now?

I took another deep breath, trying to calm myself. "Well . . ."

At that moment, I noticed a slight color change in the officer's face. It was nothing I should have noticed; it came and went in an instant. I could only think of it like a little flash of blue, disappearing as fast as lightning. As soon as I realized I was seeing it, it was already gone.

I shook my head. It was a trick of the light or I was definitely losing it. Like that time we went digging for clams in the Indian River, I stepped on a sting ray and it sunk its barb into my toe. I was convinced I'd been cut by a piece of glass, but it wouldn't stop bleeding and my whole leg swelled up. I was embarrassed, thinking I was going into shock over such a small cut—especially since I wasn't excited or upset, like now. But it wasn't shock, it was the poison. The sting ray stuck a little venom in me, making my leg throb in pain for an hour and balloon up in size. At the time I thought, how ridiculous, to go into shock from something like that. But people do. People die from shock, too. It wasn't shock, though, and it eventually passed.

This was like that. Some sort of toxin got in my system. A bad piece of cheese or maybe dehydration. I got dehydrated at Disney World once, for Pete's sake. I threw up five minutes after walking in the front gates. This had to be something like that.

I regained my thoughts. I recounted—briefly—to Officer Taggart the events as I had seen them, trying desperately not to vomit while I did. I explained about the pickup truck's squealing wheels, the woman being thrown up in the air. I gestured to where things had happened, and how the pickup truck never even slowed down.

When I finished, I summed it up: "It was like a teenager who was pissed off at his girlfriend, the way he squealed his wheels. Just burned rubber, right across the parking lot at those poor folks."

Poor folks? That wouldn't do in a statement.

The words seemed as if they were coming from the officer, but his mouth never moved and his face gave no indication he was even thinking such things.

Still, I felt uncomfortable near him.

"Yes, sir." Taggart smiled. "I'll have one of my officers come over and get your statement in a few minutes." He headed off to meet the tow trucks coming up the long driveway and glanced back at me. "Think about a wrecker. We've already called two for the other vehicles. A third's no problem."

I took the cooler into the winery lobby and felt instantly better, like stepping into air conditioning in summer after mowing the lawn. Relief washed through me.

Mallory was on her cell phone with the insurance company. "No, thank God, none of us were hurt. We weren't in the van at the time."

I debated about whether to tell her about the blue lightning. She'd only conclude I was tired from all the excitement, which was probably right.

But she interrupted me before I could broach the subject.

Chapter 7

"Since I did the original rental car paperwork, I have to be the one to go get the replacement car." Mallory looked away. She knew I wouldn't like that. On the other side of the hearth, our daughter munched on goldfish crackers and cheese sticks.

"What about their commercials?" I frowned. "Where they drive a car out to you?"

Mallory sighed. "We didn't rent from that company."

I stared at the fireplace and rubbed my forehead. What had started out to be such a nice day had really, *really* turned bad.

"I told the insurance company that our rental van was undriveable," Mallory said. "We can get another rental—a sedan—in town, or they have another minivan at the airport."

The airport was hours from here.

"They'll have somebody from the local rental office drive me to their airport location." She bit her nail. "What do you think we should do?"

There was only one thing *to* do. I shook my head. "With all the big suitcases we brought and all of the cases of wine we've been buying, it'll never fit into a regular car. An SUV, sure. But a four door sedan?" I stared out the window at the smashed van. "There's no way."

For a moment I thought about mentioning the officer volunteering to take one of us into town, but I decided against it. Something just didn't sit right about that guy now, and if any other bizarre things were going to happen today, I didn't want Mallory to face it by herself.

"Anyway, I have to give a statement to the cops. Who knows how long it's going to be before they get around to talking to me."

The cards were dealt.

"Get to the airport. I'll stay here with Sophie." I watched as our daughter carefully inspected the smile on the goldfish cracker's face. "Maybe I can find a quiet place for her to nap."

It wouldn't be the first time she had slept under a tree at a winery. We had to empty the ruined van anyway, and the stroller was in there. That could work.

"Okay." Mallory waved her cell phone. "I'll have the local office pick me up. The lady at the cash register said they have a meeting room upstairs where you and Sophie can wait, if you want."

I grinned at her as she dialed her phone and put it to her ear. She had it all figured out.

"It's about three hours each way to the airport," I reminded her. "It's going to be a long day."

She walked over and kissed me. "It's already been a long day."

I pulled her close. "Ask somebody where I can put all our stuff from the van." I kissed her again, then I went down the hallway to the front doors.

It took several trips before the winery employees realized I was unloading our van into their lobby. Then, three of them joined in. They carried suitcases, toys, and competitors' wines from our previous stops into the front hallway. I noticed the drab gray man standing there, as still as a statue, staring out the window. He had been driving the pickup truck.

As I carried the final suitcase inside, I stopped momentarily to address the old man. He seemed like a poor old winery employee who had suffered a mini stroke or something and just lost control of the truck.

be sure that the paramedics hadn't
needed treatment. Maybe I wanted to se
my daughter, even if she wasn't payi
from my father that sometimes people c
fine afterwards, and then go home a
trauma coronary. For some reason, I fe
sure that wouldn't happen to this poor
employee that was having a bad enough
surely feeling awful about the wreck he
injuries.

"How are you holding up, fella'

The old man turned and glared a
step backward. It was a fierce, hateful
face was drawn and angry.

I regained myself and persisted.
It was my friendliest demeanor. "We
attack happening to you, y'know?"

He stared blankly at me.

"You were driving the gray pick

His eyes narrowed. "Probably j
damned lawsuit."

I blinked, dropping my jaw. "Ex

"Them tourists." The old man t
window, muttering. "Some people ne
leave."

I was shocked. I expected a sy
Some remorse, not anger. It was an odd
having killed a few people. Need to
What did that mean?

A gray haired woman appeared
Mrs. Hill. Would you like to store your
Her southern upbringing and hospitality
the elderly man's were cold. "They'll b

It was a nice gesture but also a way to get the suitcases and boxes out of their hallway, where customers might trip over them. And to keep me from talking further with her employees. I accepted.

Mrs. Hill made small talk as I moved our cases of wine. The genuine article, she was a sweet woman. I was in no rush to do anything since I figured I had at least five hours on my hands. Sophie was asleep in her stroller. I had time to chat.

We talked about Mrs. Hill's grown daughter, and how enjoyable life was when her girl was Sophie's age. "It's a lot of fun, and it's a lot of effort." She sat back in her office chair, smiling. "But mostly it's a lot of fun."

I nodded. "It is. It's been a *lot* of fun." I placed the last box down and found an empty chair for myself. "Does your daughter work here with you now?"

Somehow, I already knew the answer. Of all the wineries we had visited over the years, few were able to interest their children in the business. Almost none. It was the same story every time. The kids slaved away in the winery growing up, and as soon as they were able to get out, they did.

For most winery owners, the winemaking business was something they got into later in life. The fulfillment of a dream. For the kids, however, it was a life of constant drudgery. Millions of bottles to be washed, labels to affix . . . hot days in the fields weeding and pruning and spraying. It was a life of constant work—hard work—with almost none of the benefits. The kids would have to cancel plans and fill in when an employee called out sick or quit, but they couldn't have a glass of wine afterwards. And the drudgery was never ending. Year round, there was some musty, sticky task to do. Wine was fun for customers, not for the "winery brats" or *winery rats*, as they often referred to themselves.

"My daughter helps with the register now and then on weekends, but she has her own life." Gazing at the scowling gray statue in the hallway, Mrs. Hill let out a quiet sigh. "Mostly it's just me and Mr. Hill." A pained, remorseful smile moved over her mouth. "As far as family goes."

It hadn't dawned on me until then. The drab gray man with the scowl—the driver of the truck—was Mr. Hill, the owner of Hillside winery.

Chapter 8

I accepted Mrs. Hill's offer to relocate Sophie upstairs to the meeting room while we waited for Mallory to return.

It was a large space, created as an afterthought when they were adding onto the winery's main building. Its openings looked over the tasting room and down to the front hallway. Conversations below echoed up the steps or bounced off the tasting room walls, landing in the meeting room for any willing ears to hear.

I laid out some sweaters on the floor for Sophie to nap on, then I took a seat and inspected our provisions: goldfish crackers and cheese sticks.

The far window let in the light and the magnificent view. With the sun still high in the sky, the rows of vines lit up like soldiers at attention before me. Tragedy out one window, beauty out the other. What a strange day.

I sat down and gazed at my slumbering daughter. Beauty was here, too—the very picture of a sleeping angel. I closed my eyes and shook my head. My little sleeping angel. How close she had come to becoming one today.

Pressing myself into the chair, I folded my arms and let out a slow sigh. You can do everything right. You can teach them to look both ways when they cross the street. Teach them to study hard and stay away from drugs. And still some guy in a parking lot can take them away in an instant.

I didn't know it would be so hard, this whole parenting thing. Mallory and I were almost three full years into it, and we were still just starting to figure things out.

Shifting in my chair, I thought about sleep. Then I heard someone on the steps, coming up toward us.

I jumped up from the chair to alert them before they woke up Sophie. She needed her sleep, and even if she didn't, I needed her to sleep. Five hours of a bored, whining child would be five hours too many today.

A woman appeared, looking to be about thirty, with long hair and glasses. Holding a finger up to my lips, I motioned over to where Sophie lay sleeping on the floor. The woman nodded.

"Do y'all need anything?" she whispered.

"No, we're fine." I said. "Thanks."

"Really, can I get you something to drink? A Coke, maybe, or some milk for your little girl?"

It was going to be a long wait. No reason to make it harder than it had to be. "Sure. That would be great. Thanks."

The woman smiled and disappeared down the steps, returning a few minutes later.

"If you'd like a sandwich from our floor cooler, or anything in the tasting room," she whispered, Mrs. Hill would be happy to take care of it for you."

Mrs. Hill would. Not Mr. Hill, I bet.

"That's very nice, thank you." I wasn't sure what I wanted to do. Tasting wine samples was probably a bad idea at this point. "You folks weren't hurt in the accident, were you?"

"No, no." I cracked the soda can open and licked the spray off my thumb. "We were very lucky."

She pursed her lips, folding her hands in her lap as she glanced about. She leaned forward like she was holding her breath—or holding in a secret.

She seemed to want to say more, and for some reason, I wanted her to.

I nodded toward my sleeping daughter and gave the woman my best smile. "You know, I haven't eaten all day. I could really use one of those sandwiches."

The woman stood. "Let's move to where we won't bother your girl."

At the bottom of the stairs were the offices, but by now they were empty. From there, I could listen to hear if Sophie woke up, and find out what this woman wanted to say. I lagged behind while she walked on ahead to get a sandwich out of the tasting room cooler.

When she returned, I held out my hand. "I'm Doug."

She cast her eyes downward, blushing. "I'm Janice."

I took a bite from the sandwich. "Mm, this is good, ma'am."

She smiled again.

"Do you work here, Janice?"

"Part time. I help out. I'm a friend of the family."

"You're a friend of Mrs. Hill?" Janice seemed too young for that. Mrs. Hill appeared to be in her late sixties, maybe older.

"We're neighbors. I used to babysit for them."

While I was not usually predisposed to small talk, I was aware enough to know when somebody wanted to get something off their chest. I knew the look.

I always had what was referred to as an honest face, which is, as they say, a blessing and a curse. People would tell me things they would never tell anybody else in a million years. That came in handy from time to time. They might expect you to keep those deep dark secrets. That was a little harder. One of my first jobs out of college was as a member of an investigative team of auditors. I was basically a number cruncher, but I sat through the required classes on conducting investigative interviews. It boiled down to this: when somebody wants to talk, shut up and let them.

And Janice seemed to want to talk.

As a friend and neighbor, she had known the Hills for quite a while. As a part time employee of the winery, she was familiar with their work habits. Babysitting gave her more personal knowledge of their home life than most neighbors or friends, and she was on hand to notice when work life crossed over into home life, or vice versa. Like when the winery would experience a mysterious inventory shrinkage—business talk for employee theft of wine—but extra cases miraculously appeared in the basement of the house for a party. Or were sold for cash to friends.

She was also aware of Mr. Hill's newest habit of coming home for an early lunch, already drunk.

Mostly, she noticed the changes in Mr. Hill's attitude.

"He got hurt in a car wreck a year or so ago, right?" I asked, wrapping up the crumbs from the sandwich in a paper napkin. "Maybe that—"

Janice's eyes flashed. "Oh." She sighed, shaking her head. "It started way before then."

Peering down the hallway, she folded her hands in her lap again, letting her voice fall to a whisper. "He has been getting worse and worse for years. I noticed it a while back. Years ago. Him being angry all the time, yelling at employees . . . Mr. Hill never used to be like that."

Her eyes widened. "Yelling at Mrs. Hill! Right here in the winery, in front of everybody. That poor, sweet dear." She drew a deep breath, letting it out slowly. "Mrs. Hill never did anything to deserve that. She is just the nicest lady."

I nodded. "And it kept getting worse?"

"Oh." She rolled her eyes. "It sure did. Every day he was a little more miserable to everyone than the day before. He got so bad people started quitting." She lifted a hand, counting on the fingers. "The managers, some good employees that had worked here for years . . . Good people. Family friends. They were afraid to be here, afraid of what he'd do."

I leaned forward, curious to know more about the man who could have killed my daughter that morning and who seemed to have no regrets about what he'd done to the people he hit with his truck. "What kinds of things would he do?"

"Well . . ." Janice said, catching herself. She lowered her eyes and adjusted her chair. "Mostly just temper tantrums and such."

I sat back, putting my hands in my pockets. It seemed as though Janice had run her course, so I tried to think of something conciliatory and reassuring to say.

"We all saw the senility coming, getting worse each year. Some suspected Alzheimer's, and that may have been part of it." She looked at me squarely. There was a twinge of fear in her eyes. "But the drinking and the pain killers played their role, too."

I watched but said nothing. My job was to let her talk. She seemed to need to.

She knitted her fingers in her lap, glancing around the empty room. "It's like the devil came to sit with him one day out in the fields, and never left. Like evil itself just grew and grew in him like a weed, until Mr. Hill—the nice Mr. Hill we all knew—was gone. And this angry old man who hated everyone was left in his place."

Janice stood up to leave. "He's running this place into the ground you know. Poor Mrs. Hill is always having to go behind him and clean up his mistakes."

"Alzheimer's can be—"

She shook her head, raising a hand to her temple. "This one today was a doozie."

I went for one last thing. The obvious. "Was he drunk?"

Janice watched me in silence for a long time. She took a step backwards away from the window into the shadows, nodding.

"Wow, that early in the day, huh?"

She nodded again. "*Every* day. But it's not just that. He can't control that truck of his. Not anymore. His hands can't work the controls very well, and his legs get spasms. He can't manage them at all some days."

She looked across to the hall window and the parking lot, retreating further into the coming darkness, her eyes alight with fear. "He sure couldn't manage it today."

I sat up and rested my elbows on my knees. "You know, Janice, Mr. Hill said something curious to me. After the wreck, when I came in, I saw him standing in the hall. I didn't know he was the owner. I thought he was an employee who did deliveries. He was just standing there staring out the window."

The setting sun cast long shadows over the room. Janice's eyes were the only part of her visible against the darkening walls.

Taking a deep breath, I went on. "I asked him if he was okay, and that kind of snapped him out of a trance. Then he said the strangest thing."

Janice gripped one hand with the other, saying nothing.

"He said something like 'people need to learn to get out of the way.'" I let that sink in. "Saying something like that about people you had almost killed. It seemed very odd. Very . . . inappropriate. Misplaced. You know?"

She lowered her eyes. "I'd say his mind is going, but it isn't."

"Do you think there will be a lawsuit?"

Janice stifled a sarcastic laugh. She walked to the door, stopping to look up and down the hallway. "Maybe," she whispered. "But it'll never go anywhere. His friends on the police force will see to that. They didn't take your statement, did they?"

"They're supposed to. I was waiting—"

"The police have left."

I bolted upright and peered out the window. The parking lot was empty.

"See?" Janice turned and quietly disappeared down the hall.

Soft noises from upstairs told me Sophie was beginning to stir. "Daddy?"

Climbing the stairs two at a time, I reached my daughter before she could become frightened by waking up in a strange room.

Chapter 9

My wife had never been so happy to be leaving a winery.

Neither had I.

Mallory arrived with the replacement van and had already made arrangements to get us back into the hotel we had checked out of that morning. It was now time to get a bite to eat, and to get some sleep before planning our next move. We were supposed to see more of Virginia wine country—but I wasn't sure I wanted any more wineries or any more of Virginia.

I also didn't want to ruin things for Mallory. She sat at the tiny table by the window, sifting through her brochures, but her mind seemed elsewhere.

She knew that if she even mentioned leaving to me, I'd pack up the van and start driving in the middle of the night.

"What a week we are having, huh?" I asked, attempting to lighten the mood. Sophie had drifted off to sleep watching cartoons. The only light in the room was the flicker from the TV. I picked up the remote and switched it to Sports Center. "Hey, how about some wine? I think we've earned it."

"Pfft." Mallory tossed her brochures into the center of the table and sat back in the chair, folding her arms. "I *know* we have."

I could probably guess what was on her mind, but it was better for her to bring it out on her own schedule. She sighed, pushing back from the table and moving to the bed, undressing as she went.

"Okay, madam sommelier. What did we buy that's any good?"

Mallory commenced to scrolling through her purchases out loud, trying to decide on a proper vintage for an after dinner sleep inducer. I dug around for a clean t-shirt to sleep in.

"Anything but that!" Mallory whispered intensely, seeing the Hillside Winery shirt in my hands.

"Yeah . . ." I laid it aside and sat down next to her on the bed. "I guess I already have enough souvenirs from that place." She was under the sheets but a glass of wine would still sound good to her. Better than good. Necessary.

I took a deep breath. "Let's open the champagne."

"Champagne?" Her eyes widened. "What the hell are we celebrating?"

"We're *alive*." I found the bottle and started undoing the foil over the cork. "We are alive and healthy and safe. That is worth celebrating."

"This trip has been a complete disaster."

I picked up two plastic cups from the sink area and unpeeled them from their cellophane wrappers. They were better than nothing. Placing a hand towel over the champagne bottle, I liberated the cork with a muffled pop. "This trip has been a disaster, and we are alive to complain about it." I handed her one of the thin, flimsy hotel cups. "That's worth celebrating."

We sipped our champagne, considering our different assessments of the situation, then we both spoke at once.

"You go first," I said. Mallory's shoulders slumped and she rested the cup in her lap. "I'm ready to go home. I've had enough of this trip and I don't see the next few days being any different."

As much as I wanted to agree, I held myself back. "We could do that. We could get up bright and early tomorrow and drive straight through to home. We'd be there by, say, 8 P. M. at the latest."

I took another sip. Mallory waited for the "or" that she knew was coming, and the alternate plan.

But I had no alternate plan to consider. "Honestly, I'm ready to get the hell out of Virginia." I chuckled. "Screw this place!"

We laughed together, relieving the tension for a few minutes as we sipped expensive champagne from cheap plastic hotel cups.

"We still have the rest of the week off." I sat on the back of the chair, being careful not to spill my wine. "We can goof off in the garden, maybe go to Sea World . . ."

"We have our annual passes to Busch Gardens . . ."

"And that would all be fine, you know? Sophie would love it. Heck, I would, too. So if you wanted to, we could go home and do that, but we could also stop and see a few more places—some of the special places you've already mapped out—and maybe have the best of both worlds." I sat down on the bed again. "You know, kind of salvage the trip? Only if you want to. Then head straight home."

Mallory sighed again, her eyes alight in the glow of ESPN highlights. It hadn't been a bad trip the entire time. We'd gotten some rain, and Sophie was sniffling with what might turn into a head cold, but the big downer was the wreck at the winery. Losing the car and how afraid Mallory had been thinking her husband and child had been killed. Living with that very real fear, the heartfelt possibility, even for the few minutes, had changed her attitude for the whole trip.

"Well." I watched the tiny bubbles lift off from the bottom of my glass and make a wobbly path to the surface where they popped silently. "I think years from now, the car wreck won't be the part of this trip that we remember. People tend to remember the good things."

I didn't really believe that. People seemed more likely to move on from small inconveniences, not a near death experience, but I hoped I was right.

Mallory bit her nails and stared at the TV, crossing and uncrossing her legs under the sheets. Maybe heading straight home was the best thing, the medicine she needed.

"I want to ask you something." She turned to me. "Do you really believe we were lucky today? Because I don't see it!"

I rubbed my chin in the near dark, nodding. "I do. What happened today was tragic, it really was. We all got a good scare. But in the end, here we are, unhurt, whole, healthy . . ."

She folded her arms.

"I have to look at what did happen. When things happen around you and not actually to you, you have to believe that you were lucky." I leaned over to her, putting my face near hers and kissing her softly. "That truck nearly killed four people. I watched it all, like it was happening in slow motion." I glanced at Sophie to make sure she was asleep. "The young lady should have been killed. She is feeling horrible right now but she is lucky to be alive."

I drew a deep breath. "Now, I've asked myself whether we were lucky or not. Here's how I know we were." I set my cup down. "Our daughter is never hungry. Never. It's all we can do to get her to eat. So it surprised me when she acted up in the winery today at lunch time. Maybe she was hungry, maybe she was bored and wanted attention, I don't know. But as soon as we started making our way out to the van to have a picnic, she didn't want to go."

I leaned into my wife's line of sight. "I know if we had gone out to the van like we planned, she and I would have been sitting between the two cars having a picnic. That's what was in my mind, to sit on the cooler between the cars and watch DVDs through the open van door. That's what I had planned. If we had gone when I wanted to go, that's where we would have been when that old man got into his truck." I took a deep breath and let it out slowly. "We would have been killed."

It wasn't often I would let myself be so dramatic. I let the words hang in the air for a moment, trying to decide how to explain what happened next.

"The reason we didn't go out right away, the reason we aren't in a hospital or a morgue right now, is because our sweet little princess over there threw a freaking tantrum. So I stopped to show her some t-shirts and knickknacks, to distract her. It was only for a few minutes, but . . ."

Tears welled up in my wife's eyes.

I swallowed hard. "Those few extra moments would have been about the amount of time I would have needed to get the cooler out of the car and set up shop. When the truck squealed its wheels, there never would have been enough time to get out of the way. In the hours that passed while we were waiting for you up in that meeting room, I had a chance to play it all back. There was nowhere to go. Think about the lady who was hit—she was facing the pickup truck and saw it coming. She still couldn't get out of the way. Neither could her boyfriend."

By now, I was reliving the moment in my mind, the words catching in my throat. " I might have survived, but she . . ."

My voice grew thin, trailing off, thinking the unthinkable. I swallowed again and refocused, blinking tears out of my eyes. "And why *weren't* we killed? Because our kid had to look at stupid t-shirts." I wiped my nose. "The funny ones. She asked me what they said, so I read them to her. That was the difference between having our daughter alive right now and . . . not."

Tears fell from my eyes as I strained to keep my voice even. "So, yeah, I believe we were pretty damned lucky today."

Mallory closed her eyes and leaned her head back, shining streaks flowing down her cheeks. I didn't usually feel as deeply about things as she did, but this was different. We sat for a moment, in the quiet hotel room, with only the flickering light of the TV to read each other's faces.

"I wish I could see it that way." Mallory sniffled. "But this isn't the first time things like this have happened."

"Don't connect things that aren't connected," I said. "Don't do that."

"Things like this keep happening! What if they *are* connected?"

I stood up and walked toward the door. I felt a sudden urge to vent some restless energy.

Mallory aimed her words to my back. "There was the car fire last year where you guys were almost killed, and there was the whole NICU thing the year before. Now this, a maniac who almost kills you both in a parking lot. Doug, there's something *wrong* about all of this!"

I opened my mouth to speak but had no words. My heart thumped in my chest. "Don't—" Mallory pounded the mattress, sobbing. "Am I supposed to sit here and believe that every year, some horrible thing happens almost kills our daughter—but not worry about it? At the same time of year? *Every year?*" She flung her empty cup across the room. "Stop pretending this is all just a bunch of damned coincidences!"

Chapter 10

A good cry had accomplished what the champagne could not. As frustrating as the conversation had been, releasing the pent-up emotions exhausted Mallory to the point where she could no longer fight off sleep. Now, with the bottle empty and the hotel TV switched off, I sat in the darkness considering what my wife had said.

Each year, around the same time of year, a life-threatening situation happened to our daughter.

When Sophie was born, the examining doctor had inadvertently "heard" something in the stethoscope while he checked her heart. It turned out to be a rare heart condition, one that could take her life without warning. With proper medications, people with the condition could lead a long happy life, but without getting diagnosed, the first symptom was usually sudden death.

If we had taken her home, she could have died. We never would have known why.

The next year, the "incident" was even worse.

At the time, we had two sport utility vehicles, an old Lincoln Navigator and a little Ford Escape. Since they were paid off, the plan was to drive them until they dropped. With the money we weren't spending on car payments going into Sophie's college fund, it felt noble, not cheap.

Our little Ford was a fine and roadworthy vehicle, but it was getting up there in miles. So it wasn't a huge surprise when it started acting up one day.

Sophie and I planned a trip over to her cousin's house in St. Petersburg, about an hour's drive. Sophie wanted to go swimming in her cousin's pool, so I arranged for a hamburger cookout. My brother and I could catch up and see about the Tampa Bay Buccaneers' prospects for the remaining football season.

I packed the little Escape: beach towels, swimsuit, pool toy . . . stroller. Always in the back of the car just in case, Sophie's stroller served as a reminder she was big enough that she didn't need it all the time, but when she did need it, we wanted to have it with us. She only weighed about twenty-eight pounds, but she gets awfully heavy lugging her around a grocery store or a mall. After one particularly long trek to the parking lot after Sophie conked out midday at Busch Gardens, I decided to keep the stroller handy until she started in high school.

I didn't pack any food or drinks for the drive to St. Pete because we were going to my brother's house for lunch. A quick trip across the bridge, a bite to eat, a little swimming, and then back home. Should be a nice day.

I clipped my daughter into her car seat.

"I can't wait to see cousin Vanessa!" Sophie had been asking me all morning when we were going to leave. Now it was finally time.

A few minutes later, we were on our way. At the last stoplight before the highway, I texted my brother to give him our estimated arrival time, and we pulled onto Interstate 275.

Immediately, I knew something was wrong. The car seemed sluggish. I pressed the pedal to give it some gas and get us up to highway speed, but it didn't want to do it. That had never happened before. The on ramp is only a few hundred feet long. I needed to be up to fifty-five miles per hour when it ended, or we'd get hit from behind by another driver. I gripped the wheel and stomped the gas. The Ford was too sluggish. We weren't going to make it. I glanced around as I flicked on the emergency flashers and pulled into the emergency lane. Cars roared by on my left side. I mashed the gas pedal again to clear whatever was blocking the fuel line or clogging the engine.

The little Ford made a loud hissing sound, but without the white cloud of steam that usually accompanied a blown engine hose. The car still refused to accelerate as traffic whizzed by. The next exit was coming up quickly. I pulled off.

As I decelerated coming down the off ramp, the noise lessened. When I came to a stop at the next traffic light, the noise stopped.

I considered my options.

It was a hot, sunny Florida day, and the swimming would be good at my brother's house. The kids wanted to see each other. Whatever the noise was, it had stopped. Maybe a piece of a tree limb had gotten stuck under the car and had finally come free when we turned off the highway. It had happened before, and the rubbing against the wheel had made a similar noise. In any case, it was gone now.

I glanced at the odometer—over 200,000 miles. That was a simultaneous source of pride and embarrassment. I preferred driving a new car, of course, but as long as the car was drivable and had air conditioning, keeping it was the smart thing to do.

That smart decision didn't seem so smart now.

I pulled into a gas station. Slipping the transmission into neutral, I revved the engine a few times. The car acted fine, like whatever had been clogging it was now gone. I stepped out and looked underneath. No tree limbs.

Inside, Sophie was waiting to go see cousin Vanessa.

I got back in and revved the car one more time. Nothing. I dropped it back into drive and turned around, listening for any noises. Pulling onto the road again, I cut off the air conditioning and radio, put down the windows, and listened. I didn't hear anything strange.

As I made my way to the interstate, the car acted perfect. Whatever it was seemed to have cleared itself up.

Probably a stick from a tree in our yard that got stuck underneath, and it broke free on the off ramp . . .

I got back onto the interstate. This time the accelerator responded fine. The car got up to speed quickly and my pulse returned to normal.

"Daddy, the wind is blowing too hard on me!"

I reached down and held the window switches, putting up the windows, then I turned on the air conditioning. Cocking my head and listening, the car seemed fine.

Three bridges connect Tampa to St. Petersburg. I-275 runs across the middle one, a long narrow ribbon that stretches ten miles over the bay. Once on that bridge, there are no exits until the other side. And of course, parts of the bridge were being worked on, so there might be delays.

As we approached, I still listened to see if the old car was going to tell me something or not.

I didn't hear any hissing or rattles; the accelerator was working fine . . . we came to the "last chance" exit. I thought about pulling off, but only for a moment. It seemed like whatever had been wrong with the car before, it wasn't wrong any more.

I eased my car onto the bridge. The water of the bay was beautiful, a glorious shade of blue, with a few ripples on the surface. There wasn't a cloud in the sky, and the sun was beaming down. It was hot, but otherwise, it was a real chamber of commerce day.

BOOM!

The car lurched like a cannon had been shot off under the hood. My hands tightened on the wheel. The engine hissed louder than ever—it was all I could hear.

This time, there was no handy off ramp. Construction cones and sawhorses blocked the emergency lane for miles. A strange plastic smell came into the car.

In the other lanes, cars streaked by at seventy and eighty miles per hour. Ten miles of bridge and no place to pull off. Even slowing down could be dangerous. Cars behind me wouldn't be expecting that. We could end up in a huge pile up.

The smell got stronger and the hiss got louder. Something was definitely wrong, and there were no good choices for what to do about it. I cracked open the windows to let some fresh air in.

Sophie said something, but I couldn't hear her over the engine noise.

I took my foot off the gas pedal. The car began to slow down. Once again, I turned on the emergency flashers, hoping the speeding commuters behind me would notice in the bright sun.

With the windows open, each construction sawhorse made a whoosh as we passed it. They were too close together to avoid hitting any at that speed, if I decided to try to pull into the emergency lane, and I couldn't risk slowing down too much or I'd get rear ended from another car.

A faint line of smoke streamed out from under the hood. There was no time left. I gripped the wheel and took a deep breath.

"Hang on!" I turned the car into the sawhorses. The first ones smashed into the side of the car, jolting us with rapid metal and wood crunches. The next ones slammed into the grill and piled up underneath as pieces flew into the windshield. The debris under the car clogged the front tires and threatened to pull the steering wheel from my hands.

Flames flickered under the hood. The pile of sawhorses under the car blocked the steering. Three feet away on the left, cars roared by, horns blaring. Three feet to the right, a small concrete wall and a forty foot drop into the bay.

Gripping the wheel as best I could, I hit the brakes. Splintered sawhorses flew everywhere. Construction gravel spewed all over but helped slow us down.

Now black smoke poured out of the hood. Orange flames burst upward in front of my eyes. Inside, the car filled with smoke.

I hurried to unclip Sophie from her car seat, straining backwards to reach. No good. I couldn't get both hands far enough to undo the clasps. It didn't take long to undo it, maybe it took twenty seconds, tops. That would be enough time.

I jumped out, dodging the speeding traffic on the driver's side. The wind from each passing vehicle shoved me back and forth, threatening to suck me onto the road. I reached the side door and flung it open, releasing a cloud of smoke as it did. One, two, three, the car seat was unbuckled and my daughter was free. Holding her to my chest, I rushed around the door and ran to the front of the car.

I turned back to see the flames growing larger. Thick black smoke churned upwards into the pale blue sky.

The slight wind on the bridge came from the west, so I had been driving into it. As I stood in front of the car watching the smoke pushing out faster and faster from under the hood, I thought about going to get anything of value inside. In the amount of time it took to wonder, the decision was made for me. It was only seconds before the whole car was engulfed in flames.

There, in the middle of a sweltering hot bridge, I stood with my daughter in my arms. I had no time to grab my cell phone. I hadn't packed a cooler because it was a short drive across the bridge. We stood there, with the sun scalding our heads and the pavement frying our feet, as a black column drifted to the heavens. The flames ravaged the car like a pack of starving animals.

Traffic whizzed by at seventy miles per hour or more, barely a few feet from us. There was no place else to go, so I stood there, getting tugged on every time a car went past.

I glanced at Sophie's face as she watched the car become completely engulfed in fire. Two little smudges of dirt were under her nose. They were from the smoke. The few moments we were stuck breathing it was all that were needed to lightly coat our faces and clothes, but the real danger was from inhaling it. The fire is eating the air with you, but it eats it much faster. A few seconds more behind the wheel and I would have passed out from lack of oxygen.

Then there would have been no one to get my daughter out of her car seat.

She would have sat there, strapped in, struggling against the intense heat and the acrid smoke, until the fire took the last bits of air available. The two marks under her nostrils were a sign of how close we had come to doing exactly that.

"Hey," I said.

She looked up at me.

"Let's try to blow your nose."

Holding her in my arms, I raised one hand and pinched her nose slightly with it. "Blow."

She blew. Black dirt splattered onto my hand. Smoke residue.

"Again."

More black. And more, the third time. I wiped it off on my hip. Then I did the same for myself.

It was a freak occurrence. I had just had the car serviced. Clean bill of health. But a random short in the electrical panel for that model caused a spark that happened to catch just right. They sold a million of those cars, and none of the others would have that happen. The service records showed that we had properly maintained the vehicle. Everyone, the police, the insurance inspectors, the insurance agent, all agreed: we were lucky.

Standing on the bridge in the ninety-five degree heat, we didn't feel lucky. It was hours before we got off the bridge. Other drivers had seen the fire and called for help, but it was a fire truck that arrived first. When the police finally arrived, they wanted statements and answers. They were sympathetic, but they didn't have sunscreen. The firefighters gave us bottled water, and the paramedics checked our lungs.

We were fine. Scared, but fine. And tired.

I consoled myself that I now had a good story for another time. *Sucks when your car gets burned up.*

In the dark of the hotel room, I recalled feeling something else that day, too.

Calm. Just calm.

It was a characteristic I felt I always benefited from at work. In tough situations, when others panicked, I was able to keep cool. Really, that was when I performed best. It was the same during the car fire. Before I plowed into the sawhorses, I went through the steps necessary in my head. Get Sophie out. Get clear of the car. Lack of time would not allow me to keep driving.

It saved our lives—even the firemen said so. They noted that if I had tried to drive even a few moments longer, the car would have been too filled with smoke, knocking me out, possibly crashing into the bay. At highway speeds, anything was possible.

But when I did the math in my head, I knew I only had enough time to get my daughter unbuckled from her seat and to safety if I stopped immediately. I knew I'd probably destroy the car in the process. So I just did it. It never occurred to me to be nervous. There wasn't time for that.

That was true in the NICU, too. Watching our little baby wired up to machines, and watching my wife get weaker and weaker from stress every day, not knowing what would happen or how long it would all go on, I had a strange sense of calm. I prayed, because it felt right to pray. But I never let myself consider that our daughter wouldn't be safe.

To be honest, I actually worried a little that this ability to remain calm in such dire circumstances might somehow be abnormal.

Back at the winery, I had only worried *after* I talked to Mallory. When I realized that she thought she had lost her whole family. Considering that, I felt tension. But at the time, I was almost detached. My impulse to go help the woman who had been hit was immediately replaced by the desire to protect our daughter for what she might see if I did rush over to help the victims. I let others rush in.

I did not need to be a hero. I needed to be a good father.

So why did I feel bad?

Chapter 11

The drive back to Florida was intentionally uneventful. Few stops were made; not a lot of conversations took place. Sophie's oncoming head cold would be best fought with sleep, and if Mallory was going to catch it—and riding for twelve hours next to our daughter, she would—then sleep was her best defense, too.

I just drove. The van's satellite radio let me keep up with sports and news, so I checked out the weather situation for the ride home. A tropical storm formed off the east coast of Florida, but nobody knew which direction it was headed yet. That could mean a long drive back to Tampa in the rain, or the swirling winds of the brewing storm would pull all the moisture away from Tampa and give me crystal clear skies the whole way home.

Either way, the best place for me now was Tampa, not thinking about my family getting a cold. And definitely not thinking about the three tragedies.

But long drives are long for a reason. The endless stretch of gray asphalt ribbon allows minds to wander. To go where they shouldn't.

Mallory admitted how much things looked less and less like coincidences and more and more like . . . *what*, exactly? It haunted me.

I didn't know Virginia. It wasn't fair to decide about a place after such a short period of time, but I didn't know it. I couldn't *trust* it. I knew Florida and I knew Indiana.

I knew what to expect when things happened in the places I knew. I didn't know Virginia that way. The small town law and their ways of doing things . . .

It bothered me that the officers at the winery never took a written statement. It bothered me that close friends were so ready to throw old Mr. Hill under the bus. Lots of things bothered me about that day.

I didn't have answers. I didn't understand Virginia that way. Florida, I did.

And I would get some damned answers.

I had time to make phone calls. I didn't know the rules in every state we were going to pass through—driving while talking on a handheld cell phone might be illegal in some—so I played it safe and looked up the numbers I wanted while I was getting gas. They were ready to go when we started driving again.

The first call was to our church, Our Lady Of Mercy. Although I didn't attend mass regularly after Sophie's baptism, I felt comfortable in my years of Catholic schooling to sit down with the head of the parish and discuss the connections between the strange things that kept happening to our family. It was worth a shot. Who do you go to for stuff like that?

Then, I knew that an old high school friend was supposed to be a practicing priest somewhere in the area, and I had just run into my eighth grade English teacher at my niece's wedding—he was a priest, too, and although it might make for an awkward conversation after so much time, he knew my dad and our whole family. He might be able to help.

After that, I figured I'd end up wherever this was all headed anyway. Like a boat on a river, the direction of the current would influence things. If my wife was right, if these odd happenings were related somehow, then my family was on a course we weren't directing, heading to a place we shouldn't go. We needed to do our best to not end up there.

Chapter 12

"Did you call the church?"

Mallory's words were loud enough for me to hear but quiet enough to not draw our daughter's attention. Sophie sat at the table pretending to eat while I fried a couple of eggs. I rarely ate breakfast, but I needed some energy after the long drive home.

Instead of the usual cartoons, we had the TV turned to the news. The tropical storm, now larger, was headed to Tampa. I glanced out the window toward Sophie's swing set: blue skies and green palms, still as statues. The swings weren't even swaying, it was such a calm day. I leaned down to see the oak trees. They, too, stood tall and unmoving.

I shook my head. Weather forecasters.

Some storm preparations might be in order soon, but the first order of business was breakfast. The lack of cartoons made Sophie an even slower eater than usual.

"I called the Church." I turned my attention away from the meteorologist's patented Doppler radar and back to my eggs, ignoring the colorful array of animated swirls on the TV. "I got their answering machine."

"They have an answering machine? And nobody answers at, what, nine-thirty in the morning on a week day?" Mallory grabbed the newspaper and took a seat next to Sophie.

"I know, it seems weird." I slid a spatula under the eggs and slid them onto a plate. "I can drive over later if they don't call back. I guess they're busy with, you know . . . church stuff

"I guess." She opened the paper and glanced at it, then laid it down. "Are you sure that's even a good idea? I mean, what are they going to do?"

"I don't know what they can do." I shrugged, picking a fork out of the drawer. "But it seems like a decent place to start. The Church has ideas on dealing with . . . exorcisms."

Mallory bristled at the mere mention of the word. When I mentioned it upstairs, she insisted Sophie was not possessed. I agreed. But it still launched a fight.

"It's just an example. They have rules for dealing with these types of things. If this is even one of these types of things."

Silence.

"Look." I laid my plate on the table and sat down. "You and Sophie play around the house today. Do some gardening together, have some relaxing quality time. I'll go over and see the pastor at Our Lady Of Mercy and see what he thinks."

"He's going to think we're crazy."

"Yeah, well." I took a deep breath and let it out slowly. "Honestly, wouldn't that be the best possible outcome?"

Mallory narrowed her eyes.

"To have somebody with a clear head listen to all the information and decide that there's nothing to it, and that we're being ridiculous?" I cut into my eggs. "Man, that would be music to my ears. I would love to hear we're being hypochondriacs or whatever you'd call this." Mallory lifted the paper up again. "Just go. Try not to get yourself thrown in the loony bin while you're gone."

I grinned. "I'll do my best, but I can't promise anything."

I volunteered to do the breakfast dishes so the girls could get an early start on the gardening. When the church didn't call back right away, I dug into the pile of work on my desk. After a few hours of updating reports, I took a break and allowed myself to do a little searching on the internet, looking for possible solutions to our situation. Mostly I found websites that were obvious scams, each one seeming hokier than the last, but there were a few that had possibilities.

"Help For The Hopeful." A simple black ad with white lettering, like a chalkboard, appeared when I searched *paranormal activity solutions*. A small white cross adorned the ad's middle, blinking like a tiny neon light. Something about the ad seemed remarkably understated and honest. As I went to click on it, the phone rang.

After giving my boss an update on a few reports, I pushed away from my desk. Somebody from the church should have called by now. I got up and walked over to the back window.

Mallory and Sophie had been planting a border of small purple flowers around the palm trees on the terrace. Mother showed daughter each step, taking time to ensure it was done properly. I smiled at their matching hats and gardening gloves. Sophie appeared keen to learn everything, although she clearly enjoyed some parts more than others. Digging with the hand spade was one. Patting the dirt down around the newly nested plant was another. Mallory had to redo more than a few plants after Sophie jammed them into their new home.

It looked like the project was having the desired effect—relaxation.

The clock on the cable TV box read nearly one o'clock. I definitely should have gotten a call back from the church by now.

The back door swung open. Dirty but happy, the gardeners stomped their feet to knock the mud off.

"Are you two finished?"

"Pretty much." Mallory took a large glass and a small plastic cup down from the cabinet. "We're taking a break for lunch."

I thought for a moment. Between eating, finishing their planting, and cleaning up with a bath, they would easily be busy for several hours. I grabbed my car keys. "I'm going to run out and take care of some errands."

She poured a tall glass of tea and glanced at our daughter on the door stoop. "Did the church call back yet?"

"No, not yet. I think if I just show up, they'll have to talk to me."

"Sophie, stomp your feet. Knock the dirt off."

Our daughter jumped up and down, landing as hard as she could. Mallory turned her attention back to me. "When are you going?"

"Right now."

She nodded. "Okay. Be careful."

I kissed her, then I reached down and picked up my dirty daughter. "I'm going out for a few minutes." I gave Sophie a peck on the forehead. "You be good for mommy!"

She threw her arms around my neck. "Can I come with you?"

Putting her down, I squatted next to her, smiling. "I think you would be a big help if you came along, but you need a bath first, don't you think?"

"No!"

Of course not.

"How about some tea and . . ." Mallory rattled a colorful cellophane bag. "Some potato chips?"

That got Sophie's attention. "Chips! Can I have a peanut butter sandwich, too?" She sprinted into the kitchen.

So much for going with Dad.

"Whoa! Let's wash our hands first." Mallory tapped the kitchen faucet. "Get your step stool."

As Sophie made an abrupt U-turn, I stood up. "I'll be back in a bit."

Mallory gave me a wink.

The drive to Our Lady Of Mercy was a short one. When I had been required to go every Sunday for the eight weeks before Sophie's baptism, I found the earlier in the morning the service was, the less traffic and the fewer churchgoers I had to endure.

I grew up going to Catholic schools. As a kid I attended Mass with my family every week, but when I went off to college, my attendance dropped off. I'd still go to church with Mom when I went home during the holidays, but as the college parties went later and later on Saturday nights, sleeping in became the Sunday morning ritual, not Mass.

Eventually, I stopped going all together. "I'm not a ship without a rudder," I once joked to my mom. "I'm just a ship without a port at the moment."

She did not like the comparison.

When the time came to get my daughter baptized as a Catholic, I was required to join a local Catholic church and attend services. Our Lady Of Mercy was closest to our house, so they won.

It had been almost three years since my last visit. Sophie and I attended the seven-fifteen morning service for a couple of weeks after her baptism, since we were always both awake long before then, but that was probably it. As a result, I did not expect much of a reception. I wasn't even sure we were still on the mailing list.

Our Lady Of Mercy wasn't like the large gothic church I knew growing up, and I kind of looked down on them a bit for that. To me, churches needed to be a bit more ornate to have the full effect.

As I parked and walked up to the main office, children raced around the playground. A slide and some swings, it was part of their preschool program, but Our Lady Of Mercy did not have a school. Even this late in the year, it was still hot and muggy outside. Plus, it was probably getting ready to rain. Tropical storms will dump days and days of rain, but they like teasing a little first. Some of the prettiest, calmest, sunny days would happen right before the storm, giving no idea of the shit that was about to start. That's why there are so many of those old Spanish galleons sunk off the coast of Florida—the weather was great the day they set sail.

I opened the office door and stepped inside. The cool blast of air conditioning was immediately refreshing. I had already broken out in a light sweat during the walk from parking lot. I viewed the reception room. Same couch and chairs from three years ago, and the same table full of magazines. Probably the same magazines.

The priests' offices were just through the next door, but first I had to chat with the lady behind the reception room's little window—Mrs. Clermont, according to the little fake wood placard. She wore horn rimmed glasses on her little round head and her hair was tied in a tight bun. A blue pen stuck out from behind her left ear and a pencil protruded from her right. She was practically a cartoon character. I halfway expected her to turn sideways and become super thin, like she was drawn on paper.

At the moment, a large woman was occupying the space in front of Mrs. Clermont's window, so I picked a spot on the couch and sat down.

The magazines were typical churchy fare—nothing you'd probably read at home—but a small stack of this week's church bulletins sat off to one side. Skimming through one might give me a little insight into the current affairs of Our Lady Of Mercy, allowing me to appear more engaged than I actually had been. I picked up a paper bulletin and flipped through it. The usual: Mass times, a bake sale, a clothing drive for St Vincent DePaul . . .

I wasn't sure what I was going to say to the priest, or even how to begin.

Are you unlucky if you go to a winery and almost get killed by its owner? Or are you lucky that you narrowly missed being hurt?

Are you lucky to have escaped a car fire, or are you unlucky to have been in a burning car at all? It sure didn't feel lucky that day, to be stuck on a hot bridge in the sun and heat, with a fussy child and no place to sit down, nothing to drink. We missed the cookout and the pool party.

When something bad happens, it doesn't make things better to say that it could have been worse. That's not happiness, that's only the avoidance of misery. There's a difference. Was I supposed to tell our daughter that no matter how crappy things get, they can always get crappier?

I gazed at the bulletin, but my thoughts were elsewhere.

We could have easily been overcome by fumes if I hadn't driven into the emergency barriers when the car burst into flames. That wasn't luck. That was a decision.

It might have been luck at the winery, though. I couldn't account for that. And with the doctor at the hospital, when Sophie was born, there was a fair amount of luck with us that day.

I sighed. Maybe it was luck in the car fire after all. Hitting the saw horses could have made me lose control of the car. It almost did.

Folding my arms, I pressed myself into the couch.

In movies, fires take a while to get going—because the actors need time to say their lines. In reality, a fire in a house takes only seconds to start, and within minutes the whole house is consumed. The videos of Christmas trees burning in living rooms were a real eye opener. So was the frat fire in college, when we accidentally burned down a rec room during a dance because the chimney was clogged.

Smoke gets everywhere, and it gets there fast. That was the real killer. People in fires don't burn to death, they asphyxiate on smoke. I knew that, so I plowed my car into the traffic sawhorses. I would not put my daughter at risk.

But by taking her out of the car and standing on the side of the road, we were at risk again. Cars speeding by weren't looking for people in the emergency lane.

I shifted on the couch. It was all too confusing, too interwoven between what someone might see and what someone else might want to believe.

Which is where a man of faith might come in handy.

"Sir? Sir, may I help you?"

The lady behind the little window was addressing me. "Yes." I got up. "Yes, thank you. I need to speak with . . ."

I drew a blank. I didn't have a name of a specific priest that I wanted to talk to. I hadn't been here in almost three years. I had even forgotten the pastor's name.

Crap.

I glanced down at the bulletin in my hand. The list of services showed which priest was doing each Mass. I read the first name I saw: 11 A. M., Father Joe. I looked up at the woman. "Father Joe, please."

"Father Joe?" She scanned the paper schedule on the desk. "Did you make an appointment, Mister . . ."

"Kenner. Doug Kenner."

"Mm hmm." She nodded. "Well, did you make an appointment, Mr. Kenner?"

I debated whether to lie or not, if that might get me in today instead of getting rescheduled to another time. Tough call. Mrs. Clermont probably wouldn't look kindly on things if she caught me in a lie, and then she'd be less helpful. I wanted to talk to somebody today. Now.

"I called, and, uh, I didn't make an actual appointment, because . . ."

"Father Joe is in Venezuela on a mission right now."

" . . . because Father Joe is in Venezuela on a mission."

She lowered her head to peer at me over her reading glasses. "I see."

I shifted on my feet, clutching the bulletin.

Drawing her finger across the schedule, she stopped on a highlighted square. "Well, he will be back Sunday. Would you like me to schedule you for a time with him next week?"

"Ah, actually, I was kind of hoping that I could just come in and talk to, you know, whoever was available right now."

She glared at me. "But you don't have an appointment."

"Uh . . . no."

"And you don't want me to make an appointment for you?"

I hooked a thumb toward the priest's offices. "Is it possible to maybe see whoever's available right now?"

The cartoon lady shook her head, staring at her schedule book again. "Everybody's pretty booked up today."

Doing what, I wondered. Not tending the proverbial flock.

I took a deep, quiet breath. Showing my frustration wouldn't score any points with Mrs. Clermont, and she seemed to be the gatekeeper. One misstep and it might be weeks before I saw anyone. Beads of sweat formed on my brow.

But everybody has a boss, and nobody wants the boss to get a bad report about them. Maybe I could get something going that way. This route certainly wasn't working.

I cleared my throat. "Mrs. Clermont—"

The woman glared at me. "I'm not Mrs. Clermont."

Cringing, I closed my eyes. *Of course you aren't.*

"She's out sick today. I'm filling in."

I forced a smile. "Volunteering?"

She smiled back. "That's right."

Rubbing my temple with one hand, I tapped the paper bulletin on the counter with the other. "I really feel like there should be somebody, some priest, that I can talk to."

Her chair springs groaned as she rocked back. "Everybody's booked with people who made appointments." She delivered the words with a jab.

"Well, I'm glad God keeps such a regular schedule," I said. "What do you do when an emergency happens?"

She leaned forward. "We pray."

I squeezed the paper bulletin in my fist, out of sight from the substitute troll. "Okay." I backed away, heading for the door. "Thank you."

"I can still make an appointment for you." The chair springs squealed and her little round head poked through the window.

I stopped. "When would it be for?"

"The earliest is next Wednesday with Father Joe, but you can see Father Martin on Tuesday, or Father Raul."

Tuesday. Almost a whole week away.

"Let me call you back about that." I tried to sound sincere. And nice. An appointment a week away might end up being better than nothing. I thought about going back and scheduling something as a fallback position. But I really needed answers now.

I pushed the door open into a light drizzle. Covering my head with the bulletin, I headed to the car, passing a sign.

"Confessions today 12 noon – 3 P. M."

Confession. I shook my head. What poor bastard is going to come all the way over here in the rain simply to say he swore too much this week? Confession. The church's way of spying on its members in olden days, getting them to tell all their sins and gossip to a priest.

A priest.
I stopped.
Yeah, confession.

Chapter 13

I eased open the door to the massive church and stepped inside. The metal latch echoed off the big walls as the glass door clicked shut behind me. Only three other people were visible in the rows of pews, their heads bowed in prayer. The bright, green and white windows behind the altar greeted me from their place behind the enormous wood cross.

Our Lady Of Mercy had an open floor plan like an auditorium. It was bright even on rainy days, with lots of tall windows to let the light in. That contrasted greatly with the dark, gothic St. Matthews I'd known in Indiana, full of oil paintings and stained glass windows, arched ceilings and stone columns—but ancient relics like that were built for a different time. St Matthews was erected by German stone masons over a hundred and forty years ago, modeled after cathedrals in Europe. Our Lady Of Mercy had been built in the 1970s, and it had that look.

Things tend to be done a certain way in any Catholic church, though. Holy water is located near the doors, a rack of prayer candles would be off to one side, and lining a quiet wall somewhere would be a row of confessional booths.

I crept across the back of the quiet church. To the right stood the glass partition for parents with young children, allowing the family to attend the service but not interrupt it if the baby cried. To the left was a row of wooden structures, about the size of three phone booths all in a row, with curtains. Those would be the confessional booths. The priest sat in the middle one, and the confessors sat on either side. Protocol dictated that you wait your turn by praying in the pews, but if the side curtain was open, you were being invited to come on in. Some churches even had a little light over the top of the center booth, to show that the priest was actually in there. No point in telling your sins to an empty box and having to do it twice.

Confession is a touchy thing. Nobody likes to talk about all the stuff they've done wrong. If a thousand people were at Mass, maybe a dozen would be at confession, unless a big holiday was coming up, like Lent. In places like New Orleans, confessions were standing room only after Mardi Gras.

That was sure not the case today. In a far corner, an old lady in black prayed quietly. Seems like there's always an old lady in black praying when you go to a church. That's also part of the way things are done.

Outside the confessional booths, two people sat in the closest pew. They were probably waiting their turn. I checked the time on my cell phone. There was more than an hour to go before they wrapped up the confessions. I stepped around the end of the last pew and sat on the cold, hard wood.

People get intimidated about making a confession, me included. The longer the wait, the more nervous everyone gets. With good reason. Admitting, out loud, the sins they've committed and the other things they've done wrong? Supposedly, folks feel better for having gotten something off their chest. I always just felt relief that it was over.

After a few minutes, a woman emerged from the confessional and joined the others who were waiting. They all got up and left together.

My turn. I took a deep breath and stood up, stepping sideways to the end of the pew and out onto the carpet as I wiped my sweaty palms on my pants. I made my way to the confessional booth and reached out to take its red velvet curtain in my fingers, having one last look around the spacious church. Aside from me and the old lady praying at the candle rack, the place was empty.

Good. This might take some time.

I slipped past the curtain and kneeled down, staring at the small screen that prevented the priest on the other side from knowing the confessor's identity. It had been years since my last confession, so I was antsy, but I felt relatively certain I remembered the routine.

I waited, tapping my toes. On a busy day of confessions, like a long day of interviews, the priest might need a few moments to relax before starting the next series. Who knows how long he will have to sit there listening. Hours, maybe. On a slow day, he might be in there reading Field & Stream from the table in the reception room.

Maybe I should come back later.

"Are you ready to begin?" The man's voice boomed into the confessional.

I jumped backwards, slamming into the wall. "Jesus!"

"No . . . Frank."

I caught my breath and shook my head, climbing back onto the kneeler. "Right, Father. Sorry."

"Been a while for you, huh?" His thunderous words filled my side of the little box. People in the pews could probably hear him. Maybe people in the parking lot.

Crouching, I managed a miniscule peep. "Yes."

"We'll go slowly, then. In the name of The Father . . ."

We couldn't see faces through the screen, but some movements were still visible. He made the sign of the cross. "How long has it been since your last confession?"

"Uh, a long time." I squirmed on the kneeler. "And to be honest, I'm not really here to confess. I sort of need help with a problem."

Father Frank sat motionless. "So your first confession in a long time . . . is not a confession?"

It was harder than I thought. "That's right, Father." I swallowed hard. Time for some salesmanship or he might shut the whole thing down on me. "If it's okay, I really need to talk."

That might be a good hook. Clergy are always open to helping a member of their congregation.

Father Frank was silent.

I hooked a thumb at the curtain. "If it's any help, you don't have anybody else waiting. You can check. There aren't any other . . . customers."

I winced at my own ineptitude. Through the screen I saw him close the book in his lap—hopefully it was The Bible and not a John Grisham novel. He opened his curtain and leaned forward.

I put a finger to my own curtain and peeked out a little. The church was completely empty.

Drawing a loud breath, Father Frank tapped his book. "Where would you like to talk? Here, or in the regular seats? There isn't another service for a few hours, so nobody will be coming in."

I pulled back my curtain a little wider to ensure my assessment was right. The hall was vacant, and kneelers tend to get uncomfortable quickly. Probably part of a leftover medieval torture setup during The Inquisition. A wood seat sounded like a nice upgrade. "Oh, the regular seats will be fine."

"Good!" He said, rising. "My butt was getting sore in here."

I smiled. My kind of priest.

I stood up and went through the curtain to greet him. He was a barrel chested man, dressed in plain clothes. Guess he wasn't expecting to be seen outside the confessional box so he skipped the black shirt and white collar.

I held my hand out. "Father, I'm Doug."

His massive mitt took mine. "Call me Frank." Gesturing to the empty pews with his book—The Bible—he smiled. "Shall we sit? Or would you rather walk a little?"

I opened my mouth to speak but he answered his own question. Rubbing his butt, he turned toward the exit door. "Let's walk."

I followed. Father Frank walked with a slight limp, almost unnoticeable. His shoes were old and faded.

"What brings you to me today?" His voice boomed off the walls of the empty church, making it sound that much louder. "What's the problem you need to talk about so strongly that you dare disrupt the sanctity of my confessional booth?"

My stomach twitched. I wasn't sure if he was being sarcastic.

At the door, Frank frowned. "Ah, it's raining. Damn." He turned back to me. "Looks like we'll have to talk here. Just a moment."

He took something out of his pocket and dropped it into a can by the rack of candles. It hit the bottom with a metallic plunk.

"Do you mind if Joseph listens in?" He pointed over his shoulder to the stature of St. Joseph behind the candle rack.

I shook my head.

"You're not talking much for a man who wants to talk about his problem," Father Frank noted. "Wanna know why I put that nail in the can?"

I blinked. A nail?

"I tend to swear a lot. I enjoy it. I find it helpful to me in my work. However, the powers that be within this fine institution find the use of profanity to be . . . undignified. And unworthy of any representative of the Holy Church." He grinned. "Can you imagine? And so a crafty method was devised to cure those of us with this horrendous affliction—that is, the bad habit of cussing."

He put his hands in his pockets and tipped his head toward the statue. "I have been given a hammer and some nails, not unlike Joseph here, a carpenter. Every time I use a swear word, I hammer a nail into a piece of wood in the rectory storage room."

"Does it work?" I asked.

"We don't know yet. Some days it sounds like a machine gun going off over there." He burst out laughing at his own joke, a thunderous whoop that bounced around the cavernous room.

Plopping down in the pew in front of me, he threw an arm over the back of the bench and cocked an eye. "Now, what's on your mind?"

I drew a slow breath. "Okay. But it's going to sound nutty."

"Nobody's keeping score, son."

"I have a daughter." I swallowed, searching the ceiling for the right words. "*We* do—my wife and I—we have a daughter. Sophie. That's her name. We call her Sophie."

"Cute," he said. "Go on."

"She recently turned four years old . . ."

"That's a fun age."

I nodded. "And there has been some trouble. Not trouble like she's a bad kid. God, she's a *great* kid." I caught myself. "Oh. Sorry." Using the Lord's name improperly. And in a church yet.

Father Frank dug into his pocket. He reached over and plunked a nail into the can by Joseph. "That one's on me."

"Thanks. So . . ." The words were hard to say out loud. I had thought about it and thought about it, and still I was at a loss as to how to describe what was happening. Or what might be happening. "There seems to be some sort of big event that occurs, a really bad event, every year." I looked at him directly. "We feel jinxed, or cursed or something. Possessed, maybe."

I watched Father Frank's face to see if the crazy alarms had gone off yet. So far, so good.

"It's just, things don't make sense." I folded my hands, then unfolded them. "They don't add up. I mean, if you almost get killed at a winery are you lucky because you weren't killed, or are you unlucky because you were almost killed?"

He nodded. "I see what you mean."

I was surprised. "You do?"

"Yeah. It *does* sound nutty. Have you seen a psychiatrist?"

I opened my mouth to speak.

A burst of laughter erupted from deep in his barrel chest. "Just kidding."

Relief swept through me. This guy was quite a character.

Father Frank scratched his chin. "I suppose how a person sees events like that all depends on their perspective. If you're an optimist, you see it as lucky. You weren't hurt, right? You and your family, in this winery incident?"

"No, not my family. Others were hurt, though. One lady was nearly killed."

"Mm hmm." The thick fingers massaging his jaw stopped. "Why does it bother you?"

"Because we should have been killed. It scared us." It sounded terrible when I said it out loud.

A frown crept over Father Frank's face. "Why should you have been killed? Did you do something wrong, to be punished?"

"No, nothing like that." I leaned forward and dropped my elbows onto my knees, running a hand through my hair. I had gone over this so many times in my head but it still sounded insane. "We, my daughter and I, we were walking out to the parking lot right before the wreck happened. We were going to have a picnic. We had a cooler in the van, and it was a nice day, so why not? Spend some time with my daughter while my wife sampled wines."

Frank nodded again. "Go on."

"Anyway, we went to go have our picnic by the side of the van. Only, on the way out, we got distracted."

"What distracted you?"

"Nothing really. Dumb stuff. Sophie got fussy so I read her some t-shirts."

Frank gave me a sideways glance. "T-shirts?"

"We're always encouraging her to tell us what the words are on things. Like if there's a poster or sign, we read it together. Things like that."

"Oh. Okay." He smiled. "That's cute."

"So we were in the winery, they had some wine t-shirts and I read them to her, to distract her because she was getting fussy. She was hungry. And they had some funny shirts that said 'I like to cook with wine, sometimes I even put it in the food.' Stuff like that."

"Mm-hmm."

"But here's the thing." I looked into his eyes, watching his face. "It was that little delay, reading the stupid t-shirts, that was just enough time for us not to get hit by the pickup truck in the parking lot. It smashed right into the car next to us and pushed that car, a sedan, flat up against our rented minivan. That's where we would have been sitting for our picnic. We would have been killed."

Frank let this sink in. "It sounds like you were lucky. But it also sounds a lot like a coincidence."

"I don't disagree," I said. "In fact, that's pretty much where my wife and I left it. Until we started talking about it that night. There have been other things that happened to us. They always happen around the same time of year, around our daughter's birthday. That made us start thinking that maybe there was a connection. Once they were all laid out, you start to realize there *has* to be a connection. I mean, I really don't see how it can be coincidence anymore." I swallowed hard. "That's when we started to wonder if maybe we . . . you know, if we were cursed. Or possessed. Or plain wacko."

"Well, I can see your concern." Father Frank sat straighter, adjusting his shirt. "You're her parents. You job is to keep her safe. If bad things are happening around you, around your daughter, you feel as though you aren't doing a good job." He stood. "But bad things happen. There are good things in the world and there are bad things. Necessarily."

He stepped into the aisle, pacing and shaking out his legs.

"You cannot have good without evil," he said. "You look at the embodiment of goodness in the world. A child. A baby. Is there anything that you have seen in your life that was not as good and as pure as your daughter, or any baby, when they are born?"

"I suppose not."

"You suppose correctly!" Frank boomed. "So we agree that some things are good. Absolutely good. But remember, as a Catholic, you believe that your daughter was born with original sin, yes?"

I nodded.

"And so therefore we see that the good is always accompanied by the bad. But you didn't come here for scripture. Let's look a little deeper, and from a different angle." Frank meandered past Joseph and the candles.

"If we allow that things can be good, they are only good in comparison to other things. If there was only one color in the world—the color blue, let's say—we could reason that there were no colors at all, because everything would be blue. That would be all that we know, and maybe that would not be enough information to let you understand that blue was even a color. Like air, blue would just *be*. It isn't until the addition of a second color that we can see blue, because we now have something else that is *not blue*. So that allows the comparison, and the comparison allows for the whole spectrum. Do you see?"

"I think so."

He cocked his head, apparently looking for a bigger commitment.

I gave it to him. "I'm with you so far."

"Okay." Frank strolled the aisle, gesturing like crazed professor. "Now, if we allow that something is good—and we do—then we have to allow that something is bad. Good and bad, or good and evil, et cetera." He stretched his arms out. "And between them, a spectrum. Varying degrees of goodness, and badness. Or evil. Yes?"

"Yes."

"So why is it hard to believe in God and not believe in a devil? Or in this case, if someone can be lucky, can they not also be unlucky?" He threw his hands up. "Of course they can. Usually, they aren't too much of one or the other."

Launching himself into my pew, he brandished his finger like a pirate's broadsword. "Do you recall the paintings you have seen? Of God and angels?"

I leaned away from the pointer in my face. "Like on the ceiling of the Sistine Chapel? Yes."

"Very good. Now—do you believe that they were merely imagined by the artist, by Michelangelo? That he simply made them up?"

I thought for a moment. "I suppose he was creating a visualization of something that he had read, or that had been told to him . . ."

"Again you suppose correctly!" Frank beamed, retreating into the aisle. "And let's not forget who Michelangelo's boss was. The Pope. So it's safe to say that he was getting his information from a good source."

He spaced back and forth in the aisle, his head down, one hand behind him and the other out front leading the way, stabbing the air as he spoke. "Now, if you can believe that there is a God and that there are angels, some sort of Old Testament embodiment of *energy,* that can bring down a sheep to interrupt you from sacrificing your son on the altar, like Abraham, or an aberration that can talk to this man's wife." He hooked a thumb at the statue of Joseph. "And tell her that she's pregnant, why would you not think the *other* possibility is true as well? That there are beings from the other side of the spectrum that could also interact with us? Why is that so hard to believe?"

Frank stepped into my pew and plopped down. "Most people believe the other way. They see a movie like The Exorcist and after two hours they completely believe in the devil. They'll have nightmares from that belief, and it may stay with them for the rest of their lives." His eyes fell on mine, seeming to study me. "Or, when nothing dramatic happens to them, like hovering over their bed, or their head twisting around backwards, when nothing like that ever actually occurs, they eventually shrug it off. The devil becomes a boogeyman, not a real thing, and stories they read about people who think they are possessed become things to ridicule." He sat back with a grunt. "And why shouldn't they? You only can focus on so many things, so you don't pay attention to what's unimportant or what never happens. But some of those same people can't make the leap to get their heart and mind to believe in a God, even though the proof is all around. In the beauty of a flower, in the magic of a child, on and on. What sense does that make?"

He stared at me. My turn to talk.

"Because if one exists, the other has to," I whispered. "And if God and His good angels exist, the others can, too."

His eyebrows raised at my revelation. "Aha!" Bounding up again, he went back to pacing the aisle. "You understand that there is a lot more to this."

I nodded.

"God can still exist even if people don't believe in Him, right?"

It was a rhetorical question. I didn't try to answer, and he didn't wait for me to.

"The devil and his dark angels can exist even if people don't believe in them. And until something bad happens that can't be explained any other way, most people choose not to believe in dark angels and Satan. It's pretty simple, really."

He put his hand on the back of my pew, leaning on it like he'd exhausted himself. "Let me ask you this. In the story of Abraham, he is told to sacrifice his son, Isaac, to God. Was Isaac lucky, or unlucky? Had his father Abraham gone mad, ready to sacrifice his own son on the altar, and at the last minute God intervened? God sends down an angel with a sheep, and Isaac is spared."

I shook my head. "Nobody mentions luck in that story, do they?"

Frank erupted in a laugh. "They sure as shit don't!"

He dug into his pocket and clanked another nail into the cup. Then he settled into the pew again, apparently happy with the progress we were making. I was, too.

The thick fingers returned to his jaw. "When do you think you may have seen other things like this, that make you wonder if your daughter is possessed? Aside from ones around her birthday, and even aside from being connected to your daughter at all?"

I shrugged.

"Think about that. It'll help. Maybe you've been missing things. Signs."

"But not possessed." Mallory would have none of that. "I don't believe my daughter is possessed."

"There are different types of possession. Degrees of intensity. Allow that thought in your head, too, purely as a discussion point. You want to consider—and eliminate—all the possibilities you can."

I took a breath. "Okay."

"Think about when in your life these things may have happened. Let them come to you. Then, think about those examples when they do." He lowered his voice. "This is like making tea. It won't happen just because I suggested it, but as you allow the possibility to steep in your head, you may think of something. Consider it, and what it might mean."

He glanced at his watch and stood up. "People will be filing in for the next service soon."

I followed him as he walked back toward Joseph. "Think about all of it. And then, please, come back and see me, and we will chat some more. You can talk to . . ." Frank gestured toward the church offices.

"Mrs. Clermont."

"Okay, sure." He smiled.

We walked out the door together. The rain had stopped again.

Father Frank looked at me "What does your family say about all this?"

"You mean my mom and dad?"

He nodded.

"I haven't told my dad about it. My mom passed away."

"Recently?"

"No, mom died years before Sophie was even born."

"Hmm." Frank eyed the cloudy sky. A light breeze tugged at a tuft of his hair on his forehead. "The mother is usually the religious force in the family."

"Yeah, she was," I said. "Especially when I was a kid. It's a shame that Sophie will never meet her grandmother, somebody who was so influential in my life."

"As a Catholic, don't you believe she will see her grandmother in Heaven someday?"

I squinted at him as my eyes adjusted to the brightness outside. "To be honest, Frank, I spent the first week of her life in the Neonatal Intensive Care Unit. I kinda see my job as trying to keep her from returning to Heaven for as long as possible."

"I'm only teasing." Frank patted my shoulder. "We talked about a lot of things today. You have some thinking to do."

I shook his hand. "Thanks, Frank. You helped a lot."

"Talk to my boss." He grinned. "Maybe I can get a raise."

I pulled my car keys from my pocket.

Frank lifted his face skyward, scanning the clouds. "Remember, there have been many iterations of good and evil throughout time. Fire. Dragons. All kinds of things. The original burning bush was God, and then later fire represented Satan and Hell. Nobody connects fire with God now, do they?"

"I guess not."

"Angel of light, angel of darkness." Father Frank held hands out like weighing scales. "The Church believes these things exist, and so do I. Most people just find it easier to believe one way or the other. Why not both? Why should only the bad guys get to have all the fun?" He laughed. "Fuck 'em!"

"That's a two nailer!" I said, smiling.

"At least!" Frank chuckled as he waved goodbye.

Chapter 14

She didn't hear the train coming. It was an *accident*.

Driving home from my meeting with Father Frank, I got stuck waiting for a train. That didn't happen much in Tampa, but it used to happen all the time when I was a kid.

I guess the conversation with Father Frank had gotten me to thinking. He seemed to know it would.

Anybody could have read my face and known that I was in need of answers that weren't going to come easily. Father Frank's conversation put the wheels in motion.

I sat in my car and watched the long train roll by, each set of steel wheels making a *clack-clack* as it went over the crossing. That's a noise I knew well. The rhythm lulled me into a kind of daydream, bringing back memories of Millersburg.

When I was a kid, a classmate's mom had died over the summer in a terrible accident. When people first heard about it, we were all really surprised. My parents were absolutely shocked. But I was young. Kids didn't process things the way we later would as adults.

Jenny Billen's mom had been hit by a train, along with their little baby. We knew the Billens because Jenny was in the same grade as me. Our families went to the same church, and my older brother was on the basketball team with Jenny's older brother. Our families were kind of close. When my dad felt inclined to buy an antique car, the Billens stored it at their ranch for us in an unused barn stall. I visited there once in a while. One time, Mrs. Billen gave me a peanut butter sandwich with a glass of milk that came right from their cows. I almost didn't want to drink it. Milk came from a bottle in the refrigerator, not from a bucket under a cow. I was certain it had missed some very important decontamination process that was supposed to occur before you could drink it.

When I first heard about her accident, I assumed that Mrs. Billen had probably been driving in their station wagon, and when the crossing lights began to flash, she tried to beat the striped guard pole as it came down over the road. Somehow the train must have caught her as she drove across the tracks. As kids we had heard stories like that before. On the way to soccer practice, if some teenager drove around the crossing gates to beat the oncoming train, Mom would point it out. *Look how insane that person is! That's very dangerous. You should never do that!*

This was different.

Mrs. Billen wasn't driving anywhere; she was walking. Somehow, she had managed to be walking alongside the train tracks with her little baby and gotten hit by the train.

In our small Indiana town, train tracks were everywhere. They fed the big industries that helped our town grow and thrive for decades: Richmond Chemicals, Metcalf Machinery and Mining, Atlas Engineering, among others. Most of them are gone now, but once upon a time, big thundering trains rolled through our city with the sound of progress and prosperity. When a kid got old enough to ride a bike, train tracks became a real pain in the butt. A tire might go sidelong into the two-inch dugout on each side of the steel rails at a crossing, and it would send him flying. Driving a car, a long train would ruin your mad dash to school or work. Teenagers can't budget for traffic or train delays. It's not in their DNA until sometime after age thirty or so.

As kids, we tried to flatten coins by placing them on the train tracks. Jimmy tried it a few times down near the park. You had to put a penny on the big steel rail, and when the train went by it would smash the penny flat—as thin as paper and as wide as a half dollar. Or so we had heard, anyway. We only knew about flattening coins the same way all kids learn things like that—from some other kid whose older brother had done it.

The train conductors knew kids liked to do that stuff, too, and they must have hated it. One wrong move by some dumb kid, and *splat,* the kid would get flattened along with the coins. The train's engineers were always on the lookout as they passed through towns.

Smashing coins was more difficult than you'd think. The oncoming train vibrated the tracks with such great intensity the coins moved around and fell off the rail. That meant you had to jump up at the last minute and replace your coins or they wouldn't get flattened.

Time it wrong, and you'd get flattened.

Even the rush of wind from the passing train was strong and violent. It was scary the first time I felt it, because I wasn't expecting it. From our hiding spot in the trees twenty feet away, the wind from the train was still massive and powerful. The vibrations came through the ground and into your Keds, and the suction created by the enormous train engine could pull you under its huge steel wheels.

Adventurous kids would sometimes hop aboard slow moving trains as they came to the crossings or needed to switch tracks. That often met in disaster, too, like the kids who insisted on swimming in the Indiana rock quarries every summer. You could read about some kid drowning from the shifting sands in the quarry every year, and you could find a story about some kid getting his leg cut off—or worse—trying to jump onto a moving train. They were like annual stories in the paper, only with different names each time. But I guess the draw of the cool water or the thrill of a free train ride was enough to make dumb kids take unknowing risks. Kids don't read newspapers.

As I sat in my car watching the train roll by, I thought about the game my dad would play when we were stuck by a train. He would try to get us kids to wait out the delay by counting the boxcars and coal cars rolling down the tracks. It was an old trick, and it usually met with mediocre success. It gets boring counting train cars unless there are a lot of them, and then that gets boring because there are too many.

This time, I was first in line, a front row seat. The only thing between me and the rolling thunder of the giant train was a small striped pole from the roadside train guard.

From there, even in the car, I could feel the vibrations of the massive locomotive. It made me think.

How the heck did my classmate's mom not hear that thing coming?

The trains were so big and so noisy, it seemed inconceivable that somebody couldn't hear them coming. Mrs. Billen hadn't been placing pennies on the rail to flatten them, either.

An awful, queasy feeling shot through me. Maybe she did hear the train.

A cold sweat broke out on my forehead as I envisioned what happened. She heard it coming. You can't *not* hear a train coming. And you can't be taking a walk by the tracks and not notice it from a long way off.

Gripping the steering wheel, I tried to not see, to not know. The images came at me fast, blinding me to all but the horror they displayed.

I swallowed hard, shaking my head, fighting it, but it overwhelmed me. I had to look. I couldn't *not* look.

The very thought of not seeing made my insides churn. I thought I'd throw up in my car. I was gasping, sweating, hot and stuffy—but unable to stop seeing it.

She would know the train schedules just like everybody else in town. There were the morning ones that made me late for class in high school, and the afternoon ones that made me late for my job after school. I can't tell you now what times they ran, but I could have told you then.

The scene played out inside my car like a movie projector was showing it on my windshield and all around me. Like I was there.

She put away the breakfast dishes the way she did every morning, and walked over to the high chair. Glassy eyed, she picked the baby up. I felt him squirming in my arms when she did. He was getting heavier now that he was a few months old.

The day before, she had seen her older kids off to summer camp. It was a much quieter house without them. This morning, she kissed her husband goodbye as he went off to work the cattle auction. For one week a month, he would spend the morning in town and the afternoon at the stockyards getting everything counted and ready.

She had the big ranch house to herself, just her and the baby.

She opened the window over the sink while she washed the dishes, gazing absently over the green pasture. Afterward, she dried her hands on a dish towel and slid the station wagon keys off the hook on the wall.

She drove past the small grocery stores that were closer to the farm, going all the way down to Robertson's. She found a spot in the middle of the lot and lifted the gear shift on the steering column until it clicked into park. She got the baby and walked toward the front door, but instead of going inside the store, she walked on down the covered sidewalk to the side of the building and went around the corner.

Here, the train tracks were closest to the store. There was the asphalt driveway that the delivery trucks used, then a short span of woods, and then the train tracks—a distance of maybe seventy-five feet, in all.

Waiting near the store, she heard the distant howl of the train horn as it passed the crossing two miles away at Sunset Street. The noise carried in the wind. That was her cue.

I squeezed my eyes shut, my breath coming in short gasps as I watched her step onto the asphalt driveway.

A delivery truck slammed on its brakes to avoid her. The driver honked. Mrs. Billen should have been startled, but she wasn't. Holding her baby in her arms, she looked up at the driver, paused, and then moved on.

The truck driver shook his hands in the air.

When she reached the wooded area, she paused again. The closest tree that would hide her was very close to the clearing for the drainage ditch. She wrapped her body around her sleeping child as best she could, to prevent the branches from scratching him as she pushed her way through the underbrush. Then she waited.

She could not yet hear the train but she could hear its next horn blast as it passed through each intersection, a friendly honk to drivers as the huge locomotive made its way through town.

Her breathing calm and slow, she gazed at the tracks. Simply down a small hill and up a small hill. Her pulse quickened. My heart pounded with adrenaline as a bead of sweat rolled down my cheek.

Another blast from the train horn as it crossed the intersection at Morris Road. It was getting closer. I groaned, my stomach clenched in fear as I watched.

She observed the distance to the tracks with the next horn blast. She turned to look. In the distance, the massive engine pushed its way out of the morning mist: a small white headlight surrounded by the painted yellow cat of the Chessie system train.

Right on time, she thought. Her heart was pounding now. My feet were pressed to the floor slamming invisible brakes.

The train's speed was deceptive. Objects that big don't appear to be going fast. Slowing down to pass through town, the train still moved at a brisk fifty miles per hour. As the giant steel engine rounded a small curve a mile away, Mrs. Billen stared at the tracks close by. A short run down the hill and a short run up the other side to the tracks.

Now she could start to feel the rumble of the big train. It started as a methodic clacking with a low hum underneath. The closer it came, the louder the clacking grew. The thunderous engine vibrated the ground. Its trademark yellow cat image became clear in the sunlight.

Another blast from its loud horn as it crossed Hanna Avenue a few hundred yards away. That one woke the baby. He began to cry.

I couldn't breathe. I clenched my teeth and squeezed my eyes shut, unable to stop the images all around me from continuing.

The rumbling grew louder. Her feet began to shake. Mrs. Billen put a hand on the tree to steady herself. Her baby crying, she took a deep breath.

She pushed off from the tree and sprinted down the short hill. Running with her child in her arms, each stride landed hard on the ground. She rushed across the flat span to the short hill, being careful not to fall.

The train engineer saw something move out from the trees on the left. Maybe a deer, he thought, and moved over to the left window to check.

Mrs. Billen looked up at the coming train, less than a hundred feet from where she stood. Its terrible noise deafened her and drowned out the cries of her infant son. She paused, only for a moment, as a hand frantically waved at her from the engine window.

The blaring horn was overwhelmed by the piercing screech of the metal brakes. She stepped up the short hill to the tracks, clutching her son.

She looked down at the gravel dancing under her feet from the rumbling of the massive locomotive. Then the ground was covered in a huge shadow.

She lifted her head to see the large painted cat as it leaped at her.

Closing her eyes, she braced to receive it.

I sat in my car, shaking as I cried, my shirt drenched in sweat. The churning in my stomach caused me to gag and spit. I slapped at the armrest buttons to put down a window, gulping the fresh air.

It took the train over a mile to come to a complete stop. By then, there was not much left to identify Mrs. Billen or her son. Hours later, the police finally figured out the car in the Robertson's parking lot belonged to the bodies on the tracks. The car keys at the accident site fit the station wagon door. Mrs. Billen's purse rested under the front seat.

Then a phone call was made to the stockyards, to locate her husband and give him the terrible news.

I wiped my eyes. Whatever her personal pain, her world of depression, Mrs. Billen heard the train call to her—and she went to answer it.

That's what I knew now. I knew it. I *saw* it.

She crossed over into the realm of the dark angels, the ones that push us to do the unthinkable.

She did it on purpose and took her baby with her. It was as simple as that. And as evil as that, to take the life of an innocent baby.

What other possible explanation could there be?

One, perhaps. The one they made up and gave to us kids. I remembered that.

A lie told to young classmates by their parents to protect them from the horrors of the world for a little while longer.

A lie told to the Billen kids to ease their pain and keep the good memories of their mother intact.

A method to prevent a well-meaning friend who came over to see the new calf, from asking innocent questions that would keep the torture alive.

A gift of love, really. Everyone would look the other way. What benefit was there to dwell on the truth of such a tragedy?

And what is the truth, anyway? They said she didn't hear it coming. That it was an accident. Who was I to argue? Still . . . With my bloodshot eyes and wet shirt, I now knew there were other explanations.

Darker ones. Ugly ones.

In all the years since, I never spoke about what happened to Mrs. Billen. Not to my wife, not to anyone. I never mentioned it to a living soul since the summer it happened, and I couldn't believe I thought of it now.

Father Frank was working on me.

The driver behind me laid on his car horn, yanking me out of my fog. The train had passed.

Sitting up, I put my car into drive and headed for home. My queasiness had vanished.

But I think I understood what Father Frank was getting at—or starting to. I think I may have started to grasp it. The aberrations, these dark angels or whatever they are. Maybe they do exist. I may have met one.

Once upon a time, she gave me a peanut butter sandwich with a glass of milk that came right from her cow.

My queasiness came rushing back as I realized something much worse. I may have been best friends with one.

Chapter 15

"What?" The cars were whizzing by my green Schwinn as Jimmy and I rode our bikes to Woolco. I couldn't hear his question over the noise. There were too many cars, driving way too close to us.

As adults we tend to forget these things, but being a ten-year-old kid on a bike, riding down a busy road with cars going by barely two feet away—it can feel pretty ominous.

Construction in several places along Washburn Boulevard, our chosen route to Woolco to procure more model boats, created the hazard that forced us into the street. Apartments were being built, so whole sections along the busy road didn't have sidewalks. That wasn't a big deal on our own street—the only cars that drove down Reigert Drive belonged to people who lived there. But going out to the bigger, busier roads was a different story.

A scrawny little kid on a bike feels it when a car goes past at forty miles an hour. You wouldn't think forty miles per hour was very fast riding in a car as a passenger, but a car that goes by you at that speed when you're a kid on a bike, it's a whole different ball game. Squeezed onto the side of a bustling main road with car after car whizzing by, it's amazingly fast. And *loud*. The hum of the tires make a lot of noise, especially if the cars already have snow tires on them. Trucks make the most noise. When one of the big concrete trucks rolled by, it was like a jet liner was getting ready to land on your head. The freaking ground shook. But the biggest part was the wind.

Even when the smallest sedan goes by you on your bike, the wind in its wake tugs at you and pulls you toward the road. It would grab at you and knock you off balance.

A big car going by felt like it could throw you to the ground. Asphalt roads do horrible things to hands when you fall off your bike. Not only did it sting like hell, you had to sit there and pick the little rocks out of your wounded knees and palms. Then you had to climb back on your bike, bleeding, and keep riding. It didn't matter whether you gave up and went home, or whether you toughed it out and rode on to the store, a bike was usually a kid's fastest way to get to someplace. And riding with a skinned knee or buckshot hands was the worst.

Usually, we encouraged each other to keep going and get to the store. The thinking was, as long as you already went through all that trouble, you might as well get your model boat. I bet Woolco saw more than one bleeding kid pull up on his bike on any given summer day.

So our little excursion to acquire additional warships to destroy down in the creek was made a little more adventurous—and a lot longer—by the lack of sidewalks. At least it seemed longer to us.

Amidst this chaos, Jimmy had said something to me, but I missed it. He shouted it again.

"Would you kill Hitler?"

"What, here? Now?"

Another car roared by, its driver voicing disapproval by laying on the horn as it passed.

"You wanna play *now*?"

He was crazy. This road was too busy to talk back and forth to another kid on a bike behind me. I hated this part of the ride. We needed to get to the section of the road up ahead that had the sidewalk, where we could ride safely. That's what was on my mind.

Not Jimmy. "C'mon! Would you kill Hitler?"

"Get off the road!" A motorist shouted as they sped by. We had to go on and off the street when there wasn't a sidewalk, but we obviously weren't doing it very well. This particular spot was a short section that was lasting forever.

"Come on!" Jimmy shouted. "Let's play!"

It was a stupid name for a stupid game. Irreverent, really. I'm not sure we even called it by that name. Killing Hitler. I'm not sure I remember what the actual name of that game was.

Oh, I knew all right. I remember playing that game like we'd played it only yesterday.

We didn't have wives or children or girlfriends back then to civilize us, so we played dumb games to trick each other into saying something stupid. It was a harmless game to pass the time for a couple of kids who weren't old enough to pass it in other ways.

"Would you ever steal a corvette?"

"What? Heck, no!" I gripped the handle bars and winced as my bike shuddered with each vehicle that passed.

"What if bank robbers put a gun to your mom's head, and you had to steal the car or they would kill her. You have to steal the car to help them escape, or they will kill you mom."

"Then, yes, I'd steal the car. Now shut up, you're going to get us killed."

Jimmy howled in laughter at my distress.

At times, our game was uncomplicated and pointless. Back when we were young enough to walk into the trap of questions set by the other, the opposing player wasn't usually strategic enough to ask methodical questions. We'd try to win in three moves. We had no plan. When we grew old enough to be patient, we couldn't lure the other one in. Tic Tac Toe.

The game was premised on knowing what the other person considered important, or knowing what they valued, or having a secret. But it also depended on them having similar judgment as you. And best friends spend too much time together to really keep secrets from each other, don't they?

Or do they?

I had a secret. A big one. Maybe Jimmy did, too. Maybe that's why he was always wanting to play the game, to learn mine—or to try to get me to know his. Who knows why kids do things?

What if you stole a car and didn't get caught? That changes things. When people don't get punished the first time they try something bad, they may become emboldened to try it again. Maybe shoplifting had lost its thrill so you try jacking a car—anything to see where the limits were. We knew kids who had done it. Older kids we'd see at the park. They smoked pot or went joyriding, things like that. They were tough kids who got in fights at school but didn't get beat up.

In the real world, would I ever steal a car? No, never. Hoo, boy, would I get in trouble for that! Because of course, I'd for sure get caught. My dad would kill me. I'd be grounded forever.

The other kids, the tough kids, they were learning that rules were for suckers. When you don't get caught, the rules don't apply.

Now I was starting to understand. I didn't get it back then. And if the tough kids had any clue, they ignored it. At their school, they didn't have nuns lecturing them about being good and parents lecturing them about how they represented the family in the community.

So we never tried anything. We played our game.

"So you wouldn't steal a car?" After we'd safely made it to the sidewalk, I could hear Jimmy better. "Okay, your mom has to go to the grocery store. She wants you to go with her, so you go." Then he thought for a moment. "You want to stay home and play. You want to ride your bike."

"Okay."

Patches of shade from Elm trees passed over us as we glided down the far side of the boulevard. It was a little too fast to ride with no hands, but I knew Jimmy was back there trying it.

"She wants you to help her buy things. You wanna play with your friends. It's summertime, but you go you have to go. She needs your help."

He seemed to be attempting a stealthy angle this time. Rolling along the sidewalk, we dodged the occasional low hanging tree branch.

I listened as he went on.

"After the store she wants to stop by the bank."

I rolled my eyes. "Come on, where is this going?"

"Hang on. You read your new comic book and you're miserable. You should be home. You should be down at the park, jumping ramps on the bike trails with your friends."

Jimmy liked the jerry-rigged bike ramps we made at the park. We would push our bikes to the top of one of the big hills, the same ones we would ride our sleds down in winter when they were covered with snow. At the bottom of the hill, we rigged up some plywood and old boards that we fished out of the creek. The idea was to be like Evel Knievel, racing down the hill on your bike and hitting the ramp at top speed, and then seeing how far you could fly.

The problem was, it was pretty scary coming down the hill. You picked up a lot of speed. If you hit the brakes, you might go over the handle bars and land face first in the dirt. Or your tire might skid and send you into the trees. If you made it to the bottom, you would almost certainly miss the ramp—an eight inch wide board at best—and if managed to hit it, you'd probably wreck after you got airborne. Landings were such a small part of the equation, we never planned on them. We had no place to slow down, no safety gear, and no way of getting medical attention if we got hurt.

We were typical ten year old boys.

Jimmy was still laying out his elaborate scenario while I had drifted off.

"She parks the car and goes into the bank . . ."

I shook my head. "I guess I do this before the grocery store, or the ice cream is gonna melt and the milk will spoil."

"You are in the bank, standing there," he continued, ignoring me. "All of a sudden, there's a bank robbery. They take your mom hostage. You're sitting there, so they give you the car keys and tell you that they need you to steal that car out front or they will shoot your mom. The robbers need this to make their escape."

The scene set, he asked the capper: "Would you steal it?"

"Of course," I said. "No hesitation."

"You'd get caught."

"So?"

"So you'd go to jail."

"I don't think they'd send a kid to jail in a situation like that."

"But what if they did?"

This round of the game seemed a little tortured. What was he getting at? Either he had forgotten that he had asked me nearly the same question before, or he was looking for a different answer.

I considered it, too, as I pedaled along Lummings Road. This one had a sidewalk, so we were safe.

But I was tired of the game, and frustrated from all the speeding cars conspiring to scare us. I jumped to where I thought his questions were headed. "We would all kill Hitler if we *could* kill Hitler, okay? But it isn't that easy."

I glanced over my shoulder, seeing a shocked expression on his face. "Even if you could really kill him, not just theoretically?"

"Of course. No hesitation," I said, still theorizing. "To sacrifice your life for the lives of millions would buy you a seat in heaven. It's an easy choice."

"What would make it harder choice?"

I rode in silence for a moment. It was a good question.

My family had been to my uncle's house for a birthday party for their two year old son. They fawned over that cute little kid, walking around in his overalls and t-shirt. He was their world, and it showed. To trade him away? Inconceivable. Probably for any parents, with a kid of any age, but a little kid? A helpless child? No way.

"Say you have the parents of a little kid," I started. "Their only child, on the kid's second birthday." I paused for effect, like I was making it up. "In front of all their friends and family, everybody at the kid's birthday party, you ask if they would trade their child's life to kill Hitler—you know, before he came to power. But you show them what he's going to become, and they understand it like you showed them a page from the future. They could even get away with it, Scott free. Now it's a whole different deal."

I was proud of myself. I had created a scene where there would be a real challenge to do the right thing. Young parents are hard wired not to put their child at risk. Even as a kid, I knew that. Certainly none would volunteer to lose their child for a stranger who had done nothing wrong yet, even with the promise that he would eventually come to power and be responsible for the deaths of millions of people—including millions of children. It was a beautiful dilemma.

Would you kill Hitler? Yes. What if it would cost you the life of your child in exchange? Then, no.

It changes that quickly.

No mother could ever make that choice. And she wouldn't let her husband choose it, either.

I could see the smiling look of satisfaction on Jimmy's face. In fact, I think that was his point, to get me to come up with some really challenging situations. I wondered why.

As a game, two stupid pre-teens might very well banter about this. You can still *say* yes. It's only math at that point. Lose this one, keep millions of others. Easy. As a math problem, it's a figurative child you don't know. A kid on paper.

But in reality, it's crazy. Nobody would do it. So it's not an automatic choice. The math still works, but somehow you can't do it.

I figured that was Jimmy's point. To get me to open myself to that.

Why?

I looked back at him again. He was still smiling. "Those poor parents."

He didn't mean it. He was mocking me, letting his sympathetic brain disengage from his theoretical one.

Whatever. It's just a game. Why not? It doesn't matter.

We had reached Woolco. I rolled my green Schwinn into the bike rack. "You have a dark streak, man," I said, shaking my head.

Jimmy brushed past me. "Hey, *you* came up with all that baby killing stuff, not me."

I was about to say something back to him when I stopped. He was right.

I was even a little embarrassed for having done so, thinking about the look on my uncle's face when I told him we traded his child to kill a really bad guy. Mom always said I had a vivid imagination, but to be honest, it made me a little sick to my stomach to know that I could think stuff like that up.

I locked up my bike, went into the store, forcing those thoughts out of my head

.

Chapter 16

By the time I got home from my visit to the church, dinner had been waiting. That's never good. Things were already tense enough at home, but I had to drive around a while to stop shaking. I didn't want to appear upset in front of my wife and daughter.

I'd had a roller coaster ride of emotions with Father Frank, followed by some nightmare-style daydreams, if you can call them that. The floodgates were open, and Father Frank had opened them.

There were only one or two problems.

First, he didn't really answer my question. Maybe I didn't ask it right, but I wanted to know what we should be doing about all the things that were going on. I got caught up in Father Frank's conversation allowing for the fact that I wasn't going crazy, and that was good, but we didn't take the next step. What was I supposed to do about what was happening?

Second, what do I tell my wife?

Strangely, she didn't ask. I think she knew that I'd get around to telling her eventually, but she may have also been happy not to hear if it was bad news. Or she may not have wanted her nice day spoiled. Either way, she didn't bring it up. And since we were having a good time with Sophie, who was always within ear shot, that was probably best.

Maybe the plan was to let our daughter fall asleep first, and then talk after we put her to bed. Good plan.

The only flaw in it was, since we were both full the *churrasco* steak she made for dinner, we all fell asleep on the couch after dinner. Somewhere around midnight,

Mallory woke up and carried Sophie off to bed, covering me with a blanket as I snored on the couch.

Then around 3 A. M., I woke up with my throat and belly on fire and my forehead coated in sweat. I'd like to blame the churrasco, or the howling gusts of wind from the start of the tropical storm . . .

But the nightmare about the lions in the woods was what did it.

Chapter 17

Dear Carl,

I had prepared for the death of my mother for years.

I was an adult when mom died, and afterward there were many things that reminded me of her that I could have never predicted. They came out of nowhere. My wife and I went to the Florida state fair and they had a taffy pulling machine. Mom loved salt water taffy, and whenever we were at a fair in Indiana when I was a kid, she would always get some. My first, immediate thought when I saw the taffy machine was, I should get a box and send it to mom. My second thought was, I can't because she's gone. I can never send her any gift, ever again.

Be strong for your daughter. Losing her mother at the young age of twelve will be something that may cause unexpected sadness at strange times.

Your daughter will be surprised by things like that and how they affect her, so let her know that she will have these thoughts because she really cared for her mom. I believe the amount of pain we feel at a loved one's passing is a testament to how much we loved them.

I can tell you this: when my mother died, she had been sick for quite a while—years, in fact—and we all knew she didn't have a lot of time left. Mallory and I visited, I got to see Mom one last time, and a few weeks later she was gone.

I knew it was coming and I expected it. I didn't cry when I visited her in the hospital, not when I got the news in the middle of the night, nor at the visitation.

But when I was at her funeral mass, in the church I grew up in, where I sat, Sunday after Sunday, next to her when I was a child . . . Now, in front of the altar was her coffin, cold and alone. When they started playing her favorite church song, the one she loved to sing at Mass, I cried like a baby.

I sobbed uncontrollably and unashamedly.

I wept in front of my family, my friends, and my God.

My young wife, sitting next to me, was unsure of what to do except hand me tissue after tissue and hold my hand.

I was overwhelmed. My mother was gone.

I could not stop the tears, and I didn't want to.

I loved my mother and the world is not a better place without her in it, and on that day at that moment is when it hit me, even though I thought I was prepared and I knew it was coming and I thought I was handling it well.

I believe I honored my mother that day, and I will tell you, I doubt anybody who saw me crying thought any less of me for it.

Even though I had moved away from home many years before, and I rarely visited or even called to chat, there was something nice about knowing I could. Now, even that was gone.

I would never again be able to buy Mom her salt water taffy at the fair. I couldn't spontaneously call her up at Christmas just to playfully ask the names of the Three Kings. I couldn't pop in for a quick weekend visit on my way to some fun, other place.

I couldn't do any of those things, ever again. So when I say to expect the unexpected from your emotions, that is what I mean. Ultimately, you will all be fine because you have a strong family and a great loving network. The emotions you or your daughter feel during this time are valid, so don't feel bad about having them—any of them.

At the first Christmas after my mom had died, we had our traditional family gathering. Before we all opened our presents, my brother offered a toast to those who we loved but who are no longer with us. It let everybody address the elephant in the room, have that emotion, and then move on to enjoy the rest of the day. It was a smart move, and it helped a lot.

Just like people feel guilty about the joy of having a new baby when another close relative's parent is dying of cancer, grief and joy are both allowed in the same room.

So do what you have to do. Expect the unexpected from your emotions, and if I can help in any way, let me know.

Our hearts are with all of you in this difficult time.

Try to enjoy Thanksgiving, my friend!

Doug

With trembling hands, I folded the faded, yellowed photocopy of the letter and placed it back in my desk drawer. I turned off the light and sat in the darkness, leaning back in my chair as the growing winds from the tropical storm howled outside.

Few people would make a copy of a handwritten letter they were sending to a friend, but when I finished this one I realized I'd written it to Carl as much as I'd written it to myself. The letter was like a solemn vow of some sort. Reading it was a kind of prayer.

My mind needed comfort from too much craziness as much as my stomach needed it from too much churrasco. More sleep didn't seem likely tonight.

It seemed a waste that my mother's influence would never pass to her granddaughter. Someone who had put so much effort into shaping me as a person, who went to every swim meet and soccer game, who taught me about so many things . . . Mom drilled me incessantly with multiplication flash cards so I would learn my "times tables," volunteered at our school and at the YMCA, taught me—through her actions—about our role in the real world and not book stuff like the nuns at school. What a huge benefit to my daughter, to have had that resource, but they would never meet.

And yet, they had a commonality.

I saw it in the delivery room when Sophie was born. The first time I gazed upon my newborn daughter, I remember thinking that she had the combination of a wrinkly old man's face and my mother's, a round face with dimples and bright eyes. It only lasted for a moment. When I looked again, it was gone, but it was there.

My wife didn't care much for that description—wrinkly old man—but all babies are kind of wrinkly and odd-looking when they're first born. Babies look a lot more presentable after the nurses clean them up, weigh them and wrap them in the soft white hospital blankets, and put the little hat on them.

Newborn baby gets a routine doctor's exam and get discharged, but that's not how it went for us. On the day of our planned release, to go home with our addition to the family, our examining doctor felt there was something not quite right as he pressed the stethoscope to my daughter's chest. He said he heard something that bothered him. That bothered me.

Tests confirmed his uncanny suspicion. They found a rare and potentially fatal heart condition, one that no doctor could ever have heard through a stethoscope—and yet this doctor did just that. And off to the Neonatal Intensive Care Unit we all went.

We watched, with the empty feeling of helplessness eating away at our insides, as our daughter, barely twenty-four hours old, clung to life. And we and the parents of the other babies in the NICU wept and prayed. In the midst of all that, I felt a something I had not felt before. At a time when I should have been scared, I grew to feel strangely calm.

My dad, a physician, said it was a miracle. He said that there must have been an angel on the examining doctor's shoulder that day, whispering in his ear. If we had taken my daughter home, she might have died with no warning, like so many others with the condition.

We were lucky. There was an angel on the doctor's shoulder that day. Or one on my daughter's.

I was unprepared for the emotions I would have from out of nowhere after the death of my mother, so I understood when people said they could no longer drive by a certain intersection where their kid had crashed a car and almost died. It changes you, like the NICU changed us.

The street light outside my window illuminated the falling rain. The drops came down almost horizontally in the whipping winds of the storm. I rubbed my clammy hands on my t-shirt to dry them. The grip of fear the bad dream had put in my gut had nearly subsided.

For a long time, a word or phrase that someone would innocently say to me, or something they'd do in passing, would instantly plunge me back into that cold, dark church in Indiana where I would again find myself staring at a shining coffin in the dim glow of candles. The box that now held my mother for eternity.

I'm not sure I told my mom enough that I loved her. Actually, that's a lie. I'm sure I didn't. I showed it at her funeral, and I could write about it in a letter to my friend, but I doubt I did enough to show her while she was alive. Women are different that way. I see that now, watching my wife with our daughter. A mother always wants another kiss or hug. She can't hear "I love you" enough from her child. I haven't make the same mistake with my daughter that I made with my mom. I tell Sophie that I love her all the time.

It would fall to me, then, to teach her the good things about my mother. Sure, there were many things to be learned from Mallory's side of the family. They are good and decent folks. Sophie loves them and we visit their farm all the time. She helps throw old bread to the cows and holds the basket when they collect chicken eggs from the coop. At three years old she was catching her own catfish with Mallory's father in the pond.

Sophie will build her own fond memories of childhood, and she will build her strengths and weaknesses as she does. I'm not sure how you could teach your daughter about her other grandmother anyway, especially when she can't see it for herself. I'm not sure I would even know how to teach her, or whether I could if I did know how. And that seems like kind of a waste.

I guess that's why I hang onto the copy of that letter. To help show her one day.

But that's not the only reason I keep it.

Chapter 18

By 4 A. M., I was still wide awake but the cold sweat had faded.

I silently cursed the churrasco and salsa, but that wasn't the reason. I dug through the pantry to find some Tums. Plopping down on the living room couch, I sorted my thoughts in the darkness and tried to put the lion dream behind me.

There wasn't much point in going back to the church. They weren't going to advance the ball. Father Frank had gotten my wheels turning—he seemed to think I wasn't insane, and that was a pretty good start—but a conventional church approach was never going to be the right way to go. Not for our situation.

What did I really know about whatever this was, anyway? Somehow, I had to find someone to help me connect the dots—if the dots were supposed to be connected. Father Frank seemed to think they were.

Maybe the church doesn't go into stuff like this. Maybe that stuff like exorcism is only for the movies. Maybe I should try to find some other options, and then go back and give the church another shot if those didn't pan out.

I took a deep breath and let it out slowly, rubbing my stomach. The lion dream really shook me up. Who dreams about being chased by lions, anyway? I mean, once they're older than five?

It was just a stress dream. I used to have them all the time back when I worked for this jerk of a boss, in a really crappy job. Waking up and going to work was a real downer. With a psycho tyrant manager whose goal was to find ways to ruin everybody's day, I constantly felt like I was about to lose my job. It was an ugly time.

I kept having what I called stress dreams. I had the same problem years before, when I worked for a *different* psycho tyrant boss, in a *different* job. There aren't a lot of psychos out there, but I guess they all find their way to middle management.

The stress dreams were awful things, making me toss and turn all night, then wake up more tired than when I went to bed. They made no logical sense.

I'd be in a room full of copiers, twenty or thirty of them, all whirring and popping and cranking out some important report. One by one, each of the copiers would jam or otherwise fail in some way. Maybe they ran out of paper; maybe the feeder got stuck. It was completely random, but in the dream it was my responsibility to keep that report cranking out, so I'd be running from machine to machine, hurrying to see what was wrong. Right about the time I'd get one copier working, another one would stop. Or two. And all the while, the stress was building and building. Keep the machines running! Keep them running!

It was the craziest thing. I'd sit in bed with a headache, dreading going back to sleep and hating the thought of staying awake. I'd end up exhausted, and if I went back to sleep, the stress dream would start all over again.

I didn't know what it meant and I didn't care. Eventually I got a new boss and the stress dreams stopped. Same job, different boss, no more wacky dreams. That's not to say I never had a nightmare after that. I'm sure I did. Not more than any other person, but they would happen occasionally. I couldn't think of the last time I had a nightmare. Probably a year ago, maybe longer.

Until the lion dream started happening.

It didn't make sense, but what nightmare does? I was walking down the street and when I looked up, I was in a forest. I glanced around but couldn't see a way out. However I got there, I couldn't see anything but trees and the tall brown grass of autumn all around me. The sun was high in the sky, so I wasn't worried about being lost in the dark, I was just confused about how I ended up there.

In the distance I glimpsed an opening in the trees. A big, horseshoe-shaped clearing with a large tree stump off to one side.

As I approached the clearing, the grass by the far edge moved. Not like the wind had blown it, but together, in a group, like the grass there was all connected. Then I saw eyes.

I stopped in my tracks. The surreal aura of a dream faded and the grip of real fear spread through me. The big, yellow eyes stared at me, watching. Between the long brown blades of grass, I made out the snout and ears, then the massive ring of fur around the animal's enormous head.

I held my breath. A lion, just sitting there. I might have walked right into him. I stood perfectly still, knowing if I tried to run it would trigger his chase instinct and he would attack. So I stood very still. The only sound in the woods is the chattering or small birds overhead, oblivious to the scene unfolding below.

I stared at the lion. He stared right back at me.

I had no idea what to do. Sweat formed on my forehead, my heart pounding. I could never outrun a lion, and they are better climbers than I'd ever be.

The lion's foot rested on something, a white lump in the grass. He probably wanted to keep that, whatever it was, and he needed to know I was not there to take it from him. His unblinking yellow eyes stayed fixed on me, telling me all I needed to know.

Twigs snapped behind him as something else approached. It moved through the grass, slinking between the trees. Another lion, even bigger than the first one, emerged from the woods. It nosed the first one away and off the package.

The newcomer sniffed the bundle, pawing at it. As he did, more noise reached me—from behind. The crunching of heavy feet, stalking along the leaves and sticks of forest floor. An icy wave shot through me, causing the hairs on my neck to stand. I didn't move, didn't flinch, didn't breathe. I couldn't take my eyes off the lion in front of me, but I had to know what was behind me.

Before I could look, there it was.

A third lion brushed right past me. Little flies buzzed around his ears and a pungent smell of musk filled the air. The lion's large muscles flexed under his brown coat, his claws retracted but visible with every step. He ignored me, striding straight to the white bundle the other lions had toyed with.

The growl filled the woods, a deep, guttural roar from the gaping jaws of the third lion, like a horrible, rumbling moan from deep inside a cave.

He brandished his long white fangs. In a flash, the two large beasts exchanged swipes, standing and grappling, but only for a moment. The bigger of the two, the newest arrival, staked out his domain, forcing the loser away. The third lion now stood over the little white bundle, sniffing at its cloth wrapping and pawing at whatever was inside.

I stood there, unable to move.

A fourth lion crashed through the trees. I flinched, stepping back. He opened his massive jaws and growled, a hellish, deafening groan that caused my insides to quiver. The other lions disappeared into the brush. The chattering noise of the woods became completely silent as the echo of the fourth lion's roar rolled like distant thunder through the trees. I could hear nothing but my own heartbeat.

The lion stood alone now over his prize, confident and focused, not even glancing in my direction.

I couldn't move my legs. My eyes were glued on the animal before me. With a quick swipe of its massive paw, the lion laid open the bundle, lowering his enormous head and snapping up the contents. Meat. He ripped into it with his long teeth and claws, smearing his face red as he pulled it apart. Throwing back his head, he opened his enormous mouth, emitting a growl I felt but didn't hear. Overhead, birds scattered from their trees. Everything within earshot knew he was the victorious one. With a quick flip, the next mouthful slid down his throat.

He paused, eyeing me, causing a painful shockwave of adrenaline to rip through me. I swallowed, slowly stretching my fingers to the nearest tree for support. The lion lowered his head for another bite.

On tiptoes, I strained to see what he was eating. Meat, of some sort, but what? It was small, compared to him, but obscured by the grass.

The beast drew up, part of his dinner dangling from the side of his mouth. Then, in horror, I could see.

It was a small arm. A tiny arm with a bloody string of tendons hanging from the lion's mouth.

My hearing returned for the piercing, high-pitched cry.

It was a *child.* A toddler, being eaten alive.

My stomach clutched. I looked away to avoid to not see the feet kicking as the lion's massive paw pressed downward on the body while his huge teeth ripped the child apart. I didn't want to watch. I didn't want to know.

But I did know.

Forcing myself awake, I bolted upright on the couch, panting like I'd run a mile. I was covered in sweat again and shaking, my chest pounding and my pulse throbbing in my ears.

I raced up the stairs to my daughter's room and threw open the door.

Holding my breath, I looked to her bed.

She was fine. She was right there, illuminated by her princess night light and curled up among her stuffed animals and Winnie The Pooh blanket.

I knew she would be, but I had to look anyway. Closing my eyes, I held the door frame and let my head fall onto my arm, a huge sigh filling me, washing away my panic.

I knew.

In the dream, three lions came to attack my daughter, each one bigger than the last. The attacks got worse each time, but damage was only scratches until the fourth lion showed up. He was certainly the one who would kill her.

I wiped my eyes and shook my head, going back down to the couch and turning on the TV. I needed a distraction to help my mind focus on anything other than the terrible dream. On the 24-hour weather channel, the forecasters debated about when they would upgrade the tropical storm to a low-level hurricane.

Terrific. I grabbed the remote.

Clint Eastwood, as a young cowboy with no name, finally took my thoughts from the lion dream, letting my heart settle back in my chest and my breathing to return to normal. I calmed down. It *was* only a dream, after all.

After a long while, my eyes wouldn't stay open. In a semi-asleep state, I reached over and clicked the TV remote. The set went black and I drifted off to sleep. The lions did not return.

In the morning, I was awakened on the couch by our dog jumping on me. That meant Mallory was up. Sparkles wouldn't leave her side and come downstairs if she was still sleeping.

I guess I got enough sleep. Plodding to the back door, I let Sparkles outside and then returned to straighten up the couch.

"Good morning." Mallory wiped the sleep from her eyes as she headed toward the coffee pot. Hopefully she slept better than I did.

"Good morning, honey. I let Sparkles out."

She peered at the throw pillows on the floor. "Did you sleep down here all night?"

"Yeah, pretty much."

"You look like you didn't sleep at all." Mallory disappeared into the pantry for a bag of exotic ground coffee beans and re-emerged to dig through the cupboard until she produced her favorite mug—the one with the Christmas picture of her and Sophie on it.

Pre-coffee Mallory might hear me talking, but the words wouldn't sink in right away. She idly placed her red mug under the coffee maker and waited patiently for it to fill.

I finished pushing the sofa cushions back into place as the aroma of coffee wafted over me. I stretched my arms. My back was going to exact revenge all day for sleeping on the couch. "I had a bad dream last night. Too much churrasco."

Mallory snorted. "You always say that."

"It's always true." I smiled at her. "It's your fault. You're too good of a cook."

"Hmm."

"Anyway, I was tossing and turning, having a stress dream." Placing my hands on my shoulders, I twisted a few times to work the kinks out of my spine. I figured I should tell Mallory about my nightmare so she didn't worry that I was becoming an insomniac for no reason. "It was terrible. I kept having the same dream over and over."

Sparkles' face finally reappeared at the back door. I went over to let him in. "I was walking down the street—our street, I guess—and all of a sudden I was in a forest. Then, one by one, these four big lions appeared, and—"

Crash!

I whipped around to see shattered pieces of the Christmas mug scattering all over the kitchen floor.

White faced, Mallory gripped the counter, gasping. She stared at me with wide eyes, her mouth hanging open as all the blood drained out of her face.

Chapter 19

"Oh my God." Mallory sunk to the floor, holding the countertop with one hand to keep from falling completely. "Oh my *God*!"

Her face turned gray.

I rushed past the broken ceramic bits all over the kitchen tiles. "Honey, what's wrong?" Squatting next to her, I put my hands on her face and looked into her eyes. "What is it? What happened?"

Sparkles barked, on high alert. He ran through the broken pieces of coffee cup. I grabbed him and picked him up.

"No, no, NO!" Mallory screamed, slapping the floor. She was almost gasping now. "I . . ." Then the tears started. She looked up at me with a fearful face.

"What is it?" I pleaded, my heart in my throat. "Tell me."

"The dream," she said, shaking her head. "The dream you were talking about, with the lions . . ."

"Oh, that? That was, that . . ." I wanted to sound dismissive. That dream had kept me up all night. I didn't want it to bother her. I must been telling it too intensely. "That was just—"

"No." She choked, barely getting her words out. "I had it, too."

It was like a punch to my gut. I staggered backwards. "Wh- what? What did you . . ."

She sobbed with each syllable. "I had the same dream. The lions. In the woods." Tears streamed down her face. "Tearing open a white package." Her voice cracked. "Four of them. It's the same dream you just described. I've been having the same dream!"

I sat, my mouth hanging open, unable to process what I was hearing.

"I've been having that same dream for weeks." Mallory whispered fiercely. "Weeks!"

"You . . ." I swallowed. "You must have told me about it."

She shook her head slowly, yesterday's mascara blackening the sides of her face. "No. I never mentioned it. Never."

"Are you sure?"

Her eyes went wide. "I never said a word. On purpose." Raising a trembling hand to her mouth, she swallowed hard. "I thought I was going crazy."

"You're not crazy." Stepping over the broken mug, I rubbed her shoulders. "If you are, I am. And I'm not." I whispered, kissing her cheek. "But I wonder what it means. I woke up right when the big lion started ripping—"

"Don't!" Mallory pushed me away and grabbed her ears. "Don't say it! I can't hear it right now! Not with all that's been going on."

"About the package?"

"Don't!" "Shhh. Okay, okay." I hugged her tightly, then leaned back to look into her eyes. "Listen, just . . . just tell me what you saw." I spoke slowly and cautiously, stroking her back. "Let's move to where there's less broken stuff."

I held her arm and guided her to the kitchen table, pulling out a chair. "What was your dream? Can you tell me?"

Eyes squeezed shut, she nodded.

"In my dream, the last lion rips into the package. But it turns out not to be a package at all. Is that your dream, too?" Sliding into the chair across from her, I took a deep breath. "What was in the package in your dream?"

She dabbed at her eyes with the bottom of her shirt. "It wasn't a package."

I held my breath, waiting.

"It was . . . a baby." Her head dropped into her arms and she collapsed on the table. "*Our* baby! It was Sophie! God, what kind of people have dreams about an animal killing their own daughter?" Her shoulders shook with each heavy sob. "My baby was there and the lions were attacking her and . . ."

There were no words, only a low, pained moan that squeezed out between the uncontrollable crying.

I took her hand in mine and stroked it. I wasn't sure what to do. My heart was thumping away inside me, but—

"Mommy?"

We both looked over at the doorway to the kitchen. Sophie stood there with a terrified expression on her face.

"Oh, no!" Mallory leaped up and ran to our daughter, scooping her up.

Sophie's cheeks glistened with tears. "Mommy, what's wrong? Why are you crying?"

"No, sweetie," Mallory lied, hugging our daughter. "Mommy's not crying. Mommy has a cold."

"Do you need the nebbalizer?"

"The what, baby?" Mallory sniffled and pushed her hair behind her ears, forcing herself back from the brink.

"When I was sick, I had to take—I have to use the nebbalizer."

"*Nebulizer*." Mallory wiped her eyes, smiling. "No, sweetie, mommy doesn't have to use the nebulizer. Mommy isn't sick like that."

"I wasn't feeling good before," I said. "And now Mommy isn't feeling good. So it would really help a lot if you gave her a hug. A really big hug."

Sophie complied, burying her face in her mother's shoulder.

They stood, eyes closed, rocking back and forth for a moment, as if they would never let each other go ever again.

"Mmmm! I love you. You're so sweet." Mallory cooed to Sophie, kissing her. "I would never let anything happen to you." Then she turned to me.

"Go!" She ordered. "Go now! See whoever you need to see." She stood firmly in her kitchen with our daughter in her arms. "You find out whatever you have to find out. We have to figure out how to fix this thing, how to *handle* this thing, whatever it takes."

Her voice grew more forceful as she clutched Sophie tighter. "Call the church, get whoever you talked to. Call them right now!"

She'd had enough.

"Call your church guy or find somebody else who can help us."

Standing amongst the pieces of broken coffee mug, the objective was as clear as the morning light streaming in the windows.

"Find someone who can tell us what the hell is going on."

Chapter 20

I hadn't even brushed my teeth yet and I already felt like I was behind schedule.

I convinced my wife I needed to at least get cleaned up and shaven before trying to talk to people. Especially about this.

Shampooing and scrubbing as fast as I could, I kept thinking about how things were getting stranger and stranger. The three tragedies, the dreams—like we were headed for a meltdown or something. I had no real idea where to turn or what to do.

I got dressed and headed downstairs, snatching my laptop off my desk before going into the kitchen. Mallory sat at the table with her chin in her hands, watching Sophie's every move out of the corner of her eye. Sophie, for her part, did the same, slowly and carefully eating her cereal, her movements stiff and robotic. The TV blathered on with cartoons, but my wife and daughter put on a show of their own for each other, pretending to be relaxed.

That would be good enough for now. I grabbed my keys. "I'm heading out."

Mallory looked at me. Her eyes were still red and puffy from crying. She would have asked where I was going but she probably figured I didn't really know. Maybe the church, maybe somewhere else, but I had to at least act like I was doing something.

"I'm taking my computer." I held up the laptop. "Just in case."

"Okay," she said. "Be careful."

I walked over and gave her a kiss. "I'll be back in a little while." Then I kissed my daughter. "You be good for your mother."

"Okay," Sophie whispered.

"We're going to get dressed and run some errands." Mallory leaned back and sighed, massaging her temples. "I need to get rid of this nervous energy."

"Sounds good."

As I pulled my car out of the garage, I thought about where I could go. The rain had been coming and going all morning, and the winds were getting stronger. Leaves were picked up and thrown around with every gust. Our little hurricane off the coast was making an effort to impress everyone.

A few of the websites I saw might have been helpful, but most were complete garbage. Obvious scam operations. Psychic hotlines. Stuff not even worth placing a phone call to. I hadn't followed up with Our Lady of Mercy, either, because I didn't feel they could do anything more at the moment. That left my options limited, but I couldn't convey that to my wife.

A lot of our local restaurants and coffee shops had internet access. I could stop in and continue yesterday's search. In fact . . .

I pulled over and snapped open my laptop. The screen from the prior day's searches was still up—Help For The Hopeful, blinking at me.

What was up with that little site? I'd done some bizarre searches yesterday, and it popped up in several of them. I tried to look into the meaning of lion dream, checked into paranormal activity, did some searches on demonic possessions, exorcisms . . . the little black and white ad with the tiny blinking cross was everywhere, but it didn't seem like it belonged anywhere I propped my elbow on the car window, rubbing my chin and watching the rain. The winds batted my car. On the passenger seat, the little ad on my computer continued to flash.

The Wi-Fi signal at a nearby fast food restaurant would be strong enough to use from my car in their parking lot. I didn't want anyone spying over my shoulder while I searched for bizarre stuff.

I drove to the restaurant and shut off the engine, staring at the little ad. It's line of text scrolling across the bottom: *All problems have answers.*

The tiny cross in the ad was like a miniature lighthouse, beckoning me.

I clicked the link. The page was very plain, just a local phone number and the words: *Talk with people who understand the isolation and frustration of a problem that seems to have no answers. YOU ARE NOT ALONE.*

That was all it said. No asking for money, no 900 number to call. Nothing that really said much about anything. No promises of a psychic that has all the answers, or a church that will solve the problem in ten steps. Just the tiny blinking cross and a promise of help.

Right now, that seemed a decent first step.

It would offer help, or it would be BS. There was only one way to find out.

Any internet scammer worth his salt would have a website promising to solve all my problems, that much I knew. What I didn't know was how I would avoid all the rip off artists and still find somebody who could help. And that didn't think I was nuts. If nothing panned out, I could always go back to Father Frank and see what else he could suggest.

I pulled out my phone and dialed.

A man answered. "Hello?"

I cleared my throat and sat up straight. "Uh, hello. I saw your ad . . . I was wondering if you could help me with a problem I'm having. Did I call the right place? Is this Help for the Hopeful?"

"It is." The man said. "What sort of problem do you need help with?"

I sighed. "Well . . . one that will probably make me sound crazy."

"Okay, well, first—don't worry about that. And I'm not going to ask you for any credit cards because we don't accept any money from people we help. So who sounds crazy now?"

His voice was deep and Texas-y, with a deliberate tone. Unwavering. Unquestioning. Confident. I have to admit, getting the money thing out of the way appealed to me. I leaned back in my seat. "Are you local? It looks like I called a Tampa number."

"We have an office in Tampa, but right now it's forwarded to my cell phone and I'm across the state in Melbourne. I'm supposed to be doing a little fishing, but it's not working out too well."

"Fishing?" I glanced at the bands of rain thrashing my windshield. "Oh, like fishers of men. That sort of thing. Are you part of a church?"

"No, like fishing for *fish*," he said. "The weather's not cooperating. Way too choppy. Gonna have to call it a day already."

The sunny days earlier in the week would fool a lot of people into thinking it would be calm seas. It wasn't. Sunken Spanish galleon 101.

"But, yes, I am what you could consider part of a church. A priest kind of part."

Interesting. I was tempted to ask what kind of church, but very few churches have clergymen that refer to themselves as priests.

"You never answered my question." Over the phone came banging around of some sort. He was probably packing up his fishing gear. "What kind of problem do you need help with?"

I ran my hand through my hair and took a deep breath. "I'm not even sure it's a real problem. I mean, I'm not sure what to call it, but . . . I—my family—we seem to be having a lot of bad luck that's kind of centered around certain people. And certain dates. Really bad things seem to happen every year, almost like they're on a schedule."

I held my breath and waited for the embarrassing laughter or anger—some kind of negative, degrading reaction to an obviously insane statement.

"Well that sure doesn't sound like your everyday kind of problem," the man said. "What's your name?"

"Uh." I quickly considered giving him a fake name, but my mind blanked. I wiped my hands on my pants. "My name is Doug."

"Well, Doug, it's a pleasure. I'm John Reed but my friends call me Tyree. Why don't you let me pack up my fishing gear and I'll call you back when I'm on dry land again. That'll take me about an hour. Sound good?"

An hour? "You must be pretty far out to sea."

"No, I've been visiting at one of those bars where you can pull up in your boat and now I can't find my keys."

Great. A drunk. It's still morning, even on the other side of the state. I shifted on my seat.

"They sell bait and ice, you know?" Tyree said. "I haven't been drinking. I don't drink. But with all this on and off rain we've been having, it's messed up the fishing."

That was a relief—and an immediate dose of shame for thinking bad about him. Heat rose to my cheeks. "Sure, no problem."

"Besides, they got this cute little bar maid I like to have a look at now and again."

"A man of the cloth checking out girls?" That didn't sound like a priest. My defenses rose again.

"Well, you know what they say. Just because you're on a diet doesn't mean you can check at the menu."

That was backwards. I was about to correct him when Tyree cut me off.

"I'm a sinner, Doug." More equipment noises banged in my ear. "We all are. Even you. Maybe that's the source of your problems. Wouldn't be the first time. But I'll call you back in an hour, okay?"

"Okay, Mr. Tyree," I said. "Thanks."

"You're welcome. And it's just 'Tyree.'"

"Tyree. Got it."

"Okay. One hour."

The wind let up so the rain could come straight down now. Leaves and bits of trash littered the parking lot and stuck to my windshield and the hood of my car.

I didn't know why, but as I ended the call I felt a sense of relief. I suppose getting something like that off my chest and not being laughed at eased my mind. I felt Tyree was genuinely interested in helping us—but a good con man would make a sucker feel that way, wouldn't he?

He seemed to anticipate my concerns. That was either intuitive and helpful or completely scammy. I shook my head and tapped the steering wheel, staring out at the watery parking lot. Any help is better than no help, right? Or would the wrong sort of person end up hurting my family worse somehow? Lure us in when we're vulnerable and end up scamming us?

I stared at my computer. When I was fresh out of college, I took a job at a marketing company as an assistant to one of the big producers. The first thing he'd tell new associates was, if your leads are weak, create more leads. I nodded to myself. My options were weak. I needed to create more options. I needed a plan B in case Tyree ended up going nowhere the way Father Frank did.

A gust of wind sent debris flying off the grass by the dumpster. Somebody had left it open and papers came flying out. One landed on my windshield.

It was a glossy flyer for a blues quartet, and some college kid had probably been paid to put these on all the doors in the neighborhood or the cars at the mall. In this crappy weather, the dumpster got them instead. I put down my window and reached around to peel the colorful paper off the wet glass, when the words at the bottom of the flyer lit me up like a neon sign on the Vegas strip.

My heart jumped. I started the car and raced out of the parking lot, grabbing the wheel with both hands and bouncing up and down in my seat. A new option was taking shape.

Chapter 21

If Tampa had a big sister, it would be New Orleans. "'Nawlins," as the locals there pronounce it, has Mardi Gras, an insane weeklong festival of partying and debauchery. Tampa has Gasparilla.

The Big Easy has the French Quarter, full of restaurants and bars, but also with back alleys with prostitution and drugs, side streets to eerie haunted houses, and a strange, mystical subculture of street performers and magicians.

Tampa—also known as Big Guava at times—has Ybor City.

A smaller version of Mardi Gras, Gasparilla in Ybor, pronounced "ee-bor" is a unique slice of Tampa's looser side. Like it's big sister, Ybor was part bar scene, part art district, and part loony bin, catering to the young and restless. New late night party spots stood right next to upscale restaurants that had been local favorites for a hundred years. Ybor had dancing and celebrities. Every time a Super Bowl came to town, Ybor was where you'd find the Who's Who. When the Tampa Bay Lightning won the Stanley Cup, Ybor partied 'til dawn, had a cup of Cuban coffee, and kept right on going.

New Orleans may have been the original, but Ybor City was a good local alternative. Both had the reputation of being able to deliver anything and everything a person could dream of. You want it? They have it.

Including voodoo.

If such a thing as voodoo exists, and some believe it does, New Orleans had it in spades. Marie Laveau, maybe the most famous voodoo practitioner ever, was practically the queen of the city's mystical side way back when. Voodoo was an industry in The Big Easy. The city was full of all kinds of witches and spell spinners, fortune tellers and healers. Some were allegedly legit; others were simply an obvious show for tourists. But a *mambo*, the real name for a voodoo high priestess, was serious business to believers. If I had prowled the seedy offshoots of New Orleans' Bourbon Street long enough, I would have found one who could've helped me, I'm sure.

And if they had one, we had one.

I wasn't really in a position to not consider any source I could find. Everybody knew Ybor had some mystical stuff going on late at night. Voodoo and *Santeria*, it's darker, uglier cousin, were common there, but not practiced in the light of day. And it was only a twenty minute drive away.

I pulled my cell phone from the cup holder of my car and checked the time. Too early in the day to go now, I could probably find what I was looking for tonight. Late, after midnight.

Besides, I wanted to be sure to consider everything, like Father Frank had suggested. Now I had a second option, even if Frank might not have approved of it. Just thinking it up made me feel better. Instead of going home, I pulled into a gas station to fill up and wait for Tyree's call.

Idly watching the numbers roll over as the pump churned and clicked, I laid out my plan. Tonight I could grab my keys and make an excuse to Mallory. It wouldn't matter what I said. She'd know I wouldn't have a good reason to go out at midnight, especially in a bad rain, but she seemed upset enough this morning to allow me to do just about anything. The image of her sliding to the floor in tears put a wave of uneasiness through me. I had to make some progress—any progress—and no easy answers were presenting themselves. She would be supportive, to a point.

If I waited for her to get sleepy, I could get out and back before she had time to think about worrying.

I sat in the car scratching my chin. In the meantime, what would I need? Some cash. What else? I couldn't think of anything. I headed to the bank.

Tyree said he had an office in Tampa somewhere. It might be worthwhile to drive by and check it out—if it could be found. The online county appraisal records would tell me who owed a property, and I could search for the owner's name online, but if he rented the space his name wouldn't show up. If his business was incorporated, a records search might give a name and address, but often as not those were the company's lawyer's office, not the physical location of the business or it's owner's home address. Besides, who says the Help For The Hopeful was even a corporation or a registered entity? Or if John Reed was even a real name?

Damn. Every option had flaws. Major flaws.

Still, talking to him was worth a shot. The safety of my wife and daughter were worth embarrassing myself over meeting with a con man if that's what he was. So if there was some due diligence I'd later wish I had done, now was the time to try to do it. And I had time to kill.

My cell phone pinged with a text from Mallory. *Sophie and I are going shopping. Do u need anything?*

Good. She needed to get out of the house for a while and clear her head. Glancing at the road, I tapped out a quick reply. *No. Have fun.*

The image came again, of her sliding to the kitchen floor. Our daughter crying. I sent another text. *Drive safe. I love you.*

I looked out the window. Sunny Florida wasn't so sunny today. The big storm hovering out in the Atlantic had made the weather unpredictable, raining and stopping with abandon. One minute, it was coming down like a fire hose, the next minute, the rain would stop and the sun would pop out. But the wind was getting fiercer all the time, pushing my big SUV around on the road.

Even so, I was glad Mallory was going out. She needed a distraction, and shopping with Sophie would be a good one.

The phone pinged again. *I love you too.*

About an hour after we hung up the first time, and right when he said he would, Tyree called back.

"So, Doug, tell me about what kind of problem we are dealing with." From the background noise, it sounded like he was driving.

This was it. Time to let it all out. I'd thought about what to say and even jotted down some notes, but it didn't matter. The words just spilled out. Before I knew it, I'd told him everything.

He didn't sound alarmed at all. "The tragedies all took place around the same time of year, too?"

"Yeah, within a few days of each other, really, almost like they were scheduled." I rubbed the back of my neck. "I don't know if we're unlucky or insane or possessed or what, but my wife and I both believe that it can't be a coincidence anymore. And then there was a recurring nightmare that we were both having . . ."

"Well, from what you're saying, let me tell you up front that I don't think you're insane."

I shook my head. "God, why not?"

"I've done this before. Crazies sound different. You sound upset, not insane. I believe your story."

"No offense, but you kind of have to say that even if you're scamming me, don't you?" I hated to antagonize the guy, but it needed to be addressed. I wanted help, but I was a skeptic, too, and not looking to get ripped off or make things worse.

"I understand your defensiveness, Doug. I'd have my guard up, too, if I were you. Don't worry about offending me. I'm not going to ask you for money or too much personal information. We don't work like that."

"Who is 'we'?"

"Well, 'we' is me and my associates. A loose collection of affiliations I've built up over the years through the church and law enforcement, that sort of thing. We can get into all that when we meet."

I was watching his technique from what I remembered at the marketing firm. He had called me by name, in a friendly and reassuring manner—that's supposed to build rapport and lower defenses. He'd been calm and reassuring, and seemed to be offering a solution if I agreed to follow his lead. It was all basic sales steps—and basic con man steps—and I didn't yet know which. Asking for the meeting was the next step in getting my commitment.

Those stories about an old lady who ends up giving all her money to a con man, they all start this way. He seemed trustworthy. He said he didn't want any money. Next thing you know, she's broke and he's gone.

Scammers have to model good behavior like legit people do, otherwise it's too easy to figure out they're scammers.

So my guard was up and was staying up. "Mr. Tyree, again, no offense, but do you have some references I can check you out with?"

"It's just Tyree, not Mr. Tyree. And Doug, at some point you're going to have to trust somebody. It doesn't have to be me, but it's going to have to be somebody." His voice was calm and even, not upset at all. Very matter of fact. He could have been talking about the weather. "My guess is, if you were having success doing things your way, you wouldn't have called me. And you *did* call *me*. But that's a side point. Most do that after they've tried talking to their church and their friends. Is that about where we are?"

The classic blow off. Tell them they can't have something, and people want it twice as bad. Salespeople used it all the time, like carnival barkers did. And scammers. I'd seen Christian Bale do it in that con man movie, *American Hustle*.

But Tyree was right. I didn't have a lot of options and I'd pretty much already run through them. Ybor City might not pan out, and even if it did, I'd eventually have to trust somebody to help me.

Meeting him might be a good first step towards deciding if he was a con artist or not.

"The established churches don't usually get into this stuff directly," Tyree said. "Mostly it would be the Catholic Church, and the high ups won't even do it right now."

"Why not?" Over the cell phone, I couldn't tell if he was implying "we" or "they" tone when he referenced the Church.

"Something like this can get a look when it's really clear cut. When the host nation is sympathetic, or when it's a good story. You know, something like a little girl who gets possessed by a demon, stuff like that."

I thought about that. "Isn't that pretty much what this is? A family being inexplicably terrorized?"

"Wrong country, my friend. The Vatican is a little pissed at the U.S. right now. So it's a no go. Our media is too crazy, our politics. It's a lot of things. Too bad you don't live in Guatemala. I could get you direct access in Guatemala."

"Maybe I should move."

"Anyway, in places that they feel are less hospitable, they outsource, so they can keep their hands clean."

I weighed what he said—then thought of something else. "You're making all this up, aren't you?" I asked.

"Could be!" Tyree laughed. "You're better off not knowing, aren't you? How does knowing my methods and sources help your cause? Allow me: it doesn't."

I blinked. "But the Church was helpful . . ."

"Were they? You went out and found me after talking to them, didn't you?"

Tired of the verbal volleyball, I gave up. The long night and longer day had worn me down. I had to start trusting somebody.

"Okay." I sighed. "What time do we meet?"

Chapter 22

Mallory turned the wheel and drove away from the first shop on her list, heading for the second. She sighed, working to suppress the anxiety inside her.

What a happy day it had been a few days ago. What a difference some time makes.

A few weeks ago, as she came down the stairs, Mallory quietly observed her husband and daughter at breakfast. As always, Doug had taken the chair with his back to the stairs so Sophie could watch TV. It was a bad habit, but it had started back when they were grasping at straws to get her to eat *at all*, and a cartoon turned out to be a useful distraction. Baby Sophie would watch TV and open her mouth at the right time, and somebody sitting next to her would hold a spoonful of puree up to her mouth. The system worked for everyone.

Until now, when she practically wouldn't eat unless a cartoon was on.

But there was plenty of time to work through that, Doug always said. Eating was the priority right now, and this got her to eat.

So he sat across from her at breakfast, lunch and dinner, to supervise and instruct as she fed herself. If he didn't supervise, she would skip things like vegetables—or try to. If he didn't instruct, she might not eat at all. After a while, the seating arrangement was pretty much permanent, for all meals: Sophie would sit at the corner, with Mallory next to her, and Doug across from them both. Like all parents of young children learn, meals work best if the kids were surrounded.

Mallory stopped at a red light, lost in her daydream.

Doug was strict but playful. From her office upstairs, Mallory could hear their frequent lunch or dinner battles as she took a late conference call. Mostly, it was Doug's raised voice as Sophie stubbornly refused to eat the vegetable of the day. Shouts of "Your green beans!" echoed up the stairs to her.

Just as often, though, she would catch them playing at the table while she cooked. Simple things that don't matter much and wouldn't be remembered, but in the moment warmed her heart.

From her vantage point by the stairs, Mallory stood clutching her favorite coffee mug, watching them play at the table, waiting for her. Every birthday, Christmas, anniversary, or mother's day, Doug would order a big ceramic coffee mug with a picture of Mallory and Sophie on it. By now she had quite a collection: a photo of them at the zoo, another one by the river, a favorite from when he found them picking flowers in the yard. Each photo became its own big coffee mug. It was a ceramic photo album.

All the mugs were cute, but the Christmas mug was her favorite. It was an impromptu photo, taken one day when Doug walked in after Mallory had popped a Santa hat onto the baby's head. Not even a year old, Sophie still had the big eyes and dimples of her grandmother, so the Santa hat looked especially cute. With Mallory holding her, both of Doug's ladies were in the picture.

Mallory stood in the dark by the stairs, holding her Christmas mug and watching as her husband played with their young daughter. The battles over green beans were certain to happen later, but at the moment the warring vegetable factions were allies. Sophie watched a cartoon while eating her pancakes, and Doug typed on his computer.

Sophie's chair was a bit too far away from the table. Food that she dropped would fall onto her dress—it was always a dress these days, even at breakfast—and the frillier, the better. But those princess dresses don't clean up as easily as a t-shirt and shorts.

Without looking up from his work, Doug reached under the table with his foot and hooked the bottom of Sophie's seat, pulling it closer to the table. The wooden chair sounded like a miniature car horn as its legs dragged over the tile.

Sophie checked around, her mouth hanging open. "Is that you doing that?" She was barely audible over the cartoons.

"Hmm?" Doug didn't take his eyes off the computer screen as he put his foot back under his own chair. From the steps, Mallory smiled.

Sophie leaned over, peering at the legs of the chair. "What is doing that?"

"What's doing what, honey?" His tone was exaggerated, almost lyrical.

"What was making my chair move?"

He shrugged his shoulders in a cartoonish fashion. "I don't know."

Sophie's eyes twinkled as a smile crept onto her face. "Is it magic?"

"Could be!"

"Daddy!" She pointed her pink plastic fork at him. "It's you!"

"I think it's magic!"

Sophie leapt off her chair, scurrying under the table and attacking his feet.

From then on, whenever a chair was spotted moving at meal time without the obvious use of hands, Sophie would ask if it was magic. Doug would always respond, "Could be!"

As her own legs got longer, Sophie would slide down in her seat and push back an empty chair. The noise always got everyone's attention, and she would laugh. "Look, it's magic!"

It was a nice moment, Mallory thought. Happy times.

The light turned green and she drove onto the thoroughfare.

What a difference a week makes. She glanced at the cut on her finger, a result of picking up the broken pieces of her favorite coffee mug.

After sweeping up the fragments, she'd concluded some magic was needed around her house. Good magic. White magic to fight back some of the black magic that appeared to be gathering. The happy times seemed to get taken away as quickly as the cup had shattered across the kitchen floor.

But a mug could be replaced. Her family couldn't. Like a rollercoaster going down a big hill, the dark thoughts hurled at her. Mallory's breath came in short gasps as she envisioned the winery wreck, the car fire—one horrible memory after another, as they came faster and faster.

She gripped the steering wheel and squeezed her eyes shut, shaking her head to make the terrifying images stop.

Chapter 23

Mallory heaved the steering wheel to the right and bounced over the curb into the grocery store parking lot. Sophie's toys flew up, plopping down around her.

"Wheee!"

Screeching to a stop, Mallory forced herself to take several deep breaths before taking her trembling hands off the steering wheel.

She closed her eyes again, kneading her fingers, trying to ignore the panic gripping her belly.

Relax. Relax! We're doing some shopping. Quit being afraid of the boogeyman.

She wiped her eyes and got out, rushing around to the passenger's door to help Sophie out of the back seat. Mallory's convertible was easy to get their daughter in and out of when the roof was down—the child seat harness was easier to reach that way—but today was not a top down day.

And the feeling of ensuing panic wouldn't leave her.

Throwing the passenger seat forward and leaning in past her daughter, Mallory tugged at the buckles and clips. Sophie could do them by herself when she got in and out—albeit very slowly. She had the enthusiasm but not the manual dexterity to do it quickly.

"I can do it." Sophie reached for the clasp. "It's one, two, seat belt undo."

Usually that was part of the learning process, to make a game of things and to let the child figure things out.

Mallory nodded. "Okay, you do it. But hurry, baby."

The hairs stood up on the back of Mallory's neck, as if an icy breeze had found only her. She shivered, raising her shoulders and flinching.

A man in ratty clothing and dark, sunken eyes emerged from the hedges on the far side of the lot. He stared at her.

She glanced inside the car, watching her daughter work the clips. When she looked up again, the man was still staring at her, his face an unwavering scowl.

Mallory's pulse quickened.

Some sort of derelict from the drug houses. Part of the messaging of the low-priced grocery chain was their no-frills approach. Here, it had resulted in a location near a run-down neighborhood frequented with homeless drug addicts and alcoholics. Most were harmless, but some could be intimidating, saying and doing scary things while strung out. That wasn't an encounter she wished to have with her daughter present.

"Let's go, baby." She eyed the man again as she bent over to help her daughter. "Come on."

Sophie pressed the seat belt button. "It's stuck."

"Okay." Mallory slid her hands past her daughter's, jerking on the seat belt. It jammed.

She twisted to look over her shoulder for the hollow eyed stranger. He stood near the hedges, glaring at her. "Watch out." A big push freed the jammed fastener and the seat belt unclipped. Mallory hoisted Sophie out of the seat, snatching the purse from the passenger seat and shutting the door with her hip.

"Hold my hand, honey." Mallory tried to keep her strained voice from frightening her daughter, but she felt vulnerable outside now. She grasped Sophie's hand, moving in short, fast strides. "Let's hurry."

Sophie trotted alongside her mother to keep up.

As she weaved her way between the parked cars, Mallory peered over her shoulder at the man. He kept staring right back at her like a zombie.

She walked faster, her heart pounding.

Why is he watching me?

Images of the tragedies rushed forward again. She ran a hand across her forehead.

Is this the next one? Does a demon take over a drug addict and stab us with a broken bottle?

"Mommy!"

"Hurry, sweetie." Mallory tugged her daughter's hand as she rushed across the parking lot. "Let's hurry."

Mallory felt his eyes on her. Tears welled in her eyes.

"Mommy, I can't walk this fast!"

"Sophie, hurry!"

Her heart racing, she stepped out from between the parked cars and into the driving lane in front of the store.

Sophie screamed. A car screeched to a stop next to them. Mallory flinched, yanking her daughter's arm and jumping back.

The driver yelled through the window at them as he passed. Gasping, Mallory waved absently and hurried into the store.

She grabbed a shopping cart. The bright lights of the store and the other customers calmed her. She tried to get her breathing to return to normal. Then they began to make the rounds.

"Peanut butter!" Sophie pointed at the shelves. Mallory picked up a jar and lowered it into the cart, unable to focus. At the end of the aisle, they turned. The store's big windows allowed her to see the sky dimming with the sunset. The jitters returned, her stomach tightening.

How will we get back to my car with that guy out there?

The store had no clerks to help take groceries to customers' vehicles. That was also part of their no frills, low prices image. She swallowed hard. She'd given him time to get to her car now. He'd seen it, knew which one was hers.

Now he could be waiting, hiding behind another car to grab her—or Sophie.

Mallory's hand trembled.

It was a mistake to come in.

"Grapes!" Sophie stood on the frame of the cart, holding on with one hand and plucking the bag up with the other. Leaning over into the basket as far as she could, she dropped the grapes in.

Mallory took no notice, pushing along. As they neared the front of the aisle, she peered past her reflection in the store window and observed the parking lot.

Her stomach was a knot. She scanned the cars for the man. Nothing.

Glancing at her white knuckles, she realized she'd been gripping the cart handle. She opened her hands and gazed at the deep row of red crescents her fingernails had dug into her palms.

Out of the corner of her eye, she thought she saw something move in the parking lot. A shadow disappeared behind a white van. Her heart raised to her throat. Was it him? Was he hiding, waiting for her to come out of the store to attack?

As she watched, an elderly man emerged from the side of the van. Inside, his wife pulled her seat belt as he stacked their groceries into the back seat.

Mallory exhaled, wiping her forehead with her hand.

"Mommy, can we get some of these?" Sophie held up potato chips.

She nodded. Her eyes stayed on the parking lot. The crackle of cellophane reached her ears as the bag hit the bottom of the cart.

The white van drove off. The parking lot appeared normal.

Mallory eased the cart down the next aisle. Sophie grabbed miscellaneous items as they passed. Tomato paste, toothpaste—it didn't matter, any colorful box or bag would do. The package merely needed to look pretty to Sophie. Mallory didn't care. She robotically took each item her daughter offered to her, dropping them into the cart while doing her best to keep her eyes fixed on the windows at the front of the store.

Outside, the parking lot slowly descended into darkness.

"We need to go." Mallory pushed the cart toward the checkout lanes. With one hand on the cart, she raised the other to her lips and bit her nails.

The cashier said something to her.

"Hmm?" Mallory tried to refocus on the lady.

"I asked if you were cold." The cashier eyed Mallory's hands. "You're shaking."

Mallory looked down at her quivering hands. She opened and closed them a few times to relax. It didn't help.

As she handed the money to the cashier, their fingers brushed.

"Ooh! Like ice." The lady smiled. "You need to warm up!"

Thanking her, Mallory pushed the cart over to the doorway and stared out through the glass into the dark lot. Overhead, the parking lot lights flickered to life in a dim, yellow-white glow.

A few customers walked between the rows of cars. No sign of the man who had been watching her.

She wrapped her arms around herself and clutched her purse as Sophie jumped on and off the side of the cart.

We'll wait. We'll wait, keys out, ready to run to our car as soon as somebody else leaves. We'll walk out with them. He won't try anything with other people around. Will he?

Pretending to look for her keys, Mallory rummaged in her purse until another customer finished checking out.

Then she pushed her cart through the exit doors right behind them, following them onto the sidewalk and toward the lot.

Sophie squeezed her mother's hand. "Look both ways!"

Her heart pounding, Mallory was doing a lot more than looking both ways. She looked *every* way.

They strode across the driving lane to the cars. She could see no sign of the crazy man. It didn't matter. The lot had fewer cars than when they arrived, but there were still plenty of cars for someone to hide behind.

Ahead, her convertible stood under the light. The cars on both sides had left, as had the one in front of her. With no other vehicles around hers, the convertible now seemed eerily alone and vulnerable.

She swallowed hard.

Just get in as fast as you can

Juggling the cart, they car keys, and her daughter's hand, Mallory approached the convertible's trunk. "Stand by the door, sweetie." Mallory checked in all directions. Sophie obeyed.

Across the lot, something caught her eye as it moved. Then a hard gust of wind blew, shutting her eyes against the dust it threw at them.

She looked again. There was nothing there.

"Okay, let's go." Mallory opened the passenger door. "Get up into your car seat and buckle yourself in. Mommy will come check in a minute."

She peered over the car roof to re-check the lot.

Sophie playfully crawled into her seat. Mallory took a deep breath, gripping and regripping the keys. "Honey, let's move quickly."

Pressing the trunk release on the key fob, she stepped to the rear of the convertible and shoved aside a blanket and folding stroller to make room for the groceries. "How are we doing, baby?"

"Fine."

Mallory loaded the bags and slammed the trunk lid.

There he was.

She jumped backward, gasping. The man was about five rows away, but his cold, hollow eyes pierced Mallory's insides. He stared right at her, unflinching.

Mallory rushed to the driver door and threw it open, jumping in.

Keys. Where are my keys? .

"Mommy, aren't you going to buckle me in?" Sophie held up the unfastened seat belt. The passenger side door was wide open.

The man came toward them.

Stretching between the seats, Mallory fumbling for the child restraint straps.

Sophie grabbed the buckles. "I can do it!"

"Let me do it!" Mallory yanked the straps form her daughter's hands. Twisting around to see, Mallory peered over her shoulder as the man moved closer. A wave of fear jolted through her. She shook her head. "No, no, no!"

A delivery van drove between them, momentarily blocking the man's way. As soon as the big vehicle passed, he stepped towards Mallory's convertible, increasing his speed with every stride.

She jerked away from the windshield with an audible groan, slapping at her pockets for the car keys. Shoving a hand into her jeans, she grabbed the keys and hauled them out, flipping through them to find the ignition key.

They slipped through her fingers onto the dark floor.

"Mommy!" Sophie held up the dangling buckles.

The man was almost to them.

She grabbed the keys and jammed them into the ignition, stomping the gas pedal. The engine roared to life. Slamming the transmission into drive, Mallory mashed the accelerator, lurching the car forward and causing the doors to slam shut.

She slapped the steering wheel, hand over hand, squealing the tires as the car raced through the lot. Without slowing, she swung the car sharply into the street.

"Mommy!" Sophie's toys flew everywhere.

The convertible bounded into the traffic with a bang, slamming the undercarriage onto the crowned pavement of the street. Car horns blared as other drivers swerved to miss them. She pressed the gas pedal again to leap ahead of the oncoming cars, missing a sedan by inches. Then she immediately hit the brakes.

Red light.

She swung her head around as the smoke from her tires drifted past the windows. The store lot appeared vacant of any people. The man was gone.

Mallory reached back and buckled her crying daughter, then turned and gripped the steering wheel. Her eyes stared straight at the red light, her shoulders heaved with every rapid breath.

Cars pulled up next to them—regular traffic. Regular day.

She collapsed forward onto her hands, fighting back tears.

"Mommy, what's wrong?"

She didn't look. She couldn't.

A car horn honked behind her, snapping her from her breakdown. Back to reality. She wiped her eyes and took a deep breath, then slowly drove off.

It was all she could do to keep the car in her own lane and move with the flow of traffic. She shook her head in silence. She wouldn't be telling Doug about any of this.

They took the long way home. The very long way.

Mallory drove by the mall and Target, the Polo store—all without going in. Sophie eventually drifted off to sleep.

Even with wind gusts batting her car, she could not bring herself to go into any of the shops. She pulled into the parking lots, eyed the stores, and drove on.

Too dark. Too many trees. Too many other cars.

Not *enough* other cars.

After more than an hour of driving around, she gave up. Nothing could dispel the fear and paranoia gripping her insides.

It just wouldn't go.

Chapter 24

I stared at the storage area in the back of my car and frowned, shaking my head.

I had no idea what to take to my meeting with Tyree tonight or the planned trip to Ybor City tomorrow night.

A flash light? A Bible?

A little of everything?

I had no clue. The Navigator was big, though, so even after I had loaded some stuff, it still looked empty. That made me feel even less prepared.

Mallory's headlights lit up the garage as she came up the driveway. I shut the tailgate on the Navigator and waited for my girls to pull into the garage, debating what to tell my wife about my plans for the evening.

I didn't get the chance. As my wife parked, I saw Sophie slumped over in the car seat, asleep. How kids can sleep in such awkward, uncomfortable positions is beyond me.

On nights when Sophie fell asleep close to dinner time, it was a coin toss as to whether or not to wake her up to feed her. Usually, we decided sleep was what her growing body needed at the moment, so we let her have what she needed.

I lifted my daughter out of the car seat and carried her off to bed. In the dim glow of the princess night light, a gentle tug removed each shoe, allowing me to tuck her under the pink Pooh blanket. Grabbing the proper stuffed animals, I arranged them next to her.

Brushing the hair from her face, I kissed her forehead. "Night, night, termite."

Mallory came in behind me and slipped her hand into mine. We stood there, gazing at our beautiful sleeping daughter.

"I love her so much," Mallory said.

I gave her hand a squeeze. Then we crept out of the room and eased the door shut behind us.

Like all parents, Mallory and I had long ago figured out how to eat dinner without waking a slumbering child. If Sophie was really down for the night—and it seemed like she was—a brass band wouldn't wake her before morning. Still, we kept our voices low and tried not to make too much noise. Neither of us was too hungry, anyway. Whatever could be microwaved out of the fridge would be fine.

I clicked on the TV. The forecaster updated us on the path of the hurricane. The weather would get rough pretty soon, but we knew what to do. We'd been through hurricanes before.

From the sunken expression on my wife's face, I could tell she was tired. The shopping trip didn't lift her spirits the way I'd hoped.

She seemed to have something on her mind, but history had taught me to let her bring it up. I waited, poking at my food, while she poured a big glass of wine and sat down.

"So how was the shopping?"

Mallory took a long sip. "Don't ask."

"That bad, huh? Was Sophie misbehaving?"

"Sophie was great." Mallory sighed. "I was a mess."

There was a lot in that statement. I held my breath and waited.

"My mind is all caught up thinking about everything that's happening. It's ridiculous. It's like I'm going crazy." Tears welled in her eyes.

"You're not going crazy." I reached across the table and took her hand. "You're overwhelmed. We *both* are. A lot of information has been shoved down our throats and we're trying to figure it all—"

"I almost ran over a homeless guy at Alton's because I thought he was an attacker!" Mallory threw her hands in the air. "He probably wanted some spare change."

"No, no, that's perfectly . . . okay, yeah. That's crazy."

She chuckled, wiping her eyes. "Don't do that. This is serious."

"Hit and run is pretty serious, too."

"Stop."

"Leaving the scene of an accident . . ."

She threw a piece of bread at me. We laughed.

"Look." I set down my fork. "There's a lot going on. People who find out that their kid is possessed or something, they—"

Mallory glared at me. "She is *not* possessed."

"Right. She isn't." I took a deep breath and stared at my plate. "But whatever's going on, if it's, um, an exorcism or whatever, nobody is going to believe us. Nobody. Anybody who heard what we had to say would think we were insane, or under a lot of strain from work or something. But nobody would believe the truth. Would you?" I looked her in the eye. "A few weeks ago, if one of your friends had told you a story like this, what would you have thought?"

Mallory shook her head. "I'd say they were looney."

"Yeah, so . . . I went to places I thought might *not* think that way. The church, for one." I shifted on my seat. "And I found this guy on the internet . . ."

"The internet?" She buried her face in her hands. "Oh, God."

"I know, I know. It sounded bonkers to me, too . . ."

"What is it, a psychic?"

No that's tomorrow in Ybor City.

"It's just some guy, honey." I swallowed, trying to think of a way to make it sound less ridiculous. "I think he used to be a priest. And I . . . I think he might be able to help us."

"What makes you think that?"

It was a good question. I wasn't a hundred percent certain what had switched me over from being skeptical to being open minded about Tyree.

But I couldn't tell my wife that. Gazing at her puffy, red eyes, I knew she wanted a solution. She wanted to feel safe again.

"I talked to him on the phone and he seemed like a straight shooter. And he won't take any money."

She sat in silence, watching me with sad, blue eyes. Across the room, the weather forecasters rambled on about barometric pressure and categories of storms.

I leaned forward on my elbows. "It's just one option, sweetie."

Mallory took another sip of her wine. "Where are you meeting him?"

"Not here," I said quickly. "He was across the state this morning when I called him. He offered to drive over, so I'm meeting him up off of highway 54, at the international beer garden place."

"Ugh." She set her glass down, pressing the stem between her fingers and causing the glass to turn. "Don't drink too much."

"I'm not going to drink at all. I don't think he drinks, either. It's an easy spot for him to find, and . . ."

She raised her eyebrows. "And?"

"And it wasn't here at the house. I didn't want to bring somebody like that here, a stranger from the internet. Not with everything that's been going on."

"How do you know if you can trust him, or if he's—"

"I don't. But I think I'm a pretty good judge of character. If he's not a good guy, I think I'll know. I'm only exploring options. In fact . . ." I turned around and squinted at the clock on the oven. "I should get ready. He's going to call when he gets off the interstate. That'll be any time now."

She stood up and walked around the table. I thought she was going for more wine, but she slid her arms around me and laid her head on my shoulder. "Be careful."

"I will." I nodded, stroking her arm. "Look, you can go on to bed whenever. I'll call or text as soon as I'm through talking with him, if you want. The bar is a public place. There will be lots of people around."

It didn't sit well, I could tell. I squeezed her. "Nothing's gonna happen."

"I'm nervous about you meeting this stranger. And I'm nervous about *not* meeting him." She sighed. "But I'm more worried about what happens if we don't start doing something."

"Do you want to call your mother and go over there?" I asked.

She was quiet for a moment.

"No."

It would have been an admission of weakness of some sort. Strength was what was needed right now.

I leaned back to look in her eyes. "Okay, then?"

She nodded. "Okay."

I kissed her, then I checked the time again. Whatever additional preparations I needed to do, I should start doing them. I got up from the table and headed out of the room.

"I just want our old life back." Mallory's voice quivered. I turned to see her standing, one arm wrapped around her waist, the other wiping her eye. "Our plain, boring life."

"I know, honey." I went over and gave her a hug. "We'll get there."

I went to my computer and typed a short note while Mallory went upstairs.

Meeting a man called John Tyrone Reed at the international beer house on highway 54. If anything goes wrong, here is his contact information.

I left the document open on the screen. Mallory wouldn't normally go into my office and use my computer, but if something happened to me, this is what she needed to know.

I wondered what, if anything, I should tell her about my plans to go down to Ybor City tomorrow. If she was concerned about this plan, she definitely wouldn't like that one.

My cell phone rang. It was Tyree calling.

I went to say goodbye, but she was already in bed. The cell phone screen cast enough light to see she'd crawled into bed with all her clothes on, pulling a sheet over herself and laying on her side facing away from the door.

I pulled the bedroom door shut and stood in the hallway, deciding not to bother her. She'd had enough for one night. I slid my phone back into my pocket and reached for the handrail.

Through the door came the muffled sounds of sobbing.

Chapter 25

I immediately regretted my decision.

I pulled up to the beer house, but the TV meteorologist had been right. No rain. Barely even any wind. Unusual for a tropical storm, but that's how they are—unpredictable—and the break in the rain drew the bar patrons out in force. The street side parking was all taken. The side lot was full, too.

I knew there would be plenty of open spaces in back, so I pulled around and parked.

That part of highway 54 was all new construction, so the bar was surrounded by a restaurant and some offices, none of which had been there two years ago. The rear lot had a few overhead lights, and an open view across an undeveloped patch of ground that would be a bank or dry cleaner. Beyond that stood a Hilton that was fairly busy, but overall the back lot was a dark middle ground.

I got out to stretch my legs while I waited for Tyree.

Sometimes, a thing will just look out of place. The self-defense lectures taught by off duty cops will tell you to pay attention to those things. Be aware of your surroundings. Things like that.

But I wasn't a cop. I wasn't a tough guy. I was a regular guy who was already out of his comfort zone by being in a dark parking lot late at night.

I paid attention when we took those security awareness training classes at work. Enough light reached me from the distant street pole to barely make out a couple of guys in the shadows standing next to a blue Mustang. It was a warm night, but one guy was in a long sleeve flannel shirt and a stocking cap. The other wore jeans and a white muscle

T-shirt that showed off his thick arms. There may have been somebody in the back seat. They had the hood up on the car, and they kept walking back and forth to look at the motor. In the dark.

Back and forth, from the driver's seat to the engine.

The guys in the Mustang looked at me.

The hairs on the back of my neck stood up as I looked back at them.

This wasn't South Central Los Angeles, it was Land O Lakes, Florida, for Pete's sake. Five hours ago those guys were probably hanging out at the food court in the mall. But then again, dangerous things do happen, usually when people should have known better. I had a wife and a little kid, I reminded myself, so I shouldn't do something stupid like get shot by a couple of paranoid marijuana dealers in a dark parking lot behind a bar. Not when I could easily avoid it. I should have moved, but I had a meeting scheduled there.

A car rolled up to the Mustang and turned off its lights. If they were selling crack or black market guns or something, they wouldn't think kindly of me observing their deal going down.

They kept staring at me. If they were trying to intimidate me, it was working.

Tension gripped my shoulders. I could have left and just called Tyree and found another place to meet. Why didn't I? As I pretended to be busy texting on my phone, I could make out a muted conversation coming from the Mustang guys. With a blast, the Mustang's engine roared to life. I jumped. This pleased the muscle t-shirt guy, who laughed extra loud in my direction. He wanted me to know he knew I was there. They loudly revved the engine a few times, then cut it off. A signal? My stomach tensed.

The two guys walked back and forth from the driver's door to the open hood of the car again. What part of the engine could they be checking in the dark?

After a few minutes, the second car drove off the way it came, crawling along a few hundred feet before turning its headlights on.

That had to be a drug deal move, so I couldn't make out the license plate.

I shouldn't have watched the second car so long. When I glanced back at the Mustang, one of the guys was walking towards me. Not muscle T, but somebody else, with thick arms and a shaved head. I back up half a step and peered over my shoulder to see if maybe there was somebody behind me that he could be walking toward. There was no one else in sight.

"What are you doing back here?"

My stomach leaped. I'd been leaning on my car with my arms folded, and I still had my cell phone in my hand. That would be helpful if I needed to call 911 when this guy decided to tear my arms off. He was big enough, and he was confronting me in a dark, empty parking lot at night. After a drug deal. Behind a freaking bar. How stupid am I? I quickly punched a 9 and a 1 and another 1, and held the phone in the crook of my arm, ready to press "send."

I took a short breath and tried to steady myself. "I'm waiting for someone." I was impressed with how calm I actually sounded. Inside, my stomach tightened up.

"Who?" He barked, still coming toward me. My thumb hovered above to the button on my phone that would call the cops.

"That's none of your business." I said it slowly, staring right at him, eye to eye, doing my best to not let on that my heart was pounding a hundred miles an hour.

If there was going to be a confrontation, it would be now. I had already screwed up by not leaving, but if there was a chance to get him to back down, this was the way. Try to show no fear, even if you *are* scared. Looking him in the eye would signal that I didn't intend to run, and that I might fight back.

I kept my eyes on him, not breathing. My thumb was ready to press the green send button.

He stopped and looked me up and down, sneering

"I manage that bar right there." He pointed at the bar's open back door. "So I have a right to know what's going on in my parking lot." He took a step toward me.

"Then go manage your bar." I stopped leaning on the car and stood upright, hoping a little bit of motion in his direction would stop him. It did.

A bar manager selling drugs part time. Terrific.

I was silently thankful my act was working, but inside my pulse was racing.

He narrowed his eyes. "I think you should leave."

I wasn't reacting the way he expected. "I told you, I'm meeting somebody. I'm not going anywhere."

He didn't like that. It seemed to confuse him. I wondered if it would work and he'd leave, or if it would only piss him off.

"This is *my* bar!" The slightly slurred words showed he had been drinking. "I need to know what's going on in my parking lot! *What are you doing here?*"

He was getting louder and angrier. Adrenaline pulsed through me. Some of the guys got out of the Mustang and glared at me, ready to join in like a pack of dogs. I was seriously outnumbered. Intimidation was becoming something else. Things were getting out of control.

I had no other options. I had to ride out my tough guy ploy. "Does your boss know you drink on the job?"

He hesitated, but I thought I could see his hands curling up into fists.

"Does your boss know you're drunk right now, out in the parking lot instead of managing his business?"

It was a desperate move. I figured this guy might have something to lose—a good job, a house—so I tried to remind him of that. He manages a nice bar and probably makes decent money. A fight might cost him that.

In that split moment where he hesitated, I no longer thought he'd hit me. He'd have done it already.

I glanced at his friends in the Mustang. They might change his mind.

I swallowed hard. Maybe I miscalculated.

It didn't matter. I was almost panting, I'd been holding my breath so long. Fear gripped my stomach and adrenaline pounded through my veins. I had to stand my ground now, maybe give a little verbal push back while I figured out how to get them to go away. To show them it was better to leave. I had no choice.

It was a bad calculation. Muscle T and his guys headed my way. The drunk bar manager was going to defend his territory and they were going to help.

Do I press send?

He gave me one last chance as the Mustang boys closed in. "How about I call the cops right now, and you can explain what you're doing to them?"

That was my opening. "Call the cops." I said. "*I'm* not doing anything illegal back here."

It was like the arguments I had with my older brother when I was a kid. By getting them to talk, I could lure them into an argument and away from a fight. More thinking, less fist throwing.

Usually.

The Mustang guys didn't see it that way. They weren't talking at all and didn't seem like they were going to. Halfway to me now, they moved with threatening determination. I took a quick glimpse at my phone, tucked in my arm, my thumb on the send button. I didn't know if I should press it or not. The police would never have arrived before Muscle T beat me to a bloody pulp.

This isn't what I came here for. The bar manager was ranting. Maybe he was wavering about fighting, but the Mustang guys weren't.

Another guy appeared from the other direction, shoulders squared and hands at his side like a boxer striding to the center of the ring to start the first round.

They were going to surround me like a pack of dogs, and as soon as one attacked, they all would. I had no chance.

The breath went out of me. The police would never get here in time to save me.

The boxer's appearance surprised the Mustang guys. They slowed down for a minute. The dynamic was changing so they needed to reassess things.

The stranger came up behind the manager and then made his presence known.

He didn't *do* anything. He didn't have to. When I turned my head to look past the manager's shoulder, the shadow from the parking lot lights let the manager know someone else was behind him. When the manager turned to see who it was, his jaw dropped, indicating it wasn't who he expected.

This had to be Tyree. He wasn't as big as I expected, maybe even an inch shorter than me, but he was big enough. And his attitude said he didn't mess around.

He looked at me. "You must be Doug." Then he growled at the manager. "Who are you?"

"That's my bar right there . . ."

I eyed at the Mustang guys. They hadn't moved an inch since spotting the newcomer.

"I'm here to meet this man." The stranger's voice was calm but firm, loud enough to be heard by everyone present, but not shouting. "And our meeting doesn't include you."

The stranger's height and stature were deceptive because his voice and attitude created all the authority one man needed. It made him seem bigger than he was.

The manager started again. "What are you guys doing back here?" He seemed slightly less angry now. More confused.

"It has nothing to do with you." The stranger leaned slightly in the manager's direction as he spoke. Then he turned to me, almost showing his back to the manager, but not quite. In movies, such moves are dramatic. In real life, they are not. They are subtle, but critical. This was dismissing to the manager.

I swallowed hard and eyed the man, trying to maintain an even tone. "I don't think we should have our meeting here. Too noisy."

He faced the manager. "I think we'll have our meeting anywhere we please."

The stranger's arms stayed at his sides, in a white shirt starched to a stiffness that cardboard would be jealous of, and long sleeves that looked like they never got rolled up no matter how hot it got.

"I'm calling the cops," the manager said.

The stranger didn't flinch. "You do that."

The manager glanced back and forth between me and the stranger. The Mustang guys held their ground. The stranger held his.

I held my cell phone.

"I'm calling the cops," the manager said again. This time it sounded less like a threat and more like "I'm telling mom." He backed up a step, then turned and walked back to his bar.

I took a well-deserved breath.

The stranger motioned his head toward the Mustang. "What's the story over there?"

"I'm not sure," I said.

He turned back to me and smiled. "Then let's go before they figure things out." He stuck out his hand. "I'm John Tyler Reed. Folks call me Tyree."

The fear drained out of me. I shook his hand. "I'm Doug. Nice to meet you."

He was older than me. Stockier, too, in a way that said back in the day he worked out a lot, either as a military guy or a law man. He spoke with a Texas style accent, but not a thick one, and his manner was an even split of confidence and fact. What he said, you believed.

He was the real deal. He was John Freaking Wayne. The Marines. The Cavalry.

And he saved my ass.

The drunk bar manager watched us from the back door, probably trying to decide what he wanted to do about whatever he thought *we* were up to. The idiot must have thought we were plotting to rob him or something.

"You handled that guy pretty well," Tyree said.

"Did I? He didn't leave."

"Yeah, but you didn't give him any information and you didn't back down. That's good enough in a dark parking lot."

Information? That was an odd comment. But I liked that he thought I didn't back down from a possible fight. Regular guys don't often get a chance to hear that. And that's nice, because we aren't sure we're any good at fighting. Because we aren't.

I scowled, waving at the bar. "I never thought about this being anything but a safe meeting spot until tonight. That manager's probably calling the police right now, thinking we're doing a drug deal."

The guys with the Mustang revved its engine again.

Tyree glared at them. "Well, *they* might be, but either way we need a place to talk and this isn't it now. My car's out front."

More revving.

"How about I drive you over to it and we can go someplace else?"

"Sounds good." Tyree walked to the passenger side of my car.

Chapter 26

I picked up the sodas and walked over to the table. It was time to spill my guts. "So, John, where should I start?"

Our original meeting place had been picked because it was easy to find, not because it was close to anything else. There was a twenty-four-hour donut place about five minutes away, so we went to it.

I felt like I should have been jittery from the adrenaline leaving my system. After all, I had nearly gotten into a big fight with a bunch of guys in a dark parking lot, and I surely would have lost. I expected my hands to be shaking, but they weren't. Instead, I kept focusing on the uneasiness I felt about telling my bizarre story to a stranger.

But I sensed trustworthiness in Tyree. His reassurance, *you handled that guy pretty well*, it had a calming effect. Like most people, I thought I was a good judge of character, so for some reason I thought I should trust this stranger. But this particular problem was not one to be wrong about. Not now.

Still, he had helped me diffuse a very bad situation without even knowing for sure that he had the right guy. That was worth something.

When we arrived, I went to the counter and purchased two cokes. Tyree sat down at the table farthest from the cashier. The place was empty, but the TV in the corner would help drown out our conversation from any nosy employees. More updates about the storm getting worse.

"Start at the beginning." He reached across the table and pushed a chair out for me. "And call me Tyree."

"Tyree." I nodded, sitting down. "You got it."

I thought I got lucky when Father Frank didn't laugh me right out of the Our Lady Of Mercy. Hopefully this Tyree guy wouldn't laugh me out of the donut shop.

"Your name is unusual sounding." I was stalling. "Like it's made up."

He took a sip of his Coke and smiled. "Well, it's a nickname, really."

I was sure Tyree had been in plenty of meetings like this before, and knew some small talk was usually necessary to get people to loosen up. I'd heard cops did that. Maybe he used to be one.

Sitting back in his chair, his khaki pants looked freshly ironed after his three hour drive. So did his shirt. I bet he could've beat up everybody in that parking lot and he'd still look that way.

"The name Tyree is an acronym and a double entendre, all in one."

"Doesn't sound like a typical nickname, like calling a tall guy shorty, you know?"

That seemed to surprise him a little, and he laughed, choking on his soda. "That's funny." He coughed, clearing his throat. "No, that's right, it wasn't a typical nickname. John Tyler Reed was the name they called when they took attendance in school. So the kids called me all sorts of stuff. Ty-Rod, Ty-Ree . . . but when I got into my vocation, it took on another meaning for me."

Vocation?

"I came up with an acronym. T-Y-R-E-E. Trust Your Religion for Everything."

Not an ex-cop. An ex-priest? I guessed I had some kind of nutty Bible thumper with me now, but the conversation here wasn't jiving with the guy in the parking lot who was ready to mix it up.

I thought about his explanation for the nickname. "That doesn't really work. It spells tyre. Like 'tire.'"

He took another drink of his Coke. "Would you want the nickname of 'Tire'? That's why I added the extra 'E' on the end. It stands for 'every day.'"

I'd give him five minutes, and if he was batty then I'd wrap it up and head for the door. "Yeah, well . . . I guess you're entitled to your own nickname."

"Thank you. Let's get down to business." He leaned forward, putting his elbows on the table. "What happened for you to call me?"

I took a deep breath, trying to decide how ridiculous I wanted to sound.

"Why am I here?" He hooked a thumb over his shoulder. "It wasn't just to bail you out of a fight in that parking lot. What's going on? Is the wolf at the door?"

"No, no. Not like that." I rubbed my eyes. "Not quite, anyway. It's—it's not easy to explain. I'm not sure I even understand it myself."

"If you understood it, you wouldn't need me." Tyree stood up. "This sounds like it might take some time. You drink coffee?"

"No."

"Well, I do. By the pot." He pushed his soda to the center of the table and stood up." And this sounds like a two pot story. So let me get some java, and then you start wherever you feel most comfortable starting. I have time."

Tyree strode off to the cashier while I sat there alone with my Coke, wondering what I should tell and what I should keep. Deep inside I knew I had to tell somebody, even if was only to get this insanity off my chest. And talking had always been helpful for me, in a therapeutic sense. It forced me to organize and articulate my thoughts. If I ever had a problem that needed organizing, this one did.

You gotta start trusting somebody sometime, Doug.

Tyree had already earned my trust back in the parking lot. What more did I want?

He returned with a gigantic plastic coffee mug. "You ready?"

"Sure." I nodded. "It's gonna sound pretty bizarre."

"I'm sure it will. If it didn't . . ."

"Yeah, I wouldn't have called you."

Tyree sat, holding his coffee in both hands. "You mentioned three stories on the phone. Tell me the three stories."

"Okay," I said. "Brace yourself, here comes the crazy."

Leaning back, Tyree took a sip from the big mug. "Bring it."

I started with the winery episode. By now, Mallory and I had talked about it so many times, it had its own name: The Winery Wreck. If either one of us used those words, the other instantly knew what they were talking about.

From there, I told him about the car fire on the bridge, and discovering the heart condition in our daughter. By the time I told him all three stories, more than two hours had passed. I rambled on; Tyree quietly sipped his giant plastic mug of coffee.

"Why can't it be both?"

"What?" I said. "Why can't *what* be both?"

"These things that keep happening to you and your family. Why does it have to be decisively good luck or bad luck? Why can't it be both?"

I didn't know how to answer.

"Look." Tyree scooted his chair forward and rested his arms on the table. "How does a situation appear when something good *and* bad are happening? When they happen simultaneously?" He let that sit in the air for a moment. "I think it looks a lot like what you're describing."

I rubbed my chin. "I'm not sure I follow, but let's say you're right. What does that mean to me?"

He took another long gulp of coffee. "I don't know."

I glared at him. "Well, *that's* helpful."

"No, no . . . I understand. It's not." He stared at the paper napkin on the table top. "Not yet anyway. But it's a step. Let's come back to that. Let's talk about something else. Give your mind a chance to rest from all this tragedy stuff for a moment." He stood up. "I'm getting more coffee. You need anything?"

I shook my head.

His massive mug was empty, so he went for more. I rubbed my eyes, thinking about updating Mallory. So far, I didn't have anything to really tell her. Hey, honey, I almost got beat up in a dark parking lot. I'm now sitting in a donut shop telling a stranger our wacky stories. If she were asleep, she wouldn't want to wake up for that, and if she were awake, it would only upset her.

I texted. *Everything is okay. Still talking. Will be home soon.*

Tyree came back to the table with his refill. "You probably have some questions for me. What are they?"

That caught me off guard. He was a straight shooter, though, so he would probably be prepared for whatever I asked. I thought for a moment. "Are you a priest?"

"Nope. I studied Divinity, though. I was considering becoming a priest."

"What happened?"

"I kind of had a problem with the whole celibacy thing."

That made us both laugh.

I ran my finger along the side of my soda, causing beads of water to drip off the end. "Tell me about Help For The Hopeful. How did that get started?"

"I was gonna have Help For The Hopeful put on my license plate." He blew on his coffee to cool it. "You know, 'HFTH.' People thought it meant 'have faith,' and that was nice, too."

"What about a vow of poverty? Is there any money in doing what you do?"

"Can be." He avoided saying more by taking a long drink from his mug.

I shrugged. "Seems like it could take a lot of money to run ads and meet with a constant stream of wackos, plus maintain phones and an office."

"I said I wouldn't ask *you* for any money. We have had a few grateful benefactors who were happy with our services. They have given us some gifts, from time to time."

I wasn't grasping it. Tyree put out a hand. "You do a big favor for a wealthy industrialist." He put out his other hand. "You get to call in little favors for a long time. And they are happy to help because they benefitted."

I gave him a half frown. "Does the Church know about all this?"

"Well, kind of." He gazed out the window at the empty parking lot. "C'mon, it's off track betting, a white lie."

"It's a little different from a white lie."

"That's right. It is." He folded his hands and looked me in the eye, assuming a flat, no-nonsense tone. "It's a gray lie, maybe even something with a little more color than that. So be it. I know that what I do is worthwhile. People benefit, and I get help from people who know people. It all works out. Besides." His voice softened. "I have a bit of an inside track with The Almighty. A friend does my confessions at a half price."

"He'd have to." I shook my head. "I bet you're a volume customer."

Tyree smiled again. I was relaxing, and that's what was needed. A tense mind doesn't operate well.

"The Church doesn't directly know about me, usually. In places that are uncomfortable, or places where the Church feels folks are less hospitable, they outsource.

Subcontractors, so to speak, so they can keep their hands clean."

He watched my face. His story sounded as bizarre as mine. "So, you're like the Church's CIA?"

Glancing around, he lowered his voice. "Hey, be careful. They have that."

We both laughed.

"You're quite the radical, Tyree."

"Yeah, that radical stuff was all the rage in the 1970's. Then it kinda went out of style; everybody got into making money. Even us. Damned shame. You got a cigarette?"

I shook my head.

"No?" He seemed disappointed. "Of course you don't. Figures. I quit anyway."

That struck me as an odd statement. "When did you quit?"

"This time? This morning." He folded his hands behind his head and pushed back in the chair, stretching. "When I was talking to miss Margarita at the bar where I misplaced my keys. She said she couldn't kiss a man who tasted like an ashtray."

"Margarita? Was that her name or was she a beauty pageant winner?"

"Ah, well . . . Now that you mention it, that's a good question." He dropped his hands to his belly. "How do you think your three stories connect?"

"I don't know that they do. My wife's friend originally said something about six months ago, that we were jinxes."

"Nice friend."

"Well, she was pointing out the bad stuff happens around us, not to us."

"Not yet, anyway."

I glared at him. “Thanks for that. Anyway, she said she didn’t want to catch the next disaster when it missed us. Or near-missed us.”

“The bullet would miss you guys and hit her, that sort of thing?”

“Right.”

Tyree took a deep breath and let it out slowly, his eyes fixed on his folded hands. “I think she may be closer than you think.”

My somewhat uplifting feeling vanished. “How’s that?”

“Well, how do you feel about all this? Lucky?”

“Not lucky, that’s for sure.” I shook my head. “No way.”

“Okay, but.” He raised his eyes to meet mine. “Do you feel unlucky, though?”

I thought about that. I really didn’t. “It’s hard to feel unlucky when we’d never been hurt, so no. We’ve just been close by when things happened.”

“That’s your training talking.” Tyree scoffed. “Years of social upbringing and societal norms. You have to move past that. This stuff always happens around the same time of year?”

“Seems like it.” I tugged at my collar.

“Maybe you don’t want to see what’s in front of you.” The words were heavy, like bricks stacking up on my conscience. “That’s understandable. Who would want to see a threat if they didn’t have to?”

He had tricked me, knowing I’d have to answer. *Who would want to see a threat if they didn’t have to?* I swallowed. “Anybody. Anybody with something to protect.”

He raised his eyebrows, nodded slowly, keeping his eyes fixed on mine. “And what do you protect, Doug?”

“Well, my wife, my daughter . . . my, uh, house . . . ”

"Did you always have these problems? I mean, the whole time you were married?"

"No . . ."

"When did this all start? As far as you and your wife? Have you ever thought about it?"

His words pierced me, ringing in my ears. I pushed my hand through my hair. "I—I don't know."

Tyree's eyes narrowed. "Yes, you do, Doug."

I could barely speak. "That can't be the answer."

Who would want to see a threat if they didn't have to.

"It can't be . . ."

"Why not?" Tyree asked. "Why are you afraid to see what's in front of you?"

"What are you trying to say?" I winced, turning my head away from him. "It can't be her. She can't be the cause of all this!"

The room closed in on me. The air grew stale and stuffy.

"When did it all start?" He drove his finger into the table top.

He wanted me to say it out loud.

Things were falling into place in ways I didn't want them to, squeezing the air out of my lungs. Sweat broke out on my forehead. "She's innocent."

"Who?" He frowned. "When did it start? Say it."

I glared at him and forced myself to speak, the answer in front of me like a white hot light. "It started when my daughter was born." It was barely a whisper, but it rang in my ears like a cannon shot. I slid down in my chair, dazed at how it sounded out loud.

"I think that's significant, don't you?" Tyree said.

I was a traitor. A turncoat.

Worthless.

She can't be the cause of all this. She can't be.

"She's just a little kid!" I gasped, looking up at him. I was nearing my limit. "She can't be why this is happening."

Tyree stared at me. After a long moment, he asked, "Why not?"

The words hung in the air, echoing around in my head without an answer.

Why not?

Chapter 27

I stared at the dead body. "Can I touch him?"

I had never seen a dead person before and I was a little afraid. We stood near the casket, my Uncle Glen and I, peering at a small old man laid out in a dark gray suit.

"You can touch him." My godfather put his hand on my shoulder. "He was your great-grandfather and he loved you."

I was eight years old, trying to be brave. My uncle held my hand as we stood in line, waiting our turn to pay our respects. The room was large and nearly full to capacity, but it was very quiet.

Glen spoke softly. "I think he would like it if you touched him on the hand to say goodbye."

I lifted my left hand and reached into the coffin, extending a finger, easing it past the edge of the lacquered wood.

The only place that seemed touchable was his hand. The rest of my great-grandfather was covered in his dark gray suit, except for his face. I did not want to touch his face. Even at the age of eight I knew that would be disrespectful.

As if in slow motion, I stretched out my arm and touched a fingertip to the back of his pale hand.

It was soft. And it wasn't cold; it was room temperature, like an expensive, soft leather glove. As a kid, I had seen so many monster movies with Dracula and Frankenstein, I was nearly out of my mind with curiosity, thinking about actually touching a dead person. But that was at home. As I reached out toward the hand of my deceased great-grandfather, the moment was different. None of the drama of movies happened.

He didn't feel much like a person should. I had anticipated that his hand would not feel warm—in movies they always talk about a dead body being cold. But more than that, I had expected it to be firm. But there was no living muscle behind it anymore to make it firm. And he didn't flinch or twitch as you would expect a sleeping person to do.

He just lay there motionless.

As I watched, his chest didn't rise and fall like my dad's did during an afternoon nap. He didn't brush my finger away like you might if you thought it was a fly crawling on your hand.

He didn't jump up and scream, like in scary movies. He didn't groan and slowly rise up from the coffin, sending everyone running out of the room.

He didn't move at all.

It was just the hand of a man who had moved on from this life and this body. A nice little man who always smelled like cherry pipe tobacco when we visited him. He would put out dry roasted peanuts and show us the battery operated toy monkey that would dance and bang cymbals.

He was none of the things the movies had shown me that dead people were. And I felt ashamed for thinking such things while I looked at him.

My uncle suggested that we kneel and say a prayer. I silently pretended to say the Hail Mary—one of the few prayers I knew—watching my dead great-grandfather's body remain so still, so unmoving.

That is how I knew he was dead. It was the first dead body I had ever seen.

"Finished?" My uncle gently asked.

I nodded.

I didn't even want to be in that church, much less be touching anything, but I thought it would be neat to tell my friends at school I had touched a *real dead body*. Enough of my friends watched Creature Feature on Saturday afternoons so this would be a big story on Monday.

Rising, I caught my mother's eye. I felt my cheeks burn as she smiled at me leaving the coffin. She thought I was paying my respects. She didn't know I simply had a childish and morbid curiosity about touching a corpse and bragging to my friends about it. I looked down in shame that she would have assumed was reverence.

I remember asking Mom what we were supposed to do at the visitation. She said to be respectful and quiet, and to be sure to go up to great-grandma and tell her we were sorry for her loss. A stream of her great-grandchildren coming up one after the other saying, "Sorry, grandma," in an assembly line.

When my turn came, I had remembered to tell her that I was sorry. She had lost her husband and lifelong companion. My grandmother, at her side, had lost her father. But in saying the words, it didn't feel like I was sorry in the way those words usually meant. I had done nothing to be sorry for.

I decided not to bring any of it up at school.

The service began, and eventually my mind went on to other things. But after the next funeral I went to, I never wanted to attend another funeral again.

It was only a few months later. A childhood friend had died in an unfortunate car accident. The hood of a car had flown off and smashed into the car he was riding in, hitting him in the forehead. The boys in the other car had been working on the engine and neglected to properly secure the hood before taking it out for a test drive. It cost my friend his life.

I couldn't stand the way Kevin looked in his coffin. Swelling and surgeries had changed him. The mortician's artistry had not been enough to re-make him as he was. He was a kid who had been one of my closest friends, and now he was unrecognizable to me. As an adult, when I think of him now, I first see the stark, glum stranger's face in the coffin before I can force myself to remember the true, actual smiling face of my young friend.

I could not bear to have my mother's face and memory ruined for me that way. I would not let it happen. I knew what was waiting for me at her visitation. I purposely arrived late so I could not attend, telling everybody I couldn't catch a flight in time—but that wasn't the truth. I wanted to be elsewhere. Needed to be. And I made sure I was.

It was selfish, but eternity is a long time.

I would remember the smiling face and bright eyes of my loving mother in my own way, not the mock up by a funeral director. It was my parting gift to her, and to myself. I didn't explain my absence to anyone. The only person who knew I could have made the visitation—but didn't—was my wife. She silently disapproved but likely had decided that I needed to grieve in my own way and in my own time.

Kevin was supposed to look like on TV. There, when people die, their face just relaxes and they look the same as they did a moment before. But in reality, a face may have gone through trauma from an accident, or swelling. Maybe they had to cut the person's hair to dress the wounds. Maybe the easy smile that always graced his young face just couldn't be made to appear, and the haunting, glum face and expressionless mouth would forever be burned into the memories of those who knew him—a cruel thing to do to his friend. Maybe after the gash in his head and days in the hospital, the swollen face with no smile was the best they could do.

But he didn't look like my friend anymore, and I was not about to trade a lifetime of my mother's smiles for some stupid protocol.

I knew her dimples wouldn't be there. Each of her sixty-five year old cheeks would maintain a small crease instead. The makeup would be wrong, the hair . . . I couldn't bear to carry with me for the rest of my life a vision of some undertaker's poor good efforts. The best that he could do—the best that anybody could ever do—would still be a far cry from the face I had known and loved my entire life. It would instead be a faded painting of a once vibrant woman full of energy and love and life.

I couldn't take the image of her lifeless face looking . . . wrong.

I'd prefer to remember her as she was a few years ago, when I took her picture at the kitchen table at Christmas. Smiling and happy, not the face where she was losing her fight to her illnesses. We laughed and joked, trying to get a good picture out of a bad camera—a losing battle, especially with a poor photographer behind the lens.

Then, when she thought we had finished, she made a face. She stuck out her tongue and I clicked the shutter. She was shocked that I caught her, and burst out in a glorious natural smile.

I quickly snapped another shot—the best picture I have ever taken.

And the one where I always thought she looked her best. She had a round face with bright eyes and dimples. She was cheerful and energetic and alive.

I remember the last thing I ever said to my mother before she died. My dad called to tell us that she didn't have much longer, so we drove up to say goodbye. She lay on her hospital bed, weak, her eyes closed. I leaned in and held her hand, and teased her the way I always would.

"I saw the new kitchen wallpaper, Mom." I whispered in her ear. "It looks . . . terrible."

Even though her eyes were closed, she smiled. She couldn't open them. She was too near the end.

"It doesn't go with the chairs at all," I said quietly. "When I come back up in a couple of weeks, I'll help you re-do the wallpaper. When you're feeling better."

She smiled again.

That was the last conversation we ever had.

Some people might have found it disrespectful. I disagree.

There's a smile people get on their face at the end of a long day. When they've worked hard, and they come home and they sit down, and just relax, leaning their head back in their favorite chair. And they could just fall right to sleep, satisfied, with a smile, taking a rest that has been well earned.

That was the smile my mom gave me that day. The smile that comes at the end of a long struggle, that's looking forward to a rest that has also been well earned.

An oncoming rest that God would agree was well deserved. Her eyes were closed, and there was a small smile on her lips. She was ready.

I didn't think it would be disrespectful to talk to my mother that way. I thought it would be disrespectful to talk to her any other way.

I think when you're at the end of your time, people owe it to you to be themselves. The masks, the show, the façades, are all done now. They owe it to you to just to be who they had always been to you their whole life.

So I stood before my mother, holding her hand, leaning over her as she lay on what would be her death bed, and I acted the way I had always acted my whole life. I wanted to be funny and sarcastic for her. At that time, I thought she'd like to see her son the way she always knew him. Not acting some other way in her time of finality.

I think it was a smile of appreciation, but it was certainly a smile of somebody who worked hard, who was tired, and who was ready to rest.

I made her smile. That was my farewell gift to her.

She was too weak to open her bright eyes, but I got to see the round face and the dimples. That smiling face, and the one in the photo years before, are the ones I would be able to carry forward with me for the rest of my days.

That was her farewell gift to me.

Chapter 28

"Okay, okay, slow down." Tyree had touched a nerve, and he knew it. "Calm down. Back up."

The heat drained out of my cheeks.

"Set that conversation aside for a moment and let's talk about something else. Let's shift gears. Okay?"

I wasn't sure I wanted to keep talking at all. "Okay."

"You ever play a game when you were a kid, and somebody got hurt?"

I grumbled. "Sure."

"Tell me about it. Tell me a time when you played and somebody got hurt—and you felt bad about it."

"Just, what? Anything?"

"Tell me about the first thing that comes to your mind."

"Okay . . . First thing. I wasn't even a kid. I was wrestling with the neighbor's kid." I didn't know where we were going with all this. Maybe it was his method of figuring out which of his customers were bonkers and which ones weren't.

I decided to go along. He had earned my trust back at the parking lot, but he was on thin ice.

"What happened with that?"

"He was probably about ten years old. My wife's best friend's kid. Called me Uncle Doug, and all. I was chasing him around the house, and he slipped on the tile in the foyer and I caught him. I decided to tickle him instead of wrestle him. But when I did, he twisted to get away from me and I grabbed his hand, dislocating his finger and snapping a tendon. It ruined his chance to play basketball that season. He couldn't shoot."

Tyree nodded. "Now, you said it was an accident, but you felt bad afterwards. Why?"

"He was only a kid." I shrugged. "It was my fault. You know those old guys who can't straighten out their fingers because of a farm accident or something? He could have ended up like that at age ten. I felt pretty bad about that."

"How did things end up?"

"Uh, he was okay," I said. "It only messed up part of his season and his finger healed fully. He played the next year."

"He was able to straighten out his finger?"

"Yeah, thank God."

Tyree say back in his chair, cradling his giant coffee mug in his lap. "Okay, so you could have mentioned anything, any example from your whole life. Why did you pick that one?"

I huffed. "Gee, Doctor Freud, you said to take the first thing that came to mind. I guess it was the most recent."

"Really? You never played a game with your daughter that turned out wrong? Not even when she was a baby?"

"Oh, sure, I guess so." I pulled my soda a little closer but didn't take a drink. "But nothing comes to mind. I mean, we had other things happen that we felt guilty about, like when she fell off the couch and hit her head . . ."

"You didn't feel bad about that?"

"Sure I did. But it was an accident."

"The thing with your nephew wasn't an accident?"

"It was! But it was different. I felt bad because I caused it." I thought for a moment. "And because I should have known better. He was just a poor innocent kid who got hurt by an adult who was acting like an idiot. From somebody who should have been watching out for him."

Tyree nodded again. "You didn't feel bad about your daughter falling off the couch and hitting her head? What's more innocent than a baby?"

My cheeks grew hot. I looked down. "I felt terrible about that, but it was different."

"How so?"

"It was an accident, but I didn't cause it."

"You make that distinction?" Tyree asked. "Between causing it and letting it happen?"

I couldn't tell if he was serious or not. It sounded accusatory.

"I didn't let it happen." I shifted on my seat. "She was sitting near me, then she leaned back and rolled off the couch. Nobody expected that. It was an accident, but it was different . . ."

"Okay. I agree." His tone was flat, his posture upright and rigid. In command. "Now, back to your nephew. You said that you felt bad afterwards because you should have known better . . ."

"Right. I felt guilty."

"Okay, right. Guilty." He narrowed his eyes. "What if you hadn't felt guilty?" If you *couldn't* feel guilt. What would you have felt?"

Nothing came to mind. It was the opposite of when somebody says, 'Don't think of an elephant'—an elephant is what leaps to mind. Here, the question vacated my reasoning ability. "I don't know."

"Anger?"

"Anger? No." I thought about it. "Embarrassed."

Tyree dismissed it with a wave of his hand. "Embarrassment is part of feeling guilty. What if you couldn't feel guilty? If you could not feel guilt, what would you have felt?"

"I don't know. Maybe empathy."

"That's still part of guilt."

"Well, if I couldn't feel guilt—if I couldn't feel guilt at all—then I guess I don't have an answer." I was confused. "I wouldn't feel *anything* about what happened."

"Not the way we understand feelings, anyway," Tyree said. "Who would not feel guilty over hurting an innocent person?"

"Nobody . . ." I began. "I mean, you know, a psychopath maybe. But not a human being with normal feelings."

Tyree raised an eyebrow. "Or maybe just not a human being."

"What do you mean?"

"Have you even heard the saying about angels and innocents?"

"I don't know." I raised my shoulders and turned the Coke cup again. "Maybe. Sounds familiar."

"C'mon!" Tyree snorted. "You know this. You went to catholic school for ten years."

"Twelve."

"Twelve years!" Tyree sat back and clapped his hands to his knees. "You remember what they said in a stupid personal security training seminar for work, and you don't remember this?"

"The one about the angels playing?"

"Yeah, that's it. I knew you knew it, don't BS me." He leaned forward in his chair, nearly spilling his coffee. "You know it. Tell it to me."

"Playing angels, angels at play . . ." I paused. "I don't know. I don't remember how it goes."

"Think. It'll come to you."

Those stupid nuns taught us a million things in school. I couldn't be expected to remember them all. But Tyree was right. It was coming back to me in bits. I gave it some thought.

"When angels play . . ." I squinted at the ceiling, reaching back to Sister Helen in seventh grade. " 'When angels play, innocents suffer.' Is that it?"

"Almost. That's close."

"Well, it was a long time ago. Close is pretty good." I picked up my Coke, lifting it to my lips. "Besides, you're the clergyman. Help me out."

"Are you forgetting it on purpose?"

"What? No. I—"

He stared at me.

I stopped, my soda frozen in midair. "What?"

"It's not angels," he said. "It's *dark* angels."

"It is? Are you sure?"

Tyree smiled, raising his eyebrows. "Oh, I'm sure. And it makes all the difference."

I recited it now, recalling it fully. "When dark angels play, innocents suffer."

A twinge of fear shot through me. My mouth hanging open, the soda drifted away from my lips.

And who's more innocent than a baby?

Chapter 29

I slipped into the house and eased the door shut behind me, peering around the corner at the breakfast nook. Mallory sat reading the newspaper with Sophie perched on her lap. Empty cereal bowls rested on the table, a few bits floating in the residual milk. I crept into the room and slid the box of donuts on the counter.

"Daddy!" Sophie jumped up and sprinted to me, wrapping her arms around my thighs.

As she lowered the newspaper, a smile crept over Mallory's face. She let out a sigh, as if she'd been holding her breath since last night.

Sophie peeled herself off me and ran back to the table. "This is what we want you to make for us." She held up a section of the paper. "Chocolate bread!"

The title under the image of marbled bread read *Babka*. It looked like a big, twisted pretzel.

"Chocolate bread?" I made an exaggerated frown. "Yuck. I don't want to eat chocolate bread."

Mallory set aside the section she had been reading and folded her arms, resting her elbows on the table. "It's not for you to eat. It's for *us* to eat."

"I don't want to make chocolate bread if I'm not going to eat chocolate bread."

"*We* want to eat chocolate bread."

"*I* don't want to eat chocolate bread. So I'm not making chocolate bread."

Mallory frowned at Sophie. "Daddy says 'no'."

Sophie frowned.

I was dead tired and hadn't figured out if I was in trouble for being out all night. I hadn't been partying, and Mallory knew that, but I probably looked like I had.

"I can make chocolate cake." I put my hands on my knees and turned to Sophie. "Would you like cupcakes?"

Sophie's eyes lit up. "I would like cupcakes."

"I can make *chocolate* cupcakes," I told her.

Mallory grumbled. "I want chocolate *bread*."

I shrugged my shoulders at our daughter in an exaggerated manner, and frowned. "Mommy says 'no'."

Sophie frowned.

I got a glass out of the cupboard and pulled a jug of tea out of the fridge. Maybe I should make the chocolate bread to smooth things over. I poured a tall glass as Sophie scampered over to the TV to watch cartoons.

"How did everything go last night?"

If Mallory was angry, she was masking it well. That was nice in front of our daughter.

"Good." I rubbed my eyes. "We may have found our man."

She laid down the paper. "Really?"

I leaned on the counter and gulped my tea. "I got lucky. This guy is smart. He knows the Church and their limitations and he seems to know the law. He was a good find."

"Did you guys talk all night?"

"Pretty much."

Mallory could be patient when the time called for it. She was exerting that strength now, probably wanting to leap out of her chair and ask for all the details, but holding back so as not to worry our daughter. As curious as my wife might be, though, I knew she was still afraid of hearing truthful answers to disturbing questions.

"I think you'll be happy with what I learned last night," I said. "I think you'll feel better after you hear it."

"Good."

"In fact, I should probably have him come over here and talk to both of us. He can meet you and Sophie. That might be helpful to him."

"Have him come here?" Mallory bit her lip. "Do you trust him?"

I nodded. "Yeah, I do."

"Why?"

I drained my glass. "A couple of reasons." I stepped to the table and sat down next to her, closing my eyes and laying my head on her shoulder. "I'll go over all that with you, I promise. But not now. I need some sleep." I made a loud, cartoonish snoring noise.

"Daddy!" Sophie giggled, bouncing up and down on the couch.

Mallory smiled, shoving my head off her shoulder. She wanted more, but she would wait. Opening the newspaper with a rustle, she held it high in front of her face.

I pushed it down and kissed her. "Thanks, darling." With a grunt, I put both hands on the table and forced myself to a standing position, then headed to the stairs to go to bed.

"When should we have him meet with us?"

"Soon."

"Tonight?"

I stopped and turned. "I have another appointment tonight. Another late meeting." I left it ambiguous on purpose. I didn't know how many meetings I would need.

"Another?" Mallory covered her mouth with her hand and swallowed hard, turning her eyes to our beautiful bouncing girl.

Chapter 30

Tyree yawned and slid the pot under his coffee maker. The foldout couch in the corner would be his bed and his office would be his home for a few days—if his prospective client was worth the effort. Doug Kenner seemed like a guy in need, but lots of people had problems. Tyree liked to prioritize his efforts, and wanted to see where the Kenner family placed in the lineup.

He dropped into the chair in front of his computer. Sleep would wait.

A quick search showed Doug as a freelancer for The Tampa Tribute. A few clicks brought up a contribution that had run several weeks ago. The other articles were older, with four weeks or more between them, but there were a lot.

Tyree leaned forward and rubbed his chin. Doug wasn't an employee at the Trib. Was that his choice or theirs? He browsed some of his private subscription data bases. The family appeared pretty normal.

Scrolling through to an essay in the Tribute's Lifestyles section, Tyree took a big drink of coffee and glanced at Doug's published work. One was called "I Caught Your Kiss," another was entitled "Pretend Sisters And My Daughter's Other Imaginary Friends." A third was "A Tomato Grabbed Our Car."

As the coffee pot gurgled, Tyree rubbed his eyes and settled in. "Let's see what you're all about, Mr. Doug."

I Caught Your Kiss by Doug Kenner, Tribute contributor

On Thursdays, I drop my daughter Sophie off at her grandmother's house. That's been the routine ever since Sophie started swim classes. It makes for an easier day for me, and Grandma Jenny gets to play with her granddaughter all day once a week. If you love your grandma the way Sophie loves Grandma Jenny, that's a big time treat. I'm not sure my daughter has ever eaten a vegetable over there. Certainly not on a Thursday.

Tyree smiled. This definitely sounded like the man he'd just met.

Her latest thing, when it's time to say goodbye, is to blow kisses at you and ask you to catch them. This requires you to make a move like you are catching a baseball with both hands, and then clasp them to your heart. Then she will expect you to blow kisses back at her, and she will clasp her hands to her heart, shouting, "I caught your kiss!"

The essay went on—long enough for a second cup of coffee. The lack of sleep never got to the essay's current reader.

So my wife roars on down the driveway and gets ready to pull into the street, with my daughter waving frantically at her. 'Goodbye! Goodbye!" Tears were welling up in her eyes. "Why isn't she waving goodbye to me?"

"She—she has to keep her hands on the steering wheel, sweetie. Safety first, you know?" That wasn't going to cut it. Then, a brainstorm. "Mommy will flash the car's red tail lights, to wave to you. She'll do that to let you know that she saw you waving. Watch." It was the best I could think of on short notice. Then I held my breath.

As my wife slowed down to pull from our driveway into the street, she applied the brakes and the tail lights lit up.

"There you go!" I announced in triumphant relief. "See? Mommy saw you and waved with the tail lights!"

My daughter smiled up at me, blinking back tears. "She saw me!"

"Of course she saw you! She turned on the red lights, didn't she?"

Tyree wiped his eye.

Because I realized I have to set an example for our daughter, okay? But also because it's worth it. People don't last forever, and you never know when the last time you hug or kiss somebody goodbye is going to be the last time that you ever hug or kiss them goodbye. So you have to keep that in mind.

And it's kind of the same thing with this "I caught your kiss" thing. Don't worry about stopping too soon, because it's going to stop one day, and on that day, I may wish that I had this day back. That day may be six months from now, or six years from now, or that day may never come. But I have a feeling that, like most things with my daughter, the day something stops always comes a little sooner than I want it to.

-Doug Kenner is a freelance writer and independent contractor for a local wine distributor

Setting down his coffee, Tyree rubbed his eyes and sniffled.

"Yeah," he said to the office walls. "I have to help this family."

He stood up and took one last sip of coffee before collapsing onto the foldout couch.

Chapter 31

This was the kind of weather that helped put all those ships on the ocean floor.

The big rains from the hurricane were going to come soon, and they were going to come in force when they did, but right now it was beautiful out. A little lull before the storm—because a nice, calm evening could fool anyone into thinking that all hell wasn't about to break loose in a few days.

I got into my car and headed south on the interstate.

Ybor City is funny in a way other places aren't. The things people really wanted to find aren't advertised. It takes patience, and waiting for the right moment, the right person to ask, and then *maybe* you can find what you're looking for. I had discovered that by mistake one night after a parade. Mallory's group—a *krewe*, in Gasparilla charity parlance—had a designated party bar, and we were all supposed to meet there after a parade, then a string of bar hopping would ensue. But I got there late and went to the wrong place.

The krewe started at the piano bar as planned, but it quickly proved to be too crowded and not rowdy enough. That lead to them disembarking to the first of many other packed bars, with my wife texting me which one was up next. But krewe members in pirate costume get to walk right in. We civilians have to stand in line. At busy times—like parade nights—there was a wait.

After missing Mallory and her friends at three different locations over about ninety minutes, I decided to chuck it and let her find me after the party ended. I parked it at Vespers and squeezed myself into a spot at the bar. Like every other bar in Ybor city, the place was packed.

I ordered a beer and some ice water, sliding the bartender a twenty-dollar bill on top of the cost of the drink. "I'm going to rent this space for a little while, okay?"

He nodded. I wanted a place at the bar and I didn't want him getting antsy over my lack of drink orders costing him tips while I waited for my wife.

Meanwhile, I leaned back to watch the crowd.

Eventually it got to be almost 2 A. M. On some other night, I might have been worried, but not after a parade. Folks got out, started having fun, and forgot all about the time. Mallory's krewe would be getting close to shutting down a few bars about now, and that would get her to thinking. I'd be okay right where I was waiting. The wimpier watering holes closed their doors at 2 A. M. Not Vespers. They had girls in short shorts and bustiers pouring shots out the windows to happy customers lining the street. Ybor was a mad house.

But like all things, it eventually wound down. I got a text from Mallory. *Phone dying. Will meet you or get a cab.*

That was at 3 A. M. Vespers started thinning out at 3:30, so I figured she wasn't coming. But the last thing you want to do on a parade night is to leave your wife stranded at four in the morning in the heart of party central, so I waited.

That's when a guy came up to me offering to help me find a good time. He had all the trappings: glasses that were a little too tinted for that time of night, a shiny purple suit coat and some braids. He even had a gold tooth, which may have been real or may have just been for effect—like the rest of what he was wearing. That's the kind of place this is. Ybor City, we have it all.

Now, in New Orleans, a tipster like my man in purple was a liaison to other things that sound good to you at 4 A. M. after a night of drinking and partying. Something to smoke, or snort, perhaps? Maybe a little luck with a lady if you had struck out all night. He was a commission salesman, and he got a piece of whatever action he hooked you up with.

Like I said, he was connected. He might not be the guy, but he knew the guy. He had to. It was his living, and he wanted it to pay well. In 'Nawlins, these guys know the Marie Laveau types, the voodoo practitioners who aren't there for the tourists—the ones that are the real deal. I'm not saying it's real, and I'm not saying it isn't. All I'm saying is, if you want to meet that type of operator, this is the guy to help make the connection.

My plan was basic. If New Orleans had theirs, we'd have ours. I only needed to go to the right place, wait it out, and hope I was successful. It would be like fishing. I might get a bite, I might not. Vespers might not even be the place anymore. It was a happening spot last time the krewes were out after a parade, but that stuff changes in a heartbeat. The cool club last weekend might be elbowed out of the way by a newer, hotter, trendier place this week. The waiting lines to get in would probably tell me all I needed to know.

I sat through the bumper-to-bumper traffic on Seventh Avenue, checking for the hot spots. Quite a few had people waiting to get in. Vespers looked packed. Good. I could just go park and start fishing.

Waiting in line sucks, but waiting in line to get into a bar sucks big time. My wife would kill me if she knew, but I'm happy to slip a doorman some cash to avoid an hour-long wait and sore ankles. I was wearing jeans but I had an expensive suit coat with me. That and a few bucks might be enough to jump in front of the whole line.

I parked and checked my look in a dark window of an empty warehouse. Pressed dress shirt, decent jeans, nice jacket. It was okay. I shouldn't have shaved—the scruffy look is in right now—but I put enough gel in my hair enough to pass as a guy with some money to spend. There's a window for this type of thing. At 8 P. M. I could get in anywhere because the night life hadn't started yet. At 11 P. M. I couldn't get in anywhere because I wasn't young and hip enough. I was cutting it close but I figured the cash would make up the difference.

Needing a hit my first time at bat, I palmed a fifty-dollar bill and strolled up to the Vesper's doorman, clapping him on the shoulder. "What's the wait tonight, my friend?"

He was a big guy, like all bouncers. He said nothing, just nodded at the hundred or so people waiting in line.

"Well, I'm a friend of Mr. Grant." I extended my hand. "Maybe you know him?"

He shook my hand and ignored my cash. "Sorry, my man. Mr. Grant isn't working here tonight. Maybe you know some of his other friends."

Shit.

"I know his twin brother," I said.

Big smile. "Welcome aboard, captain." He opened the rope line for me. A hundred bucks wasn't just twice what I wanted to spend to get in, it was about a hundred times that.

Oh, well, I was in. Next, I needed to find a spot at the bar. I wasn't going to be drinking or dancing, I needed to be there for a while before the lights came on and they sent everybody home. That was my play. That, and to not be too square, or for them to think I was a cop. For that, I intended to stay cool, watch the crowd dance, and not much else.

Once I wedged myself into a place at the bar, my fifty bucks was greeted with a nod by the bartender.

"What can I get you?" His nametag said Mario.

"I'm kinda hanging out for a while, Mario."

"You wanna run a tab?"

I shook my head. "I need to rent this seat for a few hours. Okay?"

Another nod.

In time, he'd ask for more, or ask what I was looking for. Bartenders were usually connected, so I'd wait for him to approach me. Until then, I just needed to hang out.

Around 1:30, things started to loosen up. Mario had gotten me three or four ice waters, and I gave him ten bucks every time he did, so he was happy. It was a message, not a tip. And the look on his face said he was getting curious.

But a seasoned bartender has seen it all. No doubt, he'd had his fair share of recently divorced guys coming in looking for companionship, but they were usually drunk or well on their way. Guys who want drugs look at the bathrooms or the parking lots. I don't know what cops do. Hopefully, they don't sit at the bar drinking ice water.

"Mario," I called to him. "I'm gonna hit the restroom."

He pointed. "At the end of the bar and to the right."

"You'll keep my seat open for me, right?" I was paying him pretty good. He'd see to it.

All that ice water had been building up, so I was glad to get rid of it. Also, I wanted to stretch my legs. Vesper's was hot and crowded, and the bathroom was no different.

As I was headed out the men's room door, a young lady headed in. "Cover your eyes, fellas, I can't hold it anymore!" She hiked her red skirt up and jumped up on the sink. "The line for the ladies' room was *too* long!"

Enough guys were watching that she had to remind them not to. It was a gutsy move for a pretty girl, and she was drunk enough to pull it off. The guys didn't care. That was more than most of them would see tonight. But I'm a dad now, so I had to ensure something like a stupid gang rape didn't happen to her. I made eye contact, making sure she saw me looking at her eyes and nowhere else. She smiled. Then she hopped down and walked to the door, which I was still holding. I opened it for her.

She flipped her platinum locks as she passed, turned to me and said, "Nice to see there are still some gentlemen left in the world." Then she winked and disappeared into the crowd.

I started back to the bar when a man in a loud suit stopped me. He looked just like I expected. Attention-getting suit, attention-getting attitude.

The stranger lifted his head and peered down his nose at me. "Hey, my man. Mario at the bar says you his boy and you a man in need."

"Well," I said. "Mario's a good guy."

"Mario's the best, man." The tipster cocked his head. "But he didn't say what you were in need *of*."

Now I smiled. "Lack of curiosity has always been his strong suit." I glanced around the crowded bar. "Where can we talk?"

He nodded at the restroom. "Step into my office."

"Not that kind of talk. I have everything I need in that area. What I need is some information. A referral."

The tipster narrowed his eyes. "Somebody in trouble?"

"Yeah, I think maybe I am." I leaned toward him. "You know a mambo?"

I leaned back to watch his eyes. It sounds racist, but it's not. He just stared right back at me. The smile was gone.

"Hey, y'all ain't some fuckaround tourist. What you want with that stuff?"

I tried to maintain an even tone. "Like I said, I think I might be in trouble."

"I don't deal that stuff." He shook his head. "That black magic shit."

I rolled the dice. "But you know someone who does."

He stared at me for a long moment. "Meet me out back in five minutes."

I watched him go, then I turned and went back to the bar. Mario had been keeping my seat clear. He smiled when I approached.

"I met your friend," I said. "He asked me to meet him out back in five."

Mario nodded.

"I'm not walking into a knife or anything, am I Mario?"

He pulled out a rag and wiped down the area in front of me, sliding a new bar napkin under my glass. "Jason's cool. Don't worry."

"Okay." I pulled out a hundred-dollar bill and ripped it in two. Mario's eyes widened. I handed half of the torn bill to him. "You get the other half when I come back in, or you check on me in ten minutes. Deal?"

He shoved the bill in his pocket. "Don't worry, I'm telling you. It's cool."

Fair enough.

"Which way is the back door?" I asked.

Mario pointed.

I went over, took a deep breath, and stepped through it.

Chapter 32

I crept into the alley behind Vespers, holding my breath and glancing around. Big shadows from the rooftops let one side of the alley remain dark despite the overhead lights. I relaxed a little. The city had done a good job of keeping Ybor safe and friendly, hoping to draw the money-spending crowds. Places that would have been dark and foreboding someplace else were decently lit here.

The street lights cast a bronze glow over the asphalt and backsides of the bars and restaurants. To the right, a man and woman chatted—he sounded drunk and she sounded like a prostitute, but they were too far away to tell for sure. Down the other way, a couple of guys were smoking next to a stack of empty wooden pallets. The occasional gust of wind let me know it wasn't all tobacco.

A few parked cars and a lot of dumpsters, otherwise the alley was empty. I folded and unfolded my hands, stepping a few feet in every direction but not straying too far from Vespers' back door. The five minutes came and went, but I couldn't necessarily expect punctuality from a guy who kept his office in a men's room.

A few shadows appeared at the far end of the alley. There were three of them, a big guy, a bigger guy, and a normal sized guy.

My pulse throbbed. They were headed my way.

I swallowed hard, glancing down the other side of the alley to make sure I didn't find myself surrounded. The smokers kept smoking, conversing among themselves and ignoring the rest of the world. Nothing else had changed in that direction. Good. I could escape that way if I had to. Despite what Mario had said, I wasn't convinced that they weren't going to rob me. My stomach tightening, I tried to maintain my breathing as the three men approached.

Their footsteps clopped and crackled on the pavement. I made out the loud jacket—the tipster was with them. The fear gripping my stomach eased down a notch. I had Mario's name, and Mario knew the tipster, so if anything happened, there were links in the chain.

When they got close enough, I stepped further into the light.

The biggest one faced me. "You Mario's friend?"

I nodded. The overhead lights behind them kept their faces in the shadows.

"What you want, sniffing around down here looking for stuff that don't belong to you?" His tone was terse. Angry. My stomach notched up again.

"I asked your man here for help." My heart was pounding but I forced myself to maintain an even tone. "I thought he could find me some."

He remained unmoving, a large black shadow with few identifiable features. "What kind of help?"

I pursed my lips. "That's complicated."

Folding his arms across his big chest, he eyed the tipster.

The tipster nodded.

"Five hundred," the massive shadow said. The breath went out of me. If they were scammers, was I supposed to give up my cash and get introduced to, what, some friend of theirs who'd pretend to be a fortune teller? No way. But if I didn't give them money, the three of them might beat me up and take it anyway.

I gazed at Vespers' rear door. It seemed very far away now. The drunk guy and the prostitute had left the alley. So had the smokers.

It was just me now, alone with the three strangers.

The uneasy feeling grew in my gut. I swallowed and braced myself. "No. You get your end after I—"

"Who are you!" His voice was like a gunshot. "To walk around here asking for that!" He stepped toward me and put his finger into my chest. "What do you want?"

Adrenaline streamed through my veins like a low fire. I had no other choice but to act angry and try to stand my ground. Otherwise it might get ugly. Images of getting beaten to a pulp and robbed flashed through my mind.

I gritted my teeth. "I told you want I want."

I stared right at him, face to face. I said it all with my eyes, but forced myself to focus on an attitude. If you hit me, I'm going to get hit. Maybe I'll hit back, maybe I won't. But what I'm not going to do is turn tail and run.

I'm going to stand here, alone and shaking, but you're not going to back me down.

Not today.

"I asked for help." I let the words hang there, wanting them to be enough on their own. He was sizing me up. I couldn't think about that. Not right now.

Everything inside me wanted to run, but something held my feet in place.

The wind tossed around some fast food wrappers and pushed an empty beer bottle from its resting place under a dumpster. The soft clinking of glass on asphalt came to us, the only other sound in the deserted alley.

"Okay," Big Man said. "Let's go." He turned and gestured down the alley. "That way."

A wave of relief washed over me. There wouldn't be a fight. Good.

I walked in front of them, my hands in my pockets. Sticking to "help" seemed to matter. It was making the difference. Ybor frowned on con artists ripping off tourists, but thieves might not care about that. If there really was a mambo, and she was legit in any sense, this might all have been to avoid a hassle from the city, nothing more.

We went a few blocks down, and a few blocks over, past the commercial side of Ybor and into the seedier, less friendly neighborhood next door. Small houses in need of paint jobs and yard work were surrounded by broken chain link fences.

The lump in my gut returned. They were luring me away from the safety of the well-lit streets up by the bars. I took deep breaths—trying not to appear to do so—to calm myself, but the farther I walked, the more I wondered if I was about to get jumped. How stupid was I being, walking around this part of town with two strangers and a pocket full of cash? When we got far enough away, we might walk around a corner and I'd get hit in the head and robbed. Or maybe they'd just demand my wallet. What was I gonna do against them? Big Man could take me down all by himself.

We were getting too far away. It didn't feel right. My breathing grew shallow as my heart pounded harder. I glanced around. Even the street lights down here seemed darker.

My pulse throbbed in my ears. Ahead, one house burned a dim yellow bug light over the porch.

This is it. This is where they grab me. We go inside and they take me apart.

I had no chance.

When we got close, Big Man spoke. "Here."

I stared up the dim front steps at the yellow door. Lights were on inside. The faint aroma of incense drifted down the steps to me.

Three concrete steps ended on a worn wood porch. Beyond that, the door.

I went up the steps and paused, not sure if I was supposed to knock, not sure if a voodoo priestess awaited me on the other side—or a violent beating.

The door opened.

Another large man filled the door frame. He didn't say anything, he just stepped back.

My guess was, the person inside didn't want anyone thinking they weren't well protected. Point taken.

Standing in the dim light, I glanced around the small living room. Beads on stringers, and a lot of African themed artwork. In one corner stood a rack of candles, like at Our Lady of Mercy.

I don't think I was supposed to look around too much, because the big guy from the front door stepped in front of me. He looked me over, then peered over my shoulder at something.

I turned around to see the mambo. The voodoo priestess.

She was tall and thin, with long black hair and dozens of bracelets adorning her wrists. Her colorful dress hung on her slender figure like a sack. She wore too much makeup, a reflection of a woman who is either trying too hard or didn't have makeup skills.

But from looking at her, she seemed legit. Something about the way she carried herself around all these guys who were there to protect her. She was cool. Like she didn't really need their protection, she just liked how it looked.

"Come." Her voice was laced with an accent from the islands. Somewhere in the Caribbean, maybe Jamaica. She walked on ahead.

I entered a small room with a tiny round table in the middle, like what you'd see in those old séance movies with a medium and a crystal ball. Candles lit this room, housed on the shelves and tables that cluttered the walls. Dark glass jars and bottles filled every available space. A tray of incense embers glowed in the corner.

But the room itself was plain and brown and well-worn. Everything here was well-worn.

In that room, it was just us. Me and the priestess. She sat down and gestured at the other chair. "Sit."

The big guy stood outside near the room's entrance. I sat.

"I am Dahlia. My friends tell me you are looking for something." She spoke slowly and deliberately, each word filling the entire room. "What . . . are you looking for?"

I drew slow, even breaths to mask my nerves. "I'm looking for help." Trying to answer as slowly as she did, my words came out sounding quiet instead.

She smoothed the table cloth. It was colorful, like a silk scarf. "Why . . . do you need help?"

"Because things are happening that I can't explain."

"What sort of things?"

I cut to the chase. "Tragedies."

That didn't faze her. She nodded, staring at the table. "Did you bring money?"

It didn't seem like a good idea to lie. Most seers are pretty good at reading people. I figured she would know if I lied. "I did."

"Who do you need to protect? Not yourself. You came here in the middle of the night." She lifted her gaze to me. "That is not the act of a person who is afraid for themselves. A person like that would stay home."

"I want to protect my family," I said. "My wife and daughter."

"But you did not bring them."

"That's right."

Her voice fell to a whisper, a low hiss audible only to me. The wind grew outside, masking our conversation from anyone else. "Why . . . do you think I can help you?"

Again, I thought honesty was the best approach. "I'm not sure you can. I told your friends I needed help. They brought me to you."

"What kind of help do you think you need?"

"Any kind I can get." I spoke softly, the uneasiness in my gut settling. "Magic. Voodoo. Religious help of some sort." I offered these words with quiet reverence. Not everyone believes, and not everyone who believes cares to have it known. But those who practice in such trades have their reasons for body guards.

Dahlia stroked the colorful table cloth, as though reading its patterns for her next question.

"Magic . . . Voodoo . . . Religious help." She said my words back to me like they were part of a mantra. "Do you have the gift?" She lifted her eyes and peered into me, a piercing gaze that made my stomach tighten. "Do you see?"

I hesitated, uncertain of how to answer.

"Your wife? Your child? Do they see?"

I looked down. "I don't think so. No."

The wind picked up, tapping tree branches against a window somewhere.

"But you believe that I see, yes?" She drew my gaze off the table and back to her eyes.

"I don't know yet," I said. "Maybe. I respect the talents and gifts that any descendant of Marie Laveau might have."

She smiled, accepting my words as a compliment.

"I do see." She nodded. "Auras. Colors, around an animal's eyes, or a person's face." Dahlia's eyes flashed wide at that. "What do you know of this?"

I took a slow breath. "I've heard of it."

She wagged a finger at me. "No, no, no. If I am going to help you, then you must tell me the truth."

"Okay." I nodded. "I know a little. About auras."

"Do you see them?"

"I, um—not like . . ." I shifted on my chair. "Like you suggested."

She stood up and slowly walked around the room, circling me. "A voodoo priestess, a mambo, sees the aura. In people, in animals. It is always there if they have the gift."

Dahlia struck a match, and held it to a candle. "If others have the gift, the mambo can see it in them, too. If she can hold items of theirs, she would see it as well." She blew out the match. "Do you understand?"

I nodded.

"The gift is inherited. But there are those who refuse to understand that they have a gift. They deny it, and push it down. Then, it can die in them."

She continued around the room with the candle. Its flickering light threw dancing shadows on the walls. "But just as a child has to learn to speak, even though there is speaking all around them their whole lives, they still must learn to build the muscles for themselves. It is the same thing with the gift. Some can be learned, but you must be born with the ability."

Sitting down, the mambo placed the candle in the center of the table. The orange glow illuminated her face, seeming to darken everything else in the room.

She gazed at the flame. "And then you must be taught. And then you must do for yourself. A coach cannot make an athlete run, the athlete must do the running. But still the athlete needs a coach to show her what she cannot see for herself. How to improve, where her faults are."

Lifting her eyes to mine, she smiled. "And there are many things we cannot see for ourselves."

I sat, unmoving, taking it in.

"The gift is stronger in women anyway. That is how it has always been. A woman listens to her body more, and will allow it to grow. A man does not do this. The gift is stronger with women because they want to believe it more. A man may give it to his daughter without ever knowing that he did so."

She eyed the candle, focusing on it like the answers lay within the flame. "That is where I got my powers. But it was nurtured in me." She looked me up and down. "You are a writer?"

I nodded.

"Did you be born with a pen and start writing? Of course not. You were taught. And for many years, you were taught just the plain, the basics. Then one day you took it upon yourself—to make it more." She leaned forward. "Do you remember when you did that?"

I cleared my throat, confused at how this related to why I was here, but following where the priestess lead. "Probably high school."

"That was the start?"

"Well, the grade school paper, I guess. I was the editor. I pestered my teacher to make it happen, to have a school newspaper."

Her eyes watched mine.

I thought deeper, going back, like drifting downward into a well. "It was earlier, though. I always wrote comics and funny stories."

"Who were they for?"

"I made them for anybody, everybody. Probably I made them for myself."

"Who enjoyed them the most?"

"My brother," I said. "He loved them."

"Always?"

I rubbed my chin. "No, that was later when he was in high school. So I was in about eighth grade."

"Think," she commanded softly, her voice nearing a trance. "Who was your audience?"

"Well." I thought for a moment. "My mom, early on. She made sure I had pens and paper—that stuff was hard to come by for a kid, and I went through tons of it. Colored pencils, art class. She even sent me to typing lessons." I laughed. "That was a bust. Typing. Boy, I hated it."

"It was not organic," the mambo said. "The natural part, you supplied yourself—and your mother fostered it."

"I guess." I shrugged. "Maybe."

"She did!" Dahlia slammed her hand down on the table. "She saw the aura!"

The mambo glared at me, her chest heaving.

"Come on." I looked away. "That's a bit much to—"

"Because you refuse to believe!" She jumped up, gripping the table and sending her chair over backwards. "When the aura is there, a man tends to deny it, even to his closest friends. A woman embraces it and her friends may not understand, but there are always signs if you know what you are looking at!" She pointed at me. "You may not be the caretaker of this garden, but the garden exists!"

"This is crazy." I stood up and reached for my wallet. "I have to go. I'll pay you."

"Pay! There is no paying with money! What do you possess that I would want?" Her eyes bore into me, her breath coming in gasps.

Putting her hand to her forehead, Dahlia turned away. Lowering her head, she sighed. "When the time comes, you will offer your gift to me. You will know what you need to do. Do not disappoint or your mojo will be cursed."

I stood there, uncertain what to do. "You will want a favor?"

She nodded, her back to me.

"How will I get your gift to you?"

The big man walked in, as if on cue. He handed me a card. Scrawled on it was a name and a phone number.

I looked at the mambo. "The tipster?"

She nodded again.

It was over. I'd blown it. Whatever she was going to tell me, if anything, I missed my chance.

But I couldn't go back to my family with nothing.

"No." I elbowed my way past the big man and approached the mambo. "I want answers first."

Big Man didn't move.

I pursed my lip. "Let's stop playing games." I moved back to the table, pulling out my chair. "Come on. If you can help me, help me. What do you see? Look here. At me. What do you see when—"

She looked back with a stern face. "Sit."

The gusting wind rattled the glass again.

I lowered myself into the chair. If she was going to be of any help to me, now was the time. She had proven to be insightful, but she was being evasive. But if she knew something that would help us, I needed to hear her out.

She took her seat and closed her eyes, slowly lifting her hands to rest on the table top. She drew several deep breaths and turned her palms up.

I didn't know if I was supposed to put my hands on the table, or on hers, or what. I wasn't sure it mattered anymore.

"Ask me." She whispered. "What you want to know?"

The wind picked up again, rustling through the trees. Light gusts of rain batted along the roof.

I swallowed, trying to relax. "Do . . . you see an aura in me?'

She nodded.

"Do you believe I have the gift?"

Another nod.

"Can it also be something else?" I clutched the table. "Something other than a gift?"

She nodded again. "A gift is a tool. You can use it for good or for evil."

I hesitated, not sure how to ask the trickier questions. For the first time, I wasn't sure I really wanted the answers.

"Ask," she said. "Ask what you want to know." She opened her eyes and looked softly at me. "You have come all this way. Do not be afraid to find the truth."

I took a slow, deep breath, held it a moment, and let it out in a huff. It was time. "Is—is my daughter . . . cursed?"

The candle flame flickered once, then remained still.

A thin smile crept over the mambo's face, her eyes aglow in the warm orange light of the flame. "No, not yet."

My heart caught in my throat. I leaned forward. "Does she have an angel on her shoulder?"

"What happened, to bring you here?" Dahlia asked.

"I told you."

"You tell the wrong things. Tell me what happened . . ." She closed her eyes. "At the winery."

A wave of shock shot through me.

She kept her eyes on mine. "Do you now believe me?"

I swallowed, my heart pounding. "Yes."

"Then tell me. Tell me what you saw."

I forced myself to continue, barely able to speak. "There was a wreck . . ."

"No," she shook her head. "Open your eyes to not look outside, but inside. You understand this. You saw a blue color flash across the face of a man at the park, as a child. Use that sight."

My mouth fell open, my mind reeling. *How could she know that?* Jimmy, the smash car, the crazy man. Her eyes seemed to peer right into me, into the things I'd hidden, like it was all there and only she could read it. My thoughts were a blur. I was falling down the well.

Her eyes flared. "And you have seen others."

The storm gathered life outside. Distant thunder rumbled and rolled.

Dahlia's voice was a whisper. "Tell me what you saw in the winery."

I squeezed my eyes shut, gasping. "I don't know. Nothing."

"Think," she gently commanded. "Remember."

"My daughter. She wanted to look at t-shirts."

"Go on. What else?"

"She—she was fussy."

"Why?"

"She was hungry."

"Was she?" Dahlia coaxed me, pulling the words out of me. "Think. *Remember . . .*"

"She . . ."

"Yes?"

I gasped, squeezing my eyes shut. "She saw the truck driver. He almost ran us over with his cart in the lobby. He wasn't paying attention."

"And?"

"And she had a fit. She started yelling about eating."

"Eating?" Dahlia's voice rose. "You must look. You must see."

Sweat broke out on my forehead. My shaking hands grabbing the table, I lowered my head. The words were coming now, whether I wanted them to or not, struggling to free themselves from me. "Um, Sophie, my daughter, she . . ."

"Go on. It is there."

"She wanted to have a picnic in the parking lot. But she didn't want to have Jello. But we didn't have Jello with us anyway. It was a crazy thing to say."

"What *exactly* did she say?" Dahlia's voice grew firm.

"She said, 'No blue Jello!' She freaked out."

"When?"

"Right after we almost got hit by the old guy wheeling the cases of wine through the tasting room." I said. "The truck driver."

"She saw him?"

"Yes."

"And then she said . . ."

I was gasping, rushing, the words spilling from me. "She saw him and then she said she *didn't* want to go outside, that the man had blue Jello on his face, in his eyes. She was ranting. She was crazy. I've never seen anything like it."

"And then?"

"And then I distracted her. I showed her the t-shirts. The funny ones. I read them to her until she calmed down."

Lightning cracked outside. The booming roar of thunder cascaded through the room.

Dahlia urged me on. "How long did that take?"

"A minute or two . . ."

"A minute or two," she echoed. "And then?"

"And then we headed out to the parking lot." I said. "That's when the wreck happened."

"Your daughter delayed you long enough for you both to be safe."

"Yes." I nodded, gasping, my insides turning over and over. I was lost, reeling. I laid my head on the table and opened my eyes to the priestess.

Her face was red in the light of the candle. The room around us had faded to black.

"That happened by chance, you think, but you are wrong." Dahlia's eyes went wide. "She sees! She saw him, like you saw, but she saw it first, and she made you stop!"

The priestess stood up, the force of her revelation lifting her. "That is why the dark angels want her! *Because she sees them.*"

I cowered against the blinding white light of the revelation. I wanted it to not be true.

I wanted my daughter to be safe.

And she was not.

The priestess pointed a long finger at me. "She has not yet learned from you how to ignore these things, and push them down, and pretend they do not happen, until the gift is finally lost."

Lightning cracked outside, lighting up the room and splashing Dahlia's face white with light. "She can see them."

It was all coming at me too fast. I was lost. Powerless.

But I knew. Inside, I knew Dahlia was right.

She narrowed her eyes. "You asked if your daughter has an angel on her shoulder."

I wiped my eyes and looked up at her. It was all I could do. The priestess wasn't really asking questions anymore.

"Everyone has angels on their shoulder." She towered over me. "Angel of light, angel of darkness. Good and bad. You choose to let them guide you or choose to push it down and ignore what you should know. Your family, your upbringing, that tells you what you believe. To some, there are many angels with us all the time. This is how I believe. To others, there is one that maybe watches over a child, or helps the sick."

Her voice grew quieter, almost inaudible. "But in the end, every time a choice comes, you make the decision, the good angel or the bad angel. In the end, if you make enough bad choices, the bad angel is all that is left."

I stared at the woman, my mind unable to fathom it all. Thunder rumbled as the rain streamed down the windows.

Dahlia took a deep breath. "Have you ever met someone where that happened?"

I forced myself up, propping my elbows on the table and rubbing my brow. "I think maybe I have."

"Then you know," she said. "That's when the dark angels have been playing with them—but dark angels don't play. When you meet that person down the road of life, they are not who they were at the beginning of the road. Young in life, they had not yet allowed the dark angels to win. Then, later on, they are not the same."

She stepped to a shelf of bottles and dried plants, leaning on it like she would fall down if it weren't there. "You don't have to go too far down the wrong path before it becomes impossible to get back to the right path."

"Impossible?" I asked.

Her shoulders slumped, her head hanging low. "For those who choose wrongly, it becomes a habit, then it becomes a way of life. Impossible. Yes, impossible."

"That seems a bit harsh."

She screamed, grabbing the table and heaving it. The colored scarf sailed through the air as the table crashed into a shelf, sending glass containers to the floor. "Do not mock the truth! Stop denying your aura. This is what make your inside feel sick when you see the policeman at the winery! Taggart."

I gasped. "Taggart! How—"

"You want to puke the whole time you are talking to that policeman. Because inside you feel his corruption, his evil. You know he will make things go away for the old man."

My head was spinning. "How . . . how can you know this?"

"Same as with the man you see in your head at the church," she roared. "And when you confront with the animal on the tree stump as a child. Always you make your body fight against itself. Against your gift. Stop making yourself not see."

I sat there, flinching and exposed in the lone chair, holding my shaking hands up in front of me. Dahlia saw it all, everything inside me.

"Life and death are real. Decisions are real." She waved her hands, her bracelets and bangles clashing together. "This is what a thousand generations of seeing have taught us. You must see. Recognize these things and understand them."

The rain thumped the old roof in a steady, rhythmic hum.

"Learn this." Dahlia rasped, her eyes narrowing. "Do not be a fool when the moment requires you to be something else."

Chapter 33

"Would you kill Hitler?" Jimmy stood with a hand on the tree trunk and the other on a high branch, balancing on a thick limb. When he moved around, it sent little shock waves out to where I sat, bouncing me and making my stomach cringe.

From our perch in the big oak tree, the crow's nest, I pretended to ignore his request to start the game. We may have only been twenty feet up, but it always seemed a lot higher. I needed to focus or I'd fall and break my arm the way he did last year. Sitting with my hands on either side of me holding the limb wasn't the best idea, but the other branches were a little too far away to reach easily.

Smiling, Jimmy bent his knees and jostled the branch on purpose. I grasped, flailing at twigs and leaves to keep my balance. Once re-secured, I scowled and picked bits of bark from my palms. Jimmy was my best friend, but he was a real jerk sometimes. And he was a better climber than me even if he did break his arm.

The insides of my legs were red and scraped, bleeding in spots from hugging the tree too tightly while I climbed. Jimmy didn't get a scratch in his ascent to the crow's nest. I smacked my stinging hands and licked a finger, running it over the little cuts on my thighs. I should have worn pants, but it was too hot out.

Not up in the tree, though. Up there, cool breezes washed through like air conditioning.

"Come on, let's play," Jimmy said.

It was a dumb game, but we thought we were smart for inventing it. I'm not even sure we did invent it. Who can remember after all that time has passed?

But I know after that day, we never played it again.

From the crow's nest, most of my childhood play area was visible. I gazed over at the sand box where we had countless G. I. Joe battles, the creek that hosted our model boat races, the big back yards where we played "army." We were as likely to play Kick The Can or flashlight tag or Hide and Seek as we were to ride bikes or go hiking.

Or climb the biggest tree in the yard and play our game.

"Okay, so even if you were sure you'd get caught, you'd still kill Hitler, right?" Jimmy started off solid.

"Right," I said. "No question."

"Would you ever kill a person for a dumb reason?"

"I oughta kill you for telling me it was too hot to wear pants today. Now my legs are all torn up."

"You wouldn't kill the President for a million dollars, though, would you?" It was more of a taunt than a question. I wasn't sure why he asked it, and there was an odd tone to his voice. "You couldn't do that."

I looked out over the creek to the hillside. It sloped down to the water, but today there was mostly puddles. It hadn't rained in a while. "For a million dollars, I bet I could."

"No, you couldn't." Jimmy repositioning himself to a higher branch. I held on tight as twigs dropped past me. "Not you. Never in a million years."

"Why not me?" I asked.

"Because you couldn't kill anybody." It wasn't playful banter. He was driving at something.

He climbed higher.

"Why not?" I blinked as fragments of bark and twigs fell on me. He answered, but I didn't hear him because I was focused on keeping tree crap out of my mouth.

"What did you say?" I held up my hand to keep the light and falling debris out of my eyes. He was right above me. He could have spit on me just by opening his mouth, and the look on his face made me think he wanted to. My cheeks got hot. I might have expected a crappy stunt like that from my brother or his, but friends or not, if he spit on me, I was going to climb up that tree and knock him out of it.

The wind blew through his hair as he looked away, squinting in the bright sunlight. "Kill somebody? You couldn't do it. Not you." His words were plain, unemotional, matter of fact. "You couldn't even kill that squirrel that one time when you took your brother's pump BB gun."

That stung. "I—Yes, I could!" My cheeks burned. I didn't know he knew about the squirrel. "I shot it, didn't I?"

"Did you?"

I looked away. "This is a dumb game."

"Did you shoot it? Did you kill that squirrel?" Jimmy stood up on his branch, out of reach.

I got up, too. To climb down.

Hugging the tree trunk, I reached out with my foot to step down to the next branch. It was farther than I thought. I moved too fast and lost my balance, dropping instead of stepping. My stomach jolted with adrenaline and fear. For a moment, I thought I'd fall. I clawed at the tree trunk, barely grabbing it, and slamming my face and chest into the hard, rough bark.

The force from my awkward stumble sent a shiver up the tree, bouncing Jimmy.

He swayed and grabbed some tree limbs to keep his balance, glaring at me like I'd done it on purpose.

I quickly moved my eyes away so he wouldn't see me looking, focusing on anything that wasn't him, and grabbed the next branch. Getting down took longer than I wanted and ripped up my hands and legs good, but I wasn't staying.

I brushed the pieces of tree bark off my forearms and face, not looking up, trying to not listen to his taunts.

My sights fell on the grassy hillside where our backyards sloped down to the creek. I spied the tall, thin tree stump that had broken off in a storm.

The one where I had once coaxed a squirrel to sit for me.

I turned and stormed off to my house, my whole head hot and throbbing, a chant of "Did you kill that squirrel? Did you?" showering down on me from the tree top.

Halfway through the yard, I stopped. "That's a dumb game and you're dumbass!"

"Screw you!" Jimmy shouted at me. "Coward!"

"Screw you! I don't have to kill stuff to enjoy it. Not like you, you stinking redneck!"

Jimmy exploded. "You didn't shoot it because you were too afraid!" His face was red with rage. "That makes you a damn coward!"

"Shut up!" I screamed back. "I'm glad you guys are moving away!" I ran for the back door. I didn't want him to see me cry. I was too old for that.

The words, clogging in my throat as tears welled in my eyes, didn't deliver the forcefulness I wanted, but they delivered the impact. They shot past the tree and across the creek, dissipating over the farmer's field.

The argument was over.

Maybe it was just how young boys dealt with their emotions. Jimmy found out that his family was moving. It was only about ten miles away, but to two kids on bicycles, they may as well have been moving across the country. We wouldn't be next door neighbors anymore. We would eventually stop being friends. Lashing out might have been our way of saying we'd miss each other.

But I was still mad. Jimmy could sit in that stupid tree all day if he wanted to, I didn't care. His stupid legs never got tired of the bark digging into them anyway, so let him. Or he could go wander through the stupid woods, like always. Stupid jerk.

At the back door, I paused. Busying myself with some of my dad's charcoal grill tools that needed my immediate attention, I faced the house and wiped any evidence of crying from my face. In the reflection of the downstairs windows, I saw Jimmy climb down from the tree and disappear.

When I was sure he was gone, I put down the grill scraper and went back.

It was halfway down the hillside, and only part of it remained, but the stump was still there. Lightning had probably been responsible for breaking it off in the first place, and at such an unusual height. From where I stood above it on the grass, it stuck up enough from the slope to almost be at eye level. When the squirrel had stood there that day, on the little flat part, he seemed to look me right in the eye.

He was amazing. Big eyes, a long fuzzy tail, and a beautiful gray-brown coat covering his fat little belly. He'd had a good summer eating acorns from our oak tree. He sat tall on the stump, his acorn in his hands, as he gnawed it, just like on TV.

I always had a good way with animals. I could approach any animal—any animal at all—and if I did it right, they would sit there and let me approach. I did it slowly, with one thought foremost in my head. That I was a friend.

It's okay. I'm not going to hurt you.

It helped to even say it out loud, in soothing tones, so the rabbit or deer would be aware I was making my presence known to them. Predators would never do that. By concentrating and focusing and almost mentally directing my thoughts to them, they could understand I was not a threat. They could feel it.

It was an amazing trick, but it was something that I rarely shared with anybody.

Once, while on vacation with my wife in the Canadian Rockies, we spied a distant moose at dusk across Waterfowl Lake. The moose had her baby with her. I spoke to them, calmly and quietly, across the water. They came all the way down to where we were, a place where the cold lake was shallow enough for them to cross. Then, the moose and her baby came over to investigate us before moving on into the dark woods.

Mallory was dumbfounded.

I completely expected it. I just kept cooing, "It's okay, it's okay." I never doubted they would come.

I guess like all mothers, the moose wanted to show off her baby.

I found out later that moose are very protective of their babies, and that such a stunt was insanely dangerous. We could have been seriously hurt, maybe killed.

It never occurred to me. It never seemed that way, not for an instant. Not to me.

I think that's why the squirrel sat there watching me. I had taken my brother's pump action BB gun rifle, which Jimmy had previously assured me would be enough to do the job. I couldn't risk taking my dad's real gun, after all. I wasn't crazy.

Maybe the squirrel was deceived by my demeanor. I spoke to him in the low soothing tones that always worked, gently moving closer as I did. Maybe he thought if he didn't move, I'd lose him in the background brush. Maybe he was scared.

I placed the stock on my thigh and grabbed the lever pump on the barrel. Twenty or more snaps of the metal pump clattered over the quiet hillside.

My pulse raced as I raised the rifle and took steady aim, lining up the squirrel between the cross hairs of the scope. I took a full breath like I had been shown, holding the heavy gun as still as best as I could. I pressed the stock into my shoulder and balanced the barrel with my hand. Letting my breath release slowly, I eased my finger onto the cold, metal trigger. I closed one eye, being careful to keep the target in the crosshairs, and squeezed.

The shot went off with a crack. The squirrel flinched but stayed on the stump. His eyes never left mine. Even if the BB didn't kill him, it had to sting like hell. Still, he just stood there, staring at me. I felt a momentary letdown, like I had failed in my stupid hunt. His gaze never wavered, seeming almost defiant.

I felt angry. And embarrassed. My cheeks burned.

With slow precision, so as not to frighten him, I pumped the rifle again, but always maintaining eye contact. This time, I did twice the pumps I'd done before.

He sat there, testing me, holding his big furry tail up behind himself. He could have run, but he didn't. He was waiting, taunting me. Stubborn.

I leveled the gun and held my breath, firing a second shot.

He twitched again. I know I hit him. I was a good target shooter. I know he was feeling the impact of the pellets. I know he had to feel the stinging pain.

But, he didn't move. He just sat there.

God damned squirrel. What's the matter with him?

Sweat formed on my face and neck. My heart pounded, making my anger and embarrassment grow. I had already committed the childhood crime of sneaking the BB gun out of my brother's room without permission and deciding to kill an innocent animal. I might as well go all the way. The nuns would say this was a sin, to kill for no reason. I knew that. But I had to finish what I started.

Sweat dripped off me as I pumped the gun again, compressing the firing chamber with each metal slap of the barrel hinge. It got harder with each pump, reaching maximum pressure. I nodded, catching my breath. I would have my trophy.

As I tried to force the lever down one last time, the stock slipped on my thigh. The barrel hinge went sideways, snapping shut on my finger.

"Damn it!" My finger bled from the tiny skin flap hanging off it. I glared at the squirrel. He still sat there. He was either stubborn or terrified, but he was still right there.

The rifle hissed, losing its pressure. I was taking too long. I wiped my temple with my shoulder and grabbed the barrel hinge, heaving it open and slamming it down. After a few pumps, the hinge went sideways, sliding off my leg and twisting my fingers.

I lifted the rifle and threw it to the ground, the metal clasp banging open in the grass.

The squirrel stared at me.

I ran at him, arms flailing. "Yaaaaahhh!"

A few feet down the hill, I stopped, exhausted.

He didn't move.

I stood there, gasping, shaking my head. I had messed up the rifle and my hand, and I still hadn't even killed the stupid squirrel. I took a step backwards up the hill, but I slipped on the leaves and fell, landing on my butt.

I dropped back on the grass and squeezed my eyes shut, my chest heaving up and down. "I quit. You win." My finger throbbed. My head ached. My butt hurt. It was too much.

I swallowed and shook my head. "I can't do it."

An empty feeling welled inside me, aching with a deep, hollow blackness. I rolled onto my side and looked at the vacant stump through watery eyes, choking on my words. "Forgive me."

If Jimmy had seen any of that, it probably would have sickened him. I hated to think about him knowing. He was a better shot than me, and a better hunter, but watching his friend fall down and cry over a squirrel, that was something he couldn't have understood.

This is what make your inside feel sick when you see the policeman at the winery! Same as with the man you see in your head at the church, and when you confront with the animal.

Confront with the animal. The mambo had nailed it.

After the fight in the tree, Jimmy's attitude toward me changed. We weren't as close as we used to be.

A few weeks later, they moved. When we ended up being down such different paths later in life, we'd never know that the first steps were taken that day.

When I walked back from the creek, I should have hidden the gun so my mom couldn't see me with it, but I didn't care. I had violated a trust, and I had misused a gift. But to me, at that age, it was just supposed to be a trick. A game.

It didn't feel like a game anymore, though. The scolding I got from my mom for taking my brother's gun—even if it was only a pump action BB gun—fell on deaf ears. All I could think about was an innocent squirrel down by the creek, standing there, shot after shot, not moving away.

That was the worst part. Worse than any scolding or punishment. All because I wanted to prove something.

I drove up the driveway, gazing at my Tampa home and its large, protective oaks in the headlights. The trees swayed and danced in the strong, rushing winds. Patches of Spanish moss clung to bending limbs or dropped in clumps into the yard.

"I'm glad you guys are moving away!"

I pulled into the garage. My dry, tired eyes wanted to close, and the couch was the closest soft spot. Jimmy hadn't been a thought in my mind for a long time, but now the echoes from the crow's nest rang in my ears.

Chapter 34

I woke up when Sparkles jumped into my lap. I had a few minutes before Mallory came downstairs—a few minutes to decide what to tell her about Tyree or the mambo. Everything? Nothing?

I had to tell her something eventually.

Maybe it was time for her to meet Tyree for herself. Then, depending on how that went, we could go meet Dahlia together in Ybor City . . .

That actually seemed like a good idea. I peered at the clock. It wasn't 7 A. M. yet, but I wasn't sure what kind of hours a guy like Tyree kept, anyway.

I clicked on the TV to get an update on the hurricane. From the constant noise of the wind and rain outside, it had gotten worse, but I wanted to see the storm's projected track. For days, the meteorologists had been going back and forth as to whether it was coming to Tampa or not. They'd have to make the call pretty soon, and there would probably be an hourly update on the news.

Sparkles nudged me.

"Okay, let's go outside." I stretched and stood up. He bounded off the couch and ran to the door, wagging his tail. I followed.

The wind yanked the doorknob out of my hand and thrust open the door. Sparkles scurried backwards. The steady rush of the pre-hurricane winds had arrived. Strong, noisy, and unrelenting.

Sparkles didn't seem to want to go out now, but he couldn't hold it until the storm passed. That could be days.

I tried again. "Come on, big fella."

I heaved the door into the howling wind. Sparkles crouched and tucked his tail beneath him, slinking out.

With some effort, I got the door closed. The gusts pushed and pulled on me, nearly knocking me over. The main feature of the looming hurricane was the constant high wind, with its incessant hum.

Everyone has been in a storm. Everyone has heard the wind howl on a rainy night. What makes this stuff different is the continuity. It doesn't stop. It's like the sound you hear when you're out for a walk and a car is coming, but it never dissipates. It doesn't go away in the morning and it doesn't go away when the rain stops. It goes away a week later when the big dark clouds of the hurricane come and rip everything to shreds.

The yard was littered with limbs and leaves. One of the neighbor's trees had already broken off in the wind and lay over part of the road.

And in the tops of the trees, the nonstop noise of the wind.

The rain had been coming in bands, but soon it would be coming nonstop—and heavy. That was often the worst part of a hurricane. Not that you would get swept up like The Wizard Of Oz, although that can happen, but days and days of soaking the ground make it turn into a muddy soup. Then when the high force winds really hit, even the largest of trees would lose their grip and fall right over. That had happened to us the last time a hurricane came through. The day after, it looked like we'd been battered by a series of tornadoes.

And the strangest part of the hurricane, aside from watching day and night as it crept closer and closer, was the eye. After causing tornadoes all over as the hurricane worked its way across the state, when the eye of the storm crossed over you, the wind and rain stopped. Not always, but usually. That made the phenomenon all the more eerie.

Afterwards—subsequent to mowing the lawn and picking up the big limbs—no one could tell that a hurricane been there. Not at our house, anyway. Some friends of ours weren't so lucky.

Sparkles was crouched by the door, ready to go back in. All this action was too much for him.

I let us both back in, wiping the rain off my arms. "Don't worry, pal. All the proper preparations happened months ago."

By now the forecasters would have a fairly good idea of where the storm was going and when it would get there. If they predicted it would hit Miami tomorrow morning and Tampa the following afternoon, it would. When things were this close, the forecasters were usually right.

And that was the mixed blessing. Because if they had just said *here it comes, everybody get out*, that might actually work. Instead, a week out they'd show a cone. It could go to Jacksonville in the north of Florida or it could go to Miami in the south. If enough people in Miami and the Keys weren't convinced it'd likely head their way, they wouldn't start preparing. Then, if the storm changed paths, they'd get trapped. Five million people around the greater Miami area couldn't all get on I-95 at the same time, and even if they could, most wouldn't have filled up their cars enough to get to safety. There would be huge lines at every gas station between Key West and the Georgia state line.

Then, the power would go out—as the winds in front of the hurricane knocked down power poles—and the folks in line for gas wouldn't get any.

The motorists, now hunkered down in their cars, would face the wrath of the 100 mile per hour winds and rain as they sat like ducks on the side of the road having debris heaved at them like rockets. Tree limbs become missiles. Roadside gravel becomes machine gun fire. And all the while, the constant drone of the howling wind.

Others geniuses would decide to wait out the storm in their houses. They might end up flooded, stranded on their rooftops awaiting rescue. And almost none of them would have enough food and clean water for any of it.

So, when a prior hurricane made us sit for three days in the brutal heat without power or cell phones, Mallory and I made up our minds to get a generator and some extra gas cans. A few sweat soaked days of muggy heat and humidity will do that to you. Inside, the house was hot and moist. There were no lights, but there was no air conditioning or fans, either. It was like standing in the bathroom while somebody took a shower. For days.

Outside, it was raining and wet, and the mosquitoes were everywhere. Mud got all over the place from all the rain, and nothing got dry. We couldn't sleep because we were too hot, and we couldn't stay awake because we were too exhausted. It was the very definition of miserable—and tempers flare quickly under such conditions, even when you're wiped out.

You'll survive, but you won't be very happy.

After three days of that, the power at a friend's house came back on. It took a few more days for the electric crews to get to us, but since our friends had power, they lent us their generator.

Electricity. Our frozen food would be saved, and we could run a fan and our portable camping TV. We could have a cold drink.

But the best—the absolute best—was the A/C. I took an old window air conditioning unit out of the garage and stuck it in our bedroom window. That night, after sweating for most of a week on the couches downstairs, the two of us slept in our bed, in chilly air-conditioned comfort. The bedroom air was cool and dry, and the mattress felt like a cloud. Like giving a man who'd just walked out of the desert an ice cream come. It was heaven.

From then on, we kept three days of canned food and water for everyone in the house, including Sparkles, and bought a small generator. With our gas grill and three propane tanks, and smaller stuff, like flashlights, batteries and candles, we were ready for whatever nature threw at us from then on.

We could also be mobile and self-sufficient, if we needed to evacuate.

As I grabbed a dish towel to dry Sparkles off, the morning TV news anchors prattled on about pressure systems and fronts.

All I saw was the big cone of the hurricane projected path. It swallowed Tampa in its center.

It was coming for us or it would pass very close by. Either way, it was time to make some decisions.

Chapter 35

"Have you lost your mind?!"

Mallory stood in the middle of the kitchen, her hands on her hips. You could say she was somewhat resistant to the suggestion of leaving our home in the middle of a hurricane.

"It's a good idea." I said, rubbing my eyes. "We can get on the road before everybody else, go to Atlanta, and rest easy. We can ride it out from a nice safe hotel room in Georgia."

"With all we—" She turned and grabbed the remote, turning up the volume on Sophie's cartoon and obscuring our conversation. "With everything that's been happening to us, you want us to drive through a hurricane and expose ourselves that way?"

"No. We have a few days before the hurricane gets here, so we evacuate early—before everybody else in Tampa gets the same idea."

"But the governor hasn't announced any evacuations yet." Mallory put a hand to her forehead. "Voluntary things on the coast."

"And he may not order mandatory evacuations. If he doesn't, we'll be holed up in Atlanta in a nice hotel eating room service for no reason. But." I took a deep breath and looked into her eyes. "If he says boo, three million people around the Tampa Bay area are gonna hit the highway at the same time. They'll start wrecking into each other in the rain and high winds."

I watched her expression. She knew that part was true.

"They'll clog any northbound road until everything is bumper to bumper, and then that's where we'll be—stuck on an interstate that's not moving, while who knows what comes for us."

Mallory shook her head. "Which is why we should stay. We have our generator, and you filled all the gas cans, right?"

"Yes, but—"

"And I filled the freezer. We have what we need to ride this out, in a house that was built to do just that."

She was right. We built our house after hurricane Andrew, under the latest hurricane construction codes.

I leaned on the counter, exhausted. "Honey, you are 100% right about all of that."

Her mouth fell open. "Then why . . . "

I peered at Sophie. She was wholly engaged in her cartoon. "Because of that." I nodded at our daughter. "Because of her. I think this is the latest part of the next tragedy."

"What, a hurricane?" Mallory was incredulous. "They're sending a hurricane after our daughter now?"

"No. I don't know. I don't know how any of this works." I sighed. "Probably not. But I didn't think they'd send an old man in his truck to mow us down in the parking lot of a winery, either."

"That's a pretty big difference. A man in a truck compared to a giant hurricane."

"It is." I slouched onto the counter and folded my arms. "So, if they didn't create the hurricane, maybe they nudged it in our direction."

"Or they want to scare us." She threw her hands up. "Make us run into the open where they can get us a little easier!"

"Okay!" I pounded the counter. "I get it." I glanced at Sophie and lowered my voice. "Maybe they want to attack under the distractions that the hurricane will cause. That might make things easier for them somehow." I looked down, shaking my head. “But they are coming for us one way or the other.”

Malory swallowed, kneading her hands together. “How do you know?”

“Do you think they’ve quit?” I glared at her. “Can you lay your head on your pillow every night for the rest of your life and assume it's all over? Because I sure don't. They're coming for us. It's only a matter of time.”

Mallory stood silent, the fear growing in her eyes.

“This hurricane,” I said, “It gives them one more opportunity to try.”

“Okay.” Her voice was a whisper. “So what do we do?”

I took a deep breath and hugged my wife, pulling her close. “We draw them out. We move before they’re ready. Maybe take the attack to them somehow.”

She turned and flung my hands off her. “This is crazy. You’re crazy!”

The phone rang. It was a good excuse for a temporary cease fire. Mallory answered it, then looked away and held it out for me. It was Tyree.

“I think we should get together, partner,” he said.

“I agree.” I stepped to the hallway. “Where are you? Back in Melbourne?”

“No, I stayed in town since our meeting. I’m in Tampa.”

“Then come to the house.” I eyed Mallory and gave him the address. His presence would help a lot—for Mallory and for me. Tyree agreed to come over by dinnertime. That was perfect. “We’ll see you then. And Tyree?”

“Yeah?”

“Pack a bag.”

“We going somewhere?” he asked.

“Maybe.”

I hung up the phone. Mallory had gone upstairs. I made sure Sophie had another cartoon to watch, then I went up to our bedroom. Mallory stood by the bed, her arms wrapped around herself, staring at the TV. Huge red bands swirled over Florida in the latest weather update.

"Tyree's coming over in a few hours," I said.

"Okay," she said, not taking her eyes off the screen.

"Look, let's get prepared, either way. Maybe we'll stay, maybe we'll leave. But let's pack up and get ready, whatever we decide. Okay?"

Her eyes remained fixed on the TV.

I sighed and turned, heading back downstairs. I had to put the propane tanks and gas cans in the back of my car and dig through our camping gear for our little propane stove. I paused at the bottom of the staircase, my hand on the banister, peeking into our bedroom.

Mallory pulled some clothes and a suitcase out of the closet.

I smiled and continued to the garage.

The rain came down in bands, whipping through the oaks with the rushing wind. Even in the garage, I managed to get pretty wet while packing the car. The low roar of the unstopping wind was an irritating reminder of the coming hurricane.

Hurricane winds are unlike any other sound a person will ever hear, and once they hear it, they'll never forget it. TV stations always describe things like a Kansas tornado as sounding like a train. It's like that when the hurricane is almost on top of you. But for days before that it's the nonstop winds. They never fade at night. They never go away during the day. They serve as a ghoulish reminder that death is coming.

Standing in my garage I could have sworn there was a long line of cars going down the street, the drone of many tires on asphalt making their way down our driveway—but there were no cars. It was just the wind, howling and battering its way through the tree tops, and it wouldn't go away until the hurricane passed.

I slammed the tailgate shut. All I had left to do was put in the suitcases. I secretly hoped Mallory might have them all packed when I went back inside.

A light flashed in my eyes. A brown sedan rolled up the driveway in the pouring rain. When it got closer, I could make out a face.

Tyree.

I glanced at the clock on the garage wall. Right on time.

Chapter 36

"**M**r. Tyree." Mallory extended her hand to our guest, but her rigid body indicated *welcome* wasn't really on her mind. "Nice to finally meet you."

"It's nice to meet you, too, ma'am." Tyree nodded, shaking her hand and stepping into the house. "And—"

"It's just 'Tyree,' honey." I said. "No 'mister.'"

A thin smile crept across her face. "Fine. Tyree. Will you be joining us for dinner?"

I put my arm around my wife. "Mallory's a heck of a cook."

Tyree grinned. "Sure. It would be my pleasure. We really should talk, though."

"After dinner." Mallory nodded over to where Sophie was playing. "When little ears will be asleep."

"Got it."

I hung his rain jacket on the banister and headed to the kitchen. "Sorry we had to bring you out on a night like this."

"Well, yeah, it's getting ugly out there. But I have my car, so I didn't get too wet. Now, if I had been on my hog . . ."

"Hog?" I pulled out a chair for myself. "You have a Harley?"

"Yeah." Tyree lowered himself into the seat across from me. "If I'd have been on that, well—let's just say it isn't exactly motorcycle weather out there."

"Softie." I leaned forward, resting my folded arms on the table. "I thought any real Harley rider wouldn't let a little thing like a hurricane stop him from a nice ride."

He and I laughed. Mallory handed me a bottle of wine and a corkscrew. I inserted the metal tip into the cork and went to work.

"Well, you're right," Tyree said, smiling. "The bike would do it. That thing has some awesome road traction, even in heavy rain."

"I knew a guy who had a little trailer and a matching rain suit." I popped the cork and handed the bottle back to my wife. "He could go out in the worst weather and never get wet."

"Oh, I have some of that stuff, but I prefer not taking those additional risks. You know, in an actual hurricane."

We laughed—again, just Tyree and me.

"I prefer not riding a motorcycle at all," Mallory said. "Harley Davidson or not, they aren't safe. And Harleys are so *loud*. Why is that?"

Tyree threw an arm over the back of the chair and faced her. "That's just how some of the more obnoxious riders like it."

"I suppose yours is a quiet one, then? Good." She handed each of us a glass of wine.

"Uh, mine? Well . . ."

I remembered Tyree said he didn't drink.

He kept the glass in his hand as he shrugged. "Mine is pretty loud. Really loud. Like it doesn't have a muffler." He grinned. "You'll know when you hear it."

I smiled, setting my glass down. "Everybody hears you coming, eh?"

"I'm not a big fan of motorcycles, I guess." Mallory leaned on the counter and sipped her wine. It was unlike her to be so challenging to a guest.

"Aww." I waved a hand at her. "I rode as a kid, on the bike trails behind our house and down at the park. Motorcycles aren't dangerous."

"You rode?" Tyree turned to me, sliding his glass to the center of the table.

"Oh, nothing like a Harley. We had little trail bikes. Kawasaki 100's. We had a red one and a blue one. My brother eventually upgraded to a 300cc street bike."

"Nice. You don't look the type."

"It was a long time ago." I helped Mallory set a platter of meat on the table, rising to get glasses of ice water for everyone. "So, y'know, I have a little experience riding. But ours weren't real loud, either. And they weren't dangerous. It's the maniacs riding them that are dangerous."

"I can attest to that!" Tyree said, chuckling.

"This guy I knew, all his motorcycle stuff matched. The little pull-behind trailer, the rain suit, it was all painted to match the motorcycle. Sky Blue. Like *baby* blue. Here's this big tough guy, riding his Harley, and all his stuff is baby blue. Not exactly a tough guy color, I don't think."

I filled three glasses with ice water and poured a plastic princess cup of milk for Sophie, then returned to the table. "He was crazy, that guy."

Tyree nodded. "They get pretty intense, some of those riders . . ."

"What about you?" I handed him a glass. "Are you that intense?"

"Uh, I have a pull behind trailer and a rain suit . . ."

"I knew it!" I slapped my knee, chuckling. "Sky blue?"

"My bike's red, thank you." Tyree said. "And it doesn't match the other stuff. The bike is red, the trailer is gray, and the rain suit is orange and black."

"What, a retro Buccaneers poncho from those ugly 'Creamsicle' uniforms in the 70s?"

"It's for visibility. Orange shows up better in the daytime. And at night."

"Oh." I cleared my throat, cheeks warming. "Well, you'll have to show it to me sometime."

"Sure thing. Besides, we can't all drive big black Lincoln Navigators, now can we?" Tyree said. "Did they let you keep that thing when you retired from the CIA?"

"CIA?" Mallory scooped vegetables from a pot into a serving bowl. "Doesn't that stand for Certified Internal Auditor?"

"Culinary Institute of America," I said. "I was a secret chef spy."

"If you were a chef, it was a well-guarded secret." Mallory was finally starting to loosen up. "Okay, you two. Time to eat. Get Sophie washed up for dinner."

"Come on, little critter." I went to the couch and hoisted Sophie up. Tyree followed.

The pre-dinner conversation had worked well to get everyone more relaxed. When we returned, we took our places at the table.

Sophie peered at Tyree. "Do you like goldfish crackers?"

He smiled. "Oh, goldfish crackers are my favorite!"

Sophie smiled back. "Mommy, Mr. Tyree and I need goldfish crackers for dinner."

"Whoa!" Tyree laughed. "Hold on. Don't do that to me."

"We're having pork roast and green beans, sweetie." Mallory said.

Sophie stuck out her tongue. "Yuck. I don't like green beans."

"Well." Tyree picked up a fork. "Maybe you and I can have some goldfish crackers for dessert sometime. Okay?" He raised his eyebrows and glanced at Mallory. She smiled.

"Today?" Sophie sat up straight.

"*Not* today," Mallory said as she sat.

"Another time." Tyree nodded. "Okay?"

"Okay." Sophie sighed, her little battle lost.

We ate, discussing miscellaneous things, and avoiding the topic on everyone's mind. When we finished, it wasn't late, but I convinced my daughter that it was bedtime. The rain outside had made it dark early, so she was easily swayed.

"Say bye-bye to Tyree, sweetie." I put my hand on her shoulder. "Then I'll take you upstairs to bed."

As he squatted down to say goodbye, Sophie surprised him with a hug. "Bye, Tyree."

"Bye Sophie."

Her face was sad. She wanted to stay up with everybody else.

"It was nice to meet you," Tyree said, standing. "I'll see you soon."

Sophie leaned toward him and whispered. "Don't forget the goldfish crackers."

"Okay, let's go." I took Sophie's hand and walked her up the steps. Mallory put the pot under the coffee maker—to Tyree's delight. Then, with Sophie in bed, we moved to the living room so we could talk.

"She's a sweet kid." Tyree took a cup of coffee from my wife and made his way to the couch.

"Thanks," I said. We sat down.

He leaned forward to me, lowering his voice. "What are you thinking?"

I guess he wanted to get the lay of the land before Mallory rejoined us.

"I was thinking about evacuating," I said quietly. "Leaving Tampa and heading to Atlanta until the hurricane passes."

He raised his eyebrows. "Wow. That's a big step."

I nodded.

"What does your wife think about that?"

I sighed. "She thinks it's a bad idea. And maybe she's right."

"Sometimes it's different for women, dealing with these things." Tyree tested his coffee. "When that whole winery thing happened, the wreck on your vacation—how did she take it?"

I chewed my lip for a second. "That was different."

"How?"

"I saw the wreck happen. Sophie and I were headed to the parking lot, but we never made it. When everything happened, she thought she'd lost both of us. That . . . kind of changes things for a person."

Tyree eyed me over his coffee cup. "Did it for you?"

"In a different way, sure." I glanced at the kitchen to make sure Mallory wasn't catching any of this. She had the faucet in the sink running full blast, rinsing some dishes. I felt bad. Normally I'd be helping do that after our guest left, but she launched in, so I guess she had other ideas. "I'm a lot more careful in parking lots. Look, what do you think about all this, the three tragedies, the timing of it all, the recurring dreams—"

"Dreams?" Tyree cocked his head.

"Yeah. What do you make of it all?"

Mallory shut off the water, and picked up her coffee, joining us in the living room.

"Well, let's put it on the table." Tyree put his elbows on his knees, wrapping his hands around his mug. "First, I don't think you folks are mental cases." He looked at Mallory. "When I look around this house, after talking with your husband a few times, and with you, this just isn't the typical crazy scenario."

He gazed at his dark pool of coffee. "I have some experience in this type of thing. And I expect people to be skeptical. But something is happening to you folks. Something . . ." He raised his eyes to us. "Supernatural."

Mallory swallowed hard, a strained expression on her face. "How do you know?"

"I don't mean to scare you." Tyree replied. "It looks a lot like what has ended up being supernatural events—when I've had to deal with it in the past."

Mallory reached over and took my hand. Hers were shaking. "Have you dealt with a lot of situations like this in the past?"

"Some." He nodded. "Enough to know what they look like when I see them."

"Whatever this is." Her voice quivered. "When you've seen it in the past . . . what do they want?"

Tyree took a deep breath, watching her eyes. "They want to hurt you."

The words hung in the air like a bell tolling at a funeral.

"Or they want something from you."

I had to remind myself to breathe. "Why? I mean, why us?"

"Why not you?" Tyree sat back, propping an arm on the back of the couch. "Doug, you're thinking about this the wrong way. You too, ma'am. Don't try to figure out why they're doing all this. You may never know the reason. They *are* doing it. That's the important thing to know."

Mallory folded her arms and stared at the window. "Oh, that just doesn't make any sense."

"Hold on, follow along with me a second." Tyree held his hands out, gesturing with his mug. "Think of a bully on a playground. What's the sense behind threatening another kid, or stealing a smaller kid's lunch money? While you try to figure out the reason, you get punched in the nose and lose your lunch money. The best thing is to punch the bully in the nose, right? Or at least to stand up for yourselves."

She continued to observe the swaying trees in the yard. He glanced at me. I nodded, mouthing the words *Go on.*

"Well." He took a deep breath. "The things that tend to do this stuff, these entities—the dark angels, we call them—they have their own reasons for doing them."

Mallory frowned, her voice falling to a whisper. "Why would they come after a little girl?"

"Maybe they destroy a child so they can become more powerful and move on to bigger things," Tyree said. "Does it matter? What matters is that it is happening. To you, to your family, your daughter. It's happening, and it's going to keep happening."

He let that sink in. "I know it's a lot to digest . . ."

"No." Mallory sighed. "It isn't. Not really. I think I've been trying to avoid realizing what it was, hoping it would go away."

Tyree nodded, sitting back in his seat. "I think if I were in your shoes, I'd feel the same way."

I rubbed my stomach. Hearing it all out loud was harder than I thought. Again. "Do you think they're after Sophie?"

"Could be. If they wanted to hurt either of you, wouldn't that be the best way?" Tyree tapped the side of his cup with his finger. "It could be that she poses some kind of threat to them, somehow."

My stomach clenched. He didn't know what the mambo told me, and I felt bad about not sharing it.

Mallory's jaw dropped. "How can a little girl be a threat to, to . . . to anyone?"

Tyree shrugged. Silence hung in the air. I had heard another answer to that question, but it seemed best to let Tyree offer his own ideas. I could tell him the priestess' thoughts later.

I rubbed the back of my neck, frowning. "Sounds like some kind of messed up gang initiation."

"More like a schoolyard bully." Tyree watched me, his face expressionless. "Without any kind of real restraint."

That comparison hurt.

"I'm sorry. That's just been my experience."

I'd had enough of that topic for the moment. There were other things to discuss. "Listen, we also need to think about what we're to do about this hurricane."

"Should we go to Orlando?" Mallory frowned and glared at me sideways.

Tyree narrowed his eyes, obviously confused. "What's in Orlando?"

"Old joke," Mallory replied, getting up.

When she had gone back into the kitchen, I explained. "The last big hurricane was a few years ago and was headed right for Tampa, so we— well, I—got the bright idea to go to our friends' house in Orlando. You know, be out of the storm. Well, we arrive and find out the hurricane turned. It was headed for Orlando now."

"Hah! What did you do?"

"We got back in the car and headed to Tampa. We weren't at their house five minutes, I'm not kidding. We said goodbye, hopped in the car, and started driving—and it's raining buckets. I mean, you can't see three feet in front of the headlights. And I realize we are the only car on the road. I-4, the busiest highway in Florida, and there is not another car in sight." I shook my head. "That's how you know you've made a terrible mistake, when you are the only vehicle on the whole highway. Meanwhile, the wind was knocking my car all over the place. It was ridiculous."

"Good grief. Then what?"

"Oh, well, we survived." I chuckled. "The next day we checked out the tracking maps. The stupid thing followed us right down I-4. Now it's a little harder to get my wife to think about evacuating."

"At least to Orlando," Mallory said. We all laughed.

I shifted on my seat. "And that's why I was thinking Atlanta."

The laughter stopped. Mallory bristled.

"It's always been our failsafe spot, right? Our disaster recovery plan? Head to Atlanta, get into a hotel, and if we are separated, send our messages to my family in Indiana until we can get reunited."

"What if the hurricane comes to Atlanta?" Tyree asked, only half kidding.

"Then we get back in the car and visit my dad in Indiana." I smiled. "Look, I'd rather be in a hotel in Atlanta dealing with this demonic possession crap than deal with it here and a hurricane too. I think it's the lesser of two evils."

Mallory huffed. "We walk away from our home? And what about Sparkles? Stick him with the neighbors and hope he's okay when we get back?"

"Well." Tyree stood. "You two have a lot to talk about, and at least a little time to talk about it." He turned to Mallory. "What are your thoughts right now?"

"I don't know," Mallory said.

Tyree nodded and looked at me.

"I think we take some kind of action." I got up and shoved my hands in my pockets, studying the floor. "They've found us every time they wanted to. There's no running from them. They will come when they're ready, not when we are. I think, we have to attack them somehow; or at least put them on the defensive." I raised my eyes to Tyree. "Are we better off here, like a small army trapped in a fort?"

"Or like ducklings in a clearing cornered by a wolf?" Mallory glared at me. "Out on the open road, vulnerable?"

"I'm not going to continue to let them come after our daughter and not fight back. I don't care how nutty it sounds or how it looks to anybody else! They weren't in that winery. They didn't see his eyes. That hollow, empty stare. I think we need to confront the dark angel. I just don't know how."

Tyree nodded. "There are ways. But for now, get some rest. Let's talk again in the morning."

I walked him to the door. The rains had gotten worse. From our covered front porch, it looked like a bomb had gone off. Branches were all over the yard, and the wind was whipping the rain into my face. It stung.

"I'd offer you an umbrella to get to your car, but it would get ripped to shreds in two seconds." I said.

"Don't worry about it." Tyree put on his jacket—the orange and black one he mentioned. Before I could be embarrassed at my prior inconsiderate comments about it, he handed me a business card. "Come by my office tomorrow at noon or so, okay? We still have some things to go over. The address is on the card."

I stuck the card in my pocket. "Where are you staying tonight? Don't you live in Melbourne?"

"I have a fold out couch in my office. I'll be fine."

I thought about asking him to stay with us for the night but knew it'd be better if I consulted my wife first—and I wasn't sure of her take on him yet.

Sophie seemed to like Tyree, though, and he seemed to like Sophie. That would make a big difference to Mallory.

He pulled the hood over his head. "I'm going to do some research tonight. If I find anything, I'll call you in the morning." He glanced at the stairs. "Is your wife gonna be all right?"

"I think so. This has all been a lot to digest."

"Let her take her time. Both of you, take your time." He looked up at the swaying tree tops as they bandied violently back and forth. "Just don't take too long."

Then he braced himself and ran to his car.

After Tyree left, I went into my office. It was late, but there were notes to write down and plans to think up.

Mallory drifted into the kitchen and away from the office lights, one hand rubbing her forehead and the other clutching her stomach.

"Mommy?"

Sophie's voice was barely audible, as if trying not to intrude, not even with her words. Mallory turned to look at our daughter. In her pajamas, Sophie peeked out from the hallway where she'd been hiding. She looked so sweet and innocent.

"Yes, sweetie?" Mallory said, forcing a smile onto her face. Her tired eyes betrayed her, but Sophie might not notice.

"I heard . . . you and Daddy—and the man—talking . . ."

"Mr. Tyree?"

Sophie nodded. "Did I . . ." Her voice broke slightly. She barely got the words out before she started to cry. "Did I do something wrong?"

I almost jumped out of my chair, but I held back to not make things worse.

Mallory pulled Sophie close. "God, no, sweetie. No, you didn't do anything wrong."

"But Daddy said—" Sophie sobbed. "Mommy, why is all this happening? What's *wrong* with me?"

Daddy said.

I swallowed hard, a large lump forming in my throat.

"Nothing sweetie!" Mallory kissed our daughter's forehead. "Nothing is wrong with you!"

Tears streamed down Sophie's face. I had never felt so empty and useless.

Her mother rocked her in her arms. "Nothing is wrong with you." It was all she could manage. Mallory began to cry, too. She hugged Sophie tightly.

“Everything that’s happening, what Daddy and Mr. Tyree discussed, it’s all just a big . . . it’s all just a problem that we need to work on. All of us, together.” Mallory pulled Sophie away to look her in the eye. “It isn’t your fault. There’s nothing wrong with you. Don’t you think that.” She blinked back the tears. “Daddy’s gonna fix it. We’re going to go away from the storm and go to Atlanta, and everything is going to be all right.”

The two of them stayed there, rocking back and forth in a hug, exhausted, my wife saying the words over and over.

“There’s nothing wrong with you. Everything’s going to be all right.”

Chapter 37

When the phone rang, I felt like I'd just closed my eyes to go to sleep. I cracked open an eyelid and peered at the clock.

8A. M.

It didn't look like 8 A. M. in the bedroom. Very little light crept in around the window shades. Not 8 A. M.'s worth.

The howling winds reminded me again. Clouds from the storm were keeping things dark.

I reached over and picked up the phone. Tyree's number on the caller ID snapped me awake. I sat up and pressed the button. "Hey, Tyree, hang on one sec."

Rolling out of bed, I slinked to the door. Mallory lay slumbering in our bed, with Sparkles on one side of her and Sophie on the other.

I sighed. Sophie still had one arm thrown over her sleeping mother. They'd hugged all night.

The rushing winds would wake everyone soon enough, but their long night didn't need to be shortened by my phone conversation. I crept out of the room and down the stairs in search of a better place to talk. My office tended to bounce conversations right up the stairs, so that was out. The living room was obviously a bad choice for private conversation after last night, and the garage was too . . . garagey. And it'd be noisy in this wind.

I went into the pantry. With boxes of pasta protecting my back and an old cheese slicer in front of me, I had a quiet bunker where I could speak freely to Tyree—without being overheard and causing another situation like we'd had last night.

I put the phone to my ear. "Sorry for the delay. I didn't want to wake everybody up."

"No problem, Doug. I'll get right to it. I have a question for you."

"I need to ask you something first." I had been thinking about the voodoo priestess and what I should or shouldn't tell Tyree about her. "I have a bill that's coming due. I met with a voodoo priestess, and I need to pay her a favor or my luck will run bad. This would be a really bad time for that to happen."

"No kidding. When the hell did you meet with a voodoo priestess, anyway?"

"Right after I met with you. The next day."

"Okay. What do you owe her?"

"I don't know. A favor. Something good."

"That could be a lot of things." Tyree was quiet for a moment. "I probably have something here you could use."

I shifted on my feet. "Whatever you have, it's gotta be pretty good."

"I'd say a relic cross fits that description. You can pick it up when you come over."

"It's a what?"

"A relic cross," he repeated. "A cross with a holy relic in the middle of it. This one is a big, heavy sucker. White, with a glass bead in the center. That holds a small patch of cloth with a tiny little sliver on it."

I knew about relics from the nuns. The patch of material came from a larger piece that touched a saint—alive or not. Creepy, to think of church elders rubbing old bones with a sheet. The sliver might be a part of a crucifixion cross or a shaving from a bone.

I slid to the pantry floor and sat on the cold tiles. "Where did you get something like that?"

"Don't ask questions that you don't want to know the answers to."

"How much did you pay for it?" A twinge of nerves shot through me. "It's not stolen, is it?"

"Calm down. It was a gift. You can't buy these things, and you can't sell them. But it might make a formidable tool for us to use against the dark angel."

Tool?

I rubbed the back of my neck, my angst and frustration growing. "Speaking of . . . that, why is it waiting? Why doesn't it come do whatever it's going to do?"

"You can't consider this only from our perspective," Tyree explained. "You have to view it differently. Time is relative. Think of yourself in a room. On one side, there's one of those giant tortoises. It's huge, like maybe four feet long. On the other side is a tiny little fruit fly that's buzzing around.

"When you look at the tortoise, he seems like he's moving very slowly. When you look at the fly, it's moving very fast—compared to you."

I sat on the cold tile floor, the phone pressed to my ear, absorbing every word.

"Now, if the tortoise looks at you, he sees you moving really fast—like the way the fly looks to you. Meanwhile, the fly probably moves so fast, the tortoise can't even perceive it.

"When the fly looks at you, he sees a tortoise. When the fly looks at the tortoise, it moves so glacially slow, it might as well be a rock from the fly's viewpoint. He probably can't see that it moves at all. To the tortoise, the fly moves at the speed of light, if he can even fathom it at all.

"All three of you—the fly, you, and the tortoise—are in the same room at the same time. But obviously, time is very, very different to each of you. So what might count as one day to the tortoise, might be a year to the fly. Get it?"

"Yeah." I nodded. "I think so." It was a lot to take in.

"That's how it could work with these dark angels. What is a year to us might only be a day to them. You can't expect things to happen on your time table. Things are working on their time table." He paused, clearing his throat. "But I have a question for you. Last night, you mentioned dreams. Recurring dreams, I think you said."

I stretched my legs out and leaned against the shelves. "Uh, yeah, that's right."

"What can you tell me about that?"

"Well." I took a deep breath. "I had a nightmare about lions in the woods. One by one, three different lions walked past me and ripped at this package. But it wasn't a package. When the fourth lion showed up, the package . . . was a child. Sophie." I swallowed hard. Just thinking about the dream again made me uneasy. "Needless to say, it was a terrible nightmare."

"Needless to say."

"In the morning, I told Mallory about it. She'd been having the same dream."

"Wow."

"She said she didn't tell it to me on purpose."

"I bet. It caught my ear when you mentioned dreams last night, but I didn't want to get into it then. A dream can be important, some kind of indicator. But if both of you are having the same dream, that's no coincidence. That's a sign."

I wiped my hand across my forehead, my stomach tightening. "Of what?"

"There were three lions that didn't really do much to . . . the package, right?"

"Right." I put a hand on the cold tile and shifted my weight.

"And there were three tragedies, as you guys call them. Now, they were all bad, I'm not saying they weren't.

You got a good scare each time—but you walked away from them, right?"

"I guess so, yeah . . ." I huffed. "Where are you going with this?"

"It was the fourth lion that ripped up the package." Tyree said. "A fourth tragedy."

My pulse quickened. I sat up, pressing the phone to my ear.

"Another event is coming. We've got a hurricane going on. It's starting to look like a coalescence of events. All that chaos—the severe weather—would make a good cover. Things have escalated with each tragedy."

I leaned forward. "And?"

"And the next one will be bigger. It will be fatal."

My mind was a blur, my pulse racing. There were a million reasons to get in the car and go to Atlanta right now, and there were a million reasons not to.

I sat on the floor, panting.

At least Atlanta didn't have a hurricane, but in a few days *we would*—maybe in less than a few days. If that was the being's cover, it could be eliminated from the equation. Which might save us all.

"Okay, that's it." I took a deep breath, nodding. "We're heading out tomorrow morning. First thing. Maybe sooner. To Atlanta."

"I think you've made a really good decision."

I pulled the phone away from my ear and glanced at the time. "We should be on the road by, say 10 A. M."

"10 A. M.?" Tyree snorted. "That's first thing?"

I frowned. "I have a wife and kid, so yeah, 10 A. M. Then we'll be traveling in broad daylight and on the highway before the roads get closed. Which all sounds pretty good to me." I squeezed my eyes shut and rubbed my forehead. "If everything goes well, we should be checking in to the freaking Peachtree hotel in downtown Atlanta around 6 P. M."

"And, you're still coming to me at noon today at my office."

"Yeah."

"Okay. See you then."

I hung up. I had been in the pantry for quite a while. Now it was time to see who else was up and around. I needed to get things moving without creating a panic.

The living room was empty. Even Sparkles hadn't come down yet. That meant everyone was still asleep and hadn't heard any of what Tyree and I had discussed.

Good.

I grabbed the remote and turned on the weather channel, rubbing the knot in my stomach. Maybe we should evacuate right now. I checked the time on my phone again. I had to meet Tyree in a few hours. Maybe I should pack everybody into the car and meet him, then keep on going to Atlanta.

Chapter 38

"Dad, what's that noise?" My daughter sat on the floor at the foot of the bed, playing with her Barbies.

"It's rain coming down hard on the roof." I pulled an extra shirt from the closet. "What does it sound like growling? Or purring?"

"Purring."

Good answer. I don't want her to be scared.

"I think it sounds like purring, too. We're not afraid of some rain, are we?"

"No."

Right answer, wrong tone. She was nervous.

"C'mere." I exited the closet and squatted down, letting her fall into my open arms. I rubbed her back as she wrapped her little arms around my neck. "I won't let anything happen to you."

She lifted her head and peered over my shoulder, whispering. "When's it gonna stop?"

I turned and stared at the swaying oaks, their limbs flailing wildly in the nonstop wind and rain. "Soon."

I got up and patted her head, trying to act natural and avoid getting everyone more scared than they already were. The plan was simple. Make a quick stop at Tyree's office to pick up the relic cross, get back home to finish packing, and head out of town tomorrow morning. Aside from a little rain and wind, what could be simpler?

To answer my question, the wind slammed another band of rain onto the roof. I flinched. Maybe Sophie should be playing downstairs.

I grabbed the last t-shirt I wanted and stuffed it into my bag, heading for the stairs. "Come on, honey. Let's play down here."

Our garage was a separate structure, attached to our house by a breezeway—a little roof section that went to a side door and offered almost no protection when the rain was falling sideways. With Sophie parked in front of the TV, I ran the short distance from the back door to the garage door, through the torrents of rain. Hitting the button to open the overhead door, I squeezed past Mallory's car to mine.

Dripping only from my head, I slipped the key into the Navigator's ignition and turned it. Its big engine groaned a little, instead of the usual growl of a V-8, then nothing.

I glared at the dashboard indicator lights. "Don't tell me . . ."

I gritted my teeth and twisted the key again. This time, a series of clicks emanated from under the hood, then silence.

I mean, *nothing.*

Dead battery.

I grabbed the steering wheel with both hands and shook it. "What the hell? What the hell!" I pounded my fist into the center console. "Is that voodoo priestess sapping my good luck already?" The wind whipped up again, the howls coming to me a little too clearly to have been obscured by a closed up vehicle. I twisted around to inspect the inside of the car. The rear passenger door was open. I had it open yesterday when I was putting the flashlights into the car, but I got distracted when Tyree drove up, and I never shut it. The light being on all night drained the old car's battery.

"Ohhhhhh." I laid my head on the steering wheel and shut my eyes. "How could I be so stupid?"

That's a nice little delay there, Mr. Planner.

I put my elbow on the window and rubbed my eyes, working to control my rising blood pressure. No problem.

We had jumper cables, and Mallory's car battery would be fine to supply a charge to mine. I'd hook 'em up and get a jump, then get over to Tyree's.

Which would be easy on a normal day. Just back the two cars out of the garage and hook up the jumper cables. But in this insane wind and rain, I'd get soaked.

Maybe electrocuted to boot. Bad plan.

I sat in my car tapping the steering wheel. If I backed both cars out a few feet, I could get access to the battery from the front and still be inside the garage. I could hook up the cables and get the Navigator started without getting wet. It would take a few minutes, but it would work.

I'll just call him and let him know I'll be late.

Good plan. I ran back through the rain to the house for Mallory's keys.

A little wetter, I called Tyree—no answer. I left a message and returned my focus to the cars.

I ran to the garage through the rain. I told myself it was faster than using the breezeway door and even though I was halfway soaked, having made three trips through the rain, I would have been just as wet going the other route.

I could still get the car jumped without becoming fully soaked, though, and without getting electrocuted.

I backed up Mallory's car, and left it running. Then I hopped in my car and put it in neutral, hopped back out and pushed it a few feet. Grabbing the jumper cables, I hooked up the two batteries.

I let the cars sit for a moment to help charge the Navigator, using the time to fling water from my arms and hair. Then I jumped back into my car to turn on the ignition.

No car keys.

Where the hell did they go?

I stared at the ignition in disbelief. I had the freaking keys a minute ago when I put the stupid car in neutral and pushed it back. I checked my pockets. Nope. Not there . . .

Maybe I dropped them.

I threw open the door and jumped out, scouring the ground. I retraced my steps: got in the car, turned on the ignition, pushed the car back. I thought I left the keys in the ignition.

I looked at the clock on the wall. I was already twenty minutes late to get to Tyree's. I scowled and checked my pockets again, ready to pull the linings out.

Where are those keys?

I looked under both cars. I looked in Mallory's car, which was still running. I looked inside the open hood of the Navigator.

I glared at the house, only a few wet feet away. A spare set of keys hung on a hook in the hallway.

I checked my pockets again. Maybe the keys would appear on the third pat down. Nope.

With a sigh of frustration, I ran through the rain again, cursing the voodoo priestess for foreclosing on my luck already. Dripping wet, I sloshed to the hallway and grabbed the keys, stomping back through the rain to the cars.

Steaming mad and soaking wet, I seriously considered stripping before climbing into the Navigator. I was drenched, and I'd get the seats drenched, too. Then I'd have to sit on wet seats the whole way to Atlanta. There was no way they'd dry out overnight. Not in this weather.

I stripped.

My underwear was still partially dry on the butt, so I didn't have to go totally commando. I yanked open the driver's door to the Navigator and climbed in. As I went to grab a fast food napkin from the stash inside the center console to dry my face, I glanced at the cup holders.

There were my keys.

I pounded the wheel, lucky my daughter couldn't hear me over the howling wind. How did I not see that on three separate checks? What is wrong with me?

I turned the key, and my Navigator roared to life.

I closed my eyes and sat back. Thank you.

I sat for a moment, wet and nearly naked, considering my next moves. It made sense to go back inside and get into some dry clothes. And to use an umbrella for the return trip to the car. Then I just needed to call Tyree and tell him I was finally on the way—after I dried off and changed clothes.

I stared at the garage clock. I was now an hour late.

Inside the house, I left another message for Tyree and dug an umbrella out of the hall closet—but didn't fully open it. If I held it close to my head like a giant hat, I could keep some rain off me without the wind ripping the umbrella open and tearing it to pieces. Opened fully, the massive gusts of wind would pop it upside down and rip the rainproof nylon from their little steel ribs.

I was bothered when Tyree didn't answer. The power was probably out, which happened at our house all the time in big storms, but still. The dull ache growing in my stomach wasn't from hunger. The cell towers were down in his area. That happened during the last hurricane, too.

I gripped the wheel tightly as I drove, leaning forward toward the windshield to see. The rain came down so hard the wipers barely made a difference. There would be a lot of wrecks from people who couldn't see in this kind of rain. Add in the sudden wind gusts and drivers would feel like the steering wheel was being ripped from their hands. Next thing you know, they're driving into a tree a hundred feet from the road.

But for now, I had some flashlights in case the power was out at Tyree's office. That was about it.

The rain was like driving in a waterfall. The wind banged away at my car, pushing it into the gutter one moment and over the center line the next. I squeezed the wheel harder, fighting to maintain control and driving slow.

Tyree's relic cross had better be worth all this effort.

The twenty minute drive took nearly twice that. As I pulled into the business park near the airport where Tyree kept his office, the flashing lights of emergency vehicles streamed across the lot. Lots of them.

I pounded the wheel and cursed. More delays.

My windshield wipers swiped away the torrents of rain, refilling instantly like some kid was on the roof pouring buckets down the glass.

I double checked the address he'd given me. Police and fire rescue vehicles were blocking access to half of the buildings.

I figured I could probably park and then walk around the cop cars to Tyree's office.

"Hey!" A loud shout assaulted my ear. I jumped, turning to the voice.

A police officer in a poncho rapped his knuckles on my window. "That way." He waved a red-tipped flashlight in the direction of the other end of the lot. "You can park over there. This area is blocked."

I nodded and pulled around to the left, grabbing for the umbrella. It wouldn't do much good in this rain—the swirling winds would smack me from all sides and I'd be drenched in two minutes—but hopefully I could get to Tyree's unit.

Bracing my umbrella against the wind, I made my way up to the traffic officer and shouted over the howling storm. "I need to get into one of these units for a meeting."

He looked at me like I was crazy. "In this weather?" His poncho clung to his frame, glued there by the incessant rushing wind. "I hope it's important. What unit number?"

"I was just thinking that I should reschedule," I said. "I'm starting to think that nothing's important enough to be out in this."

The cop nodded.

My umbrella smacked me in the head with each gust of wind. Digging the address out of my pocket, I read it to him. "Building 8, unit 8191."

He shook his head, squinting against the stinging rain. "No can do. That's the building they're here for."

My stomach lurched.

He pointed his red flashlight at the squad cars. "A break in. Pretty nasty. I don't know what unit, though. I got pulled in to help with traffic."

"Okay, thanks."

A huge rush of wind up-ended my umbrella, ripping it from my hands and tossing it down the road. In an instant, it was a hundred yards away and still moving.

I rubbed my stomach and glanced at the officer. "Is it okay if I check with the investigating officers, to see if I can get into this unit?" I pointed at Tyree's business card.

"You can try." He nodded. "Ask for officer Neil. He's in charge."

As I walked up, I could see the firemen hosing down the remains of a burned out car. The office building was roped off with plastic crime scene tape, but it had already ripped apart and now flapped in the wind like parade streamers.

The door to the burglarized office laid flat on the grass, completely broken off its hinges. I stood on tiptoes at the yellow crime scene tape, craning my neck to read the unit number on the door.

It was 8191. Tyree's office.

Chapter 39

"Please stay back, sir." The officer moved past me, one hand holding onto his plastic-wrapped hat and the other unrolling another piece of yellow tape between two trees. The plastic ribbon arced in the wind like the billowing sail on the winning America's Cup yacht.

"Sure." I had to shout to be heard over the driving wind and rain. "I had an appointment scheduled here for an hour ago. Can you tell me what happened?"

"An hour ago?" He squinted at me, blinking rain out of his eyes. "You know the man who worked here?"

"I met him. I was supposed to be having a meeting with him."

"You should be glad you missed it." Another gust whipped up. He re-gripped his hat. "There was a break in. Can't let you in. They tossed the place pretty good."

"I understand." I blinked the rain out of my eyes. "Was anybody inside?"

He nodded toward a van marked *Hillsborough County Coroner*.

An uneasy feeling welled inside me.

Another cop approached, turning his back to the wind and speaking to the first officer. I took a few steps back, but since they had to practically to yell to hear each other, I could hear them too.

"Whatever happened in there, it's hard to imagine anybody survived when there's this much blood. Did you get a look inside?"

Tension gripped my shoulders, not wanting to hear what the officers would let slip, but not daring to leave without knowing.

"I can't see anybody walking out of there." The first officer frowned and shook his head. "The walls were practically painted red. We called homicide the minute we got here."

"Where's the body?"

Body.

A crushing wave of disbelief tore through me, knocking the breath out of me and almost sending me to my knees. I stepped away and turned to the grass, my insides churning. Hands on knees, I gasped, trying not to vomit.

I could not believe Tyree was dead.

"Looks like whoever did this moved the body after they killed him. The CSIs said that's not unusual. We checked the car they torched. That was his, too."

"Anybody in it?"

"No."

The second officer looked down, wiping rain from his neck. "I had a glance in the door when I first got here. Pretty bad."

I stared at the grass, trying to inhale. I had just talked to Tyree this morning.

"Worst I've seen in fifteen years. The whole place was trashed, every inch. Just destroyed." He pointed toward Tyree's office. "They even tore open the walls. Ripped the plaster right off the walls in places. And there was blood everywhere. I mean, everywhere. The coroner's asking us to bring in a couple of extra guys."

"Okay." The second officer hunched his shoulders and pulled the rain suit collar close around his neck. "I'll call in the request."

I managed to step further back as the two officers parted, my ears ringing. Through the pouring rain, I stumbled to my car and got in.

Water dripped from my hair and nose as I gripped the steering wheel. My head was humming. Somebody destroyed Tyree's office and killed him in a very messy way.

I just talked to him this morning, a few hours ago.

I'd been leaving messages all morning for a dead man. They might even have been killing him when I was calling. That sent a shiver down my spine.

He was being killed right when I was supposed to be there. But I was late. If I had been on time, I might be dead, too. From the amount of blood everywhere, I *would* be dead.

Queasiness roiled inside me. What do we do now?

I put down the car window and stared at the office building fifty feet away. Inside the busted doorframe, a desk sat on its side and a computer laid on the floor. Papers were scattered everywhere. Cops in raincoats streamed in and out.

Adrenaline and fear pulsed through me until I could taste it in the back of my throat. I felt half numb and half terrified, but completely overwhelmed. I was more afraid than I had been at the winery. There, I saw it happen from the doorway. I knew I was safe the entire time.

Here, I'd been an hour away from getting killed along with Tyree.

My heart sank. He wouldn't have been here if not for me.

I called him in.

If not for me, he'd still be trying to fish in this crappy weather or chasing a barmaid somewhere.

I swallowed hard and started the car. I definitely wanted to leave town and go to Atlanta. Today. Now.

When I tell Mallory what happened, she'll . . .

I set my forehead on the steering wheel and closed my eyes.

When I tell her Tyree is dead.

“Oh, God.” It sounded impossible. Somebody I had just met was now dead. Gruesomely murdered by—who? Or what? Someone or something found him.

I bolted upright.

It’s going to find *us*.

Panic gripped me. My mind was a blur of horrific thoughts, each worse than the last.

If I hadn’t been late, they would have gotten me, too. In addition to him. Or, maybe instead of Tyree.

A white flash of terror crossed my brain. *Hell, maybe it got the wrong target.*

How close I’d come to being killed. How—

The floor dropped out of my stomach. Maybe I wasn’t even the target. I’d left my wife and child home alone to come to this meeting.

They were unaware. Defenseless.

What if the target was Mallory and Sophie?

I jammed my car into gear and stomped the accelerator, spinning my wheels and racing out of the parking lot.

Chapter 40

I pounded my cell phone and maneuvered my car through the torrential downpour. Each massive gust of wind tried to jerk the steering wheel from my grip. Holding my breath, I mashed the phone to my ear.

My heart was in my throat. Mallory had to answer. My wet clothes and hair caused a fog to form on the windshield. I reached over and flipped on the defroster. The burst of air caused the whole window to turn white. Gritting my teeth, I squeezed the phone to my head with my shoulder and thrust hand over the glass.

Voicemail.

My thoughts were a blur. I couldn't believe Tyree was gone. And it could have been me. Probably should have—that was the thing's intent. Lure me out . . . meanwhile, I'd left Mallory and Sophie completely unprotected and unaware.

I swallowed hard and dialed the phone again.

The streets were empty, so I ignored stop signs and red lights. I gripped the wheel and stomped the gas, panting like a marathon runner.

I rubbed my forehead with the back of my wrist. I'd gotten Tyree killed and now who knew what was happening with my family. Some demonic entity could have attacked them at the house while I was gone. It was that simple. My pulse throbbed, a cold sweat breaking out on my temple.

It waited for me to leave and then stormed in.

The home phone didn't answer. It rolled over to the answering machine.

I tossed the phone into a cup holder and punched the accelerator, racing upwards of eighty miles an hour through the rain and wind. My pulse was thumping, my hands sweating as I clung to the wheel. I could not get home fast enough.

I swerved my car onto our street. From the corner, the house looked dark. My stomach cringed with fear. The skies were black with clouds and rain. Normally, people don't sit at home in the dark.

My headlights showed our trees flinging their limbs back and forth in the screaming wind.

A broken branch hurled at me and crashed to the ground. I didn't even swerve to miss it, I just drove right through it, blasting it to pieces.

Racing up the driveway, my heart pounded in my ears. The house looked completely dark. I slammed the car into park jumped out, sprinting for the door through the whipping torrents of rain. It was unlocked. I flung it open and sprinted inside.

The living room was empty. Silent. Not even Sparkles barked. As thunder rumbled outside, I glanced at the kitchen, my office, the hallway—empty.

"Mallory!"

A thump came from upstairs. Adrenaline surging, I bounded up the steps two at a time.

The hallway and master bedroom were dark. Sophie's bedroom and the spare bedroom at the other end of the hall were dark. Water dripping from my face and hair, I stood in the hallway and held my breath, listening.

By now Sparkles should have been going bonkers, barking his head off. Even he hadn't made a peep. The only sound was my own pounding heart.

Where could they be?

From the master bedroom, light spilled out from under the bathroom door.

Another thump.

I ran to the door and flung it open.

"Daddy!"

My daughter sat up in the tub, smiling.

In front of her kneeled my wife, lathering up my little girl's head with shampoo.

"Hey, dad, look at me!" Sophie squealed, patting her head. "I have a hat!"

I had to hold the door frame to keep from falling down.

Mallory's face fell as she took in my appearance. "Honey, you're dripping everywhere."

I looked down, trying to breathe—and nearly fell. My knees couldn't hold me.

"Are you okay?" Mallory rushed to me. "You're as white as a sheet."

I leaned against the wall, gasping. "I just—"

I had nothing. There were no words.

Fear spread over my wife's face. "What's wrong?" She took my arm. "What happened?"

I shook my head, turning away. "Not in front of the baby."

Baby.

Sophie had just turned four years old. But Mallory would know what I meant. This was not for a child's ears.

She lowered her voice and leaned in, clutching my arm. "Are you alright?"

"I'm fine." I took a few deep breaths, trying to get my heart back into my chest.

"You're not."

Calm down. Don't panic everyone.

"I'll tell you everything. Finish Sophie's bath." I kissed her and pressed my forehead to hers. "But hurry."

The worried look didn't leave her face. Reaching into the bathroom, I grabbed a towel off the hook by the shower and went downstairs.

With shaking hands, I poured myself a glass of tea and leaned on the kitchen counter to think. Tyree was dead. I didn't have the cross he wanted to give me. I didn't have much of a plan except to get out of town. The hurricane was getting closer to making that impossible. The winds were bad enough on the way to Tyree's. They'd be insane by morning.

Tyree was dead.

I rubbed my eyes. God, I had gotten someone killed . . .

I picked up the towel and sloshed my way to the laundry room to peel off my soggy clothes and dry off before heading back upstairs.

Mallory finished bathing Sophie in record time and gave her the rare treat of watching cartoons in our bed. Mallory paced back and forth in front of the dresser, biting her nails. When she saw me, she held her hands out to her sides.

Holding the towel around my waist with one hand, I lifted a finger in front of my lips with the other, going into the closet. I had already packed a small bag for the trip, but there was still plenty of stuff left to choose from. I grabbed t-shirt and shorts, turning to go out.

Mallory blocked the closet doorway. "Tell me what the hell is going on!"

I peered over her shoulder, looking at our daughter on the bed. "Let's go into the hallway."

She followed me to Sophie's bedroom door.

"It's . . . bad news." I watched her face tensing up. There was no easy way to say it. I took a deep breath and swallowed hard. "Tyree's dead."

Mallory's hands flew to her mouth.

"Somebody met him at his office, right when I was supposed to be there. They . . . tore the place up and killed him."

She backed up against the wall, tears welling up in her eyes.

I shook my head and leaned against the wall, rubbing my eyes. "Honey." I put my hand on the wall to steady myself. "If I hadn't had that dead battery, I would have been there when it happened."

I stared at the floor, the vision of Tyree's office rushing back to me. The yellow crime scene tape, the torn off door, the blood.

"If I had been on time." My stomach clenched as I forced out the words. "I'd be dead, now, too."

Mallory looked terrified, still clutching her hands to her face. Tears streamed down her cheeks.

I swallowed, regaining my breath. "I thought that whatever got him, it might come here." I looked into her eyes. "I think we should go."

"Let's go." Mallory nodded. "Right now. Let's get the hell out of here." She ran down the hall and into the master bedroom. "Whatever you need, grab it. Sophie and I will be in the car in five minutes!"

Chapter 41

"Been a long time." Jimmy stared at me through the thick glass, the intercom phone filling his words with static. There was neither happiness nor sadness in Jimmy's eyes that day, just a hardness that had come from years behind bars.

His face had aged many more years than his ten years in Lima. Some of the life had been taken out of him there. I guess that was the point.

He held up a cigarette and a lighter.

A nearby corrections officer nodded. "Go ahead."

Jimmy lit the cigarette and took a deep draw. "Sorry to hear about your mom."

"Thanks." It was an unintentional whisper. I cleared my throat but didn't try again.

The phones in the federal penitentiary were accompanied by wipes, for sanitation. They needed it. The receivers smelled like bad breath and ash trays.

"I have to wonder what you're doing here." Jimmy leaned back and blew a white stream of smoke toward the ceiling. "Why today, of all days? Isn't today her—"

"Yeah." I shifted on the cold metal chair. "I was going to be in the area, and I didn't want to be at my mom's house this afternoon. Not without her in it."

"Millersburg's not exactly in the area."

"No, it isn't." I took a deep breath. "I need to ask you something."

"After all this time." He shook his head. "Don't come looking for answers. Prison isn't that kind of place."

"I'm not asking the prison. I'm asking you."

He held his hands out and glanced around at the walls. "We are one and the same now."

As a kid, Jimmy started almost where I started, but there were differences from the beginning. He went down a different path, and the step that did him in was the latest in a long series I heard about. A lot of earlier steps could have been the one to send him to the Lima Penitentiary. The one that did was almost a fluke.

He landed a lucky punch in a disagreement that got out of control. They were in a bar and the other guy swung first, but Jimmy was agile. He dodged the blow and punched the other man square in the chest, dropping him.

The only problem was, the guy had a bad heart. When he went to the ground, he never got up again. Jimmy killed him.

On the wrong side of town, with no friends in the place and a growing bad reputation, things went from bad to worse. Add in a jury that wanted to send a message, and prison was the result.

I'd say it could happen to anybody, but that would be a lie. It couldn't just happen. It needed help. In Jimmy, it got all the help it needed.

We went to different grade schools after he moved. When we were reunited in high school, we were barely acquaintances. We said hi to each other when we passed in the halls—freshman year, anyway, for the first few weeks. Time had changed both of us. I was looking forward to college and a professional life. Jimmy wasn't even looking forward to finishing high school. He skipped whenever he could, which was often.

He went back down to the park the day after we had the run-in with the owner of the abandoned car. Jimmy was always off hunting or hiking, so nobody took much notice—except for the tough kids. They noticed. A year later when I heard he had joined their gang, I was surprised. I thought we were better than that. Even if he couldn't be a better student than me, or a better artist than me, I could never be a better hunter or tree climber than him. In our own way, each of us was a little jealous of the other. I thought that was a good thing in ten-year-old boys, that maybe they ought to look up to each other a little bit.

I heard occasional rumors in high school. Stories about stealing beer became stories about stealing cars. When I went home to Indiana for Christmas one year between college semesters, my older brother said Jimmy got busted selling drugs but beat the charge on a technicality. Everybody knew a story about him being in a fist fight somewhere. His choices never seemed to catch up with him, so he kept going. The rules didn't matter.

Until they did.

"It was hard to hear about you being here," I said. "We were friends. I looked up to you."

"We were kids, Dougie." Jimmy took a drag on his cigarette. "We looked up to anybody who could throw a baseball better than us."

"I didn't become best friends with them."

"Don't start that crap. Don't get into that."

I wiped my sweaty hand on my jeans. "Why not?"

"Because all day, every day, that's what I get to think about in here." He leaned forward, pointing at me through the glass with his cigarette. "Don't try to slide in sideways and tell me that you feel guilty. My mom and my dad and my brother all came in here telling me that. They all get to feel bad because they have a son and a brother in prison. They have to hide their faces around town because they got tarnished with my sins." He sat back in the chair, tucking a hand under his phone arm. "You think you could have stopped all this somehow, right? If only you'd have been a better friend?"

I swallowed hard. "I guess so."

"Don't be arrogant. You didn't control me. You *couldn't* control me, and I didn't want to be controlled." He took a long pull on his cigarette and narrowed his eyes, glancing at a wall clock mounted in a wire cage. "Coming in here allowed me to stop the slide."

"What?" I sat up straighter. "What do you mean?"

"Do you remember in Drivers Ed class, Mr. Morgan told us to look both ways before crossing a one way street? Do you remember what he said?"

"A *one* way street?" I cocked my head.

"Yeah," he said. "You can do everything right and end up just as dead as if you'd been wrong. Because other people can screw up."

Jimmy exhaled, blowing his smoke toward the ceiling. "You aren't looking both ways, pal. You never did. Maybe guys like you don't have to."

"Guys like me?" I said. "You were a guy like me, once."

"No," he said, rising. "Not really, I don't think."

He hung up and walked toward a steel door.

"What are you talking about?" I jumped up and pounded on the glass. "Why didn't you just stop?"

A big guard approached me, his hand on his night stick. "Sir, please do not touch the glass."

Jimmy looked back at me as he prepared to make his exit. He mouthed the words. "I told you why."

I shook my head. "I don't understand."

Another guard approached. "Sir, control yourself or you'll be removed."

Jimmy said something to the officer nearest him, gesturing to the empty chair. The officer nodded.

Returning to the glass, Jimmy remained standing and picked up the phone. "I had to," he said. "I was out of control and heading full speed off a cliff."

I couldn't believe my friend could throw his life away. I pressed the receiver to my ear. "You got yourself locked up for twenty years because it was better than what would have happened otherwise? That's hard to believe."

His face took on a pained appearance, like he was remembering things better off forgotten. "I wasn't in charge of myself anymore. It was worse than you know, Dougie. Dark." He swallowed hard. "I did things. Terrible things. Coming in here for killing that guy . . . I got off cheap."

"To what?" I was nearly shouting again.

"Okay, sir. Put down the phone." The big guard gripped his baton and squared his shoulders. "Time's up."

I lowered my voice, but not my intensity. "What kinds of things? What did you do?"

Jimmy shook his head, moving his gaze to the floor. "The worst things you can think of." He raised his eyes to look at me one last time. "They locked up two of us when they put me in here."

He slid the phone back into the receiver and walked off. I didn't know what things he could have meant, and he didn't want me to know. At the time, he was right.

It would only be years later, after talking to a voodoo witch and a priest, that I would even begin to understand what he was talking about.

Chapter 42

The windshield wipers thrust bands of rain down the sides of the Navigator as I drove north on I-75. Long stretches of water ran sideways across the glass like little rivers.

The three gas cans in the back ensured we'd make it to Atlanta without stopping—on paper. The numbers worked, but the rough weather made it long a game of cat and mouse. Wind would gust up from nowhere and push the car around, and as the skies darkened with the onset of twilight, the fun was only getting started.

I checked the fuel gage and the clock. Six hours into our trek and we'd already consumed most of our gas. I'd be using the spare cans sooner than I thought. In the rearview mirror, Mallory and Sophie slept. No point in waking her for that.

Leaning forward, I squinted out the windshield. The highway curved to the left, but this section didn't have reflectors or lights. I gripped the wheel and eased my foot off the gas pedal.

Lightning flashed, turning the road white—and illuminating a massive tree sprawled across the highway.

My heart jumped. I stomped the brakes and spun the steering wheel, sending us into a tailspin. The force of the turn threw me into the side window. I yanked the wheel in the other direction as the ground disappeared out from under us.

Mallory screamed. Our big car slid sideways down the embankment. All I could do was hang on.

Don't roll over. Don't roll over. Don't roll over.

It was only a second or two, but I tried to look back to see where we were headed. The next flash of lightning showed more trees.

Lots of them.

I held my breath and braced myself. I couldn't steer while sliding in reverse.

Don't hit a tree. Don't hit a tree. Don't—

The booming crunch of metal smashing into wood met us with a massive jolt. My head slammed the headrest. Our suitcases and gear went flying.

I rubbed my skull and opened my eyes. The drumming of rain on the Navigator's roof was the only sound. Our headlights illuminated a wet hillside—and two huge ruts of mud that traced a path from the empty highway to our car.

Mallory gasped. "What's going on?"

I twisted around. Sophie was buckled into her car seat. The shattered rear window was filled with a huge tree. Splinters dotted the remaining glass and a distant lightning flash illuminated a huge gaping split in the tree trunk.

I popped open my seat belt. "We had a wreck. Check Sophie."

The car vibrated with a low groan that shook our seats, and the sharp noise of cracking wood.

"Hang on! It's coming down!" I put my hands over my head and ducked.

Mallory reached for Sophie as tree limbs suddenly appeared in all the windows.

Boom!

Half the roof compressed into the cabin, shattering the windows and scattering glass in all directions.

I unclenched my teeth and tried to lift my head. It pressed against the ceiling. Drops of cold rain fell on my arm.

Miraculously, the tree trunk had fallen diagonally across the car. It smashed the roof between the front and back seats, but didn't directly hit any of the occupants.

I peered at the front passenger seat as water splattered onto it. The tree had crushed the seat. Anyone sitting there would have been killed. Mallory's habit of riding in back with Sophie had saved her.

Sophie.

My stomach dropped. I whipped around and lowered my head to see between the seats in the dim light. Mallory clawed at the child seat restraint. Sophie's head lay on her chest at an awkward angle.

Mallory strained against her own seat belt. "Sophie! Sophie!"

I was cut off from them by the smashed roof. Mallory lurched backward and undid her seat belt, then pushed her way through the spilled cooler to the child seat.

"Sophie," she whispered, easing her hands under our daughter's chin.

Mallory gently lifted Sophie's head. I opened my mouth to caution about neck injuries, but there was no stopping her.

Sophie's eyes rolled and then opened.

Mallory froze. I held my breath.

Sophie blinked. "Are we there?"

I collapsed in relief on the console. She had slept through the whole thing.

Mallory laughed and unbuckled her. "Good girl." They hugged. "Good girl."

I sighed. We had come down the hill slow enough to avoid injuries.

"Dad." Sophie held up a wet arm. "Put the window up."

"We can't honey," Mallory said. "The window is broken. We wrecked the car."

Sophie frowned at me. “Why did you do that?”

We all laughed, including Sophie—even if she wasn’t quite sure what was funny about it.

“Good thing Sparkles stayed at the neighbors,” she added.

I instructed Mallory to check herself for any hidden pains that she might feel now that the initial shock was over, and then check Sophie as best she could. I tried to open my door. It moved a little, and with some effort I was able to pry it open. The car’s overhead dome light—now barely six inches above the driver’s seat arm rest—illuminated the wet ground.

Our headlights shined upwards toward the highway. Other than that, it was nearly black all around. Up on that curve, other drivers would be able to see our headlights. Leaving them on would attract attention.

I reached in and turned on the emergency flashers. That would send an unmistakable signal that we needed help down below.

Putting my hands on my hips, I squinted through the rain at the hill. I was probably going about fifty miles per hour when I hit the curve. It was so slight, no guard rail had been erected. I turned to face the wreck. We’d slid down the hill, losing momentum until we hit the trees.

I shook my head. Any faster and we would have been killed by the impact; any slower and we might have rolled over coming down the hill.

I pushed my wet hair out of my eyes. I didn’t know how much, if any, of the first tree was still blocking the highway. I thought I might have hit part of it, but everything happened pretty fast. I might have knocked it out of the road, but either way, the rest of it was probably still up there causing a hazard.

In the car, Mallory was barely visible under the smashed roof.

I put my hand on the door frame. "Honey, I need to go check the road and see if the tree I hit is still there."

"Why?" She glared at me. "We need you here."

"If another car hits it, they might end up down here on top of us. I just want to go check. I'll be quick." I checked around the car. It might be a while before any help came. "If you guys are okay, try to find something to keep dry with, and maybe put some of our stuff back in the cooler."

The grass near the hill was soaking wet and muddy. My feet sunk with each step. Slogging up the incline, I reached the curve.

The highway was empty. There were no cars or distant headlights coming, no road noises—and no tree, either. I must have taken it down the hill with us. I peered through the rain at the split roads to the muddy hill on the other side. I guess the tree slid off from there. A few others were leaning, like they might be coming down soon, too. Between the rain-softened soil and the wind, the heavy tree must have slipped right off.

I couldn't see much. The tree probably went over the hill with us and disappeared into the darkness somewhere.

The rain smacked the asphalt all around me, hissing like skillet full of bacon. As it rinsed the mud off the road, I stared up at the sloping hillside. That tree had to come down just right to even be on the highway at all.

A jolt of fear shot through me.

Unless it had been done on purpose.

I stared down the hill at the Navigator, blocking the glare of the headlights with my hand. Mallory and Sophie were alone down there. If the tree had been a trap, it had worked to get me to leave them alone and defenseless.

My heart pounded as I sprinted across the highway, slipping and sliding my way down the hill. The wind pushed me sideways as I pulled each mud-laden footstep from the soggy ground.

Lightning gave me a good look at the damage. The rear of the Navigator was smashed, as was the roof, but the tree had fallen onto the car and more or less rolled off the passenger side. That's why I was able to get out.

When I got to the car, it was empty. The wind whipped my face as I glanced around. "Mallory?"

"Back here!" Mallory had gotten Sophie and herself into some plastic ponchos, and the two of them were sitting on the cooler behind the car. Cold, heavy drops beat down on all three of us.

I yelled over the noise of the rain. "You guys okay?"

The plastic hoods bobbed up and down.

"It smells like gas in the car, really strong," Mallory said. "I think the spare gas cans may be leaking."

A pang of fear gripped my gut. If gasoline was leaking, it could become a fire hazard. That's why you're not supposed to drive around with cans of gas in your car. That, and the risk of explosion in a wreck.

Thunder rumbled overhead.

The Navigator was a loss as a vehicle now, but it might have kept us out of the elements. The leaking gas cans spoiled that and would ruin our spare clothes and supplies if it got on them.

I looked at Mallory. "I'll try to pull the cans out. If they did spill, it won't be safe to sit inside the car. The fumes are dangerous to breathe."

She stared blankly at me. "That's why we're out here in the rain, sweetie."

"Okay," I said, nodding. Then I turned back to the car. "Ohhhkay."

I reached through the broken rear window and grabbed one of the heavy gas cans. The smell of gasoline hit me in the face. I climbed onto the rear bumper and grabbed the roof rack, straining to pull the wet can through the broken window. They were heavy enough to lift into the car with two hands when the tailgate was operational. With it smashed shut, I strained to hoist each can over the tailgate and through the broken glass.

Overhead, the lightning intensified. The storm was coming closer.

I leaned on the side of the car, sweating and trying to assess our situation. Gas fumes aside, we would be better off in the car. Wet seats would be more comfortable than the wet ground if we had to spend the night. We'd be safer inside than being out in the storm—if we didn't get sick from the smell. Lightning was everywhere, and it might hit one of the nearby trees. If it did, the roof of the Navigator had already proven sturdy enough. If trees attract lightning, being under them was a liability.

I peered at the caved-in wreck. No windows, rain coming in on all sides, and filled with toxic gasoline fumes. I took a deep breath and stood up. Mallory and Sophie could wait by the car while I took a flashlight and tried to wave down a passing vehicle. I peered at the dark highway and sighed.

If there are any passing vehicles.

A quick check of the Navigator's floor produced my cell phone. No signal. We were either out of range or the towers were down. No surprise there—it was rough enough to knock down every tower from here to Tampa.

The nagging unease in my gut wouldn't go away. The tree, the rain—if something was determined to get us, we had allowed ourselves to become sitting ducks, just as Mallory had predicted.

I swallowed hard. *I* had allowed us to become sitting ducks. She would have had us sitting on our nice dry couch at home.

A bright flash of lightning ripped across the sky, blinding me. I crouched, almost falling to the ground. The thunder clap that accompanied it was like a cannon shot in my ears. The lightning was close, its rumbling echo rolling through the tree tops. The flash illuminated a clearing a little farther down the hill. It was horseshoe shaped, with a stump off to one side.

I breathed hard in the falling rain. The skies roared, reloading. Clouds churned and boiled while the wind whipped my face. The tree tops banged into each other like wind chimes.

I had gas cans sitting on one side of my car and a tree sitting across the other side. My wife and daughter were sitting on a cooler, cowering—and nobody in the greater Atlanta metropolitan area was out on the road. With a flashlight in one hand and a worthless cell phone in the other, I'd had enough.

I stood in the mud and cursed at the sky. "What do you want from me? What do you want?"

The skies rumbled their reply.

Stepping toward the clearing, I held out my hands. "Isn't it enough that you ruined the old man at the winery? That you nearly killed that young woman there?" I gripped my flashlight and spit into the wind. "You killed Tyree! What did he ever do?"

The wind ripped at me, pushing me—but I kept walking.

"I'm here now! Is that what you wanted?" I wiped the rain from my eyes. "Well here I am! What do you want?"

A flash of lightning blasted the ground a few feet away from me.

I jumped backward, my heart in my throat. Adrenaline surged through me.

Shaking, I continued walking into the clearing toward the stump. "I'm not afraid of you! Is that all you've got? Lightning?" I forced a laugh. "You could have used that on me at the beach! Come on, come get me!"

Each step drew me closer to the clearing and further from my wife and child.

I threw my hands in the air. "Show yourself, you damned coward!"

A blast of lightning lit up the ground, knocking me to my knees. I shook my head, my ears ringing. Mallory waved and screamed at me to come back.

I glared at the sky. The rain was coming straight down, and I could make out thick round clouds. Lightning rippled back and forth between them as the thunder groaned like a monster.

My heart was in my throat. I was never going to be much more vulnerable than I was at that moment. If the demon was here, it wasn't making its move. Why was it waiting?

I looked around. The grass of the clearing offered no cover for protection, just a stump.

I clenched my fists. "I've had enough, do you hear me? Enough running, enough being afraid." If something was going to happen, it was time to make it happen. Time to make a stand.

I gritted my teeth and bolstered myself, willing to confront whatever was coming.

And I stood, alone in the clearing, hoping to make a difference. My heart pounded. Like in the parking lot with Muscle T and the bar manager, I was ready to—

A long ripple of lightning rolled across the clouds, illuminating the clearing—horseshoe shaped with a stump. I recognized it. The one from the lion dream.

My breath left me. This was it. This was where it was supposed to happen. Here, in this wet ground—the fourth lion. The fourth tragedy.

I swallowed hard. I'd come unprepared. I had nothing to fight back with. My heart sank.

And yet . . .

I squinted at the night sky. If I was so vulnerable, why didn't it make its move?

We'd caught the demon off guard. Like Tyree had advised, the dark angel wasn't ready yet. And if he wasn't ready, he might be able to be provoked.

And nobody can provoke somebody like I can.

I pointed to the clouds. "You're a coward! You think I'm afraid of you? At least I'm here! I'm scared and I'm shaking, but I'm here! Where are you?"

The rain poured forth, ignoring me.

"You want a fight?" I tossed my phone to the ground and balled up my fist. "Come and get me!"

The wind howled through the trees, a low moan wrapped in the rustling leaves.

My heart was racing, almost jumping out of my chest. "You—you went to all this trouble to get me out in the open. It worked. Show yourself to me, dark angel. Here I am." I thumped my chest. "Come and get me!"

The wind roared again, hissing words that were almost echoes from somewhere else: *I don't want you.*

I shuddered. Alone in the clearing, I'd made contact. It was here.

Fear and anger welled inside me, shaking me. I'd fallen for the trap. I glanced at Mallory and Sophie, cowering by the car as the rain pelted them.

I widened my stance and raised my fists. "I don't care what you want. You pull all this crap to come after a little girl?" I spit the rain water out of my mouth. "You're not getting her! Over my dead body, do you hear me?"

I gritted my teeth and shook my flashlight at the sky. "I swear to God, that's not happening. You're not getting her. Not today, not ever!"

A blast of lightning ripped from the sky lit up everything around me in a blaze of white. A huge tree top exploded and crashed to the ground. Across the clearing, a second tree burst at the middle as bolt after bolt of lightning streamed from the sky. Steam poured from a splintered tree, a trail of smoke following its massive trunk as it smashed to earth. The ground shook from the impact.

A violent crack of thunder filled the air and a blinding white streak sailed past me and exploding on the ground. I covered myself with my arms and fell to my knees.

Terrified, I forced my eyes open and took a deep breath, hunching my shoulders for the next blast. My head ached and my hand was throbbing.

Laughter came in the rushing wind. Overhead, clouds moved together in a giant circle. Lightning flashed across the sky.

Heart pounding, I put a hand on the stump and righted myself.

This is it. He got us.

The thunder rumbled and rolled through the trees.

He got us all.

My shoulders slumped as a hollowness crept through my gut—an ugly, dark sadness like a cold, bottomless black well had opened inside me. I knew I was going to die right there in that field. First me, then my family. I leaned on my knee, holding back tears, knowing I'd failed to protect my daughter.

I gazed at the churning sky. Maybe one would be enough. Maybe he'd take me and spare her.

I swallowed hard, forcing myself to my feet. "Come on, then. Do it."

A loud roar filled my ears. I gritted my teeth and cringed, holding my breath and bracing myself for whatever the demon was readying for me.

The noise grew louder, coming from behind me. I bolted around to see whatever hellish thing was coming to finish me off.

A single light moved along the hillside, bouncing toward me. I squinted into the darkness. It was a motorcycle.

A really loud motorcycle, like it didn't have a muffler. I blinked the rain from my eyes.

A distant lightning bolt illuminated the scene. A red motorcycle with a pull-behind gray trailer slid sideways down the muddy hill. The rider wore an orange and black jacket.

Tyree.

My heart swelled with disbelief and excitement. He was alive.

How the hell did he manage that?

He slid to a stop behind Mallory and Sophie, jumping off the motorcycle and stumbling through the mud to them. Mallory pointed at me. Tyree nodded. After a moment, he hunched over and raced out to my position.

"Here comes the cavalry!" He plopped down next to me at the stump.

"Tyree!" I slapped him on the back. "How the hell did you get here?" I smiled and shook my head. I couldn't believe he was here. "You son of a bitch. I thought you were dead!"

"Come on." Tyree fumbled with something in his rain coat pocket. "You can't get rid of me that easily."

Thunder rumbled overhead.

He raised his eyes to the sky and winced. "How you doing out here?"

"Pretty bad, I think."

"Yeah, that's what it looks like." He jerked at his pocket, producing a large white cross. "Maybe this will help."

He handed it to me. The relic cross.

The thunder rumbled again.

I held it up, trying to see more in the darkness. "Does this thing have some special powers?"

"No," Tyree said. "But if you can get close enough, maybe you can plunge it into the angel. If you can get him to appear to you. I also brought this."

He held up a plastic bottle of water.

"Water?"

"Not just water," Tyree said. "Holy water."

I huffed. "You got this out of our cooler over there!"

"And then I mixed it with this." He held up a tiny vial. "This is holy water. You mix it with the bottled water, that makes it *all* holy water."

Lightning flashed across the sky. I flinched. "You can do that? It counts?"

"Yep. When the two waters touch, they are all sanctified. Catholic chemistry."

A loud booming thunderclap rolled across the clearing. Things were getting restless. The wind picked up. Tree branches smashed into one another.

I took the water from his hand. "What's the plan?"

"Well, again, if you can get close enough, you can douse him with it. That should do the trick. But do it with conviction. This is no time to be faint of heart."

A bolt of lightning turned the clearing white.

I raised my head from between my shoulders. "No lack of faith, huh?"

Tyree nodded.

I took a deep breath. "Okay then."

My trembling hands at my sides, I jumped up from behind the stump and shouted at the sky. "Is this your big move, demon? A little lightning? Some rain?"

I swallowed hard and regripped the relic cross, holding the mixed waters in my other hand. "What are you going to do? I'm here now. Come on. I'm not afraid of you." I widened my stance and braced for a bolt of lightning, hunching my shoulders. I was scared to death but I had to draw the demon out. I took a quivering breath and shouted. "I'm not afraid of you!"

Then it occurred to me. Maybe it was afraid of me.

I wiped the rain from my eyes with my arm. "Are—are you such a coward you can only pick on a little girl?" I frowned at the sky. "Then . . . you're not the strong one. I'm the strong one. Me." I pounded my chest with the relic cross. "I'm here to fight for that little girl. You're weak!"

The clouds rumbled.

"If you weren't weak you would've done it by now! I've got you all figured out! You tried three times, and you screwed up every time. Every time! You're a failure. You're weak!"

Tyree peeked out from behind the stump. "You're doing great, pal!"

Then he crouched back down.

Breathing hard, I took a few steps and held my arms out. "You think you beat us? You won nothing!" I looked around, shrugging my shoulders. "Here we are, in the middle of nowhere, right out in the open. Where are you?"

There was a rumble, and a flash.

I shook my head and screamed at the sky. "I am not going to live my life running from you, do you hear me? I won't. Here I am. Show yourself to me, dark angel!" I took a deep breath, as if shouting louder would summon the spirit from its world. "I'm shaking and I'm scared, but I'm here! Prove that you are not afraid of me!"

The sky lit up with lightning flashes and booming thunder. Out in the clearing, a faint flicker of light glowed. I clenched my jaw and took a step toward it.

The flicker turned blue and glowed, like a reflection of distant lightning off a deep lake. It swirled and moved, an embodiment of energy or electricity. It was the blue flash I'd seen on the face of the man in the park all those years ago.

Lightning rippled across the sky.

I crept toward the glow, squeezing my relic cross. "I'm not afraid of you." I was gasping, scared and hesitant, easing my way across the clearing inch by inch. "A person who was afraid would run. I'm not running." I swallowed hard. "I'm done running from you."

The ball hovered before me, swirling and glowing in the night.

I stared at it, shaking my head. "You can't defeat me. You don't have the power to defeat me. You couldn't defeat my daughter, not even when she was a baby in her crib."

I spat on the ground and gritted my teeth. "You're a coward and you're afraid of me."

A blast of lightning flashed again as a massive wind gust threw me to the ground.

The voice rumbled in the echoes of the thunder. *I am not afraid of you.*

Lifting myself to one shoulder, I glared at the light. "Of course you are. You've been afraid to face me. Even now, it was me who had to draw you out."

The skies rumbled again.

I rose to my knees. "Here I am. You won't get a much easier target than this. You're still a coward, hiding behind the wind, hiding in the trees like a little scared animal." I stood, clutching my weapons at my side. "Show me what you've got. Because I don't believe you can do it. You're not powerful enough."

A loud groan rolled through the clearing. Lightning cracked through the sky and another tree fell.

The voice became just a rumble. In the blue light, a pair of eyes appeared. Huge and grotesque, like fiery spheres they stared at me from the electric blue cloud. It swirled and stretched, growing to ten feet tall, then twenty, brandishing massive teeth and a wide, curled cat's maw. On the sides of the naked skull, long pointy ears made of sinew and skin, like a pig's. Flames danced behind its eyes and inside its mouth.

The ground shook and the lightning flashed at its appearance, the wind emanating outward from the beast.

I shuddered, backing up a step. It seemed amused at my shock. Then it spoke in a thunderous, booming voice.

Who are you, to dare confront me?

I blinked the water out of my eyes. "I'm the only one that matters." I held up the relic cross. "I'm telling you, dark angel, you will leave this child alone!"

It snarled. Lighting rippled over the trees.

Sloshing toward it in the mud, I held the relic cross high and put the water bottle to my mouth. I clamped the cap in my teeth. With a twist, it popped open. I spit the cap out and stepped forward, squishing and sinking in the soggy ground.

I leaned forward and brandished the cross again. "Dark angel, you will leave this family alone!"

Laughter rolled through the clearing, riding on the thunder. Heavy rain poured down upon me.

"No? How does 'fuck you' work for you, then?"

The demon growled and the blue cloud swelled, surging higher. Light bounced all around. It loomed in front of me. A ripple of lightning flashed again.

The cross burned in my upraised hand as I neared the face of the dark angel. It was a vision of Hell itself, a gaping, snarled lion's mouth with a throat filled with flames. Boiling red eyes peered out from under a mane of satanic fire, worse than any image of the devil from any Sunday school class I'd ever gone to.

A long, spindly yellow arm uncurled from the ball, pointing. *You!*

It wasn't pointing at me. It was pointing past me toward Mallory and Sophie. I looked back to see my daughter's eyes, mesmerized in the blue glow.

I turned back to the demon. He grew larger, swirling with energy.

I held up my hands and squeezed my eyes shut against the blinding blue light, running at the demon. I flung the cross high into the swirling blue cloud. As I did, I lifted the water bottle. "Holy water of God and the Church, mix with this water and become one!" I waved the bottle back and forth, flinging its contents everywhere. "Mix with this rain water and become one!"

I splashed it onto the muddy ground. "Mix with these puddles and become one!"

Then I reared back and took a deep breath, heaving the rest at the face of the dark angel.

A piercing scream filled the air. The skies flashed white as the demon's face opened wildly in a hellish scream. A brilliant shock of lightning burst forth with a deafening crash of thunder, shaking the ground and ringing in my ears.

I fell to the ground as the demon burst into a screaming ball of fire. It howled in pain as the Holy water seared it, burned it, ripped through it. Flames shot out in all directions as a gigantic explosion of thunder roared through the clearing.

It knocked me backward into the mud. I lifted a hand to shield my eyes from the white-hot flames, grimacing as the dark angel was consumed. Its scream bounced off the tree tops and folded into a distant rumble of thunder as the last of its blue embers faded into the night.

I laid my weary head back onto the wet grass and let the cold rain wash over me. The drops just floated down gently on me now, and there was silence.

In the sky, as the fading lightning flickered in the distance, I thought I saw a woman's face. A different face, warm and kind, barely visible in the outline of a cloud. A round face, with bright eyes and dimples, smiling at me.

The last traces of lightning dissipated with the wind, and the clearing was dark.

Chapter 43

I flexed my jaw, trying to get the ringing in my ears to dissipate.

"Hey," Tyree said, grabbing me. "Are you okay?"

Lifting my head, I blinked the rain out of my eyes and nodded. "I'm okay."

"Come on." He put a hand under my arm and helped me to my feet.

I stared at the sky, scanning the clouds for the face. Little flickers of distant lightning lit the horizon. The image was gone.

Tyree tugged my arm. "How about we get out of this field before we get struck again?"

I looked at him. "Struck?"

"You got straight-on blasted by lightning, amigo! A direct shot. Came right down where you were standing."

The grass around me was knocked flat, but otherwise it didn't seem any different. As the ringing in my ears subsided, I realized I was still holding the relic cross.

"Here we go." Tyree slung my arm over his shoulder. "One foot in front of the other."

The wind tugged at us as we made our way to the car. "Tyree," I said as I limped along. "I'm glad you came. I'm glad you're with us. But I have to ask. I saw your office. Nobody could have survived that. The blood—"

"Animal blood." He shook his head. "It was pig's blood or something. Supposed to scare me."

"It sure scared the heck out of me!"

"Nah. When they broke in the front door, I went out the back window. Then they trashed the place and burned up my car."

I cocked my head. "Who did?"

Tyree stopped and looked at the sky. "I'd say it was some friends of whoever was doing all this with you. Like how they did with that winery guy."

"And here you are." I trudged through the mud. "Riding in on your loud as hell Harley to save the day."

He smiled. "I said you'd know it when you heard it."

I still couldn't get over his being here. "How did you find us?"

"I got your messages." He held up his cell phone. "The cell towers were out because of the hurricane, so when I got to a pay phone, I called in and checked my messages. By then, I couldn't call you back. I went by your house and saw that you were gone, but you'd already told me that you were going to Atlanta, and to what hotel." He shrugged. "When I spotted your big old Navigator CIA car wrecked down here, I knew it was you guys."

It was all very matter of fact. Pure Tyree.

When we got near the car, Mallory and Sophie ran out and greeted me with a big hug.

"Are you okay?" Mallory squeezed me. There was concern in her eyes.

"I'm okay, I'm okay. Don't worry." I pulled them close and looked at the clearing. "We're all okay. It's over. The dark angel thought we would run, or that we would be too afraid to do anything. It didn't think we'd fight." I reached down and patted my daughter's head. "It was wrong."

I reached out to shake Tyree's hand. "Thanks for all your help, my friend."

He grasped my arm and leaned in, whispering. "How do you know for sure it's over?"

"Well . . ." I gazed up at the clouds. "Let's just say a little bird told me."

Tyree grinned. "You saw something out there, didn't you?"

I smiled back. "They can't win this game. They'll move on to an easier target, or they'll quit, but they won't be back."

"Son of a gun." Tyree chuckled. "That's good news."

He peered over at where he had left his motorcycle. A tree had fallen on it during the storm, crushing it.

"Oh, are you kidding me?" Tyree groaned.

A car horn honked. Several drivers had pulled off the highway and were waving to us.

"Hey," I said. "Looks like we might be able to catch a ride and get out of this rain."

Tyree nodded, grumbling. "I'll go check it out." He stared at his Harley and made the sign of the cross. Then he moved off toward the hill.

I took a deep breath and scanned the grassy field again, holding my wife and daughter close. The lightning had moved on and the rain had lessened. The light, cool drops felt good on my face.

I patted Sophie's shoulder. "We're not afraid of some rain, are we sweetie?"

Her big eyes peered up at me from under her poncho as she clung to my waist. "Maybe a little."

I laughed. "Okay, maybe a little."

On the highway, headlights from a few cars lit the cab of a trucker on a CB radio.

"I'll wait for the police and the tow truck, honey." I kissed the top of Mallory's head. "Why don't you and

Sophie catch a ride with Tyree and one of these other drivers, and go on ahead to the hotel? Get out of this weather, get dried off?"

She squeezed me tighter, shaking her head. "I don't want us to be split up right now. Even if we have to stay here in the rain."

I sighed. She was right. "Somebody should go, though."

Tyree sloshed toward us. "I'll go!" He looked around sheepishly. "I mean, if that's okay. I'd like to get out of this weather. That rain suit was worthless."

"It's a good idea," I said. "Go on to the hotel in Atlanta, check in and order us all some hot food. I'll take care of the police reports and the tow truck, and then we'll be there. Maybe an hour or so, tops." I glanced at his crumpled motorcycle. "I'll have the tow truck take care of that, too."

Tyree gave me a thumbs up and ran toward the waiting cars.

Sophie tugged on my leg. I knew what she wanted.

"Tyree!" I called after him. "Get some goldfish crackers!"

He hustled up the muddy hill. "Will do." A car door opened as he approached. He hopped in and they were off.

"That was nice." Mallory pulled her poncho back and looked into my eyes. "He'll appreciate that."

"Having to track down goldfish crackers?"

She smacked my arm playfully. "Getting to go on to a nice, dry hotel!" She put her head on my shoulder and hugged me. "With a hot shower and a warm bed and room service."

"Oh." I nodded. "Hey, nobody said anything about room service."

Her smiling face was illuminated by the headlights of the highway patrol car and a tow truck as they appeared on the hill.

Chapter 44

Two large room service trays lay empty on the floor of our hotel room, along with several empty packages of goldfish crackers.

Sophie and Tyree, all clean and wrapped in their plush white Peachtree Hotel robes, watched cartoons on the TV. Mallory, perched on the large bed in her robe, worked the phone to pursue a rental car for us. Everyone looked safe, warm, and happy.

It was my turn to get cleaned up before saying goodnight to Tyree and sending him to his own suite next door. I went into the bathroom and got in the shower, letting the warm water bring my body temperature back up to normal. Steam rose over the bath curtain and drifted along the low bathroom ceiling.

I leaned against the tile wall expecting to feel different, to look different somehow, from all that had transpired.

And I was different, but I was also the same.

We used to play a game when I was a kid. A game that me and my friend created. We made it up, and gave it a name.

But you would not kill Hitler.

Even if a person could get away with it and nobody would ever know it happened, people wouldn't do it. Most folks wouldn't even talk back to their boss. They could never commit murder.

Our game was a naïve pastime for little boys who wanted to play at being brave. And there is a cruel irony in knowing what needs to be done and not being able to do it.

Jimmy was right. I couldn't kill Hitler. If an act were to occur that no one witnessed, that no one else would ever know about, it exists only in the minds—only in the personal realities—of the people involved. Dreams exist there, and everyone knows that dreams aren't real.

Besides, Hitler had to be killed before he became Hitler, before he became the powerful dictator that sent millions of people to their deaths. Because if you wait, you have failed. If you have the power to act, to avert a monstrous thing, you act.

And if you do . . .

If you act in a way to save five million people, the ones who do not die will never know they had been saved. Only if the millions perish would it ever be known you failed them. No, you must act before Hitler becomes Hitler, and save them all.

And therefore, you aren't really killing Hitler, are you?

Not the Hitler the world has come to know and despise. You have killed a clerk or a small time political hopeful, before he came to prominence.

A nobody.

You would not be a hero, you'd be a madman raving about how in the future blah, blah, blah . . . who would listen to such a person?

I wouldn't.

If some guy were to start blathering on about "needing" to kill someone so that a future horrific event wouldn't happen, why, they'd lock him up. And I'd be the first one to agree that he should be locked up. A smart guy would do what needed to be done, and then if there were no witnesses, he'd shut up about it. That would be the smart thing to do.

In a faraway field, in the middle of nowhere, in the middle of the night, a guy does what needs to be done.

Whatever it was that he did, if anybody saw, they'd be keeping quiet. That's almost the same as if nobody saw. And if nobody saw . . . can we say it even happened? Why, once things get back to normal at home, it would all seem like a big crazy dream.

Who's to say it wasn't?

So I did not kill Hitler. And I can live with myself about that.

Chapter 45

The next day, the storm had passed.

I looked out over the Atlanta skyline as Mallory and Sophie slept. 6 A.M, my usual wake up time—but not theirs. It was nice to think that things would start getting back to normal now.

The skies were sunny and bright. Pastel colors beamed out from the puffy white clouds. It was a beautiful day. Heavenly, one might say.

I had decided about something, too. We were lucky. We were absolutely lucky.

There had been an angel on the doctor's shoulder that day. There was one with her at the winery, and with us at the car fire. Maybe other times, too.

My daughter *does* have an angel on her shoulder. And I had come to feel that I knew who that angel was. Watching out for my daughter, and still watching out for me. Giving things a little nudge here and there. Or throwing an elbow. Giving me a dead battery at the right time . . . Maybe an angel had been helping me all along, I just didn't see.

I was glad she would play a role in my daughter's life after all. Like Father Frank said, why should the bad guys get to have all the fun?

At breakfast, I asked Tyree for a favor. An old friend, who was getting out of prison soon, would need some guidance in rebuilding a life for himself. He would need help finding a different path than the one he'd been on. Tyree was more than willing to head on up to Lima, Ohio, and start his next project.

Meanwhile, I had some driving to do myself. When the rental car showed up, we packed it with the few remaining items that hadn't been ruined in the wreck or doused with gasoline.

That, and a few bags of goldfish crackers for the ride home.

It was another big van. I wondered if maybe Mallory was trying to tell me something.

On the long drive south, we talked and sang songs, and watched cartoons on the car's DVD player until boredom and fatigue eventually put my wife and daughter to sleep again.

I was content. I knew that Dahlia would appreciate my gift of the relic cross and the story that came with it. That would more than satisfy my debt with her, and maybe even rack up a little house credit—not that I planned on needing any. The cross was valuable before, but like all weapons, once it had seen battle, it had become even more precious. I felt the mambo would see that it went to good use.

That only left one person to thank.

I pulled out my cell phone and called Our Lady Of Mercy. Mrs. Clermont answered.

"May I speak with Father Frank, please?" I asked.

"Who?" Mrs. Clermont's voice crackled with static as I drove. Maybe all the cell towers weren't back up and running yet after the storm.

"Mrs. Clermont, may I speak with Father Frank, please? Is he in?"

"I'm sorry, sir, we don't have anyone here by that name."

"I think we have a bad connection from the storm, ma'am. I'm trying to reach Father Frank. Is he available? Or can I make an appointment with him?"

"No, I heard you, sir. There's no Father Frank here. Do you have the right number? This is Our Lady Of Mercy."

"Mrs. Clermont, I just spoke with him a few days ago. Father Frank. He was doing confessions—"

"Sir, we have no Father Frank here." Mrs. Clermont replied cooly. "In fact, we have nobody on our roster named Frank at all, first name or last. And I've worked here for ten years."

I set the phone down, speechless, staring at the highway stretching in front of me.

Then I remembered.

Why should the bad guys get to have all the fun?

I almost drove off the road.

THE END

If you enjoyed this story, please leave a review on Amazon. Thank you!

About the Author

International bestselling author Dan Alatorre has 17 titles published in over a dozen languages.

From Romance in *Poggibonsi* to action and adventure in the sci-fi thriller *The Navigators*, to comedies like *Night Of The Colonoscopy: A Horror Story (Sort Of)* and the heartwarming and humorous anecdotes about parenting in the popular *Sophie Stories* series, his knack for surprising audiences and making you laugh or cry—or hang onto the edge of your seat—has been enjoyed by audiences around the world.

And you are guaranteed to get a page turner every time.

"That's my style," Dan says. "Grab you on page one and then send you on a roller coaster ride, regardless of the story or genre."

Readers agree, making his string of #1 bestsellers popular across the globe.

His unique writing style can make you chuckle or shed tears—sometimes on the same page (or steam up the room if it's one of his romances). Regardless of genre, his novels always contain unexpected twists and turns, and his endearing nonfiction stories will stay in your heart forever.

25 eBook Marketing Tips You Wish You Knew, co-authored by Dan, has been a valuable tool for upcoming writers (it's free if you subscribe to his newsletter) and his dedication to helping new authors is evident in his wildly popular blog "Dan Alatorre - AUTHOR."

Dan's success is widespread and varied. In addition to being a bestselling author, he has achieved President's Circle with two different Fortune 500 companies. You can find him blogging away almost every day on www.DanAlatorre.com.

Dan resides in the Tampa, Florida area with his wife and daughter.

Other Books By Dan Alatorre

Novels

The Navigators

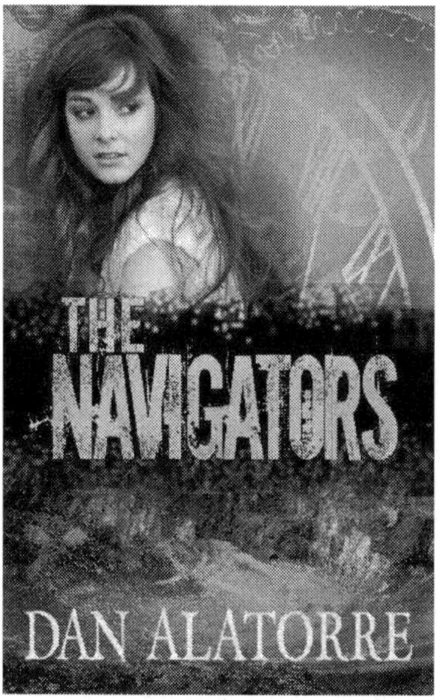

A freak landslide at a remote Florida mine uncovers a strange machine to Barry's group of paleontology students. Rumors spread about the discovery of a time machine, creating risks everywhere: a trusted classmate betrays them, and a corrupt school official tries to sell the machine to another university. When power company executives learn it may contain a unique fuel system that would put them out of business, possessing the machine becomes a matter of life and death. Now on the run, Barry's team struggles to keep their amazing discovery—but using it has consequences more severe than anyone can predict. Buy now on Amazon or FREE with Kindle Unlimited. *Also available in paperback!*

Poggibonsi: An Italian Misadventure

When family man Mike Torino lands a project in Italy, home of naked art, Valentino, and taxi-crashing yoga pants, he brings along his wife, hoping to rekindle their marriage. But romance gets derailed by head colds, constant bickering, and assaults from ankle-breaking cobblestone streets. Their daughter develops a gelato addiction. Mike's Italian partner has a coronary. And as for amore . . . Mattie tells Mike to handle things himself—and storms back to America. Mike is trapped. Leaving Italy will blow a promotion; staying might cost him his wife and family. While reeling from Mattie's frantic departure, a replacement liaison is assigned—a top-notch, beautiful young Italian woman who is instantly smitten with Mike and determined to reveal the passions of her homeland—whether he wants to see them or not! Normally immune, Mike is tempted—but is headstrong, voluptuous Julietta worth the risk? Buy now on Amazon or FREE with Kindle Unlimited. *Also available in paperback!*

Family Humor

Savvy Stories: funny things I learned from my daughter
The TERRIBLE Two's: funny things I learned from my toddler daughter
The Long Cutie

Short Stories

The Short Years
There's No Such Thing As A Quick Trip To BuyMart
Night Of The Colonoscopy: A Horror Story (sort of)
Santa Maybe
A Day For Hope

Children's books

Laguna The Lonely Mermaid
The Adventures of Pinchy Crab and Ramon D'Escargot
The Princess and the Dolphin

Cookbooks

All American Favorites: 35 Delicious Family Recipes That Will Make You The Star Of The Show
35 Great Recipes You Wish Your Mother Made
35 More AMAZING Recipes Your Mother Would be Proud Of!

Marketing (available to newsletter subscribers only)

25 Great eBook Marketing Tips You Need To Know!

94398641R00189

Made in the USA
Columbia, SC
01 May 2018